BLACK
LILIES

JODI PERKINS

Elicia ~
Enjoy the
Sequel +
Merry Christmas!
♡ Jodi Perk.
12 - 2019

SILVERHAND
PRESS

First Edition: August 2019

Editor: Dylan Devine

Cover art by Najla Qamber at najlaqamberdesigns.com

To Trinity,
my sweet little Assassin Bug

One

*Do you think the universe fights
for souls to be together?
Some things are too strange
and strong to be coincidence.*
Emery Allen

March 31, 1876

THE THREE BOYS—the youngest almost ten years old, the eldest eleven—tried to keep their faces solemn as they placed their chosen treasures into the small wooden box. Moonlight left shiny streaks on their cheeks and an impish glint in their eyes.

"Let us now state the items we chose for the cache, and why we chose it," George announced, wiping a stray lock of black hair from his forehead with his grubby fingers. He was the smallest of the three boys, yet often the most articulate.

"You sound like Teacher," William noted as he moved the last of the bricks.

Kade rubbed the dust from his hands onto the knees of his trousers. "Really, George. Do we have to make a production of it?"

"Our items are being left for the good folks in the future," George said. "This is history in the making, worthy of being honored by a few words."

Kade hid his grin. He had come tonight because burying a treasure chest sounded more entertaining than an evening of knucklebones with his sister. But George's flair for dramatics made it hard to take things seriously. "Alright, you go first."

George straightened his posture and picked up his treasure. It was a small pewter soldier, standing proudly, ready for battle. "This little figurine used to belong to my pa. I chose it because I think it represents me, the soldier I will someday become."

The boys nodded as George placed the soldier into the box. He faced Kade. "Your turn."

Kade plucked a coin from his pocket. "This is an Indian head penny, freshly minted. I chose it because it is inscribed with the date. Supposing a person in the future finds our cache, this will inform him how long the contents have rested here." Kade placed the penny in the box.

"That is quite…uh…practical," George said. "You were supposed to choose your greatest treasure, remember? A treasure with little monetary worth but with sentimental value."

"Given my father will hang me when he learns I stole this penny from his coin collection, it *is* sentimental."

"Very well." George, rolling his eyes, turned to William. "Your turn then."

William picked up a small pocket knife and twisted out the blade. Its lustrous carbon steel captured the moonlight as he held it up for his two friends to behold. The handle was dark polished oak, with the words "American

Centennial" inscribed in a light feathery script.

"That's the latest Schrade pocket knife," George breathed. "And I see you had Mr. Vaughn inscribe it. My father loves his work. Are you sure you want to part with it?"

"I can get another," William said, folding the blade and placing the knife back into the box. "You told us to bring something special. I chose this because it marks our first centennial."

"Right, then" George smiled, clearly enthused about William's contribution. The Indian head penny also marked the date, Kade noted, but evidently it wasn't as special.

George placed the lid on the small box, and Kade, whose arms were longer, slid it deep into the depths of the broken masonry of the almost-finished clocktower until the box was no longer visible.

"Are you sure it will be safe?" Kade asked.

"Yes," George said. "My father says that the mortar is being applied to the brickwork on the morrow. By then our cache will be sealed within."

"And the town will get to vote on the clock tower's name," William added.

Kade gazed up at the face of the clock, a radiant copper that glowed like the sun. It reminded him of a story his ma used to tell him when he was five or six years old, about an ancient chief. In the story, the chief's mother complains that her bark cloth can't dry because the days are so short. The chief, wanting to please his mother, climbs up a mountain and lassoes the sun's rays as it rises, using a rope made from his sister's hair. The sun pleads for its life and agrees that the days shall be long in summer, and short in winter.

The story was Kade's favorite—he loved the idea of

wrangling the sun. He suspected Ma loved the story too, because it showed the depth of a child's love.

Now, lost in the clock's face, Kade wished the town would name the clock after the ancient chief in the story. Ma would love that. But he highly doubted the town would vote for a name submitted by a not-quite-ten-year-old boy, much-less a name so strange and foreign. The townsfolk would want to give the majestic clock an appropriate name that honored their rich American history, like the *Lincoln Clocktower.*

No one would want to name it "Chief Māui" after the captor of the sun.

But, regardless, he decided then and there he would suggest the name.

Perhaps his father would allow him to take a photograph of the clocktower as well. Pa was quite possessive over his expensive Sanderson Camera and all of its delicate glass plates, but just last week Kade had started to read books about photography and, with the help of his ma, was now training in the complex mechanics and art of creating a photograph. Kade would love to capture a close-up of the clock's massive, regal face.

If he could only convince his father to give him a chance.

A train whistled in the distance, breaking Kade from his trance. Kade helped his friends place the bricks back, piece by piece, until the masonry at the base of the clock looked untouched. A minute or two later, the train sounded right behind the clock tower, its throaty chug-a-chugging vibrating the air around them. George and William, eager to get back home before they were caught missing, waved a hasty goodbye. Kade lingered back. The train finally departed into the distance, and the thick silence serenaded him in the strikingly bright night. He contemplated the clock. The giant hands sat motionless, the hour hand frozen on the roman numeral VII, the minute hand poised between the III and the IV. The hands wouldn't budge until tomorrow, when the mayor would do the honors of winding them for the first time. Staring up into the massive golden face, Kade wondered what the clock would look like once it was alive, ticking away the minutes and singing away the hours.

A current of air ruffled his hair, and he caught a flash of white in his peripheral vision. He looked down and saw it— some kind of crumpled thing, scuttling across the dirt from the base of the clock where moments before they had just planted their cache. It moved with the breeze, and Kade lunged down to grab it before it fluttered away.

He examined it. It was some kind of…stationery. Curious stationery, of a brightness and variety that was unlike the parchment his ma often penned letters on. He unfolded it and carefully smoothed it out, further perplexed to see thin blue lines spaced perfectly apart along the creased page, lines so straight it was hard to believe someone had drawn them. One red line traveled vertically down the page, and there were three holes punched along a fringed edge. He wondered what the holes were for. Flipping the parchment, he noticed writing. Curly and slanted and fine, in violet ink.

Violet ink. Such an oddity.

He blinked again. Squinting at the page, he began to read.

Dear Kade,

I know this letter will never reach you, but as I stare at the Face of Maui, this amazing thing that you named, I feel like you are here with me, somehow….

His heart thumped and he dropped the letter. No. It was impossible for this letter, written on foreign parchment in peculiar violet ink, to be for *him*. Perhaps it was for a different boy, someone else with the first name Kade. There were no other Kades in his town, but the letter might have traveled a long way in the recent storms. Or perhaps it was George and William playing an early April Fool's Day prank on him, since everyone would be too occupied at the unveiling ceremony tomorrow to bother with hoaxes.

Yet the words "Face of Maui, this amazing thing you named…" struck him in the chest. He had only conceived a name for the clock minutes ago, and hadn't shared it with any person. He turned around, suddenly feeling watched.

The paper began to skid in the breeze, and he reached down to retrieve it. Flattening it again, he skimmed down to the end of the letter to find the closing salutation.

Yours Faithfully in Time,

Aviva

He let out a breath. That confirmed it. He didn't know anyone with such an exotic name. *Aviva*. She must be a foreigner.

Curious now, he went back to read the letter in its entirety. The beginning was confusing, and some parts made him chuckle. But by the time he reached the end, his eyes were fogged with moisture, and his skin felt hot. He was glad that William and George had gone home so they wouldn't witness him behaving like such a pansy.

He carefully folded the letter and stuffed it into his pocket. The letter wasn't meant for him.

But why, then, could he not shake the feeling that it was?

Two

To contemplate is to look at shadows.
Victor Hugo

Monday, January 21
The Candlelight Vigil
Present Day

"OW!" I YELPED as my dad eased his F150 alongside the curb. "Seriously Phee, can't you put your damn elbow somewhere else?

"Aviva, don't say damn," Daphne chided from the front. "You don't get 'damn' until your sixteenth birthday."

I stifled a laugh. My stepmom Daphne believed in allotting mild curse words for birthday gifts. I got 'crap' for my thirteenth birthday, and 'hell' for my fifteenth. It would be another two months before 'damn' made its way to me with a big shiny bow.

"Sorry Daphne." I tried wiggling away from Phee's sharp elbow. "But Phee, seriously."

Amber light poured into the dark space of the backseat where I was currently smashed between my two sisters, and I could see Phee rolling her eyes.

"Sure, sure, let me just pluck this sucker off and move it

somewhere else. Hey Dad, can your glove box store an elbow?"

Krystal huffed to my left, while Dad shook his head.

"We're getting out anyway," Daphne said from the front passenger seat. "Now remember, we're here for Taz."

I immediately sobered, recognizing Daphne's thinly veiled message. *Shut up and take this matter seriously. Someone that Taz cared about died.*

And not just someone. According to Taz, it was a little girl.

Ugh. It was just…heart breaking.

Still, a big fat selfish part of me didn't want to be here. I had never met the little girl who died. I didn't belong. I felt like I was infringing upon someone else's private moment, someone who actually knew her and cared about her. The whole thing felt awkward.

Plus it was a school night. I had a big chemistry test tomorrow.

Okay, that couldn't sound more self-centered. A little girl was dead and I was worried about a stupid test. But when I was honest with myself, it wasn't about the chemistry test. I just *don't do* death. Thank God we weren't entering a cemetery or I would be diving head-first back into the truck.

The parking lot at Mel's Diner was overflowing with a procession of cars lining the street for the candlelight vigil. I slid out of the truck behind Phee. The cold air greeted me with a startling and welcoming slap. Stryder and Taz were already hurrying across the street toward Mel's as my sisters and I took a minute to stretch. A small, limp plant was bathed in frosty moonlight near the curb, and I reached down to touch it. Almost immediately its branches stiffened

8

and leaves perked up. A thrill coursed through my body as buds dotted the plant, then bloomed with tiny lavender flowers.

"Aviva!" Phee whisper-scolded.

Reluctantly, I allowed my hand to drop from the plant, fighting a sudden rush of dizziness and fatigue at having used my powers. I turned to Phee, planning to remind her that I saw her cheating with the rules a few days ago when she used her powers to heat her cappuccino at Copper's Kettle. Instead, I gasped.

"What?" Phee said, looking toward the streetlamp where my gaze now hovered.

"I saw…uh…I thought I saw…." I let out a breath, realizing I was stammering. I didn't know how to explain to Phee why I was gawking at a streetlamp. There was nothing more than a dark smudge, small and unimpressive, cowering at the base of the lamp. An itty bitty shadow. Big deal.

Yet something about it spooked me.

It vanished. Probably chased away by the surrounding light, as is the nature of shadows.

I shook my head. "Never mind. It's just nerves. Vigils are not my thing."

"Well I don't think they're anyone's *thing*," Phee said. "I cancelled my date with Eric tonight so I could freeze my butt off outside some restaurant and pretend to mourn over someone I've never met."

"Phee!" I said, shocked by her callousness. And ashamed, too, because I felt the same way. I looked over my shoulder. "Don't let Daphne hear you talk like that."

"Yeah, okay, sorry. You're right. That was rude. But really, I don't get why we're here. And you know, I never once heard that report that Taz told us about. The one on the radio that said that little girl died. Lisa during lunch mentioned something about an officer getting shot, but that's about it. Isn't it weird that we didn't hear more about this little girl?"

"Yeah, I guess," I conceded. "But Taz and Stryder both said it happened. Even Dad said it happened."

"Yeah, I know, that's what Daphne said too, but still…" She coughed as Krystal walked up, Dad and Daphne right behind her. I didn't have to ask why she dropped the conversation. We both knew it was awkward talking about anything Taz/Stryder-related with Krystal around.

The crowd thickened as we drew closer to the diner. I spotted Taz in Stryder's arms, the two locked in a kiss. No wonder they wanted the head start.

Krystal stepped up beside me, her face scrunched in revulsion.

Phee walked closer to the love kittens, crossing her arms and waiting to be noticed. Finally, she coughed. The two pulled apart. Taz smiled breathlessly when she saw us.

"If you two are about finished, we have some respects to pay," Phee said.

Taz's smile darkened and she nodded. Stryder dipped his head in greeting to us, his face somber. She and Stryder turned toward the growing crowd. The half-moon hung solemnly as we approached the group huddled in front of the diner, shedding silver splotches across the asphalt like withering leaves. A large gold picture frame sat directly in front of the diner, along with large clusters of yellow chrysanthemums, white lilies and baby's breath. Someone had placed two tall ivory pillar candles on each side of the memorial, and their soft light cast golden shadows across the picture frame. I adjusted my glasses, trying to see the portrait.

That's when I saw the shadow again. It was nothing more than a small smudge, hardly noteworthy. Yet my muscles tensed. It was on the picture frame....but no. Unlike the other shadows playing on top of the frame, the smudge looked like it was floating in front of the frame.

Can a shadow float mid-air? It has to land somewhere, right?

As if reading my mind, the shadow wiggled back and slid down the frame onto the cluster of flowers, absorbing the light from the lilies, steeping them in black. My eyes followed the shadow as it flickered and slid away from the memorial. The black lilies slowly returned to their pristine alabaster color as the shadow crept further away.

I blinked, but it was still there, barely discernible, slinking along the diner's walls. I blinked again, shaking my head.

The shadow was gone.

"So what exactly broke the curse?" Phee asked Taz, shifting from one leg to the other. "And please don't say 'true love's kiss.'" She stuffed her hands into the pockets of her jacket.

Her question broke my trance. I knew I was psyching myself out because I was at a vigil. The smudge wasn't anything ominous. It was just a shadow. Nothing more.

"Aww, Phee, don't be such a cynic," I said, trying to take my mind off my nervousness. "What's wrong with true love's kiss?"

Without thinking, I squinted back into the dark, wondering if the smudge-I was-convinced-was-nothing would reappear.

Nope. Nothing.

"It's just *so* cliché. You'll never see me waiting around for some stupid smooch to save me."

"I bet it really was true love's kiss. What else could it be?" I tried to concentrate on the conversation. "Taz and Stryder are so lucky. They have the most romantic story *ever*."

Seeing something flutter in the distance, I glanced back into the dark. It was nothing more than a flower petal caught in a light air current, scuttling along the diner's wall. *Ridiculous.*

"Yeah," Taz reached over to squeeze Stryder's hand, her face lit with amusement. "Soooo romantic. Especially the rat-kissing part. And the part where I threw a tantrum and broke a multi-thousand dollar chandelier…and smashed a car or two…and Stryder served time in prison for a hit and run he didn't commit, and"—

"It was only one day in juvenile hall," Stryder shot her a grin. "But I like your version better. Much more dramatic. I really come out as the unsung hero."

I laughed, forgetting for a moment about the shadow-smudge.

"It doesn't matter anyway, girls," my dad said. "I'm afraid true love's kiss was not the answer to the curse."

"No?" Taz asked, coughing awkwardly. "What was it, then?"

I leaned in as if I was listening, when really my mind was a hundred miles away. Or at least twenty yards away, searching for the shadow. My dad prattled on in his science-teacher voice about Taz's and Stryder's curse. Krystal punched Dad in the arm and everyone burst into laughter, so I joined them, though I wasn't exactly sure what we were all laughing about.

And then my stomach turned. The smudge was back. I watched as it flitted on the same part of the wall where it had disappeared from before, sliding onto the ground like something gelatinous and alive.

What was it? I narrowed my eyes, adjusting my glasses again. It was moving at a snail's pace across the asphalt.

Moving towards *me*.

I stepped back, putting my arm on Krystal's. She raised her eyebrows at me, and I pointed over at the shadow. She followed my gesture, and then turned back to look at me.

"Aviva, what's wrong? There's nothing there."

"Are you sure?" I whispered, not wanting the rest of my family to hear. They were all engaged in a new conversation about Dad's relatives sensing time disturbances, or rats, or something.

"Yes, I'm sure. What do you *think* is there?"

"I, uh, I don't know. I keep seeing a shadow." My eyes skimmed the dark asphalt. Once again, the shadow was gone.

"With all this candlelight, there're lots of shadows."

I sighed, not knowing how to explain to her that this one was *different*. "Yeah, okay. I'm just jumpy, I guess."

She patted my arm. "Yeah. This is making me a little crazy too."

"Sorry, Krys," I said, remembering again how uncomfortable this whole thing was for her.

A hush trickled over the group of mourners as the candles were lit, one by one. A cute dark-haired guy with his arm in a sling limped toward our group and started talking to Stryder and Taz in low tones. I thought I heard Stryder call him "Joe," but after that I stopped eavesdropping; I was too distracted by the golden flames dancing around me like awakening fireflies in the sleepy dark. If I didn't hate events having to do with death so much, I might actually enjoy being outside at night-time surrounded by all these mesmerizing candles.

And if I wasn't worried about being the first person in the universe to be eaten alive by some tiny carnivorous shadow.

A man in a decorated police uniform began talking over a P.A. system, his voice crackling through the speaker. Everyone bowed their heads to pray. At the end of the prayer I opened my eyes to see a little girl standing between Taz and Stryder.

"Grace," I heard Taz whisper.

Grace…wasn't that the name of the five year-old who Stryder and Taz claimed died in last night's shooting?

Every fiber in my body buzzed with the certainty that I was somehow witnessing a miracle. I had a thousand questions. But before I could open my mouth to ask even one of them, my euphoria nose-dived.

The damn smudge was back. (It's a good thing Daphne can't read my thoughts lest she find out I opened my birthday gift early.)

Ignore it, I willed myself, turning away from the smudge. I wanted to bask in the beauty and wonder of the little girl Grace being alive, not obsess over some meaningless shadow. But it fluttered on the fringes of my peripheral vision like a dark, exotic moth, demanding to be noticed.

Unable to resist, I snuck a peek. My eyes widened as the shadow spread and grew, the formerly small blob stretching thick dark fingers outward and upward, metamorphosing into a wobbly shape. Heart slamming in my chest, I yanked my glasses off, rubbed them clean with my jacket, and smashed them back onto my face.

Saliva stuck like glue to the roof of my mouth. *I can't be seeing this right.*

The shadow now looked like it had been carved into the shape of a man. A blurry, obscure, flickering man. And the shadow-man-figure wasn't standing. Rather, it was…*hanging*; squirming and dangling from some kind of dark shadow-rope. A dark feeling of horror and injustice poured over me, drenching me with hopelessness. The dark figure seemed to turn on the rope. Without thinking, I reached for it, wanting more than anything to touch it. To touch *him*. To help him, somehow.

With a long arm, he reached for me.

Coming to my senses, I choked on my scream and jumped back, nearly tripping on my feet. I felt a hand grab my elbow and I almost screamed again, before I realized the hand was trying to steady me.

"Whoa, there. Are you okay?" It was the cute dark-haired guy with the sling. Joe, I thought. His brown eyes were deep and warm against his olive complexion. "You look like you've seen a ghost."

I gratefully accepted his hand and righted myself, trying to control my breathing. Heart beating like a drummer on steroids, my eyes darted around the space where the shadow-man had hung. He—it—was gone.

The grand clock in Pendulum Square, the one we Sezonians call *The Face of Maui*, tolled in the distance, its deep bells cutting through the night. Ten soulful chimes, each slipping into the dark like a shadow.

I swallowed hard and looked up into Joe's concerned face.

"I think I *did* see a ghost."

Three

…a ghost,
must be spoken to a little
before it will explain itself.
Charles Dickens

Wednesday, March 20
Present Day

MY BIRTHDAY DAWNED on a gray and drizzly morning, with dim muddled light filtering through my half of the window. Years ago Krystal and I couldn't agree on our curtains, so Daphne said we each got one panel. Krystal's half of the window was draped in a ruffled curtain in solid black, while mine was a light, sheer panel in sunshine yellow. Likewise, my half of our bedroom was decorated in springy greens and bright yellows, while Krystal's half was in deep purples and black. Our room was quite the conversation piece whenever we had friends over.

Happy Sweet Sixteen, I mumbled to myself, rolling over to hit the snooze button on my alarm. Burying myself back into my comforter, I was feeling the warm tendrils of sleep wrap around me again when the door burst open.

"Happy Birthday!" a chorus of voices yelled. I groaned and opened my eyes to a squint. Dad, Daphne, Krystal, Phee, and Taz were standing in front of my bed, Daphne balancing a tray of breakfast goodies.

"Happy birthday to you, happy birthday TO YOU…" they belted out at the top of their lungs. "Happy birthday dear Aviva…!"

I buried my head under my pillow. Something clutched my toes beneath my blanket, and an icy chill coursed through my foot.

"Aughhh, Krystal!" I yelped, jerking upright in my bed.

"Oh, come on, Aviva," Taz said. "We know you love it."

I chuckled. "It's true," I admitted. "I mean, the breakfast in bed part. Not the Krystal-freezing-me part."

Krystal smiled wickedly.

"Well, eat fast," Daphne said, shoving the tray in my sleepy arms. "We want you to have time to open your birthday gift before school." I took the tray, eyeing the contents. Runny eggs, burnt bacon, mushy pancakes swimming in a sea of syrup, and a frozen blob of orange juice in a metallic green cup.

"That's fresh-squeezed orange juice," Krystal offered, seeing my look of skepticism. "I made it myself, and Phee made the bacon."

The bacon looked more like bits of charcoal. I shook my head, the motion jiggling the tray and sloshing orange juice slush onto my comforter. "You know you guys can use a pan and a stove to cook like normal people, right? No offense, but your powers make some crummy food."

"I tried telling them that," Dad ran his fingers through his silver-shot black hair, sighing. "I'm ruing the day I agreed to let you girls practice using your powers at home."

17

"Oh come on," Taz said. "It's not that bad."

"Not that bad? Your sister lit Daphne's robe on fire."

"I was trying to be nice." Phee snagged a burnt bacon-chunk from my tray and popped it in her mouth. She swallowed and grimaced. "I wanted to make it warm and toasty for her. It was chilly that night."

"See, her motives were pure, Dad," Taz pointed out, "and at least that was better than what Krystal did to your fish tank."

Krystal cringed while the rest of us dissolved into laughter. I still remembered the way those poor fish looked, frozen solid in the five-gallon aquarium in Dad's office. Nothing like a goldfish popsicle to start off your Tuesday morning.

"What about you, Aviva?" Krystal cut in. I wiped my moistening eyes to look at her. "Yeah. I saw you yesterday morning on the patio, healing that cockroach."

"Ewwww!" Phee shrieked. "Aviva, you didn't."

My cheeks burned. "I swear I was just practicing. I didn't think it would actually work. Better to practice on an injured roach than an injured bird or something, right? What if I, like, blew the bird up or something?"

My sisters burst into more giggles and ewwwws.

"Great," Daphne said. "Now I'm going to find that roach's grandkids in my garden. It's good to know you're using your powers for such altruistic causes."

I gave an apologetic shrug.

Dad shook his head, sighing again. I swear he had aged by five years in the past couple months, not to mention he kept getting struck with migraines. I asked him a few days ago if he was okay, and he said "I think your pops is just getting old."

"Can you actually get old?" I had asked him.

He had answered me with a strange look. "Oh yes, ladybug. Indeed, I can." He never offered any further explanation, and I didn't ask. Not for the first time I was struck with the feeling that he was hiding something from me and my sisters. Harboring yet another secret. A bigger secret. A few hours before the candlelight vigil two months ago, he told us the truth about who we were in a conversation that was too mind-blowing to be fiction. He explained that he was the human form of Father Time. And according to him, my sisters and I are somehow the flesh embodiment of the four seasons. My entire world had spun off its axis that night. Yet, somehow, at the same time, I was overcome by a feeling of acceptance. Taz said it's because Dad had confirmed something that I already knew. She said she had revealed the truth of who I was at the hospital during one of her loops, and apparently I used my powers to try to save Stryder's life. I didn't remember any of that, but it sounded familiar—and real—somehow.

But I think my feeling of acceptance was because I *finally* had a reason to explain why I was so weird…why I was born with my odd gift—my gift of revitalizing things, of bringing strength and energy and renewal…of giving *life*.

Because, as it turns out, I'm Spring. As far as seasons go, I think I got a pretty great one. Even if I don't really like flowers and stuff.

How does Spring herself not like flowers?

Though I do love reviving them.

That same night, after my sisters and I recovered from Dad's big revelation, he gave us permission to start practicing our abilities in the privacy of our home. Since Taz's life-absorbing powers nearly tore her and Stryder's time loop apart, Dad decided that his previous approach of pretending our powers didn't exist was a folly. "Power in the hands of teenagers might be risky," he said, "but power in the hands of the ignorant is downright reckless."

I *loved* playing with my powers. Sure, I still had to keep them a secret from the world, but the mere fact that I could now be myself in the privacy of my home had quickly turned home into my favorite place. I couldn't even walk ten steps without getting an itch to perk up some wilting leaves or revitalize a sluggish insect. That's what my sisters couldn't possibly understand about the roach. It's not that I had some bleeding heart for roaches (just…ewww). It was more this strong compulsion to intervene. I see something injured, I want to heal it. Just like Krystal and Phee (Winter and Summer, respectively) feel compelled to chill and heat things.

And now we could. Between gaining the freedom to use my powers, and witnessing the miracle of that little girl, Grace, popping up alive and well, January 21 should have been an amazing day. But then I remembered the shadow-man hanging from a rope in front of Mel's Diner that night. Even though it had happened two months ago, the terror that had poured off him in waves still felt vivid and raw; the way he had slowly turned to face me, then reached for me…

I shuddered, sloshing orange juice on the covers again.

It was only your imagination, I told myself for the gazillionth time. *Spring hates death. Your inner-season was protesting to being at an event honoring the dead. That's all.*

I shoved the tray back into Daphne's arms, not feeling particularly hungry for runny eggs. "So what's this about a birthday present?" I threw my comforter aside and hopped out of bed, eager to think about something other than creepy shadows.

Daphne grinned and set the tray on my nightstand. "Okay. Follow me."

I saw Taz's and Phee's eyes light up when they realized Daphne was escorting me to my birthday gift, and Krystal had her hand over her mouth as if she was trying to contain a squeal. Whatever this gift was, it was something they couldn't bring to me, which meant it had to be big. Huge, even. I dared to hope…could it be a car?

No. I instantly dashed my own hope. Dad refused to resort to that kind of extravagance. Especially since he had *four* daughters, all in their teens. He'd have to mortgage our house to buy us all cars. Plus both Phee's and Taz's sixteenth birthdays came and went with no sets of wheels.

But what else would have Krystal so excited?

I followed Daphne and my sisters from the bedroom. As Taz passed Daphne's large ficus, vibrant in its red pot beneath the skylight, she stared at it, and narrowed her eyes. The leaves sagged and wilted, shrinking into themselves. She continued down the hall.

I grazed the plant's leaves with my fingertips as I passed by. The ficus sprang back to its current beauty.

Phee turned around and let out an exasperated sigh. "You and Taz are so annoying."

I grinned.

Rather than turn to go downstairs like I was expecting, Daphne and my sisters rounded the corner and continued until we reached the linen closet—a dead-end.

"Okay…?" I wondered aloud.

Daphne reached up to pull a slender gold chain from the ceiling. A wall partition slid forward, and she pulled down a ladder.

"Oh, I get it. You hid my present in the attic."

"You could say that," Daphne grinned. "Go ahead."

Confused, I climbed up the ladder. I had only been in the dark attic a handful of times in the last few years when my dad needed me to fetch something from the cramped, sweltering space. When we were little, Taz and I used to sneak up here to play, but Dad put an end to that. Since the space was unfinished, he was worried about us slipping through the insulation or hurting ourselves on exposed beams.

My curiosity growing, I popped my head through the ceiling opening. My mouth dropped open. I scrambled up the rest of the ladder until I was standing on shiny, hardwood floors. I turned a full 180 degrees, trying to take in the open, sunny space. The previously skeletal walls of the attic had been insulated, dry-walled, textured, and freshly painted. Two of them—the one to my left and to my right—were a crisp cornflower blue. The third wall, the one housing the small round window, was the color of rich, creamy buttermilk. The three walls slanted to greet each other in a sharp point at the roof. A blue shag rug spread across the floor, and I stepped forward so my bare feet could luxuriate in the softness of its fibers. I spotted a brand new comforter set in striped blue, spring green, and yellow folded neatly on the hardwood floor in front of the window where I assumed my bed would go. A free-standing stack of shelves that looked like it was built from tree branches stood to my right. I was already imagining what my book collection would look like on those shelves. A small heater, installed neatly into the wall, hummed to my left, adding a feeling of warmth and life to the space, with an antique trunk—possibly from Uncle Kiel's shop, sitting below the heater.

Dad, Daphne, and my sisters followed me up the ladder, and they all stood beside me now, grinning like happy gargoyles.

"You guys, oh my gosh," I stammered, barely able to talk in my excitement. "Is this—is this *my* room?"

"Your dad did all the work himself that weekend you went horseback riding with Elisa," Daphne beamed. "Well, except for the painting and designer touches, of course. That was me and your sisters. Actually, Phee didn't do much—"

"I told you, I was supervising," Phee said, plucking a speck from her shiny gold fingernail.

Daphne ignored her. "Obviously we still need to bring up your bed…your dad's going to have to take it apart to get it to fit. And I'm sure you'll want to decorate it yourself, but —."

I flung myself into Daphne's arms before she could finish. "I have my own room!" I shrieked, and spun around, jumping up and down and hugging everyone like a crazy person. I couldn't believe it. Krystal and I, being the youngest in our family, had always been forced to share a room in our modest four-bedroom house. Not that Krystal was the worst roommate in the world, but her quiet obsession with dark and dreary things did get on a person's nerves after a while. Plus she always complained about my glass tanks of ladybugs, or grasshoppers, or whatever critters I happened to be raising at the moment. She never let me live down that one time my collection of silk worms, who had been snug in their cocoons for three weeks, hatched into moths overnight. I thought it was kinda sweet being greeted with fifty-some fluttery moths flocking our bedroom that morning, but Krystal was NOT happy, even though I told her it was an accident (how was I to know that the book I was using as a lid had slid over by two inches?).

But now I had my own room, and I could host moth-invasions to my heart's content and no one would complain. And aside from a few quirks, like the fact that the entrance to my room was a ladder, and the fact that the bathroom was now a mile away, my new room *rocked*.

I was running late for school by the time I finally tore myself away from my birthday gift. I took a four minute shower, threw on a pair of skinny jeans and my favorite flannel shirt, braided my wet hair, shoved my steamy glasses on my nose and jumped into Dad's truck in the knick of time, reviving another two houseplants that Taz had tried to kill along the way. Dad usually left for school early, so I figured he must be cutting me some slack since it was my birthday.

Light rain streaked the windshield of Dad's truck on the way to school. His oldies drifted softly through the muggy cab as Krystal and I chatted about this and that. Phee had hitched a ride with a friend, and Taz now rode with Stryder every morning in what they referred to as his "rusty blue chariot." They had all sorts of inside jokes and phrases that I didn't get. I ignored the twinge of jealousy.

No matter. I have an entire attic to myself. My joy-o-meter was through the roof this morning and I was determined to keep it that way.

Once at school, I bypassed my locker and hurried into Mr. English's class (Mr. English teaches Algebra, but if you try to point out the irony to him you get awarded with a scowl). I sank into my desk right as the bell rang, hoping that my friend Brett, who sat to my right, brought his book so we could share.

"Hi Aviva," he grinned, his teeth bright white in contrast to the dark stubble on his chin. For the hundredth time I wished I had Brett's sunny smile. He could be in a toothpaste ad. "Happy birthday," he said, passing me a card.

I beamed at him. "Thanks, Brett."

The front of the card displayed a colorful hand-drawn anime character I didn't recognize. I opened it, trying to decipher his slanted writing.

Naruto's orange,
Sasuke's blue,
you're someone special
I really like you
Happy Birthday

My face heated. Brett was always walking this line with me between 'friend' and 'something more.'

"What's Sasuke?" I asked him, trying to avoid the awkward parts in his poem. "Is that a flower?"

Brett burst out laughing. "You really don't know who Sasuke is? Come on, he's like Naruto's partner in crime and arch nemesis! Don't ask me how that works…."

I was about to ask him who Naruto was when Mr. English chose that moment to tell us to pull out our math homework. Relieved, my face still warm, I dug into my backpack to find my homework. When I sat back up, I noticed a new student, some tall guy, sitting two desks over, one row up—in the same seat that used to belong to my friend Elisa before she moved to Denver to live with her dad.

The class was crowded, and I might not have otherwise noticed the new guy if not for his clothes. While most of the boys at my school preferred their name brand jeans with button-up shirts or t-shirts, the new guy was wearing a strange outfit…some kind of old-fashioned suit.

Curious, I adjusted my glasses to examine him closer. From what I could see, his jacket wasn't really a jacket…it was more of a coat—a topcoat of sorts—charcoal-colored with the front edges meeting one button in the middle, creating an upside-down 'V' and curving into a pair of tails behind. And his pants definitely weren't jeans. They were black and gray striped…trousers? Like the ones I had seen on that old show that Daphne DVRed…*Little House in the Meadow* or something.

Who wears striped trousers to school?

He must be in the Drama Club, I decided. Probably a student who transferred from another class, dressed-up for a performance his club was doing today. It was the only explanation I could fathom for the guy's bizarre clothes.

But as my eyes unwittingly roved over his strikingly pale profile, I realized it was more than his clothes that gave me a weird feeling. A faint stubble shadowed his jawline, and his lips, though relaxed, were pursed slightly. His dark sandy blond hair was parted on the side as if he had started to fashion it, but gave up, his slightly mussed locks careening down to the edge of his coat collar. His physique was more solid and filled out than the softer, rich boys in my class. I could barely make out his eyes, but they appeared to be squinting lazily toward the front of the room as he tapped his long fingers impatiently on one of his legs.

There was a certain air about him that I couldn't quite pinpoint. He exuded arrogance and…sophistication. He was probably the most mature-looking sophomore I had ever seen. If it wasn't for the awareness that lit his features, I would swear he had flunked a few grades, as he looked closer to 20 than 16.

Brett coughed next to me, and I whipped my head to face him. He turned his gaze toward the new guy, and looked back at me with raised eyebrows, his question lingering between us. Embarrassed that he had caught me staring, I offered him a sheepish smile and flicked my hand through the air, as if to say *oh, that? That was nothing.*

I reached down into my backpack and pulled out a spiral notebook, determined to take some pretend-notes to shake the awkwardness. Mr. English was discussing the importance of math in the real world, as he often did before starting a real lesson, this time telling us how our forefathers in Sezona Hills had used math to build a railroad in the early 1870s. "They not only worked hard physically," he was saying, "but they made sense of problems, and persevered in solving them. Because of it, Sezona Hills was amongst the first townships to have a railway, which led to industrialization, and, by extension, to prosperity."

Mr. English eventually collected our homework, then launched into the quadratic formula, which had nothing to do with railroads. Burying my nose into the task of taking notes, I plowed a full five minutes into his lecture before risking another peek at the new guy.

He was still staring ahead, tapping his fingers on his knee, his lips now moving in concentration. Then, to my surprise, he stood.

"This lesson is quite tedious," he announced, facing Mr. English, his voice rumbling deep and smooth. "I should like to hang myself before listening to another minute of your drivel."

I took in a sharp breath, my eyes darting back and forth between Mr. English and this new guy who obviously had a death wish. Never mind my earlier assessment—there was no way this guy was an inter-school transfer. Everyone at Clagan High knows you don't get lippy with the stern algebra teacher.

And his speech. Who uses words like *drivel*? So weird.

I tensed, waiting for Mr. English to light into him. To my bewilderment, the teacher ignored the outburst, continuing his lesson as if nothing had happened. Confused, I glanced around the room, waiting for someone else to say something, or to laugh, but no one spoke. No one reacted. No one so much as paid a glance to the guy standing tall in the middle of the room.

An uneasy feeling uncurled in my stomach.

Unperturbed, the guy turned with smooth deliberate movements to walk out the door. He took two steps when he caught my stare. Against his pallid skin, his eyes were a deep indigo blue. He gazed at me with such brazen openness that I squirmed in my chair, finding it difficult to breathe. Almost immediately I felt annoyed by my own reaction. If he had the audacity to stare, then two could play at this game.

I stared back.

Why wasn't anyone else acknowledging him?

With a sudden air of purpose, he beelined straight to my desk.

"You see me," he said, leaning over me, his bright eyes boring into mine.

I opened my mouth to blurt out "Of course I see you,"

but snapped it shut. Oh *crap*, I thought, dutifully pulling from Daphne's list of approved swear words. *Am I not supposed to see him?* My eyes darted around the room again. No one was watching our little exchange, other than Brett, who kept looking back and forth between me and his notes. But nothing in Brett's expression revealed that he could see this guy up in my grill, so close I could see the lightning-like veins in his throat.

I shook my head a little, my body pressed rigidly back against my chair, trying feebly to deny to him—and to myself— that I could see him, though recognizing the irony in that gesture right away.

"By God, sweet girl, you can see me." His lips spread into a triumphant smile, and then he glided past my desk. "We'll discuss this after your mathematics lesson." I swallowed hard, my hands clutching the side of my desk, my stomach stuck somewhere in my throat.

"What's wrong?" Brett whispered next to me two beats after the strange guy had left, snapping me out of my trance as he touched my arm. "You look really pale, Viv."

I already knew the answer, but I needed to be sure. "Brett, has anyone new been assigned to Elisa's desk?"

"I don't think so," he said, glancing in that direction. *"It's been empty since she moved.* I saw you looking over there earlier. What's up? Do you miss her? I know you two were good friends."

"Um, yeah, I think I'm just missing her more than usual today," I forced the words out. "She came up for horseback riding a couple weeks ago, but it feels weird not having her here on my birthday."

I hoped my voice didn't betray the panic flooding me at Brett's words. It's been empty since she moved. I couldn't be the only one who was able to see and hear the oddly-dressed stranger. I couldn't be. Because that would make me crazy.

Or it would mean I was seeing a ghost.

As if those two aren't the same.

Four

*Maybe all the people
who say ghosts don't exist
are just afraid to admit that they do.*
The Neverending Story

Wednesday, March 20
Present Day

I WORMED MY way through a cluster of students as I exited Mr. English's class, going with the whole "safety in numbers" theory. Assuming the strange guy was one big fat hallucination, I felt pretty confident that the distraction of noise and crowds would prevent me from imagining him again. And if the strange guy was indeed a ghost, well…in all the ghost movies I had ever seen, the victim was never haunted in broad daylight smack dab in the middle of a bustling hall. Really, as long as I stayed away from dark abandoned corridors, old creaky stairs, damp cellars, and apparently Mr. English's class, I should be fine, right?

I continued toward my locker, stopping once to confirm slumber party plans with my friends Liz and Mikayla. We were all bummed that Elisa wouldn't be there.

"Aviva!" someone shouted once I reached my locker, and I jolted. It was only Brett. Man was I jumpy. He hurried to catch up with me.

"Hey," I said. "Oh, sorry for taking off so quick. I meant to tell you that I loved your card."

"Really?" A smile spread across his face. "Even though you have no idea who Naruto is?"

"Yeah, I really don't," I admitted.

"One of these days I'm going to get you to cross over to the dark side of anime with me."

"Yeah, anime's not really my thing. Krystal likes it though."

"You say that, but I bet after three episodes of Sword Art Online I'd have you hooked. That's like the gateway anime. After that you can't get enough, and you need deeper and darker stuff."

"Are we talking about anime or drugs?"

"The two are pretty much the same. SAO is pot, and Garden of Sinners is cocaine. And Yuri on Ice is basically meth."

I raised my eyebrows toward him, and he changed the subject. "So what are your plans for your birthday tonight?"

"Just going out to dinner. On Friday night I'm having a slumber party with Liz and Mikayla. Why…you wanna crash my party?"

"Ooh, that could be fun. Girls in skimpy nighties having pillow fights…"

I punched him in the arm. "Seriously, where do you guys get your information about slumber parties from?"

"There's a 4chan thread for secret slumber party meet-ups."

"No way."

He grinned. "I'm kidding, Miss Gullible. My information comes from my hopeful imagination."

I laughed. "Well sorry, it's March and freezing, so you can kiss your skimpy pajamas fantasy goodbye. Plus my bedroom's in the attic. I don't think you want to climb two stories."

"Two stories to see a bunch of girls sitting around in bulky sweat pants…yeah, I think I'll pass."

"What's a slumber party?" a new voice said to my left. A deep, smooth voice. A voice I had heard only one time in my life but would probably never forget. My body jerked as I swung to look at my pompous hallucination, who continued to talk as if he were perfectly real.

"To slumber means to sleep," he was saying. "How do you reckon having a social gathering of sleeping folks? The very notion is nonsense—."

"Hey, you're doing that pale-thing again," Brett said to my right. "What are you looking at?"

I pointed tentatively to the apparition, hoping, somehow, that Brett would be able to see what I was seeing.

"The Valentine's Dance poster?" Brett asked, gesturing to the bright poster taped to the wall beyond my hallucination.

"Yeah," I muttered lamely. "It's been over a month since that dance. You'd think they'd take that poster down by now. It's an outrage."

"Uh, okay…" a look of question flickered across his features.

"Ha! Shrewd evasion, sweet girl," the apparition said.

"I've gotta go to the bathroom," I blurted, swinging around before Brett could respond.

I ran to the ladies room, the tardy bell ringing as I hurried inside. The bathroom was empty, with students getting settled into their second period classes.

Great. I was officially late.

I walked straight to the counter and dropped my book bag on the floor. The counter was lined with four sinks and a large mirror that spanned from wall to wall.

"Why are you hallucinating?" I railed at the mirror.

"This is a washroom, yes?" The apparition appeared about three feet behind me in the mirror, and I just about jumped out of my skin. He turned and sauntered to the nearest blue stall door and peered inside. "What is this space? A water closet? I've heard rumors about these being built in New York and Chicago, but have never seen one myself. Seems a little extravagant if you're asking me."

I mentally batted away my confusion and swallowed hard. I wasn't going to give into this figment of my very active imagination.

He turned to face me again in the mirror. "But what I really wonder is, why can you see me when no one else can?" He stood with his arms crossed and a smirk playing across his face. "You can chew the rag with that mirror all day long, sweet girl, but I'm no dolt. I know you can see me. It's written all over your face."

I gritted my teeth. If this thing called me 'sweet girl' one more time I might be the first person on Earth to strangle a hallucination. I looked at the apparition in the mirror, trying to dislodge my heart from my throat.

Then I was struck with an idea. Maybe this thing was a hallucination; maybe it was a ghost. Either way, if I convinced it—and myself—that I couldn't see it anymore, maybe it would go away.

I forced my eyes to *unfocus* on the apparition—to look beyond it.

"Well at least it's gone now," I said to the mirror, hoping my voice wasn't overly loud and fake. I tried to adopt a genuine look of relief. "Hopefully for good."

A shadow of uncertainty crept across the apparition's pale face, though I had to force myself to peek for only a moment lest he guess what I was up to.

I grabbed my book bag and swung around to leave, keeping my eyes trained ahead toward the door, purposely walking as close to the apparition as possible in an invasion of personal space that would be unnatural if I could actually see him. He stumbled to the side, his brows furrowed.

Yes, he bought it. I hurried to second period, forcing myself to avoid the impulse to turn around in case he was following me. Or floating after me, or whatever hallucinations do.

"Ms. Aevos, I'm going to have to mark you tardy," Ms. Frost announced when I entered the class. She tapped a few keys on her laptop. "Looks like this is your first one though, so this one's a warning."

I bobbed my head, relieved. "Thanks, and sorry, Ms. Frost."

She nodded and continued her lesson. "Now to practice characterization, I want you all to pull out a sheet of paper...."

I sank into my chair and pulled out some paper, allowing myself to feel a sliver of peace, and triumph, over my recent victory with the hallucination, or whatever the strange guy was.

What was he?

I considered the possibilities. If he really was a hallucination, he had to be a product of my own imagination. Which meant that everything about him—his weird clothes, his arrogant air, his bizarre speech—all came from me. Was that possible? Am I really that creative? Would I use words like 'drivel'? (Maybe I had heard that word from *Little House in the Meadow*, too?). Would I call myself 'sweet girl'?

If he was a hallucination, something had to be wrong with me. Like, a giant tumor was growing in my brain or something.

But if he wasn't a hallucination, he had to be a ghost, right? That was a tough pill for me to swallow, considering I didn't buy into the whole ghost-thing. Even as a little girl, I would ooh and ahh and shiver during my friends' ghost stories, all the while believing they were exaggerating, or that their senses had been confused and what they thought was a ghost was a simple trick of lighting. Even the dark shadow-man hanging from the rope at Mel's Diner hadn't changed my mind about phantoms wandering around in the afterlife. After a good night of sleep, I was sure that the shadow-man was a figment of my neurotic imagination.

But what else could this guy be? If he was a ghost, what did that mean for me? That I could see spirits now?

The tumor theory was suddenly starting to sound more appealing. At least a tumor could be sliced off.

"…You'll start by drawing a Venn diagram comparing and contrasting two real-life people from history," Ms. Frost was saying. "Choose one that you would consider to be a hero—a protagonist—and one that you would consider to be a villain—or antagonist. Come up with at least six character traits these two people have in common, and six that are different. Any questions?"

Jackie to my left raised her hand. "Can I do the Angel Killer for my antagonist?"

"If you're up for the challenge, I say go for it," Ms. Frost told her. "Just keep the details PG rated."

Jackie grinned and grabbed her pencil. I thought she was crazy. I had only half-listened to the assignment, but I was already planning to choose people easy to describe, like Attila the Hun. The problem with the Angel Killer is no one knew his true identity. He was a notorious killer from the late nineteenth century who murdered fourteen women in Sezona Hills and the surrounding areas in a period of nine or ten years. The Angel Murders—thusly named due to the fact that the killer used either charcoal or blood to draw a halo around each of his victim's heads—was still one of the biggest unsolved serial murder cases in American history. Up until the Mel's Diner shooting, the Angel Murders was the only major crime Sezona Hills had ever experienced.

I knew it was morbid, but something deep inside me was intrigued by the idea of my town having such a dark history. Not that I would ever wish that kind of fate on anyone. But sometimes Sezona Hills, with its bright lamp posts and model citizens, felt stifling. The smooth porcelain perfection was a constant reminder that there's not a whole lot of acceptance if you deviate from the norm. More the reason to hide my powers. Shoot, at my school, I was teased for wearing flannel shirts…I could only imagine what my classmates would do if they saw me perking up some daisies. So, yeah, a horrible part of me was fascinated by the fact that there was this big, fat smudge on our quaint little town's past.

And here Taz was worried that she might be evil because she absorbed life from things. What was wrong with me?

Brushing off thoughts of the Angel Killer, I contemplated who to choose for my protagonist, finally scratching

'Abraham Lincoln' on one side of my paper. A generic choice, but my heart really wasn't into this assignment anyway.

"Hello, clever girl."

I jerked. My hallucination with the striking blue eyes was sitting on my desk. *On my desk.*

Well at least he had upgraded me from 'sweet' to 'clever'.

Jackie raised her eyebrows at me, probably wondering why I was throwing my body to the back of my chair as if a rattlesnake was uncoiling in front of me.

I will beat this, I thought. I forced my muscles to relax, leaned down, and scribbled "Osama Bin Laden" as my antagonist.

The apparition stared at me. "You are keeping with this act of yours that you can not see me?"

I ignored him, writing the word "Influential" next to Lincoln and surrounding it with a bubble. He folded his arms across his chest. "Very well." He stretched his legs out, stood up, and walked to the front of the room.

Uh oh.

Ms. Frost, busy on her laptop recording grades, didn't acknowledge the apparition as he jumped on top of her desk. His eyes sparkled merrily as he stood straight and tall in the front of the room.

He threw his shoulders back. *"Oh say can you seeeeeeeeeeeeeeeeee, by the dawn's early liiiiiiiiiiiiiiiiiiiighhhhht….."*

Oh my gosh. He was singing the Star Spangled Banner. Or screeching it, I should say, as I would hardly classify the awful sounds coming from his mouth as singing.

"What so proudly we hailed at the twilight's last gleaming…"

I put my hands over my ears as he continued to serenade me and the class with the worst rendition of our nation's anthem that I had ever heard. Jackie, who had been scribbling on her paper, tossed me another strange look.

"Headache," I mumbled.

"*AND THE ROCKET'S RED GLARE*," he belted out at the top of his lungs—assuming he had lungs. "*THE BOMBS BURSTING IN AIR....*"

"Really bad headache," I amended.

"*GAVE PROOF THROUGH THE NIGHT, THAT OUR FLAG WAS STILL THERE...*"

I swear a cat trapped in a car wash had to sound better than this. I smashed my hands harder against my ears, but to no avail.

"*OH SAY DOES THAT STAR-SPANGLED BANNER YET WAVE—.*"

"Shut-up!"

Ms. Frost, startled, looked up from her laptop. There was a gasp in the class, and everyone turned to look at me.

Oops.

"Alright," the apparition said, his eyes glinting. "As soon as you admit that you can see me."

The class was still staring at me, and I could feel heat creeping up my neck. "Um, sorry," I croaked to Ms. Frost, my cheeks burning. "I think I'm having a migraine. Mind if I go to the health tech?"

"Yes, please do," Ms. Frost said. "Better take your stuff in case they decide to send you home." She paused. "Next time, Ms. Aevos, simply raise your hand to let me know you're not feeling well. No need to shout."

Limbs trembling, I nodded and grabbed my backpack. I snatched my assignment from my desk and hurried out the door. I continued to walk down the hall and around the corner until I was sure no one could overhear me 'talking to myself.' Who knows, maybe the apparition was gone. I turned around.

No such luck.

He was standing there, arms crossed, smugness lifting the corner of his lips. "Ready to admit that you can see me?"

Despite being out of breath, I pinched my lips shut, still trying to recover from my outburst in class. From this short distance, I was astonished by how...solid he looked. His face was definitely paler than most of the boys at Clagan High, with light blue veins caressing his neck, and shadows tracing his prominent jawline. He towered a full head over me, with broad shoulders that seemed a bit out of place with his finely trimmed, tailored suit, and solid arms straining against the sleeves of his jacket. Dark blonde stubble shadowed his fair features, as if he had missed his last shave or two.

I had to admit, if he was a hallucination, I had a damn-fine imagination. I couldn't decide if he was handsome or not, but he was definitely compelling to look at.

"Well then," he said. "Where did I leave off on the Star-Spangled Banner? Let me see...."

"Fine," I bit out. "I can see you. Okay? What do you want from me?"

He stared at me. "Nothing. Why do you ask?"

"Because you're following me. Aren't you? What are you? Are you a ghost?"

Confusion masked his features, and his blue eyes deepened as he considered my questions. "I am certainly no phantom."

I looked at him, perplexed. "Are you sure about that?"

His gaze was sharp. He shook his head as if to clear it. "What's your name, girl?"

"Girl?" I crossed my arms and stepped back in a show of defiance. "I'm not some little kid. And I'll tell you my name as soon as you tell me who you are, and what's going on." The assignment that was crumpled in my hand fell over my fingertips onto the linoleum floor. Moving quickly, I reached down to pick it up.

"I've seen this stationery before," he said, leaning forward to look at my paper.

"It's not stationery, it's my assignment. It's what I'm supposed to be working on right now, but I'll get an 'F' now because of your performance of the *Star Spangled Banner.*"

"Let me see that."

Why would he want my paper? There was barely anything written on it. I shrugged. "Here."

He reached for it, and I noticed a long puckered scar on the flesh of his palm beneath his thumb. Before I had time to contemplate it, he changed his mind and pulled his hand back. He leaned in instead, examining my assignment closer. His mouth gaped open before he quickly snapped it shut. His body seemed to freeze. "I know this longhand." He jerked back, his fists clenched at his side. "Tell me your name, girl."

I stood silent.

"It is you, is it not? You're Aviva."

My mouth fell open. I blinked, and he was gone.

Five

Ghosts take shape under moonlight,
materialize in dreams. Shadows.
Silhouettes of what is no more.
Ellen Hopkins

Wednesday, March 20
Present Day

CUSTOMERS WERE ALREADY flocking
D'Argentino's when we pulled up to the elegant parking
meter half a block down the street. This place was almost
always crowded, even on weeknights. Thankfully Dad had
made a reservation earlier. I had suggested going to a more
down-to-earth place, like Janie's Cafe (trying to avoid Mel's
Diner, for Taz's sake, who still couldn't enter the restaurant
without having a panic attack), but Dad said he wanted to
treat me to something nicer. "It's not every day your little
girl turns sixteen," he explained. I didn't have the heart to
tell him that country fried steak sounded better to me than
some sort of eggplant-tortellini-linguine-thing, so here we
were now, at Clockwork's fanciest restaurant.

The restaurant's lobby flickered dimly with warm
candlelight as we entered. The hostess escorted us to a large
block table in the center of the restaurant, boasting enough

seating for ten. I was pondering where to sit when I heard a jovial voice boom behind me.

"Where's my birthday girl?"

I swung around, my face breaking into a giant grin. "Uncle Kiel!"

I ran to my uncle and flung myself into his outstretched arms.

He swung me around, his cane gripped tightly in his fist, his brown eyes dancing with warmth. "Happy Birthday, Ladybug. Did you get my present?"

"The trunk in my room, right?" I said.

"Yes, and be sure you peek inside later. There's other goodies in there too."

I grinned. "Thanks. The trunk is awesome."

Uncle Kiel settled himself in the dark walnut chair between Krystal and my dad. I was about to prod Uncle Kiel for more hints about what else was in the trunk when Taz and Stryder walked in. Taz introduced Stryder to our uncle, and after everyone said hello, the two sat across from me. We looked over our menus.

"So kiddo, how does it feel to finally be sixteen?" Uncle Kiel asked once the server had brought us our drinks and taken our orders.

"Pretty much the same as being fifteen. Except for, did you hear? I got my own room!" My cheery words sounded hollow and forced, even to my own ears. I was trying desperately to push the encounter with the ghost—or hallucination—or whatever the strange guys was—out of my mind and just enjoy my birthday, but at this point, it was getting more and more difficult to pretend he wasn't real. Ever since he disappeared from school earlier, I couldn't get our conversation out of my head. His brazen stare, his confusion, the way he spoke my name... I felt an impulse to ask my dad about what I had seen, but I was afraid they'd all think I was crazy. Plus a birthday dinner might not be the most ideal setting for discussing ghosts.

"Speaking of birthdays, here Aviva," Stryder said, pushing a flat gift across the table. It was wrapped in shiny blue and orange paper, instantly reminding me of Brett's orange and blue Naruto poem from earlier. "Taz wrapped it," he added. "Good thing, or else it would look like some sort of trash sculpture."

I smiled. "Thanks." I took the gift, trying to hide my surprise that he had given me one.

I peeled off the paper to find a white box labeled Jade Garden Ant Factory, with a colorful picture in the front of ants tunneling through sand held between glass, all framed in black wood. "It's an ant farm!"

"Taz told me you liked taking care of little critters" he explained, giving me a tentative smile. At those words, I felt both awkward, and warmed. Even though it had been nearly four months since New Year's Eve, I was still trying to thaw around Stryder...to trust him. Taz said that Phee, Krystal, and I had forgiven him during one of her loops (apparently right after Phee set an icy bouquet of flowers on fire—not sure how that works), but I had no memory of that event.

"I love it," I grinned at him. "Thank you."

"So, I'm surprised to see someone outside the family at your birthday dinner," Uncle Kiel remarked. His voice was nonchalant, but was tinged with a trace of disapproval. "I have to say young man, you seem to be quite accepting of my nieces'...*talents*."

"Well, you know, getting trapped in a time loop by your

girlfriend's dad gives you an open mind about things," Stryder told him conversationally. "How long have you known about their abilities?"

"Uncle Kiel likes to pretend he just found out about us," Phee said, waving her hand, "but really, he's known all along, just like Dad. Right, Uncle Kiel?"

Uncle Kiel's lips quirked. "To be fair, you girls didn't do the best job of keeping your powers a secret when you were little. No one could deny the strange little occurrences happening around my antique shop."

"Like what?" Stryder asked.

"Like the time I poisoned the weeds in front of the shop, and the next day they looked bigger and healthier than the day before." He chuckled. "Oh, and the time I found my car keys melted on the counter top."

"Melted?" Stryder's voice was incredulous.

"Yes, indeed. Though she was only six at the time, that one had little Miss Phoenix written all over it."

Phee grinned.

"Do you have any abilities yourself?" asked Stryder.

Uncle Kiel, unfolding a napkin, paused, considering the question. "Well, I can make a mean meatball sub."

We all burst into laughter.

"Laugh all you want, but who are you going to come running to the next time you're hungry? Someone who can perk up weeds?"

I tried not to spit out the gulp of water I had just drank.

"He's being modest, girls." Dad grabbed a breadstick from a nearby basket. "Kiel can do a lot more than make a sandwich."

Daphne nodded her agreement. The thought struck me that Daphne seemed so calm about all of this magic-stuff, even though she wasn't blood-related to any of us and had no gifts herself. Come to think of it, none of us really knew how Daphne and Dad even met. That's a pretty big thing to simply not know. Honestly, it felt like she had always been there. I made a mental note to ask her later.

Uncle Kiel, responding to Dad, flung his hands up in a surrendering gesture. "Okay, you got me. I make a killer macaroni salad too."

Daphne laughed while Dad rolled his eyes. "Seriously, Kiel, at this point I think it's safe to show the girls at least one of your tricks."

My heart leapt. Ever since I found out about my dad's powers, I had suspected that Uncle Kiel had powers, too. Dad and Uncle Kiel were brothers, after all. I leaned forward.

"Horace, I don't think that's a good ide—".

"Oh please, Uncle Kiel?" I begged. "It'll be my birthday present."

"Hey, I already got you a trunk for your birthday with an antique leather journal and some cool pens—". He froze, realizing he had spoiled my gift.

Stryder and my dad boomed with laughter.

"Really?" I said. "That's such a nice gift! But…."

"You still wan't me to show you a trick."

"Well, it *is* my Sweet Sixteen. You're supposed to go the extra mile."

Phee laughed. "And you guys say I'm manipulative."

"Spoiled ladybug," Uncle Kiel agreed. "Very well." He glanced around to make sure no customers or restaurant staff were eavesdropping. "As is the case with your father, it's difficult to put into layman's terms who and what I am. My real name is Hveðrungr."

"Hammanda-what?" I reeled at my uncle's use of a foreign tongue.

"Hveðrungr. Though maybe the Danish name would be easier for you to say. Lokkemand."

I sighed.

He grinned. "See why I go by Kiel? Much easier."

"So what can you do?"

"A variety of things. One of my powers is similar to Taz's."

"You can make things fall? Or decompose things?"

"Make things fall, or not fall."

Taz set her fork down. "I don't get it. Why would making something *not* fall be a power?"

"My powers are limited to working within the laws that govern discord or chaos."

I'm sure Krystal, Phee, and Taz's look of confusion mirrored my own.

Stryder leaned forward. "Wait, our substitute teacher just showed us a video on the theory of chaos last week. It has something to do with certain things in our universe being vulnerable to cause and effect, or something like that, right?"

"Close," Uncle Kiel said. "The theory of chaos is the branch of mathematics that deals with complex systems whose behavior is highly sensitive to slight changes in conditions, so that small alterations can give rise to strikingly great consequences." He paused. "Okay, I may have memorized that definition from Google."

Taz and I giggled.

"Isn't chaos *bad*?" Krystal, who had been relatively quiet thus far, piped in.

"Sometimes," Uncle Kiel looked over at her. "It can be

good or bad."

"How does it work?" I asked.

"Well, exactly how the definition states. If there is any condition in the universe in which a small altercation—that is—one small change—can greatly impact the outcome, I can inflict that change to bring forth the outcome I desire."

Uncle Kiel must have noted the foggy expression on our faces. "Here, let me illustrate. You see those plates over there?" He pointed to a small tower of salad plates stacked in the server's station. "Given that they are positioned in a short, sturdy stack in the center of a large counter, my powers of discord would be rather impotent in this situation."

"Okay…?" I tilted my head, still not understanding.

"But the restaurant manager over there, on the other hand…." He pointed toward a man with salt and pepper hair wearing black slacks, a dark blue shirt, and striped tie. The well-dressed manager appeared to be helping his staff get some orders out. He finished loading up a large tray with five or six steaming dishes, then propped the edge of the tray on his shoulder, reaching for a tray stand with his free hand. Uncle Kiel continued. "His quick movements and posture suggest he is a seasoned veteran when it comes to carrying large trays, but the beads of sweat on his forehead suggests he is currently stressed. Also, note how the edge of the tray is on the bottom curve of his shoulder, rather than tucked into his shoulder blade closer to his neck where it would offer more stability. Furthermore, his hand should be holding the tray from the center to maximize balance, yet due to his sense of urgency, he is holding it closer to the edge. When you consider all of the possibilities and probabilities—impossible for most mortals to do, by the way—that manager has a 36.2 percent chance of dropping that tray. Likewise, he has a 63.8 percent chance of not dropping the tray. Because the universe has already calculated a certain risk of that tray falling—I can use my powers to shift the balance the way I will."

"No way," Krystal said, staring at the manager who was now turning away from the food window with his heavy burden.

"Indeed, yes." Uncle Kiel flicked his hand. At the subtle motion, the tray slipped from the manager's shoulder and crashed to the ground, sending a loud clatter ricocheting through the restaurant. A few customers gasped, whipping around in their chairs to see what was causing the commotion.

I jerked, trying to tamper down my shock.

The manager was now crouched down, his face beet red as he scrambled to clean up the mess. Two bussers hurried to help him.

"Kiel!" Dad seethed, keeping his voice low. "When I said to show the girls a trick, that didn't mean to wreak havoc on an innocent restaurant worker."

"How do you suggest I demonstrate my powers, Horace? If I used my abilities to make that tray not drop, it would appear as if I did nothing at all, given that the odds were in his favor."

"Whoa," Stryder and Phee uttered at the same time.

"Your power seems sort of…" I trailed off, trying to find the right word.

"Wrong," Krystal supplied.

"Now all those people have to wait twenty more minutes for their food," Taz added. "And you probably ruined that guy's night."

Uncle Kiel nodded. "Sorry if my power has alarmed you girls. I can't lie to you and say that it doesn't have the potential to be bad. That's why I compared my power to Taz's earlier. We both have abilities that can harm others, if we choose to use them that way. But we can also do a great deal of good, too. I could have just as easily flicked my hand to ensure the manager never dropped his tray. If a child steps out onto the street chasing after her ball, with a mere flick of my wrist I can ensure she escapes the truck barreling down upon her. If a bomb may or may not explode, I can shift the odds to ensure it doesn't explode. As long as I have some probability to work with, I can do a lot of good things for humanity."

An uneasy feeling settled in my stomach. Uncle Kiel kept saying what he *could* do, not what he does do. How many times had he actually used his powers for the good of humanity? He didn't seem to think twice about taking down that manager's tray.

My uncle had always been a bit of a prankster, which was a fun little nuance back when I thought he was a normal person. But now that I knew he was some kind of… *probability shifter*…the prankster thing seemed less cute.

"I've seen you make your orb glow," Krystal pointed out, gesturing to his cane leaning against the chair, which was topped with an emerald green orb. She must have felt uneasy, too.

"Nahhh, you girls always liked to believe that it glowed, but that's simply the way the light hits it," he explained. Then he said in a deep sinister voice, "Or IS it…?"

We all started giggling again. Me, a nervous giggle that I hoped no one else picked up on. Thankfully our server chose that moment to deliver our soups and salads.

I had just stuffed a big blobby bite of mixed greens and blue cheese into my mouth when a deep, unwelcome voice nearly made me spit it out.

"Now this suits me better."

I gagged, then coughed.

"This is a most splendid dining room," he continued. "Far more superior than that pitiful excuse for an eating establishment within your schoolhouse."

I forced myself to swallow down my bite, which now felt like a large lump. *Was this some kind of cosmic joke?*

As if discovering that my uncle could bend events to his will wasn't enough, my ghost was back.

Six

*You hover like a hummingbird;
haunt me in my sleep.
You're feeding on my energy.*
Of Monsters and Men

Wednesday, March 20
Present Day

IT WAS ALMOST funny, when I thought about it. I mean, this seriously was the most ridiculous birthday dinner ever. I might have even laughed, if it wasn't for the gravity of the situation. You know—the fact that a ghost had popped up in the middle of D'Argentino's on my birthday and was now talking to me while I choked down my salad.

"I thought you were only haunting my school," I said through clenched teeth.

"What's that, Aviva?" Stryder asked.

"Nothing," I said.

"So today is your birthday, sweet girl?" the ghost asked rhetorically, eyeing the gift wrap crumpled on the table in front of me. "You should have told me. I would have sang *For She's a Jolly Good Fellow* to you earlier, instead of the *Star Spangled Banner.* Even though you're not actually a fellow. Or good, that I'm aware of." He moved toward the empty chair at the foot of the table.

"Darn, I'm sorry I missed that," I said in the softest voice I could muster. "I guess the *Happy Birthday Song* doesn't exist where you come from?"

He sat down. "The Happy Birthday Song? Never heard of it."

Taz was talking with Krystal and Uncle Kiel, but Stryder leaned across the table, his gray eyes narrowed. "Aviva, who are you talking to?"

I glanced over at the ghost. His hands were folded across the table, and he leaned forward, a small smile quirking his lips. "Yes, clever girl, to whom are you speaking? I'm interested in hearing your response to this inquisition myself."

I froze, considering my options. Back when my sisters and I were keeping our powers a secret, I would have never told anyone that I was being haunted by some arrogant, old-fashioned guy that no one else could see. And even now, I wasn't eager to let my family in on my latest brand of crazy. But given the fact that my family was now open with each other about who we are, and the fact that we just learned some interesting revelations about my uncle, there didn't seem a reason to keep my ghost a secret. In fact, compared to my uncle's tray-tipping performance, a ghost might not even be the weirdest thing that happened tonight.

Plus I had watched too many movies in which the main character could have solved all of her problems in the first twelve minutes if she had simply *told people* what was happening. (Mean kid bullying you? *Tell school authorities.* Psycho-stalker got you down? *Call the police.* Weird ghost following you around? *Get magical family involved*).

Mainly, I was hoping someone could shed some light on

what was happening to me.

Decision made, I pointed to my ghost. "I'm talking to him."

"Uh, the chair?" Stryder asked.

The ghost smiled and leaned back. "This ought to be interesting."

I ignored him and tried to answer Stryder's question. "Yes—I mean no—I mean yes." I grabbed my napkin, using it to cover my heated cheeks. The decision to tell the truth was obviously a lot easier in theory than in practice. I felt like an idiot.

"Everything okay?" Dad asked. I peeked over my napkin to see eight pairs of eyeballs staring at me. I guess they were done talking about Uncle Kiel's cool powers. My ghost, on the other hand, had a look of such bemusement on his face, you would think he was watching a comedy unfold.

"Um, well, I don't know," I stammered. "Dad, since we're on the subject of powers, I was wondering…the fact that we're seasons and all that…can we see ghosts?"

Phee let out a loud guffaw, and Uncle Kiel started at the question.

"Seriously, sweet girl, can you get off this whole phantom theory? I am not a ghost," my not-a-ghost said.

"Then what are you?" I lashed at him. He clamped his lips in a straight line.

My dad eyed me as if trying to gage if I was actually being serious. "You're seeing ghosts?" he asked slowly.

"And talking to them, too," Stryder remarked, biting off the tip of a breadstick. "Never a dull moment with the Aevos family."

"Here-here," my ghost agreed. "Granted, this is my first supper with them, but I am thoroughly enjoying myself."

I glared at him.

"Look, I'm not seeing *ghosts*," I clarified, "Just one ghost. As in, singular."

"Wait, Viv, you're serious?" Phee asked, her face now clouded with disbelief. "How long has this been going on?"

"It started this morning. He was sitting in my Algebra class. He started following me when he realized I could see him."

"Wow," Taz said breathlessly. "So you're really seeing a ghost."

"Or hallucinating…?" I suggested.

My ghost sighed dramatically, tapping his fingers against the tabletop. "Your hallucination theory suggests I'm not real. And trust me sweet girl, I am real."

"I don't think you're hallucinating," Taz said. "That seems like a pretty elaborate head trip."

"Yeah," Phee agreed. "Sorry, but you're not that creative."

"Gee, thanks," I said.

"See, the ladies agree. I am not a hallucination," my ghost stated simply.

"Is he a scary ghost?" Krystal asked, her thickly-lined eyes shining with hope.

At this, my ghost scrunched his entire face into a grimace, rolled his eyes back, and stuck out his tongue. I laughed. Krystal cocked her head.

"Sorry," I said. "He's trying to be scary."

I watched as my ghost (when did he become *mine*?), now restless, stood from his chair at the foot of the table and sauntered closer to Stryder and Taz. He leaned across Stryder and examined the basket of breadsticks. Dad was still glancing between me and the empty chair with a look

55

of deep concentration. "So he's over there?" Dad pointed to the foot of the table. "In that chair?"

"He's standing behind Stryder now."

Stryder jumped from his chair so fast it nearly tipped backwards. "What?!"

Phee laughed. "What happened to 'never a dull moment'…?"

"Sometimes one little dull moment might be nice," Stryder muttered. "Is he still there?"

Taz slid her chair over about a foot, staring intently behind Stryder, trying to see the so-called ghost. The ghost stepped closer to her, peering at the ice cubes in her drink, but then stopped. His body flickered, and he let out a soft groan.

"What's wrong?" I asked.

"Something in the air over here. It's…draining me."

He jerked away from Taz and moved to the other side of Stryder. "That's better."

I looked toward Taz. "You don't have to worry about him getting super close to you. Your powers seem to have a bad effect on him."

"Interesting," Dad and Uncle Kiel uttered at the same time.

Taz looked unconvinced as she moved her chair even further from Stryder.

"Where's he now?" Stryder asked, still loitering behind his chair.

"He's next to your chair. He seems interested in the bread basket."

My ghost nodded his agreement. "Why would the cook choose to make bread so slender?" He reached for a piece, but his fingers glided through the basket. "By the way, it's rather amusing to hear you narrate my every movement."

"He just commented about the bread sticks," I told the table, trying not to do a double-take at the way his hand glided through the basket. "He also likes it that I'm narrating him."

"Typical guy," Phee said. "Such egomaniacs. Even ghost-guys."

My ghost snorted.

I realized how badly this conversation was digressing. "Wait—you guys actually believe me about the ghost?"

Before anyone could answer, our server walked up to our table and set a giant serving tray onto a stand. He moved around the table, placing dinner plates in front of us, but stopped when he reached Stryder. "Uh, sir, would you like to take your seat so you can enjoy your meal?"

Stryder looked at me, his eyebrows raised in question. I gave a small shake of my head. "He's in your chair," I mouthed.

"Nope, I'm good," Stryder told the server. "I, uh, prefer to eat my meals standing. Apparently."

The server gave Stryder a strange look before sauntering off with the tray.

Once the server was out of earshot, Stryder swore under his breath and moved to the foot of the table, sitting down in the empty seat. "Can't believe my chair got jacked by a ghost…"

"Tell him I apologize for being so inconsiderate in acquiring the seat that was clearly his," the ghost said. "But I desire to sit here where I can see your face."

I coughed uncomfortably.

"Though I'd appreciate if that young lady—your sister, is she?—would keep her distance lest she make me ill."

"What'd he say, Aviva?" Taz asked, still looking over at Stryder's former seat like there was some kind of lethal virus attached to it.

"He said he's an ass and he knows it. He also says you should move closer to him...."

"Oh, clever girl," he clucked disapprovingly.

"Aviva!" Daphne admonished. "Ass is *not* an approved curse word. And where are your manners? You don't talk like that. Even when talking to...to...wait—does he have a name?"

Wow, I couldn't believe I never thought to ask. This whole time I kept considering him a "thing"—an apparition; a hallucination. Not an actual person with a name.

I almost didn't want to ask. Learning his name would make him real.

Daphne stared at me expectantly.

"Um," I looked over at the ghost. "Do you have a name? Like Casper, maybe, or the Ghost of Birthday Present...?"

"I go by Kade," his eyes twinkled.

"Kade...what?"

"Kade..." he trailed off, and the twinkle vanished from his eyes. "Just Kade."

Everyone at the table was staring at me and the "empty" chair across from me with unabashed curiosity now. I couldn't begin to imagine what this looked like from their point of view.

I stuffed a bite of lasagna in my mouth, gathering my thoughts, then swallowed hard. "Look, um, Kade," I lowered my voice. "Can you please be quiet for a few minutes while I talk to my family and try to figure this out?"

He stared at me with an impenetrable gaze before nodding. "I'll try, sweet girl, but no promises."

"Thank you." I turned to face the table. "His name is Kade. No last name. So…can someone please tell me what's happening?" I looked at my dad and Uncle Kiel, figuring they would have the most knowledge about this kind of thing.

"I'm not sure," Dad said, still looking with astonishment at the empty chair. "It's normal for your powers to get stronger around your sixteenth birthday—it happened to Phee and Taz like that—but according to the Laws, there are no such things as ghosts."

"See, I told you I wasn't a ghost," Kade said, a smug look on his face.

"You said you'd be quiet," I snapped at him.

"I said I'd try."

"Try harder."

"Horace, don't lie to her," Uncle Kiel said quietly, interrupting my and Kade's bickering. I looked up at him, startled by his soft proclamation. "You know ghosts exist."

"Kiel," my dad's voice was full of warning. "You know what I mean. Ghosts don't exist in a literal sense."

"What do you mean Dad?" I asked. "Do they exist or not?"

He sighed, practically glaring daggers at Kiel. "I mean, it's possible that something so heinous can happen, something so tragic and erroneous and…*wrong*....that it's very memory leaves an essence behind."

"Like an echo?" Taz asked. She had more experience with echoes than any of us.

"Yes, exactly," Uncle Kiel chimed. "And sometimes the echo can be so strong and contain so much energy that it actually forms into something substantial. In other words, a ghost."

"Are they really trying to argue that I'm nothing more than a 'substantial' echo?" Kade scoffed.

"Shush," I waved him off, trying to listen. Stryder and my sisters raised their eyebrows at me, still trying to adjust to the invisible person who had joined us for dinner.

"So theoretically," Dad was saying, still scowling at Uncle Kiel, "ghosts can exist. But neither one of us has ever seen one before. In the same way echoes are invisible and intangible, ghosts are too. That's why it doesn't make sense for you to be seeing one now, Aviva."

"You're wrong again," Uncle Kiel said. "It makes perfect sense. Think about it, Horace." He gestured toward me, making me feel like an imposter in my own conversation. "Aviva is Spring. She brings life. Likewise, she abhors death. This makes her more sensitive—more attuned if you will-- to anything related to death, including the ghost that is evidently following her."

"What does he mean when he says you are Spring?" Kade asked.

I ignored him, not wanting to get into that right now. I could not have loved Uncle Kiel more than I did in that moment. Not only did he believe my ghost story, but he actually explained it in a way that didn't make me sound crazy. And he was treating me like an adult, instead of sugar coating things like my dad.

Dad's brow furrowed. "I can see how a ghost might be drawn to her," he conceded. "But you know as well as I do Kiel that there would need to be some kind of connection between Aviva and this so-called 'ghost' for him to be following her."

"Not necessarily," Uncle Kiel replied. "Again, Aviva is Spring. A strong enough spirit would be able to sense the life-giving energy she exudes. If my theory is correct, such a spirit would be drawn to Aviva like a magnet."

"Like, he's dead so he's attracted to the fact that Aviva brings life?" Taz clarified.

"Exactly," Uncle Kiel confirmed. "Ghosts covet life. They lust for it. The more this ghost lingers around Aviva, the more he will draw from her energy, and the stronger his apparition will become. Likewise, he will avoid Taz like the plague, as she consumes life."

"I wish I had Taz's power," Krystal muttered.

Kade's appearance did look less pale than he had this morning. He looked…realer. Less ghosty. Was that because of my "life-giving energy"?

Across from me, Kade shifted uncomfortably in his chair.

"Is this the first time you've seen a ghost?" my dad directed his question to me.

"Yes," I answered, before remembering something. "Well…I did see a weird shadow at Mel's Diner the night of the candlelight vigil. It wasn't anything obvious though. I thought it was my imagination."

"Interesting," my dad said thoughtfully.

"What?"

"Back at the turn of the nineteenth century, Mel's Diner wasn't a restaurant."

"What was it?" I asked.

"A courthouse."

I turned that thought over in my head.

When I looked toward Kade again, he was nowhere to be found.

"He's gone," I announced to the table. I waited for relief to flood over me, but instead I felt a small pang in my stomach.

"Good," Stryder said, moving back to the chair next to Taz. "Here I finally get your sister to date me and somehow ghost-boy gets to sit next to her."

"He *was* awfully cute…" Taz ribbed him.

"Do you think he's gone for good?" Krystal asked.

"Maybe," I said. "He seemed uncomfortable when we were talking about ghosts."

"What's he look like Viv?" Phee leaned forward.

"Ask Taz. She just said he's cute."

"Come on. Seriously."

"Um, well, he's not *bad* looking."

"Oh my gosh, he's gorgeous, isn't he."

"I don't know Phee, he's a dang ghost."

The dinner conversation, to my relief, eventually moved away from non-ghost-related stuff, my family forcing the change of subject for my benefit, I suspected. Krystal talked about her science fair project idea, in which she planned to procure some stomach acid and test the myth that if you swallow gum, it sits in your stomach for seven years. Afterwards, Daphne, who works as a forest ranger and a park protection dispatcher, talked about various calls she responded to last week, which included three illegal campfires, one group of poachers, and—my personal favorite—two incidences of unsolicited squirrel feeding. "It's my fault," Daphne explained. "I'm supposed to bust people for feeding the squirrels, but every time I see those fat, happy critters enjoying an all-you-can-eat buffet provided by generous campers, I walk by and pretend not to notice. So now it's getting worse and worse." She scrunched up her face. "Don't tell my boss I told you that."

My family and I laughed.

"Your crimes will never leave this table," Stryder

reassured her.

It was one of Daphne's quirks. On the one hand she was always pushing my sisters and I to use good manners—almost to ridiculous measures ("Did you thank your teachers for your quality education today?"), but on the other hand she was often confused by what was considered socially acceptable standards of behavior. In her head, there was nothing wrong with feeding a hungry animal—never mind the environmental impact, or the fact that it might have rabies. There was also nothing wrong with handing out swear words as birthday gifts. I guess Daphne was a bit of an oddball, but it was hard to tell since she's the closest thing to a mom I've ever had.

Finally my cake arrived—a chocolate messy heap that Daphne had baked. (Did I mention she's a horrible cook too?) Everyone sang Happy Birthday, including the wait staff. I tried to get in the spirit, but I felt…off. I couldn't push my ghost out of my head. Kade.

Sixteen candles melded into one glowing blaze on my cake as the song faded to its end. Everyone looked at me expectantly.

"Make a wish, Aviva," Daphne prompted.

I closed my eyes and, before I could stop myself, I wished that Kade would come back. Now that I was accepting the idea that he was a ghost, I wanted to know more about him.

I blew out my candles. One candle flickered stubbornly a moment longer than the others. Before anyone would notice, I took a smaller breath and snuffed it out.

Seven

There's an energy when you hold me;
when you touch me, it's so powerful.
Ellie Golding

Saturday, March 23
Present Day

"ARE YOU KIDDING me?" My stomach heaved as I gaped at the dead frog in the fridge, its chest spread open with pins labeling its various organs. I grabbed the jug of cranberry juice and slammed the door shut. "Do you guys have to put your dead reptiles right next to the eggs?"

"Amphibian," Joe corrected, highlighting something in his notes.

"Maybe you can revive it?" Taz suggested innocently without looking up from her textbook.

I frowned at her and cast a sideways glance toward Brett and Joe. Neither seemed to notice Taz's slip. I wasn't so worried about Joe—Stryder and Taz had told him their bizarre time loop story (minus the tidbits about our dad being Father Time and all of us girls having powers) and apparently he half-believed them and half-didn't—but I definitely didn't want Brett to know about us.

"There's seriously a frog in your fridge?" Brett said, flipping a page of his manga. "Too cool. We should chop off the legs and eat 'em. Rich people do."

I gaped at him. "Yum."

At least Joe had the decency to look apologetic. "Sorry Aviva. That's our frog for anatomy. Your step-mom told us we could keep it there. I have to tutor your sister on all the parts for Friday's midterms. She's hopeless."

Taz nodded. "Truth."

"Not to change the subject, but check this out, Viv," Brett held up his manga for me to see. A curvy anime girl was springing across the page wielding a glowing sword, her purple hair flying behind her.

"Um, what exactly am I looking at?"

"You'd look great if you dyed your hair like that," he pointed out. "Maybe some streaks? It would go awesome with your white hair."

"My hair's not white. It's just really light blonde. It's called 'platinum.'"

"Well, whatever. It'd still look awesome." He set his book down. "Why is your hair so pale, anyway? Did you get super scared as a kid? Like, it shocked the pigment right out of you?"

"You're one to talk," I pointed out. "Your hair looks like you stuck a fork in a socket."

"Hey, don't be hatin' on the 'fro." Brett patted the top of his frizz. "Not everyone can rock this look the way I can."

Taz laughed.

"This is the worst study group ever," I mumbled, pulling out a glass and pouring myself some juice. Midterms were coming up, and Brett had asked me the day before if we could study together. Daphne had said yes, with the condition that we studied in the kitchen. "No boys allowed in your room," she said, which was fine by me. It would be awkward having Brett in my bedroom. Unfortunately the only studying we had managed to do so far was examining dead frogs and boobalicious anime girls.

To be fair though, I was feeling more irritable than I should. My ghost—Kade—had never returned after he disappeared from my birthday dinner. Now I was left burning with a heap of questions and a sense of unease. I was learning that I didn't handle lack of closure well.

Or maybe I was just crabby because I had been up so late last night for my slumber party. Mikayla, Liz, and I hadn't crashed until around 4:00 a.m this morning. They left around 10:00, and instead of taking a much needed nap, I was forced to study.

I should feel grateful that Kade McGhost hadn't shown up during my slumber party. Now that would have been a pain.

I set the juice jug on the counter, not feeling particularly eager to open the fridge again. "Hey, where's Krystal?" I asked, changing the subject.

Joe immediately sat up straighter. Taz and Joe didn't have to ask why I was wondering. Ever since Joseph Tanning started hanging around our house, Krystal almost always made excuses to join him and Taz in whatever they were doing. More than once I had noticed Joe staring at Krystal, and vice-versa, then coyly looking away. It was adorable and annoying. I bet Krystal couldn't wait to turn sixteen so she would officially be allowed to date.

Joseph Tanning—or Joe, as we called him—was the same cute dark-haired guy who had showed concern for me at the candlelight vigil. His arm had finally healed from the shooting at Mel's Diner, but sadly he had a permanently deformed foot due to a hit-and-run accident last spring involving Stryder and a girl from my high school. Joe and Taz had discovered two months ago that they had a few of the same teachers, but for different periods, so now they often studied together. I asked Taz once if Stryder was bothered by the time she spent with Joe. "Stryder trusts Joe with his life. And mine," she had stated matter of-factly. The details still confused me, but apparently in one of their alternate timelines, Joe pulled off some heroic antics in Mel's Diner that forever put him in the category of "trusted friend." Taz also said that Joe had been there for her when Stryder had been shot in one of her loops. I couldn't lie; the whole thing had given me a touch of FOMO syndrome. Taz and Stryder had experienced this entire other reality that no one else could relate with, and I knew the experience made them close. The most I could ever hope for was a guy who might like the same music as me. Or a guy who thought my hair would look great in purple.

"Krystal is over at Staci's," Taz answered my question distractedly as she squinted down at her giant anatomy textbook. "Joe, I'm gonna need to take a look at Prince again. I can't tell the difference between the pancreas and gallbladder."

"You named your frog 'Prince'?" I swallowed another gulp of juice.

Joe walked to the fridge and pulled out the large tin tray, plopping it down on the dining room table. "Yeah, but don't try to kiss him. He'll be the stuff of nightmares if it works."

I laughed, took one last swig of juice, and put my glass in the sink. Brett's phone buzzed and he took a break from his manga to glance down.

"Shoot, I gotta run." He stuffed his books into his backpack. "My mom has to run errands and needs me to babysit Keandra. Can we study some more tomorrow?"

I raised my eyebrows at him in a look that I hoped said "You call this studying?"

He put his hands in the air. "Okay, less manga tomorrow. I promise."

"And are you going to quit trying to convince me to dye my hair purple?"

"Are you going to apologize for making fun of my 'fro?"

"No."

"Well…" he saw the look on my face. "Okay, fine. I won't bring up purple hair. No guarantees on pink or blue, though."

I smiled in spite of myself. "Alight, fine. We can study again. See you tomorrow."

Brett grinned and hurried out the door.

The stench of formaldehyde was making me dizzy. As Joe pointed out the nuances of Prince's pancreas to Taz, I grabbed my books and headed upstairs to my room. A little music and a nap sounded heavenly.

The heater was humming when I entered my attic, and thanks to the scented oil Daphne had plugged into my wall, the room smelled like warm vanilla—a huge step up from the chemical cloud brewing downstairs. My room was still messy from last night's slumber party, with pillows and blankets all over the floor and a large popcorn bowl propped on my bed. The ant farm Stryder had given me for my birthday was set up across the room on my dresser, and I noticed the tiny black specks were finally burrowing tunnels. I watched them for a minute, then walked to my nightstand and picked up the ivory comb sitting there. Pushing aside the popcorn bowl, I sat down on the edge of my bed, running my fingers over the comb's smooth surface, kneading it like a worry stone. The comb, an antique, used to belong to my biological mother. It was made from ivory, with an inlay of a butterfly-half, complete with a gold filigree antenna and a sapphire eye. It was part of a matched set, and even with the other half missing, one could tell that the two halves placed together would form the whole butterfly.

Though I had no memories of my mother, I felt like someone who owned something this beautiful and elegant must have been a lovely person.

I would have to return the comb to my dad's room before he noticed I had swiped it. Although at this point he was probably getting used to my kleptomania when it came to pretty things that used to belong to her.

"Hello, sweet girl."

I jumped about a thousand feet, nearly dropping the comb, and spun around.

His arms were folded casually behind his head, looking utterly relaxed in my bed. He looked even more solid and tangible than he had three days ago. Was this more of my life-giving energy, like Uncle Kiel had said, making him look whole? His face appeared more flushed, his eyes a sparkling blue. Dark blonde stubble dotted his prominent jawline, and his lips were quirked in a half-smile.

I found myself wondering if he truly was a ghost. Did I really have the power to make a spirit look so real without even trying?

I took a deep breath, hiding my shock over his presence and the tiny prickle of excitement that shot through my spine. "I was starting to think that I had dreamed you up."

"Ahhh, but you have it backwards, little one."

"I have what backwards?"

"I am the one who is dreaming about you."

I stared at him blankly, not understanding. I set the butterfly comb down on my nightstand. "Where'd you go these last few days?"

He stared up at me. "I was absent?"

"Yes. The last time I saw you was three days ago. At my birthday dinner."

His eyes registered his confusion, but then he waved it off. "For me, it has been mere minutes. I guess that is the nature of a dream. Skipping hours and days. Time tends to travel non-linearly within the slumbering period."

The dream-thing again. "You think you're asleep?"

"Not so much asleep as unconscious, in a state of fever." He sat up on the bed and planted his feet on the floor. "In my waking world, it is not uncommon for folks to fall victim to a fever, or plague."

"Like the Bubonic plague?"

He gave me a strange look. "You are speaking nonsense, but since you are a product of my subconscious, I will humor you."

I opened my mouth to argue, but he continued to talk.

"Those who are unfortunate enough to be struck with a plague suffer through a severe feverish state that can lead to vivid hallucinations. I've heard men describe incredible visions of things that clearly were not there when in this unfortunate state."

"Okay...?"

"I finally deduced that I myself must be catatonic with illness. And you, this world—it is all a figment of my fevered imagination."

I shook my head. "So you think you're lying in a bed somewhere right now, unconscious with fever? And this is all a dream?"

"Yes. One great, vivid delusion brought on by my illness."

"That makes no sense."

He leveled a patronizing look at me. "Why ever not?"

"Well, for one, you were pretty shocked when you saw my English paper the other day. That's not normal for someone who's dreaming. You can't take a dreaming person by surprise since it's his own imagination creating the events that happen."

Kade blinked at me, quiet. "An astonishingly sound argument, little one. But you forget; on some level I'm in control over all that happens. In that moment my subconscious wanted me to be surprised. It was simply part of the script."

"So the fact that you recognized my writing was part of the script too? And Ms. Frost called me Ms. Aevos, but never Aviva, yet you knew my name without me telling you. How?"

"Because you're part of my delusion. I simply gave you the name I wanted you to have."

I sighed and tried to refrain from rolling my eyes. "Oh, really? Then explain to me, why would you choose to give me the name 'Aviva'? I highly doubt that name exists anywhere in your 'waking' world."

It was a shot in the dark, but I had a good feeling I was right. I'd seen Catherines and Ediths and Winifreds next to black and white photos, but no Avivas.

"Because I've yearned to know you my whole life," he

explained, "so I obviously conjured an image of you in this vivid dream I'm experiencing, and called you by that name."

I wondered if Kade knew that the more he talked, the less he made sense. "What do you mean, you've always wanted to know me in 'real' life? I don't understand."

"I found a letter penned by you when I was a child. This I remember from my real life, though I do not remember much else. When I discovered your letter, it was signed with the name Aviva. I was never entirely sure if the letter was intended for me, for I do not know anyone by that name. But when I saw your penmanship on the English paper crumpled in your hand, it was the same handwriting as the letter I received as a child. I was momentarily shocked, thinking I was finally meeting my mysterious Aviva, the girl who has been an enigma my entire life. Until I realized it is all part of an elaborate dream."

"That's impossible. I've never written you a letter. I didn't even know you as a kid."

He looked at me as if I were a small child. "Of course it's impossible. Have you not been paying attention, little one? Everything that happens in your world is impossible, because *this is all a dream.* But yes, the Aviva I'm referring to in my waking world really did pen a letter, and it traveled to me through the wind. I found it in front of a clock tower. Though I feel like I lost it, somehow, or locked it away..." he frowned, trying to remember. "Nonetheless, it was signed with her—your—name."

"And it was addressed to you?"

"Yes. It opens with *Dear Kade.*"

I laughed. "Maybe you really are delirious with fever. There's no way I would start a letter like that."

Actually, I couldn't think of an instance where I would even write a letter. A text, maybe, or a DM…and those usually opened with "Hey."

"That's what I've been striving to tell you. I'm delirious. But the letter is real. Your English paper, however, was not real. That was a product of my imagination. My mind simply applied the handwriting that I have memorized in my waking world to that paper in my dream."

"Okay, forget about the letter for a minute. You seriously think this is all some mass dream?"

"Yes, I do. It's the only theory that explains why I seem to skip from place to place, and why time seems to have no construct here. And it's the only thing that explains this world and all of its magic."

"Magic."

"Yes. These frames and windows with pictures in motion, the peculiar candlelight that glows without a flame, the water that flows with a mere touch, all of your places of worship marked with golden arches, the strange attire—"

I laughed. "Those aren't places of worship. Those are fast food restaurants. People eat there."

"How is food 'fast'? Food does not move. It remains stationary upon a platter."

I sighed. "Okay, I get it. The 'magic' you're referring to is simply what we call 'technology.' You're obviously from the far-past."

He shook his head. "No, it can not be so. This place is far too extraordinary to be real, even for the future."

"What do you mean?"

"Well, consider those small magic boxes everyone holds, which evidently allow folks to project their voices from a great distance away."

I picked my cellphone up from my side table. "This?"

His eyes lit up. "Yes, that! It has amazing power. I saw a group of young people at your institution of learning posing for what appeared to be a photograph, holding that contraption an appropriate distance away with a long stick. Imagine that, capturing a photograph with that tiny thing!" He gestured toward my phone. "That is far too astonishing to be the future."

I laughed at his description of a selfie stick. I tilted the phone toward him and pointed toward the tiny camera icon. "See? They were using the camera app to take pictures."

"...app? I thought you captured pictures with a camera."

I leaned close and held the phone up to his face for him to see. "See these little pictures? These are called 'apps.' They're how we control what the phone does. This one controls the camera, but this is just the app. The camera itself is this little lens on the front," I flipped the phone around.

He drew closer to my phone. "How many apps does this cell-contraption possess?"

"Well, mine has at least fifty. But there are thousands out there—maybe even millions—that can be added to a person's cellphone."

"And everyone in this place carries one?"

"Pretty much."

Astonishment shone on his face. "Incredible."

"Yet you still think you're dreaming all of this? Are your dreams usually so detailed?"

His brow furrowed. "Yes. I am being flooded with... knowledge, in this moment."

"You remember who you are?" I couldn't tone down the

excitement in my voice.

"No. No memories. Only knowledge."

I let out a disappointed puff of air. "Knowledge of what, then?"

"Photography. It's as if gazing at that tiny camera inside of your magic box has granted me access to information." He paused, as if trying to work through the sludge in his head. "I'll be damned, little one. I am a photographer! I must be. I can feel how well-schooled I am in this subject. More-so than the average person. The complexity of developing glass plates...whoa." He put a hand behind his neck. "I tried an experiment once to develop dry gel on paper to replace the photographic plate so that a photographer would no longer need to carry boxes of plates and toxic chemicals around and...my God, it worked! I invented a camera that anyone can use! It is truly revolutionary."

I gazed down at my cellphone, a touch of sadness fluttering against me like the soft wings of a lost butterfly.

Noticing my shift of mood, he, too, gazed down at my phone. "It *will* happen," he said softly. "Yes, that amazing camera in your hands makes my invention look like a whiffet's toy, but all of this is only a dream. I will wake up any second and realize that I am still me, and I am contributing wonderful things to my world."

I coughed uncomfortably. Then it occurred to me. "Hey, that whole experiment thing you described is a memory! What else can you remember?"

He sighed. "Nearly nothing. It is so odd." He gazed upward, his eyes squinting in concentration. "I admit, I am ashamed to recall so little. I do know the ladies do not wear trousers where I come from, as you are. The men wear similar attire to that which I am wearing. There is land, and farms, and nothing—," his arm swept the room—, "of this. Men and women understand how to speak. Speech here in this dream is…abrupt and peculiar. And everything is slower in my waking world. Much slower. This world seems quite…fast. Much like your food. It over-ornates the senses. Perhaps that is why I disappeared. Even in my catatonic state this dream world is much to endure."

"What's your full name?"

He seemed agitated by the question. "I remember only Kade."

"You remember the opening line of a letter I supposedly wrote you when you were a child, and a bazillion facts about old-school photography, but you can't remember your full name?"

"I am certain the fever has given me partial amnesia. I can fathom no other reason why my mind is choosing to hang onto some memories whilst discarding the rest. I only hope my memory-loss is not permanent."

"You don't have a fever," I argued. "Not anymore, at least. You may *have had* a fever, and that's why you're a ghost now…."

He glared at me.

"How'd you get that scar?" I changed the subject, pointing to the puckered gouge at the heel of his hand. The scar was lined up almost perfectly with his thumb, traveling down at least two inches until it nearly touched his wrist, its pearly-lavender color standing out starkly against his skin.

His eyes drifted up, trying to remember. "I do not know. But it has something to do with pumpkins."

"Pumpkins?"

"Indeed, pumpkins. Or perhaps only one pumpkin."

"Okay…" I pressed on. "Where are you from?"

"The township of Sezona Valley."

Now we were getting somewhere. I made a mental note to research whether Sezona Hills used to be called Sezona Valley. It would make sense, given that our little town featured not a single hill. Really, Sezona Hills should be called There-iz-no Hills.

"Do you have a family?"

"My gut tells me I have a family, but I can not generate an image of them in my mind. I have friends, too. Dear friends. I can think of two by their first names only. George and William."

"And a girlfriend?" The words blurted out before I could stop them. My cheeks instantly burned.

"A *girl* friend? I have lady acquaintances, yes. I am sure of it."

I sighed with relief, realizing that the term girlfriend didn't have the same implications for him that it did for me.

He paused, thinking, then continued. "I feel like I have made a commitment to someone in my waking world. Perhaps I am betrothed?"

I didn't know what to think about that. Why wouldn't he have someone special from wherever he came from? He seemed like he could be a catch. Well, aside from the fact that he was stalkery, arrogant, and probably dead.

"How old are you?" I finally asked.

He gazed at me, quiet for a moment. "I'm a young man of marriageable age. That is all I know."

What did that mean? 17? 19? 28? Without knowing what time period he was from, I had no idea what constituted a "marriageable" age.

Suddenly my skin grew hot with self-awareness. I was

sixteen years old, alone in my bedroom with a "young man of marriageable age."

So much for Daphne's "no boys" rule.

Did ghosts count as boys?

I squirmed beneath his steady gaze.

"You have extraordinary hair," he said out of nowhere. "It's like alabaster streaked with sunlight. I've never seen anything like it before." He reached out as if he wanted to touch it, but then dropped his hand. "I can not touch anything. But it's nice to know I can imagine such vividly beautiful things."

A warmth spread through my chest. It wasn't uncommon for my pale hair to draw attention from time to time, but it was usually things like "What brand of hair dye do you use?" ("None") or "Do blondes really have more fun?" ("I don't know—I've never been anything but blonde"). Or, the latest, "Hey, nice hair. You should dye it purple." Never once had I been told that my hair was like "alabaster streaked with sunlight." I liked the way the word 'alabaster' rolled off the tongue.

I cleared my throat, trying to figure out what to say. "This isn't your imagination. I promise you, I'm really standing here."

"A part of me wishes that were true. But the bigger part of me knows it is not, and is exceedingly grateful for that fact. Take no offense, but if you are real, what does that make me?"

I looked at him hard. "Remember how offended you were when I thought you were a hallucination? Because that meant you're not real? Well now you're doing the same thing to me. You're saying I'm nothing but a dream. Which means I'm not real. That's pretty insulting, you know." I crossed my arms. "I've been called a nerd before. Even a freak. But not once has someone accused me of not existing."

I paused. He stared.

"Does anything I'm saying make sense to you?"

"No."

Irritation rubbed my nerves like sandpaper against rust. He was so cocky! He couldn't step out of his little self-righteous box for two seconds to see that I might be right. "Look, Kade, you don't have a freakin' fever, okay? This isn't a hallucination. I'm real. This world is real. Look, touch me." I held my hand out.

"As I have previously stated, I can not touch you. Behold." He went to grab one of the twigs from my branched shelf, and his hand went right through it as if it were a hologram. "I can sit on chairs, and lean against things, and even climb things. But I can not deliberately touch things with my hands. Even people. People walk right through me. When I reach out to touch others, my fingers travel right through them. It's becoming a torment for me."

This explained why he refused to take my English paper from my hand in the hall. I also recalled during my birthday dinner, he was able to sit perfectly fine in the chair across from me, yet his hand went right through the bread basket as if he were a projection.

"Isn't that the exact characteristics of a ghost?" I pointed out.

"Or a dream?" he countered.

"You sure have to jump through a lot of hoops to convince yourself that your theory is true…" I trailed off, seeing a shadow cross his face.

"What difference does it make?" his tone was sharp.

"Either way, there seems to be only one person in the world who can hear me and see me. You. For this reason I can not leave you."

My stomach dropped. "What? You're not leaving? What exactly is your plan? To follow me around forever?"

"Not forever, sweet girl. Only until I wake up from this bizarre daydream."

"What if you don't wake up until I'm seventy-two years old?" I railed.

"It is not greatly laborious to follow you around. Indeed, it is quite easy. And you are but a dream, so it is not truly bothersome to you."

"Arghhh!" I pointed to my door. "Get out!"

"No. I shall stay." He laid back down on my bed.

I groaned and collapsed on the blue shag rug.

He jumped up. "Are you not feeling well?"

"Of course I'm not feeling well!" I lashed out. "How could I possibly feel well when I'm doomed to be haunted by a ghost for the rest of my life? And you don't even care! I'm nothing more than a dream to you."

He stared at me. "Forgive me for causing you distress, sweet girl. Even though you are a delusion, you are an exceedingly convincing one, and I do find myself disquieted by your suffering."

"Gee, thanks. That's awfully kind of you, to want your delusion to be happy."

His blue eyes darkened. "What can I do?"

"Leave."

"I can not do that."

"Why not?"

"Dream or not, this place is too lonely when it is devoid of the only human who acknowledges my existence." He paused. "I start to lose grip of myself when I am alone."

I sat up and crossed my arms. "If you won't leave, then at least stop referring to me as a dream, okay? You don't have to agree with me, but simply *consider* the possibility that I might be real. That I exist. That all of this exists. Consider the possibility that you really are a ghost. That way we can move forward. We can try to figure out who you are and why you're here."

His eyes grew hard, his face stoney.

"I can not do that either."

I stood up. "For someone with such fancy speech, you are the most clueless person I've ever met."

His body began to tremble. "Stop."

I had touched a nerve. Emboldened, I stepped closer. "Look Kade, it's time to face the facts. I'm real. I belong here. You don't. You're from the past. You're a ghost. Look hard into yourself for the truth. Would your imagination really be able to create all of this?" I gestured around me. "Quit this stupid denial crap. Why are you so hell-bent that you aren't a ghost when all the evidence says you are?"

"Because I can't be dead, Aviva!" he roared, lunging forward and grabbing me right below the shoulders. "I refuse!"

I yelped as electricity jolted through me. It wasn't painful, it was just…shocking, like a concentrated rush of static electricity being dumped from his hands into my body. He jolted backwards and the blood drained from his face. Blood that shouldn't be there for a ghost.

"Bloody hell. I felt you." He gazed at me. "How is that possible?"

I stood in place, still buzzing in the after-shock of whatever just happened.

"Is it because I lost my temper?" he wondered aloud. He moved toward me again, his stare piercing me, his lips straight and determined.

I stepped back.

"Please Aviva, forgive me. I will not harm you. I am calm now. I need to try this without the frustration."

I nodded mutely, my heart drumming in my chest. His hands reached for my face, and I froze, watching his face enraptured in concentration. My breathing grew hard. His fingertips grazed my cheek, feather-light. Electricity vibrated the nerve endings of my skin, spreading across my cheeks like a warm, delicious fire. Growing braver, he cupped my face into his hands more firmly, his thumb tracing my jawline as his fingers stretched across my temples and gently gripped the hair right at my neckline. His electric current hummed through my body. He peered down at me, his question lingering between us.

"I feel you too," I whispered.

Eight

Why do they say ghosts are cold?
Mine are warm,
a breath dampening your cheek,
a voice when you thought you were alone.
Julie Buntin

Sunday, March 24
Present Day

"SO WHAT FLAVOR do you want?"

Stryder scanned the colorful options beyond the glass.
"I'm thinking Rocky Road."

"Not you." Taz punched him in the arm. "I'm talking to
Grace. What flavor do you want?"

Grace's nose scrunched in concentration as she
considered all of her options. "Ooh, look at that one. It's
pink...with gum balls!" She pointed at the pink goo.

I chuckled. The same kid who pretended to be a kung-fu
ninja earlier now wanted pink ice-cream. "Watch out
Grace," I told her. "They always sucker you in with pretty
colors. Then you find out later in life that chocolate is way
better."

Grace looked up at Taz, her face serious. "Is that true?"

"Kinda," Taz laughed. "But pink with gum balls is still

pretty dang yummy."

We placed our order and left Sweet Clouds Creamery with heaping cones, strolling toward Pendulum Square. It was an unseasonably warm day for March, with puffy clouds—much like our ice-cream—piled into a spruce sky, and a hint of moisture in the air. Stryder and Taz had been babysitting Grace every Sunday for a couple months now. Shelly Sanders, Grace's single mother, was more than grateful to have Taz and Stryder so willing to watch Grace while she worked her busy Sunday morning shifts.

"Thanks again for letting me tag along with you guys," I said, tilting my cone forward to keep my mint 'n chips from dripping all over my shirt.

"*Letting* you tag along?" Stryder took a giant bite of his Rocky Road before continuing. "Pretty sure we insisted."

Taz nodded. "Seriously, one more hour by yourself, Viv, and you would have had the neighborhood looking like something from a Home and Gardens magazine." She licked her ice-cream. "Though at least you deal with depression better than Krystal. It was pretty cool to see you revive that dove. Now we know you can heal things larger than roaches without blowing them up."

The dove was a local resident of our yard who had recently laid eggs in the eaves of our backyard patio. This morning, Taz and I found her waddling into some shrubs near the street. Upon catching her, I discovered that she had been shot with a pellet gun. The small hole went clear through her wing and shoulder blade, with an exit wound on the other side. Without thinking, I concentrated all my energy on the dove's injury until all that was left were two rough little scars. Luckily Taz was there to catch me when I passed out, and she dragged me back into the house. Once

Stryder arrived with Grace, the two decided I needed some fresh air.

We reached the wrought iron benches at Pendulum Square. The brick planter in front of the square's fountain was vibrant with orange and yellow snapdragons popping from a cloud of white lilies. The thick, sickly-sweet smell of the snapdragons assaulted my senses. I could smell all sorts of flowers when my sisters couldn't—it must be part of the whole spring-thing.

Taz narrowed her eyes at the snapdragons, and they began to wilt.

"Dang it, Taz." I hurried and leaned over the flowers, touching them to counteract her death-wish until they sprang back to life. I wished my power worked by narrowing my eyes the way hers did. It'd make things much easier.

"I can't take you two anywhere," Stryder sighed. "It's one nonstop power struggle."

"Sorry," Taz said. "I don't want the flowers to die; it just feels so good to mess with things. At least I leave them with enough life so Aviva can revive them."

"So you can kill them again," I retorted, even though I knew exactly what she was talking about. Lately the compulsion to bring energy to every plant I walked by was almost too intense to ignore. Dad said that teenage hormones aggravate our cravings to use our powers, and we'd mellow out once we were older. But that didn't help me and Taz much now.

"Should I be worried that my girlfriend likes to kill things?" Stryder said, pulling Taz into his arms.

"Not as long as you're nice to me," she winked.

The bench directly in front of Maui was occupied by two

women and a stroller, so we settled for two benches across the square. I sat on the one facing the large fountain, a six-tiered marble monstrosity with carved angels holding up each tier, and two noble lions sitting proudly upright on the bottom tier shooting arches of sparkling aqua water from their mouths.

Taz sat down next to me. "Feeling any better?"

"Oh, yeah. This is great," I reassured. "Sorry that I've been all weird lately. It's just…." I trailed off, not sure how to finish my thought. I was the only thing Kade could touch, and it made me feel confused, and restless, and distracted. But how did I voice these things aloud when I couldn't form the thoughts in my head?

Taz nodded her understanding to my unspoken words. "Is he…" she looked around, as if that mattered, "…here, right now?"

Grace, with her ice-cream cone in tow, tugged at Stryder's hand and pointed toward the fountain. "Can we make a wish?" she asked.

"As soon as we finish our ice-cream," he told her. I could tell he was stalling, interested in my and Taz's conversation. He perched himself on the wide stone rim of the fountain, facing us.

Grace balanced her half-eaten cone on the rim and climbed up, holding her arms up in the air like a bird getting ready to take flight. "Look, I'm a moth!"

Stryder shot a grin at Grace. "A moth? Why not an angel or a butterfly?"

"I want to be a moth."

"Be careful that you don't fall, little moth girl," Taz warned her before returning her attention back to me. "So is he?"

I swallowed a bite of ice-cream. "No, he's not here, but he was at church with us this morning."

"Really? You did a great job pretending he wasn't. I couldn't even tell."

"He was actually behaving himself for once."

Stryder leaned in. "I bet they take church seriously where he comes from."

I nodded my agreement. "I think you're right. He was actually singing along with some of the older hymns."

I didn't bother telling them that he belted out Amazing Grace with a voice so strong and beautiful that it had sent shivers down my spine. He had officially confirmed my suspicion that his horrible screeching of the Star Spangled Banner was a ruse. Now his startling voice was playing on repeat in my head.

Along with the sensation of his touch last night.

"When did he leave?" Taz bit into her cone.

"When we all crammed into Stryder's truck. I'm starting to think he doesn't travel. Every time I get into any kind of vehicle, he disappears."

"That means if you ever need a break from him, all you need to do is get into a car."

"Yeah, but then he eventually finds me in my new hiding place."

"Who finds you?" a familiar deep voice asked. I leapt a foot from the bench. Speak of the devil.

"Oh my gosh, he's here!" Taz squealed.

Stryder straightened and clasped his hands together.

Did those two have to look so thrilled about the poltergeist haunting me?

Once my heart beat calmed, I looked over at Kade, perched on the fountain next to Stryder, and rolled my eyes.

"Who do you think?"

A look of confusion rolled over Stryder's features. "Your ghost, Viv. Isn't that who we've been talking about?"

"No, I'm talking to him now."

"Oh, yeah. Sorry." Stryder glanced over to his left where my eyes were focused. "Hey, Kade. What's up?"

"Peculiar question," Kade remarked, gazing at the sky. "Is your friend's vision so impeded that he can not see the sky is 'up,' along with the clouds. Oh, and that curious bird soaring in the distance."

I didn't bother telling him that the 'curious bird' was actually an airplane. One thing at a time. "It's just a greeting, Kade. Like a casual way of saying hello."

"Ahhh. Very well. Tell him good day for me, and 'what is up' as well."

I looked back at Stryder. "Kade says hey."

Kade's lips quirked. I think he was getting used to my lousy translation skills. "What is this pastry you are nibbling on?" He moved toward me and peered down at my half-eaten cone, but then flickered and groaned, clutching his chest.

"Your power," I told Taz. Her eyes widened and she leapt back, perching herself on the fountain near Stryder. "Sorry."

Kade's body re-solidified, and he straightened. "It's ice-cream. See?" I held it out toward him. "It comes in all kinds of flavors, but mint 'n chip is my favorite."

His eyes lit up. "Ice-cream is all the rage where I live, but I have never heard of mint ice-cream. I love the freshness of mint. My mother acquired a recipe some time past for mint sugar sticks." His eyes widened and he scratched his head. "Alas, that memory occurred to me quite abruptly. I have a mother! I mean, I suspected as much. But now I believe my mother is still alive. And I am quite fond of her. I can not recall my father, however…" he frowned. "Anyhow, George's family made mint sticks with crooks on the top for Christmastime and adorned their tree branches with them."

Candy canes. I could barely contain my grin. Another clue. Whatever period of time Kade came from, candy canes were just making an appearance into the world.

"Is that what your mint and chips taste like?" Kade asked, before I could ask him if he remembered anything else.

I considered his question. Describing flavors to someone who had no ability to taste them was like trying to describe the color purple to the blind. (Although at least a blind person wouldn't tell me I should dye my hair purple.)

I wished I could share the ice-cream with him.

"Yeah," I finally answered, "I think it tastes like your mint sticks, but colder, and creamier, with a hint of chocolate. It's like…" I thought for a few seconds, "…it's like that moment as a little kid when you're feeling silly, and spontaneous, and carefree. Mint 'n chip ice-cream tastes like that."

Kade gazed at me.

"Wow Viv," Taz said. She and Stryder were both leaning forward, engrossed in my one-sided conversation. "That was the most poetic thing I've ever heard you say."

Of course the first time in my life I burst into poetry is when I'm describing ice-cream. Go figure.

"Why is Vivi talking to that blurry thing?" Grace's curious voice piped in. Her arms were now swinging back and forth as she mastered her moth navigation skills on the fountain.

Stryder and Taz both gasped.

"Grace, do you see something by Aviva?" Stryder asked slowly.

"Yes, silly" she said simply, pointing toward Kade. "Right there. See?"

My breath came out in excited puffs. "What *exactly* do you see?"

She stopped swinging her arms and squinted her eyes toward Kade. He held very still.

"A smooshed spot," she finally said, then continued to swing her arms and prance around the fountain.

"Does the 'smooshed spot' have a shape? Like, the shape of a person, maybe?" Stryder prompted.

Grace stopped and looked toward Kade again. "Nope. It's just a smudgy thing."

I sighed. Damn. I was so hoping someone else could see Kade too, even if that someone else was a five year-old girl. I was grateful that my family and Stryder believed me about Kade, but his presence still had me questioning my sanity. One other pair of eyes confirming Kade's existence would be awesome.

Kade stood up and moved back toward the fountain. Grace's eyes tracked his movement.

"The smooshy-thing is by Stry now," she sang out, then continued her dance around the fountain.

Hope welled up within me again. "She's right," I told Taz and Stryder. "He just moved back to the fountain. She's not seeing Kade as a person like I am, but she definitely sees him."

"Whoa," Taz mused. "I wonder if it's like the echoes."

Stryder nodded. "Yeah, I remember your dad saying that time has less hold on little kids. You think the same is true about ghosts?"

"Yeah, maybe," Taz twirled a lock of auburn hair around her finger, her lips pursed in thought. "Though I still wonder why Grace only sees a smudge…."

I stopped listening as a fragment of a thought wiggled through the peripheral of my conscious. At Mel's Diner, the night of the candlelight vigil, I had seen a shadow that I could only describe as a "smudge," too. Up until now I had assumed that I was just seeing things that night, but was it possible that the smudge had been Ka—?

A splash interrupted my thoughts.

Grace!

Kade lunged for the fountain and dove in.

Watching normal flesh and blood people swim through water already looks like something ghostly. The water is transparent, and their bodies shimmer and ripple like something ethereal. But nothing can describe the way a ghost looks moving through the shallow waters of a fountain. The water sparked against Kade's skin, then jerked away from his body with the speed of a lashing whip. This effect created a violent, flashing tunnel around Kade, his own galvanized water tube.

It was clear he didn't belong there.

Another splash sounded, and Stryder was now in the fountain, too. He heaved himself out a moment later with a soaking wet Grace tucked beneath his arm, her curly brown hair tangled and plastered to her forehead, her sky blue pants pressed against her legs like a baggy second skin. Towering behind them was a perfectly dry Kade.

"Oh my gosh, Grace!" Taz ran up to the trio. "Are you okay?"

Grace rubbed her nose and eyes with her clenched fist, blinking in shock. Then she snorted and giggled. "I got water up my nose."

Stryder planted Grace's feet to the ground, steadying her. His jeans and the bottom of his shirt were soaking wet. "I think that's enough flying for you today, Lil' Miss Trouble." He wiggled his cellphone out from his drenched pocket and pushed a few buttons on his home screen. "Dead," he mumbled. "Good thing I'm filthy rich."

"Sorry, Stry," Grace offered meekly, though she could barely contain the grin spreading across her face at having gone for a lovely impromptu swim in the square's fountain. "I wanted to spit water back at the lions, and I fell."

I wondered how Taz and Stryder were going to explain her wet clothes to Grace's mom.

"How'd you get so soaked?" Taz asked Stryder. "The fountain's only like two feet deep."

Stryder rolled his eyes. "I panicked and lunged on all fours to grab her."

Taz and I laughed.

Kade was looking back and forth between Stryder and Grace with an entirely different expression on his face. He looked…dismayed.

"What's wrong?" I asked him.

"Well my phone is dead for one, not to mention I look like I've pissed myself—" Stryder stopped, seeing me shake my head. "Oh, you mean Kade."

Kade met my gaze. "I am utterly powerless. I can not so much as rescue a small child in danger. I—I have no purpose."

I felt a pang in my chest. In his life, he was probably used to being the hero. Saving the damsel in distress. And now he felt useless. Kade might think this was all a dream, but I knew it was real. Ghost or not, his sadness was real too.

"Come on," I said, grabbing his hand. "Let's go for a walk." A current immediately pulsed from his hand into mine. I jerked, but forced myself to maintain my grip. After a few seconds, the current subsided to a steady, pulsing warmth.

I waved goodbye to Taz and Stryder, who were still messing with Stryder's fried phone. Grace waved back. "Bye Vivi! Bye Smooshy!"

Once I pulled Kade away from the bench and across the courtyard, I dropped his hand. I couldn't be seen by other pedestrians, after all, holding on to thin air.

"You may continue to hold my hand if you are so inclined," he turned to me as we sauntered up toward Maui, mischievous sparks lighting his eyes to a cerulean blue, much like the water in the fountain. "I am enjoying your warmth."

"In your dreams, Smooshy." I could barely contain my grin at his newfound nickname. "But hey, since apparently you are dreaming, why not just command your imagination to make me hold your hand?"

He paused and squeezed his eyes shut, his whole face a mask of concentration, his lips slightly moving.

He opened his eyes. "My attempt appears to have failed."

"You need to dream of easier women."

We passed another brick planter, the blossoms in this one still closed, probably due to a nearby hedge casting shade upon the flower bed. I leaned over and touched the nearest bud, and it eagerly opened its petals to greet the morning.

"Do my eyes deceive me?" Kade asked, his voice unable to contain his wonderment. "This dream gets more and more strange with each passing minute."

I laughed, feeling unconcerned that he had witnessed me

using my powers. Our weird-ometer was already maxed out with him being a ghost and all.

"I give energy to things," I told him.

"Energy? As in, life?"

"Yes. But it's not like I can bring dead things back to life. There has to be at least a spark of life for my powers to work."

"Do all of the people in this place have powers?"

"No. Just me and my family, that I'm aware of. My sisters and I each have a different power."

He stared at me in awe. "You're an angel."

"Trust me, I'm not an angel." I explained to him how I was the human embodiment of a season, and told him about my dad.

"Ahhh, that is why your uncle referred to you as Spring during your birthday supper," he remembered.

"Exactly."

"And your sister—Taz?—she absorbs life? This is why I feel unwell near her?"

"Yep. You nailed it."

Kade processed this. "Amazing. I have an incredible imagination."

I opted not to argue the matter, knowing the whole dream vs. real life debate would get us nowhere.

The golden face of Maui loomed ahead, and we paused in our stroll to take in the view. Troubled creases tracked across Kade's forehead.

"Are you okay?" I asked. I elbowed him gently in the arm, ignoring the sharp zap of static that shuddered through my funny bone. "Are you freaked out over my power? Or is it still bothering you that you couldn't pull Grace out of the water? She wasn't in any real danger anyway, Kade. It would have only taken her another few seconds to realize she could stand on her own."

He didn't answer.

"Hey, if it'll make you feel better, I can throw myself into the fountain and you can save me—"

"No, it's not that," he finally said. "Well, I was indeed disturbed by that a few minutes ago. But now…it's this clocktower."

"What about it?"

He squinted his eyes as if he were trying to bring it into crisper focus. "I'm familiar with this timepiece."

"Well, we have been sitting right across the courtyard from it."

"No, I mean I *know* it. This is from my world. I remember this. And I remember those railway tracks over yonder." He pointed toward the abandoned tracks beyond the clock. "Though they seem more…desolate now."

"Oh, you have a Face of Maui too, in your Sezona Valley…aka, the Faraway Land of Wide-Awake People?"

He ignored my ridiculous classification, his face lighting up like Christmas morning. "The Face of Maui? You call it by that name as well? My goodness, yes! I was the one who bestowed the clock with that name!"

"Wow, and I thought you were arrogant before…"

He took my hands and clutched them within his own, his current vibrating hotly through my arms. An elderly couple walked by, staring at me oddly. Okay, this had to look weird. With no other recourse, I stared hard at the cute little hunched-over lady until she politely turned away.

That's better.

"No, little one, you do not understand," Kade said, still clutching my hands. "It is quite hazy, but I remember submitting the name 'Chief Maui' at the clock's unveiling ceremony. The clocktower was only just constructed. The name I suggested was thought to sound rather primitive. The townspeople, however, were quite fond of the backstory behind Chief Maui, thus voted to keep the name 'Maui' alone."

I felt nearly woozy with excitement over this information. I craved to know more about the backstory Kade referred to, but we now had more pressing things to think about. "Kade, this means we can figure out the time period you're from! All I have to do is research when The Face of Maui was constructed, and *voila*! Mystery solved." I stopped, feeling a seed of hope. "Unless…do you remember other things about your life now? Or at least the date you…um… fell asleep?" Perhaps remembering the clock had opened the floodgates to Kade's other trapped memories. He had, after all, recollected memories about candy canes earlier. Isn't that how it worked with amnesia patients? A woman would remember her favorite cereal was Lucky Charms and bam, she suddenly remembered her Aunt Hilda, her cat Marmalade, and Freddy, her pet goldfish?

His eyebrows furrowed. "No. It is so peculiar. A torrent of memories associated with the clock are occurring to me now, but nothing more. Not even my birth year."

So the clock only triggered memories about the clock. Just like my mint 'n chip ice-cream had only prompted memories about mint and Christmastime. Well that was a nifty little nuisance. If that's the way it was going to be, I'd have to take Kade all over town to try to pull out more memories. I sighed, but then immediately perked up. No big deal. At this point we must have enough information to figure out Kade's identity, even if he never recalled another detail about his life. One quick internet search would solve everything. As soon as Kade and I finished our walk, I'd find a quiet place to chill out with my phone and see what I could find.

Kade seemed to perk up too. "I must remind myself that this is all a spectacular dream. And to simply enjoy the experience."

"Wow," I muttered. "What's it like living in Denial Valley?"

He looked at me quizzically. "I live in Sezona Valley, silly one."

I shook my head. "Let's keep walking. Maybe you'll remember something else."

"Wait."

I watched as he continued to stare up at the clock.

"I think there is more."

Curiosity nibbled at me. "Okay…?"

He rubbed his chin thoughtfully. "Yes…I placed something inside."

"Inside the clock? I'll be honest, I don't even know what that means."

"Before the final mortar was applied to the brickwork, I placed something within the masonry," he pointed. "There, at the bottom." His face was rapt in concentration. "I feel that my dearest friends did as well. It was a…a cache of some sort."

"Cash? Like, money?"

"No, not money. Though…perhaps some coins. I am uncertain." His gaze drifted to the bottom of the clock. "No. It was a cache of simple objects. Items of interest for future persons to discover."

"Oh, like a time capsule," I supplied. "We did one of

those during our sixth grade camping trip. We all put one 'treasure' into a storage box and buried it, with instructions to open it in a hundred years. We left newspaper clippings and notes describing what the world is like today."

"Yes!" Kade's eyes lit up. "I am not acquainted with the phrase 'time capsule', but that is an apt description. I am positive that is what we deposited into the masonry."

"Well let's go get it!" I started to move toward the clock. Kade wrapped his fingers around my forearm, gently, but the sparks of heat vibrating through my arm were enough to stall me mid-step.

"No, sweet girl. I do not recommend you attempt to recover the items. It would require the very unladylike act of tearing apart the brickwork. What tool would you use to perform such a feat? And it would make for quite the spectacle, and would, furthermore, damage the base of the clocktower."

I tried to suppress my smile. "Do I look like a 'lady' to you Kade?"

His eyes traveled from my hastily braided hair, to my sky blue "I need sunshine in my life" t-shirt knotted over faded skinny jeans, and landed on my brown, worn ankle boots. "I confess, you do not. Your hair is unkempt and you are dressed like a wagtail."

I avoided the urge to give my butt a little shake.

He put his finger on his chin, thinking. "But I'm convinced that in spite of your deplorable appearance, you are indeed a lady. Or perhaps despite your marriageable age, you are more like a child, lacking in the sophistication to be concerned with grace and etiquette. But it is not hopeless for you. Etiquette can be learned. You could very well mature into a lady."

"Um, thank you?" I cocked my head. "So, I'm of marriageable age?"

"In my world, you, little one, would already be preparing for wedded bliss. Though with your spirit and lack of refinement, you would require a husband with extraordinary patience."

Before I could express annoyance over his elegantly-worded criticism, he returned his gaze to the base of the clock. "I feel as if I returned here as an adult. Replaced an item in the cache. But why would I do that?" His expression looked thoughtful. "Is this place of some significance to you?"

"This place? As in, Pendulum Square?"

"Yes."

"Other than the fact that it's been around my whole life," I answered, "not really. Why?"

"Because the letter you wrote me...it was here that I found it."

"Ohhh yes, your make-believe letter."

"I assure you, it is as real as you are."

"Which by your own admission is not real at all."

He tilted his head, evaluating me. His eyes dimmed, slipping into shadows as a cloud drifted across the sun. "My confidence concerning my original assessment of this situation is beginning to slip."

Triumph made my heart skitter. "Are you saying you think I'm real? Even with my crazy reviving powers and everything?"

He sighed. "I still believe I am dreaming. But I also think that somehow you must be real. Both of these things must be true."

"I'll settle for being the girl of your dreams, as long as you admit I exist." I teased.

He grinned. "Very well. I admit it. You, sweet girl, definitely exist."

Nine

*To be haunted is to glimpse a truth
that might best be hidden.*
James Herbert

Sunday, March 24
Present Day

THE THICK AROMA of ground coffee and spicy cinnamon permeated the interior of Copper's Kettle. I hunched over the small wooden table, tuning out the grinding and whirling of various machines as I clicked through websites on my phone.

As I suspected, it took me less than ten minutes to narrow down Kade's time period. According to a history tab I found on the Sezona Hills Chamber of Commerce page, the Face of Maui was unveiled to the Township of Sezona Valley on Saturday, April 1, 1876. But here's where it got tricky. Kade said he was a child during the unveiling ceremony. Did a child mean five years old, or twelve, or what? And what about now? How old was Kade? 17? 22? The way he talked and his graceful movements made him seem older, but the smooth lines of his face beneath all that stubble could be young.

Who exactly is my ghost? Or who *was* he? I adjusted my glasses, straining to read the information on my phone's tiny screen. My heart sank a little further with each swipe.

Nothing.

This should be so easy. At this point I had more clues than Detective Pikachu when he solves a case. I think Pikachu solves cases, right? I'd have to confer to Brett on that one. Either way, I kept hitting walls. I'd read through every Sezona Valley obituary I could find from 1876 to 1885, but there was none written for a person named Kade. Maybe I needed to try the library. I remember them having some sort of ancient machines that let you look through old newspapers.

Sighing, I typed in my next search query: "Sezona Valley obituaries 1886." A few links popped up. I clicked on the first one. It was for a man named Clarence Barnes, 42 years old, who died of pneumonia.

Nope.

My cellphone pinged a low battery alert for the dozenth time. Ignoring it, I clicked on the next link and waited for the website to load. Fractured lines of a black and white photo slowly fused together on the screen. A woman in a lace-trimmed dress emerged, stiff and elegant, her mouth turned down in the somber expression that seemed to characterize photos from this era. Frustrated at yet another dead-end, I hovered over the 'x' to close the page. Something made me pause. I glanced over the woman's photo again, noting her dark, swept-up hair and smooth eyebrows. She really was beautiful. Though her sophisticated hair style and pose made her look older, I realized, looking at her smooth face, that she probably wasn't much older than me. I wondered what happened to her.

Gripped by curiosity, I began reading her obituary.

January 19, 1886
The Township of Sezona Valley, Illinois
Miss Marguerite Broderick, aged 18, died at the McCleran Stables after being stabbed by an unknown attacker on Sunday afternoon. Services will take place tomorrow morning at Singing Creek Episcopal Church. Interment will follow in Singing Creek Cemetery. Revs. J. W. Sunderland and H. R. Gallin will officiate. Marguerite is survived by her parents, Mr. and Mrs. Edwin Broderick, one sibling, William J. Broderick, and her betrothed, Mr. Thurston K. Oaks III.

In that moment I decided I hated obituaries. Here this poor girl, a mere two years older than I, was murdered in cold blood, yet this short toneless paragraph couldn't muster up even a shred of emotion as it gave its dispassionate report.

Stabbed. I shuddered. So much for Sezona Hills' glowing bubble of perfection. With the Mel's Diner shooting last year, the infamous Angel murders, and now this, my prestigious little town had quite a dark shadow cast on its bright, shiny facade.

Wait. I tapped my fingers on the oak table, something nibbling on the corner of my mind. The Angel Killer… didn't his reign start in the late 1800s? In my head that meant the mid-to-late 1890s, but was it possible that the killings started earlier—as early as 1886?

I tapped the words 'Marguerite Broderick murder' into my phone's search bar. Good ole' Google knew exactly what I wanted, spitting out a newspaper clipping from the

Sezona Valley Herald. I waited as the same grainy black and white photo of Marguerite loaded, along with an article that was significantly longer than the obituary. It was dated Monday, January 18, 1886. My phone chirped its low battery alert again, so I hurried to scan through the text.

According to the article, Marguerite was enjoying brunch and tea with acquaintances after church, when she left to meet her betrothed, Thurston Oaks, for a horseback ride. The town sheriff received a report of a loud scream coming from the McCleran property at approximately 3:20 p.m.

I paused for a second. 3:20. My birthday was 3/20… March 20th.

So? I thought, then continued scanning the article.

The Sheriff arrived to investigate, where he found Marguerite dead on the stable floor. The report claimed that Thurston Oaks was hovering over her, covered in blood. Thurston was taken in custody and was considered to be the prime suspect in the assault and murder of Marguerite Broderick. His trial was scheduled for the following day.

I took my glasses off and rubbed my overly strained eyes. So Marguerite's death wasn't related to the Angel Killer after all. One key detail of the Angel Killings was the fact that it was the biggest cold case in Sezona Hills' history. No one knew who was responsible for those murders. Given that this Thurston-guy was practically caught in the act, Marguerite's death was obviously an isolated crime.

Or was it? Another key component of the Angel Killings was the halo that was always drawn over the victim's head. In any serial murder case, there's always that very *first* murder, right? What if the Angel Killer simply hadn't drawn a halo that first time? Or maybe he did, but no one knew to check for it?

Could Thurston Oaks and the Angel Killer be the same person?

No, I answered my own question. Thurston was caught in that stable red-handed. He was arrested, and, according to the article, was scheduled for trial. If he were indeed the Angel Killer, there's no way he would have been able to murder fourteen more women after his arrest. He would have been serving time in jail, or worse. I wondered if he ended up getting the death penalty for what he did.

I hope the jury fried him.

Before I could search out what happened to Thurston Oaks, my screen went black. Frustrated, I tossed my dead phone into my bag and exhaled a puff of air. Though the murder of Marguerite Broderick was darkly interesting, I was wasting too much time researching things that had nothing to do with Kade.

Though now that I thought about it, Sezona Valley was a small town—not even a town, but a 'township'—in the late 1800s. As revolting as I found the notion, there was a chance that Kade and Thurston knew each other. They might have even been friends.

"There you two are," a familiar voice broke my reverie. I looked up to see Stryder approaching my table.

"It's just me now." I nodded toward the empty chair. "Kade disappeared in front of Maui when I started hinting around that he's a ghost again. He hates that. Hey, can I borrow your phone?"

He pulled his phone from his pocket and pointed at the black screen. "Fried by the fountain, remember? Besides, Taz is ready to get going. She's got that paper due for English tomorrow."

I sighed.

"Oh hey, what's wrong?" He pulled up the empty chair and settled himself across from me.

I gazed at him, unsure of how much I wanted to say. "I just…don't get it. I can't find anything about Kade. It makes me feel like…like he's not real. Like maybe I really *am* going crazy."

Stryder gave my hand a quick squeeze. "Aviva, you're not crazy. After all of the stuff Taz and I went through, one thing I know is that there's so much in this world that we *don't* understand. Your ghost is part of that, somehow. Plus even Grace saw him, remember?"

"Well, yeah…."

"So trust me. Kade's real. And he's here for a reason." His gray eyes were soft with concern. "We'll figure this out. Okay?"

Stryder's words wrapped around me like a warm blanket. I nodded and forced myself to smile. "I can't believe I ever thought you were a jerk."

He grinned. "I am a jerk. I just behave for you girls."

My forced smile blossomed into a real one.

"Now are you ready to get out of here? I left your sister with Grace at Patty's Critters. If we don't get moving soon we're going to end up going home with a mob of ferrets and guinea pigs."

"Would that be such a bad thing?" I joked, grabbing my bag.

"I JUST DON'T GET what makes haikus special," I grumbled, erasing the line of poetry I had scrawled for the third time. "They're no better than me globbing a bunch of paint on a canvas and calling it art."

Brett paused in his writing to look up at me. "Are you feeling okay?"

"I'm fine. Why?"

"Well, you've been huffing and puffing ever since we got here, and I think you just erased an entire hole into your paper."

"Ugh. Sorry." I finished erasing my disastrous line. "I'm just tired."

"More coffee, you guys?" Joe stood at our booth as if on cue, a small stack of dirty plates in one hand and a carafe of coffee in the other.

"Thanks Joe," I mumbled. "You're a life-saver. Oh, Krystal says 'hi' by the way."

A big grin spread on Joe's face as he refilled our mugs. "Tell her hi back for me. Is she…um…has she been feeling okay lately?"

"Yeah, why?"

"It's just that…she seems sad a lot."

I pulled my mug closer. "That's just Krystal. She's happiest when she's sad."

Joe cocked his head, confused.

"It's like that episode of Dr. Who," Brett offered, "where Sally Sparrow's best friend wonders why Sally loves looking at the weeping angels, and Sally explains to her that sad is actually happy for deep people."

I nodded my agreement. "I have no idea what he's talking about, but it sounds right."

"If you say so," Joe nodded, though he didn't look entirely satisfied with that explanation. Turning around, he limped toward the swinging door that led to the kitchen.

I thought about the accident that led to Joe's crippled

foot. "Don't tell Taz we came here tonight, okay?" I forced casualness into my voice, brushing eraser debris off my still unformed haiku.

Brett sipped his coffee. "How come?"

"She doesn't like this place. I just don't want to bring it up."

I didn't like this place either, but I decided to keep that to myself. When Brett suggested coming to Mel's Diner to work on homework, I almost said no. The echoes of what happened here didn't haunt me the same way they did Taz, but I still felt…something, about this place. And I couldn't get the image of the shadow-man out of my head. His despair….

But I had given in to Brett, deciding that despite my hourly ghost-interruptions, I still needed to keep up with my school work, not to mention my small but reliable social life. Daphne and my dad said I could go, as long as I was home by eight.

"So what's keeping you up?" Brett changed the subject.

"Huh?"

"You said you've been feeling tired lately. What's keeping you up at night?"

I peered over my paper, the words "a ghost" on the tip of my tongue.

"I think it's my new bedroom," the lie slipped easily from my lips. "I love it, but I'm still not used to sleeping in an attic."

"Yeah, that would be kind of weird." He returned his gaze toward his poem. "Should we get back to this?"

I frowned.

"Oh come on," he encouraged. "I used to think haikus were lame too, but now I kind of like them."

"What changed your mind about them?"

"Well, there's this scene in *Avatar: The Last Airbender* where Sokka accidentally stumbles onto a poetry lesson going on in the girls' class, and he and the salty teacher go through a crazy Haiku battle. It's epic."

I rolled my eyes. "Of course anime is the reason you love haikus."

"Nickelodeon's stuff doesn't count as anime. But yeah, it's still a great scene. Now I can create a haiku in like, thirty seconds flat."

"No way."

"Is that a challenge?"

I raised an eyebrow. "Maybe."

He lifted his pencil. "If I can't write a haiku in thirty seconds or less, I'll buy you dessert."

"And if you win?"

He grinned. "Then you have to kiss me."

I couldn't stop the smile from spreading across my face. "Deal."

I pulled out my cellphone and set the timer for thirty seconds. "Ready, set, go!"

He scratched some words on his paper, his forehead creasing in concentration. Ten seconds passed, then twenty, then, right before the timer rang, he handed me the creased paper. A flush crept up his neck. "I won."

It took me all of five seconds to read his haiku.

I love our friendship—
Aviva, can we be more?
You're my everything.

My heart lurched. I dared to peek up at him, pricks of

moisture springing to the corner of my eyes. His eyes, shining with hope like new copper pennies, were searching mine. "Brett—"

"Hello, sweet girl."

Ten

I wonder if I am even human anymore.
Have I turned entirely into a ghost?
Do I merely exist to haunt you?
Thomas Mattheos

Sunday, March 24
Present Day

SERIOUSLY, your timing couldn't be worse," I snapped at Kade, who had materialized in the booth next to Brett.

Brett's face dropped. "I'm sorry Viv, I just—"

"No, not you, Brett. I'm talking to…I'm talking to myself." I planted my face into my hands. "I'm so sorry. I might be going crazy."

Brett's expression softened. "Oh hey, it's okay." He reached for my hands and pulled them gingerly down from my face, cupping them within his own. "Talk to me."

Kade, his lips pinched shut, seemed to flinch at the contact.

Did I imagine that?

I peered up at Brett, my hands curled up warmly in his palm. Before I could second-guess myself, I leaned across the table and kissed him. Not a long kiss, nor a quick chaste kiss. It was something in the middle, soft and warm, with my lips lingering over his for a few slow seconds.

Before Brett could register what was happening, I pulled away, my pulse racing. "Well you did win, after all."

Kade was now standing over our booth, arms crossed in front of his chest, eyes boring darkly into mine. I ignored him.

Brett's eyes, on the other hand, were lit with awe. "Wow. That was…wow."

"The thing is…."

"Oh no," his face fell. "This is sounding like a "I like you, *but*…."

"Arghh. Sorry. It is."

He sighed.

"The thing is, I love our friendship. Just like you said in the poem. Honestly, you're kind of my best friend right now. I know it's selfish, but will you keep being my best friend? Please? I don't want to lose you."

Disappointment flickered across his face, but he contained it quickly. "Of course I'll be your best friend." He squeezed my hand. Then he grinned. "Any chance we can do another haiku bet though? You're a good loser."

I laughed, relieved that he was already bouncing back to his normal goofball self. "Was it good? That was my first."

"Five stars," Brett said. "And I have lots to compare it with."

I punched him in the arm. "Shut up. No you don't."

He laughed, but then his face grew serious again. "Seriously Viv, if you're going to friend-zone me, then… well…it's cool that you gave me your first kiss. At least I have that."

I smiled. "No worries."

A few awkward seconds passed between us. "So, hey,

mind if I take you home now so I can nurse my wounded ego?" Based on the red in his cheeks, I knew he was only half-kidding. "Or should we keep practicing haikus?"

"Go ahead without me," I told him, deciding to spare him any more embarrassment. "I'm going to run over to B-Mo's before they close and look for a book of haikus." I scooped up the poem he had written for me and waved it at him. "They're sort of growing on me now."

Another lie. But the touched look on Brett's face made it worth it.

"Are you sure? How will you get home?"

"I'll just call my dad to pick me up, or hitch a ride with Joe."

B-Mo's—or "Burning the Midnight Oil" as it was known back in the day before someone decided that was a ridiculous mouthful—was an indie bookstore across the street and around the corner, right at the southeastern entrance to Clockworks Village. Though I loved their selection of quirky titles, I had no intention of actually going there tonight. My real plan was to hang around so I could talk to Kade. After my fruitless search at Copper's Kettle earlier, I yearned to jog more of his memories.

Brett and I stopped at the cash register to take care of our checks, then he walked me outside. I prayed Kade would follow us. He looked like he was definitely in a mood. I reminded myself to not bring up the ghost-issue, or else he'd disappear again.

"Want me to give you a ride to B-Mo's?" Brett asked.

"Oh, no, it's only like a three minute walk," I reassured him, trying not to look like I was in a rush as I glanced around him, searching for Kade. "I kinda want to clear my head anyway."

"Um, okay. I'll see you tomorrow." He leaned forward and gave me a quick hug.

"Bye Brett," I smiled. "Thanks again for the poem."

After he left, I scanned the parking lot. It was almost 7:00, and a few pedestrians were out and about, passing by with shopping bags and laughing in the brightly-lit night. But there was no sign of Kade. My heart sank.

Where was he?

"I found what you are seeking, little one."

I whirled around, my heart in my throat. "Kade. You scared me."

He gazed at me, wordless, the lines of his face more serious than usual.

"What do you mean, you found what I was seeking?" I asked.

"In the bookstore. A faded blue and pink hardcover volume titled *Blossoms in Moonlight: A Collection of Ancient and Modern Haiku*." His voice was low. "Back of the store, left side, third shelf from the top. I tried to retrieve it for you, but, alas…" he reached out to touch the To-Go parking sign next to him. His fingers glided through.

"You went over to B-Mo's?" I asked, incredulous.

"That was your intended destination, was it not?" His voice had a bite to it, as if he were irritated.

I felt a little ashamed to tell him I was lying. Especially after he had taken time from his busy stalking-me schedule to go haunt the bookstore and memorize the exact location of a book, all for my sake. "Thank you," I said, my voice lit with wonder. "But I wasn't actually looking for a poetry book. I just wanted to stay longer so I could talk to you."

"So speak and be done with it," he said sharply.

Irritation clawed at me. "What's with the attitude?"

The look he threw my direction could only be described as a 'glare'. "What attitude would be considered appropriate after witnessing your brazen behavior with that young man?"

"What?" I asked, confused. Then I realized what he was talking about. "You're upset that I kissed Brett?"

"I thought you were a lady."

Heat fanned flames of annoyance through my body. "That's on you," I bit out, my cheeks growing hot. "I've never once claimed to be a lady."

"Obviously. I can hardly believe your world permits a young woman to be in the presence of a man without an escort. One can see where that leads."

Anger and embarrassment knotted together inside my stomach. I wished his opinion didn't bother me, but it did. "You don't understand the way things work in this century," I snapped. "The fact that I'm sixteen years old and have only just now experienced my first kiss practically makes me a saint. And what right do you have to follow *me* around anyway, passing judgement on the way I live my life? If I want to make-out with a dozen guys, that's *my* business. If you don't like it, go follow someone else."

A soft giggle drifted through the tension-thick air. I looked over to see a teenage couple staring at me and Kade from the sidewalk. I recognized both of them from school, but couldn't recall their names. The dark-haired girl looked at her boyfriend, as if they were sharing some inside joke, then back at me, smothering her laugh beneath her hand.

I cringed, realizing they weren't staring at me and Kade. They were staring at *me*, the crazy girl, arguing with herself in the parking lot.

Ugh! I swung around and stormed toward the unlit side

of Mel's Diner, wishing the building would swallow me whole. I suddenly regretted not taking Brett up on his offer for a ride.

Rounding the corner, I felt a current of electricity on my elbow. I turned around to find Kade inches from my face, his eyes capturing little glimmers of light in the dark space.

"Perhaps it is unfair for me to judge you based on the standards from my world."

"Yeah?" I prompted.

He hesitated, as if gathering his thoughts, before continuing. "If a man from early-medieval Spain were to see the women of my day not wearing veils, he would accuse them of witchcraft, or think them harlots. So… perhaps standards for women behavior are relative, dictated by period- and region-specific norms."

"Is this your way of saying sorry?" I asked.

A smile played on his lips. "Yes."

I took a deep breath and tried to reel in my temper. "Is that kiss still bothering you?"

His smile fled. "Yes."

I didn't know what to do with that information, so I settled for staring at him for a few seconds before coughing uncomfortably. "So why did you really go to the bookstore? Was it to find me that haiku book? Or was it because you were annoyed by that kiss?"

Kade paused. "I believe I felt a compulsion to escape this place."

This got my attention, considering Mel's made me feel squirmy, too. "Why?"

"I am uncertain. Something about this dining hall is familiar, but not in a friendly way. It is causing me great unease. Perhaps if we step to the front of this structure again, I can focus more and try to remember."

"Okay," I agreed, wondering if it was something from his own memories causing him to be uneasy, or if he was picking up on some of those 'echoes' of death that Taz had talked about. "But let's stay here for a few more minutes. I could use a breather."

Really, I just wanted to make sure those kids from my school were long-gone. The darkness on this side of the diner was comforting. Not only did it allow me to talk to Kade in peace, but the front of Mel's was too glaringly bright. Light is supposed to chase away shadows, but sometimes it gives birth to them. The dark, on the other hand, quietly buries them.

"Very well," he stated. "You wish to talk with me?"

Oh yeah. So many questions I had for Kade…questions that were so important to me a few minutes ago, but dimming now. I forced myself to focus. I thought about everything I had learned about Kade's time period. I wanted to ask him how old he was when he planted the time capsule, or have him tell me more about the Face of Maui. Or maybe I could give him some keywords to jog more memories of his home life, the way the mint 'n chip ice-cream had.

But all I could see was the pretty, solemn face of the girl who was murdered. Marguerite.

"Do you know a guy named Thurston Oaks?" I finally asked.

Kade's body jolted. His eyes widened.

"What?" I asked, excited that I may have triggered another clue, hopefully something bigger than a candy cane. "What are you remembering?"

"Thurston Oaks…." he tripped over the words.

"That's…that's the name of my father."

The shock of this revelation nearly knocked me over. Kade's dad was a killer?

"And I—I am—" his body keeled over.

Before I could register my alarm, he straightened, and his features darkened. I took a step back, even though I knew whatever he was remembering had nothing to do with me; he was looking at something distant that I could not see.

He started talking, his voice far away. "I am the third generation. Everyone calls me by my middle name to avoid confusion with my father."

"So you remember him clearly now?"

He eyed me, his face shadowed. "Yes. Not there is much to remember. My father has always been too occupied with his ambitions and burying my family in debt to care about any of us."

"Kade, was your dad a murderer?" That would explain why Kade had blocked out his past.

But then something occurred to me. If Kade's dad killed Marguerite, that meant his dad was engaged to marry her. The article said Thurston Oaks was Marguerite's betrothed. It didn't add up. Kade with an eighteen year-old step-mom? If anything it made more sense for Marguerite to be betrothed to Kade…

My heart thumped sickly in my chest. Kade's words resonated from the recesses of my memory. *I feel like I have made a commitment to someone…. Perhaps I am betrothed….*

I froze, fear clutching my chest. The name—the full name—in my mind's vision, rose in bold print from the Sezona Hills Gazette.

Thurston K. Oaks III.

Third generation.

Everyone calls me by my middle name to avoid confusion with my father.

Kade.

No wonder I couldn't find his obituary. The ghost standing in front of me had only ever given me his middle name.

I opened my mouth, maybe to gasp, maybe to scream. Before I could find out which, Kade lunged forward. Static electricity burned every pore of my skin as his body pressed against mine and his hand sealed over my mouth.

"Shhh. Aviva. You do not want to garner the attention of pedestrians."

To hell with that. I definitely wanted to "garner" their attention. I'd even take those gawking teenagers from my school again. I shook my head, panting heavily into his hand, my arms pinned between his body and my own, the wall of Mel's Diner rough and cold against my back. Hot currents surged through my limbs. Fear squeezed my heart.

A ghost couldn't actually *hurt* me, right?

Kade must have seen the panic in my eyes. He loosened the hand that was pressed up against my mouth, though barely.

"You…you're Thurston K. Oaks," I panted into his hand. "You killed Marguerite. You and your dad have the same name. Kade is your middle name. It wasn't your dad. It was you. You…oh my God!" I could hear my voice go shrill as the hysteria seeped in, but I couldn't seem to stop it. "You were supposed to marry her! But you killed her!"

He tightened his grip. I thrashed against him, but he leaned against me, and I was no match for his heavy frame. How could a ghost feel so solid? And how could his breath, coming out in heavy puffs against my cheek, be so humid and stifling?

I waited for him to say something. *Anything.* I squirmed against him, trying to shake his hand from my mouth.

"Aviva, stop fighting me. I will release you, but you must be quiet."

Though his words might have been construed as bossy and overbearing, the way he pushed them out—in a kind of rushed whisper—sounded desperate. I forced myself to breathe evenly, despite his vibrating palm pressed against my mouth; despite my body going numb with his currents rushing through me. He could have hurt me already if he had any intention of doing so, I rationalized. Was there any reason for my fear?

I forced my muscles to relax, and I gave a tight nod in agreement. Slowly, he slid his hand from my mouth.

"Why aren't you denying it?" I asked after an unsettling minute had passed, trying to keep the shrill note from creeping into my shaky voice again.

"Defending myself makes no difference." His voice was like stone.

"Did you ever even love Marguerite?"

His body flickered and he took a step back. Light rolled through him, making him glow like a prism.

"Kade," I gasped, my pulse speeding up again.

He finally returned his gaze to me. "I died." Streaks of variegated light continued to flash through him.

I swallowed hard. "What's happening to you?" I stared at him, realizing that I could now see through his body. "You're…you're turning into a ghost…."

He backed up another step. His body flickered again, like a picture on an old TV with lousy reception. Fear spread cold fingers through my chest. Fear not of Kade, but of something else.

"I died here. At this place." He pointed toward the parking lot. "Right over there. *That's* why I feel so unsettled here. And you—" his voice hitched, his body flashing. I watched and listened, paralyzed. "You were there. I saw you. You were an angel with alabaster hair, glowing with light. This whole time, I believed I was dreaming. I thought this was a fever-induced delusion. But this is real. You were correct all along, little one." His last words were stated with grim finality. "I am dead."

"How did you die?" I whispered, my words choked. I knew what he was going to say, even as I prayed that he wouldn't.

He eyes locked onto mine. His body was like water now, so transparent and fluid that his eyes were the only thing I could clearly see.

"I was hung for the murder of Marguerite Broderick."

His liquid-body shimmered, then dissolved. But unlike the other times he had disappeared, this time was different. This time I knew he would never come back.

Eleven

*The worst lies
are the lies we tell ourselves.*
Richard Bach

January 8, 1886

ANYTHING ELSE I can help you with, miss?"

Gazing into the full-length mirror, Molly patted her hat upon her coiffed hair. Dark, glossy tendrils curled softly around her neck, resting upon her high lace-trimmed collar. Smoothing her dress, she turned her body, admiring how the dress's bustle and gathered skirts gave her a curvaceous silhouette, and how the sky-blue material set off her dark hair and eyes.

"Thank you Maude, that will be all," she dismissed her lady's maid with a nod.

Donning her shawl and grabbing her parasol on her way out of her bedchamber, Molly sauntered into the garden to look for Charlie. Her brother was attending to business today and could not escort her, so Charlie—always happy to be at her beck and call—had gladly offered to take his place. Molly had been invited to the home of her betrothed, where she would be dining with his family and enjoying an evening around the piano. Maude was efficient in helping Molly ready, and she was now thirty minutes early, but she felt eager to be on her way nonetheless. She wanted to see her fiancé's eyes light up when he beheld her elegant beauty, and she looked forward to further charming his family. *They are quite smitten by me already*, she smiled to herself.

Her smile quickly dissolved. Unfortunately her betrothed wasn't wooed by her the way his family was. Daily she tried to deny it, but it was a cold, hard truth. Even the townspeople knew. They never said as much—they were far too polite for that—but she heard the prescribed pity seeping from their shallow questions and bits of conversation.

At least he was always good to her, and gentle, and chivalrous…he performed well in his role of good future-husband. But he was distant. His mind was perpetually a million miles away. She was accustomed to having men's undivided attention with a bat of her eyelashes, a coy smile, or a wave of her fan, so his lack of attentiveness wounded her pride.

Surely tonight this would change. Tonight he would notice her. Tonight he would feel fortunate and blessed to be marrying her.

Ten minutes of searching the property yielded no signs of Charlie. Impatience crawled over her. Did he forget his commitment?

Of course not, she chided herself, remembering that he had twenty minutes more before they were supposed to depart. He was probably readying the carriage.

Sighing, she circled back toward the stables. She stopped when she heard voices drifting from the old outhouse building that housed various horse tack and supplies. Why would anyone be in there at this hour?

Father better not be with that servant girl again, she fumed.

It was a well-known secret in her family that her father often snuck away to dally with the housemaids. Though no one ever discussed the matter—such conversations were taboo—Molly wasn't so blind that she couldn't see the way her father's eyes lingered on the female servants; the way he would excuse himself to leave while her mother's face reddened.

Lifting her skirts, Molly tip-toed toward the building, following the sound of the voices. She peered inside, her eyes struggling to adjust to the dim light. She made out the silhouette of the family's housemaid, Clair, her dress rumpled and hair disheveled. She was standing with her back toward Molly, talking in a hushed voice to someone outside of Molly's line of vision. Molly stepped out of view and strained to listen.

"….hugely inconvenient," Clair was saying, "but it feels like a part of me now. I don't know what to do."

A masculine voice uttered a response, but the hushed voice was further away, too low for Molly to discern. *Is it Father?* she wondered. Or perhaps it was Charlie. She had heard through the gossip mill that Charlie had designs on Clair.

"How can I?" Clair asked, her voice shaking. "An unwed servant? The scandal it will cause. You know I will be sent away."

Molly strained to hear the other side of the conversation, but to no avail.

A sob escaped Clair's lips. "No, I—I can't. This child is part of me. Part of both of us. I want to keep it."

Molly reeled backwards, her hand flying to her chest. Clair was with child! Eavesdropping this conversation felt horribly intrusive and wrong. She moved to sneak away before she was caught. As she turned away, she heard Clair speaking again.

"….with me," she was saying in a choked voice. "We can run away and raise our son together."

Molly knew without a doubt there was no way Father, or any wealthy man for that matter, would leave his privileged life behind to be with a soiled servant girl. But Charlie didn't have wealth at stake, so he might be willing. Her curiosity got the best of her. She turned back around and leaned forward again, interested now as to how the mystery man would respond to Clair's plea. All she could make out was his low soothing tones, but no words.

"Oh my darling, do you promise?" At least Clair's side of the conversation could be easily heard.

A feeling of uncertainty settled in the pit of Molly's stomach. Though she was missing half of the conversation, she knew Father would never honor a promise to keep the baby. It must be Charlie. No wonder she couldn't find him anywhere.

Clair began weeping again. "I can't. I can't." Her sobs grew louder. "We can't deny ourselves true love! And I will not deny our babe his father." Her voice stalled as she broke down. The sound of her crying was muffled, as if she were weeping against a shoulder.

"Hush now, my love."

Finally! Molly could hear the other side of the conversation! The whispering voice had moved closer for a moment, and Molly froze when she suspected who it belonged to. She strained to listen more.

"…one more time. Are you truly unwilling to rid yourself of this—issue?"

Molly's arm hair prickled at the odd note that had crept into the man's hushed, barely discernible voice.

Clair sniffled. "I love our baby too much."

"Very well."

A cut-off shriek, followed by a strangled, gurgling sound, sent a cold chill racing down Molly's spine. She stumbled backwards and, nearly tripping over her skirts, spun toward the house and ran. She didn't stop running until she reached her bedchamber. She shut the door hard behind her and sank on the floor in front of it, her bustle smashing painfully beneath her. She panted as she clutched her crumpled shawl to her chest.

It sounded like Clair was…was…

No! She thought. The notion was preposterous. She never actually saw anything. The noise she heard might have been a dozen different things. What sounded nefarious might have been Clair gasping as she was pulled in for a passionate kiss. Or maybe Clair's crying had taken on a noisy sort of desperation. Jumping to the conclusion that Clair had been hurt was dramatic and rash.

Fear threatened to paralyze Molly. That whispered voice….

In an act of sheer will, Molly stuffed what her ears had heard into a private sector of her mind where she could pretend it didn't exist, along with the fear. Because that's what her family did with information that didn't assimilate properly into their ideal world; they kept frozen smiles plastered on their faces as they gracefully continued on with their lives. So when Maude knocked on her door fifteen minutes later, hollering "Miss Broderick, Charlie says your carriage is ready," Molly's response was a cheery "Indeed, Maude. Let me find my parasol and I will be out in a jiffy!"

And with that, Miss Marguerite Broderick—or "Molly" as she was affectionately called—continued to pretend all was right in the world, even when the family's housemaid, Clair Whitaker, was never seen or heard from again.

Twelve

Ghosts have a way of misleading you;
they can make your thoughts as heavy
as branches after a storm.
Rebecca Maizel

Sunday, March 31
Present Day

"THE TRUTH WILL set you free. John 8:32." Pastor Alvarez's voice peaked in intensity as he concluded his passionate sermon. "Remember that folks, and let it bring you comfort. You will know the truth, and the truth will set you free."

But it hadn't for Kade, the thought invaded as we bowed our heads for prayer. Instead of setting him free, the truth made him disappear. The truth freaked him out and made him vanish into oblivion. The truth left me aching, a bundle of nerves, with a thousand unanswered questions and a hopelessness that settled on me every night, blanketing me the way sleep once had.

I should have noticed it from the beginning, the fact that the more Kade learned about himself, the more inclined he was to disappear. I should have known that once Kade finally discovered his true identity, he would vanish for good. Maybe denial is what makes a ghost a ghost. Maybe it's just like it is in the movies, where a refusal to accept what is happening is what traps a spirit in the same plane as the living. Maybe it's only when a ghost is forced to come to terms with his death that he is released from his self-imposed prison.

Maybe the truth really did set Kade free, and I was just too miserable to accept it.

What's wrong with me? I asked God, since He was the person I was supposed to be talking to at the moment. *Why do I keep looking behind my shoulder, hoping Kade will be there?* I tried to turn off my thoughts and listen for an answer. But the thoughts raged in my head.

I didn't know what to make of anything. Kade and Thurston were the same person. Thurston Kade Oaks 'the third', to be precise. Even if all my research wasn't enough to convince me that Kade had killed a person, Kade admitted it himself. *I was hung for the murder of Marguerite Broderick.* The words drummed against my temples.

Kade was a cold-blooded killer. And I felt empty.

I can not miss him. I can not miss a murderer, I told myself.

But that was the problem. Despite all of the evidence to the contrary, my heart whispered to me that Kade was innocent.

Your *heart*? I chided myself. Really? How stupid can you be?

Maybe I didn't actually miss him. Maybe I just needed closure. He disappeared so fast, and left me with so many unanswered questions.

Who was I kidding.

He had seen me that night. That was probably the most powerful revelation of all. I never told him about my shadow-man at Mel's Diner. I shivered, thinking about the way the shadow seemed to hang, then turn around and reach for me. He was the shadow. He was the one reaching for me.

You were the angel with alabaster hair, glowing with light.

At a vigil surrounded by candlelight, I could see how a dying man might mistake me for an angel.

But how could two people over a century apart possibly see each other at the same moment in time?

"NO. ABSOLUTELY NOT. No." My dad shook his head vehemently behind the wheel of his truck.

"But, Dad—"

"Aviva, have you gone mad? There's no way I'm sending my sixteen year-old daughter to the 1800s so she can be a Nancy Drew wannabe and try to clear some guy's name."

I didn't know who Nancy Drew was, but his point was loud and clear. "I'm not asking you to send me. I just want to know if it's possible."

"For the sake of this discussion, no, it's not possible."

"But it *is* possible, isn't it?"

He gave me a sideways glance. "Aviva, listen. I've talked about this a lot with your uncle Kiel recently, and we think we understand more about what's happening, and why your ghost disappeared."

"Really?"

Dad returned his gaze to the road and turned left, heading toward Clockworks Village where we were meeting the rest of my family for brunch. I had asked my dad if we could drive separately so we could talk, which worked out in the long run anyway given that there were too many of us to take one car.

"Those last few seconds that Taz and Stryder were trapped in their curse," Dad was saying, "their universe was rewinding by nanoseconds. They were lucky to survive. If your sister wasn't who she was, she and Stryder might have died. But the extreme concentration of that time loop did cause damage. According to your sister, the Face of Maui exploded during their final rewinds. But that was nothing compared to the unseen consequences." He turned left, then continued. "Kiel and I have theorized that Taz's and Stryder's final loops were so concentrated and powerful that they actually tore a rift into the universe."

"What's a 'rift'?" I asked.

"It's a fissure. Like a rip. Or a crack. In this case, the crack serves as a doorway from Kade's time to our own. I looked into Thurston K. Oaks' past, and he was hung right where we were standing during the candlelight vigil. His hanging took place on the same night as the vigil, but in 1886."

"I figured that out, too. But why would Kade be hung in a diner parking lot?"

He shook his head. "It wasn't a diner back then, remember? Mel's wasn't built until the 1960s. Before that, the original courthouse stood in its place. It wasn't uncommon in the past to hold public hangings right outside of the town's courthouse, especially in small towns where hangings were rare. Unfortunately—or maybe fortunately —the courthouse burned down in 1948 due to an electrical fire, and a new one—the one we know today—was built next to Town Hall.

"Whether he's guilty or innocent, Kade experienced a traumatic death in his time period, and with a freshly torn rift nearby, his spirit couldn't resist slipping through, straight into our time period. Like your uncle Kiel speculated on your birthday, it would be only natural for a ghost in denial over his own death to be drawn to your life-giving aura."

I tried to digest this. "So the shadow I saw at the candlelight vigil…that was Kade." I already knew I was right, since Kade said he saw me at his hanging, but I wanted to be sure.

"Yes."

"I still don't understand why Kade was only a shadow when I first saw him. Originally I thought it was because of what Uncle Kiel said; that his form was getting stronger the longer he was around me. But I remember when I saw him as a shadow, he was hanging on a rope, and it felt like he was reaching for me. That doesn't make sense because he couldn't have been a ghost yet. He would have still been alive."

"True," my dad speculated. "But he was dying. His spirit was fighting to go through the rift, while his physical body was fighting for life. A spirit in that kind of discord might appear to you as a vague shadow in the beginning. His shadow might have moved along the very path to the gallows that his real life body had walked in 1886. But, as weeks passed and as his denial and disillusionment grew, his ability to project himself as a flesh-and-blood human being to the one person who could see him also grew stronger."

My dad's words were baffling, yet somehow made sense. Then something occurred to me. "Dad, if Kade was able to slip through the rift into my time period, I can do the same! Doors work two ways."

My dad sighed. He pulled over, easing the truck to a stop on the curb, then turned to look at me. "This is really important for you to understand, Aviva. You can't go into that rift. Rifts are dangerous and unpredictable."

"How so?"

He stared ahead, gripping the steering wheel tightly. "This isn't the first rift that's ever been torn into the fabric of time, and your uncle and I have learned a few things about them. First, they are invisible, which makes them very difficult to find. This rift, though we know it started at the Face of Maui and stretched as far as Mel's Diner, could be anywhere by now. Second, even if you could find the rift, it's nearly impossible for a corporeal being to slip through. If you don't know the trick to making the passageway work, you might as well be banging your head against a wall. Third—and this one is the most important—rifts are temporary. They're unnatural and not meant to be, and the universe knows it. A rift is a nasty gouge cut into the skin of Time. Time will do everything in its power to heal the cut, to seal it back up so that all is right and whole again. That's the dangerous part."

"How long does it take for a rift to close?" I breathed.

"Some rifts take mere minutes to close, others take months. I suppose in the same way the severity of a cut determines the time it takes to heal, the same is true for a rift. Without knowing how deep this rift is, there is no way of knowing how long it will take to seal shut. But I strongly believe Kade's sudden disappearance shows that this particular rift's healing has begun."

A rush of hopelessness ran through my body. "It's just…

Dad, I...I feel like I'm meant to do something."

He squeezed my hand and looked me directly in the eyes. "That doesn't matter. If you try to follow Kade into the rift, you could be trapped forever in the past."

"WHAT'S GOT YOU down, kid?" Uncle Kiel asked, pouring syrup over his pancakes.

My uncle didn't always join us for Sunday brunch, but he did about once a month. We were now piled into two booths at Janie's Cafe. Tables large enough to seat all of us were a rare luxury during the after-church rush, so Dad and Daphne were sharing a booth with Krystal and Phee, while I sat with Taz, Stryder, and Uncle Kiel. Thankfully Grace and Shelly were out of town this weekend, or else Grace would have been crammed into our booth, too.

I raked my scrambled eggs into a pile with my fork, then looked over at Uncle Kiel. "Nothing. I'm fine."

"It's her ghost," Taz said, tearing a large bite from her sandwich. "He hasn't come back all week."

"Taz!" I threw her a murderous look.

"What? He already knows about Kade. We talked about it on your birthday, remember?"

I huffed. She was right, but I still felt like a mental patient talking about it in front of people.

"It's okay," Uncle Kiel encouraged. "This whole topic actually fascinates me. Do you mind me asking for the latest developments regarding your ghost?"

I took a bite of cold scrambled eggs and swallowed hard. "Didn't you and my dad already talk about it?"

"Yes," he looked slightly taken aback that I knew. "But I'd rather hear your version."

Letting out a puff of air, I gave in and decided to tell him everything that had happened since my birthday, all the way to Kade's body liquefying into thin air.

A hush settled over our table once I finished my long monologue. It was like everyone was holding their breath. They either thought I was nuts, or they were totally enraptured by my story.

Taz finally broke the breathless silence. "You don't believe Kade killed Marguerite." She didn't pose it as a question, but stated it as a fact.

I squirmed in my chair. "I, um…" I took in a breath of air. "No, I don't. But it makes no sense. All the evidence says he did. Even *he* said that he did. I think. His words at the end are kind of a blur. Anyway, he didn't. I know he didn't."

My own words surprised me. I didn't realize I felt this strongly about Kade's innocence until I said it aloud. But now that the words were out, I couldn't deny the truth behind them.

Uncle Kiel was staring intently at me, as if trying to form his next words.

"If only I had more time with him," I said. "If only there was a way to prove that he didn't do it. Kade and I saw each other the night he was hung. We saw each other from two different periods in history. I thought he was some weird shadow, and he thought I was an angel. That has to mean something, right?" I mumbled the next part, knowing I was taking things too far but unable to hold the thought in any longer. "Maybe I'm supposed to save him. Like the guardian angel he thought I was."

"Oh, Aviva…" Taz reached over and clutched my hand. "Stryder and I thought the same thing about Grace, and it turns out we were never supposed to interfere."

"Yet you did, and because you did, she's alive," I pointed out.

"Yeah, but not without a price. A cop died who was never supposed to die. We really messed things up."

"Would you do anything differently, if you could go back?"

Taz stared at me for a few silent seconds. I knew she was thinking about Grace; all the Sundays they spent together. She dropped my hand in defeat. "No."

The table grew quiet again.

"Well, this is all pointless anyway," I said quietly. "I can't go back and save Kade."

Stryder frowned. "Have you thought about asking your dad for help?"

Taz snorted. "Seriously? You know more than anyone how he is. All that 'Intervening with the natural course of events can blow up the world' and stuff."

Stryder scoffed. "I seem to remember *you* being the one who thought messing with time might blow up the world. Your dad just thought it could have serious consequences." He took a sip of coffee, then nodded. "But yeah, you're right. He won't be willing to help."

"I already asked him for help anyway," I said, keeping my voice low so my dad wouldn't hear me from the next booth over. "He says Kade came in through a rift—created by your loops, by the way, so thanks a lot guys—" I nodded toward Taz and Stryder, "—but I can't follow Kade through because I'm not a ghost. And because it's closing. I might get trapped."

I tried not to look as crestfallen as I felt as I reached for my orange juice.

"That's not entirely true," Uncle Kiel voiced.

My orange juice teetered in my hand. Uncle Kiel flicked his wrist, righting my glass. My eyes widened as I felt the pull of his magic tingling around my fingers. I snapped my attention to him. Stryder and Taz looked at him curiously.

Uncle Kiel didn't seem to notice he had used his powers to save my drink from spilling. His stare lost its intensity. "On second thought, your dad's right. Messing with rifts is like playing with fire. And as attached as you are to your ghost, you have to use your head to rationalize this. This Thurston-guy was convicted in his time period for the murder of a young woman. Things happened exactly the way they were meant to happen."

I stared at him. If his goal was to comfort me, he failed. I tossed my napkin on top of my plate. "Excuse me." I didn't even attempt to hide the shortness in my voice. "I have to use the restroom."

I escaped the booth and, thirty seconds later, stepped into the ladies room. I turned on the faucet and let warm water pour over my hands while I stared in the mirror, wishing Kade would pop up behind me.

If he did appear behind me, would I be happy to see him? Or afraid? Or both?

After lathering my hands with citrus-scented soap and drying them, I straightened my slumped shoulders, then marched out of the bathroom into the hall. I made a mental note that it was time for a change of subject once I got back to our booth.

"Hey, Ladybug." I swung around to find Uncle Kiel leaning against a discolored wall that looked like it had once housed one of those old-school pay-phones.

"Oh, hey Uncle Kiel," I said unenthusiastically, looking

around him to see if he was waiting in line for the men's room. "What're you doing?"

"Thinking."

"Um…okay."

"You really ought to let it go."

"Let what go?"

"Your ghost."

"I thought I had no choice but to let him go."

"There's always a choice."

I tilted my head at him. "What are you getting at, Uncle Kiel? Can you help me?"

"Do you have any idea what it's like to be me, seeing all the chaos lurking right below the surface? Seeing so many people drift by for years, floating on their fifty or sixty percent chance of success, only to have chaos burst into their lives in some crippling way?"

"No, I…I guess I don't."

His eyes grew distant. "I always see it coming. Not necessarily in a prescient way, but I'm always a witting bystander, watching as the odds catch up with them. I might not know if Frank or Lucy is going to die in a car accident or a plane crash, but I know that a fiery death is looming for so many people. The odds. Those merciless odds Aviva…I can see them so clearly. I can feel them in my bones."

I blinked, stunned. "I'm sorry. It sounds…awful."

"Don't be. I've been who I am for a long time. I've come to peace with it."

I hesitated. "Can you feel the odds of my success in saving Kade?"

He gazed at me darkly. "Yes. They're very slim."

"But…you've come here to tell me you'll help."

He leaned against his cane. "If that is your wish."

I stepped forward, curious. "Can you use your powers for this?"

"No. I have no control over probabilities from the past. But I do have knowledge."

I tried not to let my disappointment show. "Okay, what knowledge can you give me?"

Uncle Kiel glanced around, as if to be sure no one was listening. "Your sister and her boyfriend did a lot of damage to the fabric of Time. This particular rift is the biggest one I've ever known to exist. There is no way to physically "see" it, but your dad and I can feel its presence. Your dad is right to be concerned for your safety. He's your dad, and that's his job. But…"

"But…?" I encouraged.

He peered down the corridor again, then continued. "From an objective point of view, this rift is not going to close anytime soon. The healing process has begun, but this one's a monstrosity. It's going to take months to heal completely."

"Really?" I whispered, hope brimming inside my chest. "So it should be okay for me to go through it?"

"Yes," Uncle Kiel replied. "But Aviva, while I feel confident about this, you know I would never put you or your sisters in harm's way. So I need you to know that, despite my confidence, there's always a risk."

I nodded. Something hummed beneath my skin. An uncertainty. Almost an omen. "Uncle Kiel, why are you telling me all this?"

His eyes pierced mine. "Because I was young and in love once, too."

My mouth dropped open. "I'm not in love!"

Uncle Kiel's lips quirked.

My face warm, I considered his words. I thought about the beautiful little haiku Brett had written me, and how I rejected him. Brett and I were so comfortable and happy together. He was cute, and fun, and would be an awesome boyfriend. Yet I had friend-zoned him. Why? Was it because of Kade?

"Oh, God," I whispered.

Uncle Kiel nodded knowingly. "If there was a way that I could have been with my first love—even if we were destined for a tragic end—I would hope, Ladybug, that someone would have told me how. So against my better judgement—especially given your narrow margin for success—I'm doing that for you now."

My thoughts were a muddled whirlwind. Shoving the whole loving-Kade-thing aside, I took a deep breath to compose myself. Somehow Uncle Kiel helping me felt... wrong. Sort of like the tray falling. Yes, I understood his motives, but I couldn't stop a small seed of distrust from sowing itself into my gut.

Stop, I told myself. Uncle Kiel was treating me like an adult, pure and simple. That was his way. He was giving me the information I needed, and letting me make my own decision. Unlike my dad, who was a control-freak. A lovable control freak, but still. I should feel grateful toward Uncle Kiel, not doubtful.

"How do I find the rift?" I finally asked. "And how do I get through? Dad said there's a 'trick'."

"I can't offer much help in finding the rift, other than to advise you to start searching in its place of origin."

"Pendulum Square? That's where Stryder and Taz spent their final loops."

"That would be a logical place to start. But keep in mind that rifts are finicky, and fluid. They stretch; they move."

"Dad said something similar." I pictured a rip in a skirt, or dress, shifting as the fabric sways. Or a small tear in a pair of nylons, running out of control the second the nylons are stretched.

"As far as getting through," Kiel was saying, "incorporeal beings can go in and out of them easily. Your ghost likely had no clue he even stumbled through a time rift. But it's different for mortals. You can't simply walk through. Like your dad said, there's a trick. It's stupidly simple, and simultaneously complicated."

Curiosity nibbled at me. "What is it?"

"You must touch the rift while holding an item belonging to a person from that time period. This act turns the object into a talisman. The talisman will pull you through the rift and take you to the person you seek."

"That's it?" I said. "Just hold an object?"

"That's it," he affirmed. "But it's not as easy as it sounds, Ladybug. The object you choose must belong to that time period, and can only take you to its owner. To find Thurston K. Oaks, you must hold an object that belongs to him. This is a challenging endeavor given that he died well over a century ago."

He paused, looking over his shoulder again. "We need to go back now. We've been away too long."

I started to follow him back to the table, when he turned around. "One more thing. Talismans aren't perfect. Sometimes they behave erratically. That's the thing with magic…it is never truly controlled. Chaos is built into the very nature of the universe. Learn to accept it and it can bring peace. Fight it or ignore it and it will crush you like a bug."

Before I could ask my uncle more about this bug-crushing business, he was already limping back to our booth.

I walked back, slowly, pondering everything Uncle Kiel had shared with me. It was clear that my odds of going back into the past were slim-to-none. But that didn't matter to me. Tunnel vision was taking over. I now had a clear idea of what I needed to do.

I was going to find something that belonged to Kade. Then I was going to find that rift.

And despite my uncle's attempt to be secretive, I was going to ask my sisters for help.

Thirteen

Ghosts don't haunt us.
That's not how it works.
They're present among us
because we won't let go of them.
Sue Grafton

January 11, 1886

I WISH I COULD simply love her. The words chewed through Kade's thoughts as his gaze traveled over Molly's lovely face. She twitched, holding her eyes steady on the path stretching out before her. Her shawl did little to hide the faux curves created by her bustle as she glided down the path, her hips sashaying gently back and forth. She knew he was watching her, he guessed, but was pretending otherwise. She was talented at feigning ignorance concerning a man's attention as she was quite accustomed to having plenty of it.

Why couldn't he just love her? Or if he could not muster up feelings of love, why could he not at least feel content that such a pleasing young lady was gracing his side? She was delicate and poised and charming, everything a man could want in a future wife.

As if she could read his thoughts, she said, "Darling, why do you never hold my hand or arm as we walk? I admire your chivalry, but we *are* to be married at the end of the month. I promise I won't bite," she added teasingly.

He forced a gallant smile and, as a gentleman escorts a young lady, latched onto her elbow. "Is this more to your liking, my dear?"

"Much. Imagine what a perfect picture you and I look together," she beamed. "Now tell me about your week. It has been a few days since we last walked together! I have to admit I am glad your family has decided we no longer require an escort."

"I, too, am glad for that, though sadly I have not much to tell. Although, I am happy to report that the trials for the new camera are going quite well. Things are looking bright for my father."

"Oh, come now darling, your father is not the sole possessor of your success," she spun her parasol over her left shoulder. "Once we marry, you know that your design will be an investment in our future, as well. We will be able to live in a home even more grand than my parents'!"

"I am glad that thoughts of our future fill you with happiness," he said, then, changing the subject, "How is William doing? I heard from various sources that he is courting a young lady. I believe the scoundrel is trying to steal our thunder," he laughed.

Molly's expression clouded.

Kade halted her on the path, facing her squarely. "Is something bothering you? You know I'm only jesting about your brother. He may be a scoundrel, but he is one of my closest friends."

A rawness drifted over Molly's face that was more "real"

than Kade had ever experienced from her before. There was something so relatable in her vulnerability, and for a few brief seconds, he felt a connection with her. But her polished mask slipped quickly back into place, and the moment was gone.

"Ahh, no darling. I was only thinking about how much I am going to miss my brother once we marry and move to a separate household. It is a silly notion though, as we can not live as children with our siblings forever."

Kade frowned, taking her elbow and continuing their stroll. There was something else going on, but Molly had already closed the subject. Was this what married life would be like? A series of masked smiles and empty conversations?

At least they would have a grand house, fashionable clothes, and luxuries that would make them the envy of the town, Kade thought. A beautiful, frivolous, manufactured life. What else could a person ask for?

Without thinking, Kade reached deep into his coat pocket and grazed the battered letter with his fingertips. The letter he had been carrying since he was nine years old. He wondered if conversations with the allusive Aviva— whoever she was—would feel this hollow.

As if on cue, Molly said "So, my darling, can you believe this unseasonably warm weather?

"HOW WAS YOUR walk?" Kade's mother asked as he hung his coat and hat on the stand in the foyer. She was polishing their finest set of silver flatware on the credenza near the dining room entrance. Ever since they had let go of most of their servants, his mother had taken on more of the household chores. They still had one servant left,

Griselda, who had been with the family for as long as Kade could remember. But Griselda was struggling to keep up with all of the cooking, cleaning, and laundering on her own—tasks she hadn't done in a good decade and a half—so his mother helped when she could.

"Hello there, Ma," Kade leaned in to give her a peck on the cheek. "It was a fine walk. Molly anticipates with excitement being married."

"And how about you? Have you come to terms with it?"

Kade's eyes widened. He had never told his mother his insecurities about his upcoming nuptials. "How—" he stuttered, not sure what his next words were going to be. "How long have you known?"

"I've always known, son." She glanced up from her polishing to give him a knowing look, compassion tracing her features.

"Did you love Father when you married him?"

She set down a spoon and turned to face him. "I knew him not well enough to love him, but he had many qualities that I admired, and I felt certain that I would grow to love him." A sad little puff of air escaped her lips. Kade pretended not to notice.

While his father was faithful to his mother in the strictest sense of the word, he was emotionally absent from her life, and from his children's. Kade had no fond memories of his father trying to teach him something new, or showing him or his little sister Bess any affection. Once, when Kade was young and fascinated by the large camera in the family's studio, he asked his father if he would show him how to use it. His dad simply looked at him like he was an imbecile, rolled his eyes and walked away. Kade never forgot how foolish he felt that day. Later, Kade's mother, seeing his interest in photography, bought him some books on the topic, then she and Kade learned how to work cameras and capture beautiful photographs together.

Once, and only once, did Kade bring up the issue of his father to his mother. It happened when Kade was nine years old, and he showed his father the first photograph he had developed from the family's glass plate camera—a picture of his sister Bess, laughing brightly in her Sunday dress. She had tried to adopt a serious expression for the photograph, but Kade had taken so long to capture the picture that she lost her resolve and laughed. The developing process was complex—most chemists would struggle through it—and Kade was beaming from ear-to-ear at having done it. But Kade's father had barely glanced at the photo, muttered "Uh-huh," then continued his work without another word. Kade ran to his mother, tears brimming his eyes, and told her, "Father doesn't love me."

She took him in her arms, and explained to him that her father was a changed person from the man he used to be. It was then that she told Kade that he used to have a brother. Thurston Benjamin Oaks, or Ben for short. Ben was the elder Thurston's pride and joy. He was going to ride championship horses someday, and take over the family's photography business.

One day, when Ben was nearing the age of three, he came down with Typhoid Fever. The doctor couldn't save him. Kade's mother was pregnant with Kade when it happened, and upon his birth they carried on the family name 'Thurston', but it didn't matter. The morning Ben died, something in Kade's father died too.

"On some level your father loves you," his mother had said. "I think he distances himself from you—from all of us

147

now—because he never wants to feel a loss like that again."

Even at the young age of nine, Kade wondered if living a life in which you never allow yourself to love anyone was worth living at all. His father had plenty of enthusiasm for money and luxuries; it was only he, Bess, and his mother that he failed to muster up any affection for.

Sometimes Kade thought that his father committing infidelity would be an easier problem to contend with; at least that was something a person could put a finger on. And at least the bastard would feel guilty about it and possibly treat his mother with love. But his father's coldhearted distance—his complete apathy for his family— was a more subtle issue, and more difficult to define.

Occasionally his resentment would overwrought his sense, and he would ponder whether his older brother's death—as tragic as it was—was merely an excuse, and perhaps his father was simply an ignoble man, worth less than the gullyfluff found in the pockets of the Barnard boys. But he would never say so much to his mother.

"She's a fine young lady," his mother ventured, steering the conversation away from Kade's father.

"Agreed," Kade said, his fingers tracing the cold skin of a recently polished brass horse. "I wish I could give her the affection she deserves."

He could feel his mother's stare. "Kade. This is a difficult position for me. I'd never wish you to marry Molly if it brings you unhappiness. But consider the issue carefully, as the consequences of breaking off your engagement are many."

He looked up, surprised. Not marrying Molly had never once been presented as an option. "For curiosity's sake, what would the outcome be if I dissolve my marriage agreement with the Brodericks?"

His mother shook her head. "You already know, son. Do you merely want to hear the words from my lips? Very well. Mr. Broderick is a proud man. If you break your marital contract, he will be so insulted that he will refuse to merge our two businesses." She paused. "But I am starting to question whether financial gain is worth my son's happiness."

Kade sighed. He didn't doubt his mother's predictions for a second. Mr. Broderick was an arrogant man, and unyielding in his dealings. Kade had no doubt that Mr. Broderick would cut off his family in a heartbeat if he perceived an offense. The man was already filthy rich without Kade's invention; he didn't need the Oaks. The Oaks needed him.

If only I hadn't invented that damn contraption. The Oak Box, as revolutionary to photography as it was, had started all the trouble.

Kade's family owned the one and only photographic studio in the county, which had always earned them a decent living. Once he learned the trade, Kade took pride in operating the highly complex cameras, and he spent his early teenage years extending his father's business to cover outdoor events, town ceremonies, and even the occasional wedding, in addition to still-shots performed in their studio. Middle-class and elite folks throughout the region travelled to Sezona Valley to utilize their services. The Oaks never shared the same wealth as the Brodericks, but they were fortunate enough to have a properly decorous house, a nicely-appointed buggy with a matched set of thoroughbreds, an array of servants, and a respectable social life.

Then one fateful day, Kade tried to explain to little Bess the complex mechanisms of their studio's glass plate camera and how to capture a photograph, when a wild thought occurred to him. *Suppose there was a camera simple enough for everyone to use?* Thus dawned Kade's new obsession.

Two years later, the first Oak Box prototype was born. When Kade's father was first shown the capabilities of Kade's new camera, despite its glitches and hodgepodge construction, he knew a road to wealth when he saw one. He immediately pooled all of the family's money and resources, then took out hefty loans to finance Kade's invention. The new camera, with the slogan "Now everyone can be a photographer!" was destined to be hugely popular if channeled correctly. Kade wanted to believe his father was going through all of these measures because he had faith in him and his amazing invention, but it soon became clear that this wasn't the case. Kade's father constantly referred to the camera as if it were his idea, and his obsession for wealth was taking over his family's lives. Now, the Oaks family was out of money. Kade's mother was forced to lay off the household staff and mend older dresses to stay afloat—a fact that would be social suicide if leaked out to the townsfolk.

Fortune shined down on them six months ago when Kade's father demonstrated the Oak Box Camera to Mr. Broderick, a sharp, savvy businessman. The two, over brandy and cigars, decided to merge the two families through the marriage of their children, Molly and Kade, and to forge a business agreement. Given that Mr. Broderick was an industrial mogul with ties in the east coast, the new camera could now be distributed quickly and efficiently to a wide range of industrialized cities, including

Chicago and New York. Kade's family had truly struck gold. The Oak Box Camera would not only pull them from financial downfall, but would indeed make them wealthy, and Kade was now betrothed to the most beautiful young woman in town.

The only problem was Kade felt no love for his bride.
Ridiculous problem, he mused.

"It's important to consider Molly, too, in all of this," his mother said, bringing him back to their present conversation. "If you break off your engagement, she will suffer the consequences of a ruined reputation because of her previous behavior."

"What previous behavior?"

"Everyone knows that a couple can become more intimate once they are engaged," she explained. "Stroll out alone, hold hands in public, take unchaperoned rides, visit alone behind closed doors…. It matters not whether you have actually done these things. In the eyes of the town, you have, because you are Mollys fiancé. This is why an honorable man rarely breaks an engagement, so as not to cause the girl discomfiture."

Kade ran his hands through his hair, mentally prattling off the list. If he broke off his engagement with Molly, Kade's family would have to sell off their photography business and possessions to pay off their debtors, they'd lose their social standing in town, and he would ruin a young woman's reputation. His mother would live in poverty without so much as a loving husband to help her endure.

He almost laughed.

"Why on earth are you smiling?"

He grabbed his coat and hat from the stand and turned to face her. "I suppose I find it amusing that it almost seemed like I had a choice in this matter." He strode towards her and pecked her cheek. "I love you, Ma."

"You only just arrived home. Where are you off to now?"

"To the clock tower. I need to take care of something that I should have done a long time ago."

Fourteen

Sunday, March 31
Present Day

THE DOOR SLAMMED in my face. Well, maybe "slammed" was too strong a word. But it was definitely shut with enthusiasm.

"Grrrrrrr," I growled.

"That went well," Taz kept her voice light, turning from the front porch. "On to the next one?"

Phee groaned. "Remind me why I'm wasting what's left of my weekend visiting some dead guy's relatives?"

"Because you're a nice person who cares about your sister?" Krystal offered.

Phee arched a brow. "Does that sound like me?"

"Fine. Because you're the only one of us with a car," Krystal amended. "Though just so you know, Taz almost has enough saved to get one too. Pretty soon we won't need you anymore."

"Hey," Taz interjected, "For the record I'm not gonna be your guys' Uber once I get my new car."

Phee smiled and crossed her arms. "Ahhh, how the tables have turned. You were saying something about not needing me, Krys?"

Krystal scowled, though she knew her comments hadn't actually offended Phee. It was nearly impossible to get her older sister down when she had been glowing for the last three days over her new set of wheels.

"Let's move on to the next one," I interrupted, trying to get my sisters back on track. I looked at the typed list in my hand. "Evelyn Norton. Dang it. She's the last living relative in the area. Most of the others live near the West Coast."

No way any of us had enough gas money for that kind of road trip. I had already used my allowance to pay familyancestry.com to dig up Kade's living relatives. Since Kade never had children in his time period, I was left with a pretty bleak list. A small handful of his sister's descendants was about it. And so far the ones we visited either had no idea who he was, or did indeed know of their notorious ancestor but didn't have anything belonging to him. Or this last one, a Daryl Somebody, who knew all about his great great great great (give or take a great) uncle being hung for murder, and was furious that I had the nerve to bring up such a sensitive subject...hence the enthusiastic door-slamming.

Now I was down to one last name. My nerves twisted inside my stomach.

"Well, let's make this last one count, then," Taz said, opening the passenger door of Phee's Honda Civic.

"Fine. But I'm hanging out in my car for this last one," Phee grouched. "At least I can listen to some music while you're getting doors slammed in your faces."

The rest of us piled into her car. With the help of her

navigation app, Phee made the drive to Poplar Glen, a small town right on the edge of Jayne County.

Twenty-five minutes later, I rang the doorbell of a small white Victorian house. Taz narrowed her eyes at the yellow potted daisies by the door until they collapsed into crispy brown. I quickly leaned down and revived them. I glared at her.

"Sorry," she whispered.

I took a deep breath. The door swung open. A bright-eyed elderly woman wearing a light turquoise jumpsuit stood on the other side.

"Hello," I said. "Are you Evelyn Norton?"

Her eyes narrowed, causing the corners to crinkle. "Yes…" she said suspiciously.

"I'm sorry to bother you," I said. "My name is Aviva. This is my sister, Taz," I gestured beside me. Krystal and Phee were waiting in the car. "I know this is strange, but are you familiar with an ancestor named Thurston K. Oaks?"

She cocked her head at me, curious.

"You might also know him as Kade Oaks," Taz added quickly. "It's…kind of important."

I nodded toward Taz gratefully.

Evelyn's expression softened. "I'm sorry sweetheart, but anyone with the last name 'Oaks' would be related to my husband Parker, not me. That's his side of the family tree."

"Oh, okay. Can we talk to him?"

"He passed away three years ago."

My stomach dropped.

"I'd invite you girls in for a cup of tea, but I'm leaving for Bridge at the Lebowitz Center. Is there anything else I can do for you?"

"Um, no," I said, unable to hide the deflated tone in my voice. "I'm really sorry for your loss. And thanks for your time."

Taz put her arm around my shoulder and gave me a sideways-hug as I plodded back to the car. "I'm so sorry, Viv. But at least you tried, right?"

I gave her a sidelong glance. "I'm not done trying."

"I'M DONE TRYING," I moaned two hours later, letting my styrofoam cup drop onto the table at Copper's Kettle. A splash of coconut macchiato splashed out from the hole in the lid. "I don't understand how it can be this hard to find one measly item belonging to someone from the past."

"Why not try to clear Kade's name in the present?" Krystal suggested, using her napkin to wipe off the coffee I dribbled on the table. "We know his full name now. We can hit the library archives, look for evidence that shows he's innocent. It won't change things in the past, but at least his family tree will lose its blight."

"What's 'blight'?" Phee asked as she used a compact mirror to fix her lip gloss. "Here, you look like you could use this more than me," she shoved the tube of gloss into my hand.

I rolled my eyes at her.

"It's like fungus or mildew…like when a tree starts to wither with disease," Krystal told Phee. "Aviva should know that since she heals things."

"Just because I heal plants and stuff doesn't mean I heal family trees or know what words like 'blight' mean," I grumbled, flicking the lip gloss on the table until it was spinning. "Taz is the blighty one. And if I can't go into the

156

past to clear Kade's name, it's pointless. He still dies. It's not about improving his reputation. I want to save his life."

At least my sisters didn't know what Uncle Kiel had said, about me being in love with Kade. I didn't think I could handle that right now. Until I sorted out my feelings for my mystifying ghost, I would let my sisters believe my reasons for wanting to save him were totally altruistic.

"I hate to say it Aviva," Taz hedged, "but this is starting to feel like one of those things you're not supposed to change."

I stared at her over my cup. "Easy for you to say. You already got to play hero and save a little girl."

"You keep bringing that up, like it makes me some kind of hypocrite to disagree with you about Kade. But Grace was different. Maybe we were wrong to interfere. I mean, an officer died in her place, and that's something I have to live with every day. But either way, there was a hundred percent chance Grace was going to die if we didn't get involved." She took a long drink from her Tazo tea.

"If I don't interfere with Kade's hanging," I pointed out, "there's a hundred percent chance he will die, too. He already has. So what's the difference?"

"The difference," Phee cut in, dropping her compact back in her purse, "is Grace was the innocent victim of a crime, whereas Kade might be a killer."

Her words punched me in the stomach. "I thought you guys trusted my feelings on this one," I accused.

"We do trust your feelings," Taz assured. "It's just that there's more at stake here. Even if you could go back and save Kade, you might be freeing an innocent man. But you also might be freeing a murderer. At least the little girl Stryder and I chose to save wasn't surrounded by all this doubt."

"*Chose* to save? Like I could make a better choice, somehow?" I crumpled the napkin that had been serving as a coaster for my macchiato and tossed it to the center of the table. I grabbed my bag and stuffed the lip gloss into my pocket. "Well I guess it's a good thing that all three of you think I'm an idiot for wanting to save him, because I can't do it anyway."

"Oh come on, Viv," Krystal said. "We just spent all day driving you to all of Kade's relatives because we *do* believe you—"

"It's fine," I bit out, turning to leave. I knew I was behaving like a spoiled brat, but I needed to get away.

"Aviva—," Taz protested, but I was already charging for the door. "Dang it Phee," I heard her sigh. "That was *my* lipgloss."

I would have laughed if I wasn't mad. Phee did laugh.

A cool evening breeze nipped at my face and ruffled my hair as I left Copper's Kettle. My feet took on a life of their own, stepping down Greenwich Drive until I turned into Pendulum Square. Maui loomed ahead, casting her long shadow across the courtyard, her face glowing regally in the twilight.

Her? Not according to the clock's namesake, Chief Māui. I smiled sadly, remembering the story that Kade had told me about the clock's name.

It was here, in front of Maui, that Kade confessed that he thought I was real. Warmth spread inside me for a few seconds before it was replaced with the numbing knowledge that I would never see him again.

I perked up a few flowers in the square to try to cheer myself up. It didn't work. Feeling light headed from using my powers, I plopped down on a bench facing Maui. I wished so badly I could talk to him. I wished I had known the last time I saw him would be the very last. Maybe I would have done something differently.

Unzipping my messenger bag, I pulled out the spiral notebook I had used last week to practice haikus with Brett. I tore out a sheet of paper, placed it on top of my notebook, and dug for a pen, finally pulling out a purple one that I had found in the birthday trunk Uncle Kiel had left in my room.

Dear Kade, I scratched out, deciding to use the same greeting as the fantasy letter Kade claimed I wrote.

A sharp gust of air lifted the corners of my paper and played havoc with my hair. I slipped a hairband from my bag and used it to pull my hair back into a sloppy ponytail, then tilted my notebook up toward the glow of the nearby fairy lights. Tapping the top of my pen against my chin, I thought about what I wanted to say.

Dear Kade,

I know this letter will never reach you, but as I stare at the Face of Maui, this amazing thing that you named, I feel like you are here with me, somehow.

Or maybe this is just wishful thinking.

I'm not elegant with words like you are. In fact, I think in our short time together, I only understood about half of what you ever said. Given that one of those things was the fact that I'm hopeless and unladylike ("a wagtail", I believe you put it?), I probably shouldn't like you.

But I do, Kade. Despite your arrogance and your insistence on treating me like a dim-witted child, I more than like you. I feel… something stronger than 'like'. My uncle calls it love. Is it possible to feel love for someone I barely know? For someone who I've never met in the flesh?

I don't know. But I do know that your disappearance is a stabbing ache.

I regret feeling fear the last time we were together, because I know now that you would never hurt me. You would never hurt anyone. I know you are a good person. I feel it down to my core.

It's crazy for me to assume this letter will somehow bring you comfort as you eventually take your last breaths, but somehow, someway, I hope it does. A time might come when you will be forced to pay a price you don't deserve. If that happens, I'm begging you, please let these words wrap around you, and protect you from pain. And remember as you look across a sea of mocking, accusing faces, that I'll be with you. I'll be an angel watching over you. Find me, and take my hand Kade. We'll get through this together.

Those around you might betray you. But I'm here. And I believe in you.

Yours Faithfully in Time, Aviva

My eyes stung as I signed the letter.

The letter gave breath to my most deeply-seeded longings, yet Kade would never read it.

Adjusting my glasses, I reread what I had written. So heavy and dramatic.

Stupid. I crumpled the letter and tossed it toward a nearby trash bin. As it hit the rim, a gust of wind caught it, propelling it toward the ground.

Loud laughter captured my attention. I whipped around on the bench. A group of rowdy teenagers were walking by, more kids from my school. I slunk down on the bench, hoping they wouldn't notice me.

Once they passed, I flipped my wild bangs out of my eyes and stood up to retrieve my crumpled letter, deciding it was time to leave. The wind was picking up, and unless my sisters ditched me (I would if I were in their shoes), then they were still waiting for me at Copper's Kettle.

The letter scratched the pavement as it scuttled toward Maui in the breeze. And then, touching the clock, it vanished.

I blinked. Of course it hadn't *vanished*.

I walked toward Maui and circled the base of the clock, searching for my letter, but it was nowhere to be found. That last gust of wind must have carried it away. I hoped no one who knew me would find it. It's not like 'Aviva' was a common name.

Shrugging to myself, I turned to leave. But something was niggling at me. Didn't Kade tell me that when he was a child, he had found a letter I had written him? Right in front of the clocktower?

No. It was impossible.

I stepped up to the clock tower again and grazed it with my fingertips.

Nope. Nothing. No magical vibrations. No vanishing into thin air.

The bricks were cool and rough. I leaned forward and rested my forehead on them. A tear slipped down my cheek. I tried to comfort myself in the knowledge that once upon a time, long ago, Kade had once sat here, before this same clock. I closed my eyes and tried to bring myself to that moment. If we had co-existed together for a moment during his death, could we co-exist for a moment in his life? I reached out with my will, stretching fingers of thought to him, telling him I was here, that I believed in him, that I knew he wasn't a murderer.

"I miss you Kade…" I whispered.

At least, I missed the relentless ghost who had followed

me around since my birthday. But what about flesh-and-blood Kade? I never met him. Real-life Kade was an enigma.

Before I had time to ponder the matter further, my eyes flew open. Words Kade had once said whispered in the corners of my mind.

"Before the final mortar was applied to the brickwork, I placed something within the masonry…"

I reeled back.

The time capsule.

I am such an idiot! All of this searching, all of these dead-ends, when an item belonging to Kade was right under my nose the whole time. Kade and his friends had hidden a time capsule inside the clock.

I lunged toward the base of the clock and started digging into the masonry. My fingers scraped painfully against the rough bricks, my nails tearing into the craggy grout.

Come on, come on!

I knew it was futile, but fanned by my own fervor, I couldn't stop. I clawed and clawed at the mocking bricks until my ragged nails began to bleed. I was so close….

"Miss—are you okay?" Someone touched my shoulder.

I gasped, looking up into the concerned face of a middle-aged man. A woman and two kids stood behind him, their mouths gaped open.

"I…I…." My neck and cheeks burned. I must look like a disaster. Hair sticking out wildly from my ponytail, ragged breath, bleeding nails…."Sorry. I was just looking for something."

The man threw me an odd look.

Before he could say anything else, I stood up, brushed off my jeans, grabbed my bag and quickly walked away, refusing to look behind me at the family's incredulous expressions. I wandered toward the backside of Maui. I would just hide here until the family went away. I rested my back against the clock tower, pulling out my cellphone and trying to look busy just in case anyone saw me loitering back here. The wind was finally subsiding, but the chilly air was sharper, now that the hot exertion of trying to tear bricks apart was leaking from my body. I shivered.

From this angle I could see the abandoned railroad tracks that Kade had pointed out during our walk. I tried to imagine what it was like to have a real-life train chugging through the edge of Pendulum Square. Gazing at the tracks, an idea occurred to me. Stuffing my cellphone back into my purse, I edged my way closer. The tracks were lined with railroad spikes, each one hammered into the edge of the rail about a foot apart.

I closed the distance to the tracks. Crouching on the ground, I reached forward and tugged at one of the spikes. It was stuck. I tried another, then another. The third one was loose. I yanked it out, feeling like I had struck gold.

Time for an episode of Railroad Spike vs. Brick.

BREAKING OFF THE first brick was much harder than I expected. It didn't help that I was interrupted half a dozen times by people meandering in and out of Pendulum Square. Each time someone came near, I would jump up, hide my railroad spike beneath my sweater, and casually stroll away. By the time I finally muscled the brick out, I was breathless and sweating.

The second brick, loosened by the absence of its partner, came out quicker, and I was only interrupted twice.

It was a school night, and with the sky darkening by the minute, Pendulum Square was starting to clear out by the time I started on brick number three. Thank goodness some of the grout was already crumbling with age…it was making my job much easier. My arms throbbed and my legs were aching from squatting for so long, but fueled by how close I was, I wedged the spike beneath the brick and continued to dig, scrape, dig…until I finally pried the brick from the base of the clock.

Three bricks down. It might be enough.

I bent down and peered inside the rough opening I created. The interior was too dark. Swallowing hard, I got on my hands and knees and blindly reached inside the hole, hoping there were no spiders. I grimaced as my hand brushed against a web.

"Remember how many of your cousins I've healed if you're tempted to bite me," I murmured to any spiders who might be listening, forcing my hand to keep moving forward.

My fingers grazed something solid. Yes. Groping around, I finally found purchase on the corner of the object. I gripped tightly and slowly slid it out, kneeling on my knees to examine it.

It was a small, splintered box. Awe washed over me, and I realized a part of me thought the time capsule was a fantasy; that it wouldn't actually be there. Heart thumping, I used my blood-crusted fingernails to pry off the lid.

Two objects rested inside, on top of a folded sheet of paper. I was a little underwhelmed, having expected an entire trove of treasures. I reminded myself that the items didn't matter. One of these objects would take me to Kade, if I could only find the rift. Taking a deep breath, I removed the first item. It was a small, rustic pocket knife with an inscription carved into the handle. I tilted the knife toward the fairy lights glowing in the nearby shrubs. *American Centennial.* Wow. This thing was probably worth a mint.

I carefully set it aside, then moved onto the second item. A miniature soldier. I rolled it between my forefinger and thumb. The figurine reminded me of those little green plastic soldiers in Toy Story, but this one was made from a dense metal. Pewter, maybe?

I placed the soldier on the pavement next to the knife.

Okay, so one of these items belonged to Kade. But which one?

Sighing, I went back into the box and pulled out the folded paper. Maybe it listed who had contributed what.

The paper was brown and brittle with a crumbling, burnt edge. I unfolded it slowly, worried that one wrong move might cause it to disintegrate into pieces, and began to read.

Dear Kade,

I know this letter will never reach you, but as I stare at the Face of Maui….

My body convulsed. I dropped the paper.

Impossible. No. Impossible.

With shaky hands, I picked up the letter and continued to read.

…as I stare at the Face of Maui, this amazing thing that you named….

It. Can't. Be.

But it was. Though the previously white paper was now decrepit, and though the purple pen marks were now a gritty shade of gray, this was beyond a doubt the letter I had written for Kade.

I felt sick to my stomach.

I had just written this letter. And then it had blown away. How could it be here, sealed inside a time capsule within the Face of Maui? I had broken apart these bricks myself. Not to mention the condition of the paper revealed that the letter was now much older. It looked like it was a hundred years old.

You penned me a letter when I was a child. I never knew who you were.... Kade's words when we first met serenaded me now.

...it traveled to me through the wind. I found it in front of a clocktower....

I had assumed Kade was just a rambling lunatic. But here it was, the letter I had written him, the reason he knew my name over a century before I was born.

It was signed with your name...

I clutched the letter to my chest. I tried to stand, but painful pins and needles tingled through my now sleeping legs. I wobbled, then leaned against Maui's cool bricks.

A shocking vibration zipped through me. A burning pierced my body. I tried to recoil, but I was frozen. I screamed, the sound paralyzed somewhere in my throat. I felt my glasses fly off my face as the ground tore itself from my feet. The courtyard around me began to spin, turning Pendulum Square into a vibrant whirlpool of streaks and whirls.

What's happening?

Fifteen

Sometimes it's hard to tell
where the ghost ends and real life begins.
Nathan Ballingrud

January 11, 1886

KADE SCRAPED OFF the last of the mortar, then scrubbed the bricks with a wet rag to remove the thin drying film of cement coating the surface. Once finished, his disruption of the bricks was virtually unnoticeable. He eyed the base of the clocktower one last time, then dropped his rag and tools back into his bag.

Fingering the Indian Head penny in his pocket, he stood back, waiting to feel some sense of accomplishment. He had finally buried the last of his childhood fancies. He was at last a man, ready to shoulder the burden of adulthood. To do what was right for his family. Should he not feel some honor in this?

Instead he felt a gut compulsion to rip the bricks apart and retrieve his letter.

He had tried to burn the letter, to the point where the flame licked the edges of the parchment with its searing tongue. It was the right thing to do. Molly deserved a man whose attention and loyalties were directed to her alone, not a man infatuated with a fantasy. He refused to be a distant, unfeeling husband to Molly the way his father was to his mother. If he didn't love her the way he should now, he was determined to learn how.

But burning the letter proved to be too much for him. At the last moment he had yanked the parchment back from the flame and smothered the tiny smoking embers between his fingertips. Remembering his childhood cache of treasures, he decided it was time to retrieve his dad's Indian Head penny and exchange it for something far more valuable.

Let the people of the future puzzle over the mysterious Aviva.

A chortle of laughter rang through the crisp air as three boys sauntered into the town square, bundled in coats and scarves. Kade recognized them as Mr. Barnard's--the tallow maker's--sons. Normally at this time of the year the town was buried in snow, with men venturing into town only for provisions and goods. But this week the sun was shining, which inevitably led to youngins, all-overish with boredom, emerging from their homes to play.

The Barnard boys waved hello to Kade with their mitted hands before crouching in front of Maui to scoop up snow. They were either preparing to build a snowman, or readying for a snowball fight, neither of which he cared to partake in. He offered the boys a cursory wave and turned to walk home.

Some distance away from the square, he heard a commotion. He swung around and saw the three boys standing in front of the clock, shouting and pointing excitedly at something on the ground.

A lizard or whatnot, Kade decided, turning to continue his walk home. Mid-step, he stopped. Lizards generally don't scurry about in the dead of winter. Plus something about the boys' voices seemed oddly excited. He swung around, squinting his eyes against the sun. One of the boys was prodding a bundle on the ground with his toe.

Kade hurried back to the square to see what all the fuss was about.

"What's the commotion?" Kade asked as he approached the small circle of boys. He inhaled sharply at the sight in front of him. The body of a girl lay on the ground. "Oh." Kade crouched over her and placed his hand on her chest. Feeling the soft rise and fall, he breathed with relief. "She's alive."

"Why is she wearin' trousers, Mr. Oaks?" the youngest Barnard boy asked, staring down at her.

Kade gazed at the girl, taking in her disheveled appearance. Her flaxen hair, so pale it was nearly white, was pulled into an unkempt updo. Her light blue chemise and denim trousers were more akin to men's attire, yet the way they clung to her skin was scandalous. Her boots were dark and slouchy with no ties or heel.

"I don't know." Kade's brow furrowed. "I have never seen such disreputable clothing on a woman before. She'll likely catch her death of a cold with those thin garments. Where did she come from?"

"She fell from the sky," one of the boys answered.

"No," Kade scolded. "The truth."

"He ain't jestin' you, sir," the youngest Barnard interjected in a high voice. "We were scoopin' up snow when the clocktower shook, then poof, there she was."

Kade frowned, trying to make sense of the boys' story.

"She's a witch!" the eldest lad shouted.

Kade stared hard at him. "Now don't you go stirring up trouble with some backwards claims, young man."

The boy flushed and scowled. "She showed up out of thin air. We all saw it."

Kade opened his mouth to argue, but snapped it shut when he realized he had no explanation.

The other Barnards, excited by this theory, bandwagoned with the eldest. "Witch! Witch! Witch!" they chanted.

Kade returned his gaze to the frail girl. Witch hunts were a thing of the past, but the boys' chanting made him uneasy. It was difficult to rationalize the girl's bizarre clothing and appearance, and there were enough small-minded people in this town to cause trouble for her if they believed the boys' theory.

"One of you lads go fetch Dr. Harris," Kade said. "I'll keep an eye on her."

The youngest boy turned to scuttle away when Kade noticed something clenched within the girl's closed fist. He bent down to examine it. Some sort of parchment. He gently pried her fingers open and removed the fragile paper. Smoothing it out in his palm, he began to read it.

Dear Kade...

His heart stopped.

Impossible. He had sealed this letter within the clock tower mere moments ago.

"Come on back here, son!" Kade hollered, trying to control the tremor in his voice. "Change of plans."

"What's wrong, Mr. Kade?" the eldest asked. "You look like you've seen a ghost."

It was likely the greatest act of self-control Kade had exhibited in his entire life, smoothing his features into a calm expression and acting as if the universe hadn't just played the biggest trick on him.

"All's well, lad," Kade stated, toneless. "It merely occurred to me that my family has plenty of provisions to show some hospitality to a young woman in need." He dropped the letter carefully into his supply bag. He pulled his coat off, tucked it around the girl, then secured his bag strap over his shoulder. Leaning down, he scooped her up into his arms. Her head lolled back. He adjusted her weight so that her head was resting in the crook of his elbow. Her pale matted hair trickled over his arm.

"What're you gonna do with her, Mr. Kade?" the youngest piped.

"Get her warm, for starters. If she requires medical attention once she awakens, I will call Doctor Harris and have her treated in the comfort of a bed rather than the ground here." Kade looked levelly at the boys, hoping his next words would carry the weight of his warning. "If any of you start spreading rumors that this girl is a witch, I'll have your mother wash your mouths out with soap and salt until those slanderous tongues of yours are clean."

The boys glanced at each other as Kade stepped away, looking visibly wary over his threat.

Little did the boys know that Kade himself wasn't convinced of his own words. What else but some kind of sorcery could describe why this mysterious girl was in possession of a letter that he had just sealed within Maui? A letter that looked to have aged by a hundred years in a matter of minutes?

He wanted answers. Until he had them, he had no intention of allowing her to escape his sight.

He turned and, praying that no one else besides the

Barnard boys would be out and about on this glittering morning to see the load he cradled, started the slow trek home.

Sixteen

People will do anything,
no matter how absurd…
to avoid facing their own soul.
C.G. Jung

January 11, 1886

I KNEW SOMETHING was "off" before my eyes opened. Was it the chill in the air? Or the texture of the fabric pressed against me? Or maybe it was that erratic *tap tap tap* flitting about my ears.

Either way, I sensed the strangeness of my surroundings seconds before I actually woke up, so when my eyes finally did pop open, the gasp was already flying from my lips.

"Shhhh," a deep voice soothed. "You lost consciousness, but you are safe now."

I bolted upright, clutching onto the blanket on top of me. "Who are you? Where am I?"

Embers in a corner stove cast a soft glow into the space, but its subdued light was not far enough to reach the dark blurry figure leaning over my bed. My hands flew to my face, feeling for my glasses. My fingers hit the bare skin of my nose. *Great.*

"Is it not I who should be asking who you are, little one?"

Recognizing the voice, my heart skittered. And then I remembered, I found the rift! Time used the letter I had written to Kade as a talisman. The letter, after all, was his. I flung the blanket aside and leapt out of bed, ignoring the dizziness that pounded my temples.

"Kade! Oh my gosh, I found you!" I lunged at him, planning to throw myself into his arms for a bear hug.

But instead of wrapping his arms around me, his large hands gripped me right below the shoulders, keeping me at arm's length. I was immediately struck by how…alive he was. His skin, which in my time period had been pale with his ghostly pallor, was now tan and seemed to glow with life. His eyes blazed with a fiery blue.

"Explain to me how you know my name." He leaned forward and leveled me with a dark stare. "Or better yet, explain to me how you came into possession of *this*."

He let go of my shoulders and turned to grip an oil lamp from the nightstand, shining it on a crinkled, yellowed sheet of paper spread out on the end table. I squinted and leaned forward, then frowned when I recognized my letter. "I don't understand it either. I had just finished writing that letter when it disappeared in the breeze, then I found it later in your time capsule. How could that have happened?"

His eyes narrowed. "You are speaking gibberish, child."

"You're joking, right? Kade, it's me. Aviva." My pulse was still skittering at the sight of him, and I was baffled at his lack of familiarity with me. "I'm 'the girl of your dreams,' remember? Or do you have amnesia again?"

His eyes widened as he grabbed the letter. "You're…you're her? You're Aviva?"

And then I realized how stupid I was. Kade didn't know me. Of course he didn't. Why would he? He hadn't died and become a ghost yet, so we had never met. He only knew the name on the letter.

Before I could open my mouth to respond, he closed the gap between us and gripped my hands, turning them back and forth in his own as if trying to gauge my realness. I felt a laugh bubble up at the notion that even when he was alive, he refused to believe I was real, but my humor quickly dissolved in the distraction of his touch. My breaths grew shallow as he continued his exploration, his thumbs caressing the soft flesh of my palms, and then moving up to my wrist and lower arms. It reminded me of the very first time he had touched me in my bedroom, when he was trying to understand how he was capable of feeling me, and I him. Just like then, his eyes sought mine every few seconds, his expression a mask of curiosity. It struck me that I could no longer feel electric vibrations course through me as I had when he was a ghost, yet there was a tangibility to his flesh and blood touch that sent my nerves humming in a completely different way.

Then he pulled me forward, and my shoulders were in his vice-like grip again. "If this is some kind of prank, so help me little one, I'll—"

"Kade," I stopped him before he could finish his empty threat. My head was spinning. I couldn't tell if it was his proximity making me dizzy, or my crummy vision, or maybe just a side-effect from traveling through the rift, but either way, I needed to sit down. "Are all the guys in this century as grabby as you are?"

He stared at me, making no move to release me.

I sighed. "I'm dizzy. Do you mind if I sit down?"

Understanding dawned on his features. "Forgive me. In my confusion and curiosity I am behaving like a scoundrel. Despite how chirk you appear, I should have known that you are not completely well."

I yelped as he leaned down and scooped me into his arms, cradling me like a child.

"Did I hurt you?" he glanced down at me.

"Uh, no. It's just...I only wanted to sit down. I don't need to go back to bed, and even if I did, my legs aren't broken."

He chuckled. "Well allegedly we men in this century are quite 'grabby.'" He carried me over to the bed, where he lowered me onto the soft mattress. "Lie down until you are feeling well. Would you like me to fetch you something to eat?"

At the mention of food my stomach rumbled. When was the last time I ate? It was hard to deduce time when you spliced right through it.

"Food sounds great!" I grinned.

"You are quite transparent with your enthusiasm."

"Is that a bad thing?"

His lips twitched. "In these parts it is considered unladylike."

I laughed. His head cocked questioningly.

"It's not the first time you've accused me of being unladylike," I explained. "In my time period you called me a 'wagtail.'"

"Similar things were stated in your letter. Though it is all drivel to me. Are you certain you do not need sleep?"

I sighed again, realizing living-Kade couldn't possibly understand a word I was saying.

"No. Food first. Then we'll talk."

He nodded, his eyes glowing a deep cobalt in the

candlelight. "Agreed. In all sincerity, little one, I have waited my entire life to talk with you."

My heart galloped.

Calm down, I told myself. He is simply curious about the letter.

I leaned my head back against the pillows, waiting for my dizziness to pass. Drowsiness tugged at my consciousness and before a minute passed, I slipped into a dreamless sleep.

A FEATHER-LIKE touch grazed my arm. I opened my eyes to see Kade towering over me with a tray of food. "I knew you needed to rest," he noted. "You have been out for awhile."

Shaking off the drowsiness, I felt my eyes widen at the shock of having fallen asleep when I was finally reunited with Kade. Man, this time-traveling business wipes a person out.

"Thanks," I sat up and took the tray he offered, balancing it on my lap, squinting to deduce the contents. I wished I had stuffed my glasses into my pocket before traveling through the rift. The food looked like bits of pork, corn, and beans, a chunk of bread, and a china cup brimming with a steaming creamy liquid. A step up from the runny eggs and burnt bacon I had last eaten in bed.

Kade sat stiffly in the nearby rocking chair, watching me eat. I tried to slow my shoveling down to more ladylike nibbles, taking breaks to sip what I now knew was tea. The hot beverage warmed my inner core, leaving me feeling cozy.

"Mmmm," I set the cup down on its tiny saucer.

"I was unsure how you take your tea. I surmised sugar and cream was a safe gamble."

"I don't know how I take my tea either. I just order whatever sounds good at Copper's Kettle or Starbucks."

"Starbucks?"

"Never mind."

I finished my meal, sneaking peeks at Kade from time to time. One hand was resting on the nightstand, long fingers tapping restlessly against the surface, eyes on me. That must have been the tapping sound I heard earlier. I could tell his patience was wearing thin.

"Okay, I'm done." I set the tray on the nightstand, then turned my body so I could face him.

"Very well," he said. "Let us discuss our situation. You claim to be Aviva. How is that possible? Where did you come from? How did you write me a letter when I was a boy, even though we had never met? Furthermore, based on your appearance, you would have been a mere toddler when you wrote that letter, which is obviously absurd. But most perplexing, why are you in possession of the letter now, when I sealed it within the clock tower only this morning?"

"Whoa. That's a lot of questions."

He narrowed his eyes. "I've waited a long time, Aviva."

I put my hands up in a surrendering gesture. "I'll try my best, okay?" I leaned over to gulp one last swig of tea. "I'm from the future. The twenty-first century. Sometime in your own future—wait, what is the date right now?—anyway, you're going to die, and your ghost will visit me…" I trailed off. His brows were raised in a doubtful she's-gone-mad way. "Okay, I know how all this sounds."

"As if you're hysterical?" he offered.

178

"Ugh. Okay. Let me start over. You came to my time period as a ghost. My dad says it's because you experienced a traumatic death, so you slipped through a rip in the universe from your time to mine. He says you were drawn to my 'life-giving aura.'"

"I don't understand."

"Well, the life-giving aura thing is because I'm Spring. I can revive things. Since you were dead, you were attracted to that. Here, grab me a houseplant or something, and I'll prove it."

He cocked his head to the side, his eyes boring into me, as if trying to assess my sanity.

Did they even have houseplants in this century?

"Okay," I admitted, "that part is really confusing. I'll come back to that later. Anyway, you found me in my time period and you and I became…" I paused and swallowed. "…friends. We were friends, for a short time. You couldn't remember much about your life, not even your own age— hey, how old are you anyway?"

"I will be twenty years on March 4th."

So he was nineteen. The fact that we were both technically teenagers pleased me, though I didn't care to admit it. "Anyway, you did remember a few things. You told me that your mom used to make candy canes. And you named the Face of Maui after a famous chief from a childhood story. Oh, and you and your friends buried a time-capsule inside of the clock tower. I wonder…" I thought about the letter, but then decided to file that thought away for later. "I started to figure out how you died, and when I confronted you about it, you…you changed into a different person, and it scared me, but I think you were the one who was truly scared. Then you

179

disappeared." My eyes misted. "I miss you. I mean, I miss your ghost. I know that sounds weird, but I do. Even though you followed me everywhere and treated me like a hopeless kid and were all weird and formal, you were also fun, and funny, and you thought my hair was like ala—"

"—Alabaster streaked with sunlight," he whispered, reaching out to touch it.

My heart skittered. "You remember?"

"No. But it is what I am thinking now."

He slowly dropped the lock of hair and we stared at each other.

I finally broke the silence. "When you disappeared, I wrote you that letter," I nodded toward the decrepit paper flattened on the nightstand, the faded script disappearing into crinkles and shadows. "I felt silly after writing it, so I crumpled it and tossed it into the trashcan. Only—the wind caught it, and carried it toward the clock. Then it was gone."

"That's where I found it." A note of amazement laced his voice, his eyes wide. "I was a boy…only nine years old. We had just finished burying the cache of keepsakes. I found the letter drifting in the breeze near the clock. It's as if…as if…." He took an unsteady step backwards.

"As if the letter slipped from my time to yours," I breathed. "Do you remember the date you found the letter?"

"It was the eve of April Fool's. I remember because at the moment I found it, I thought perhaps George and William were playing a prank on me."

I swallowed hard. I had written and lost the letter at sundown on March 31st. The eve of April Fool's. He had found the letter on the same exact night, but as a child in his own century. I sank into my pillow, feeling dizzy again. "Maui's the rift, Kade. My letter slipped through the rift and found you. It's like Time knew it belonged to you."

He lowered himself into the rocking chair, scooting the chair closer to face me, his face lit in awe.

I sat up. "Wait. Right after the letter disappeared, I dug out your time capsule and found the same letter trapped inside. That doesn't make sense. Why would it be there? You just now said that the time capsule was already buried in the clock by the time you found the letter."

"I kept that letter close to my heart every day," Kade said quietly. "I used to dream about meeting my mysterious Aviva. Until today, when I decided it was time to let you go for the sake of my upcoming nuptials."

My mysterious Aviva. *I decided it was time to let you go…*I felt both warm and cold at the same time.

He continued. "This morning I broke into the masonry of the clock, pulled out the cache, and re-sealed your letter within. It was the perfect way to rid myself of the letter forever, without destroying it."

"And I found it over a century later, minutes after I wrote it."

Our eyes locked. "Incredible," Kade said.

I glanced over at the letter, sitting so unassuming beneath the flickering glow of the oil lamp, having no idea how special it was.

For the next half hour I told Kade most of everything I knew. He listened raptly the entire time, though I couldn't tell if he believed me or not. At the end of my monologue, I exhaled and sank back into the bed.

"When do I die?" he finally asked. I wondered how much exertion it was taking him to force his voice to sound so calm.

I searched my memory, thinking about the conversation I had with my dad. "January 21,1886."

He swallowed hard.

"What's the date now?" I asked.

"Monday, January 11, 1886."

Ten days. We had ten days to unravel the mystery of Marguerite's death. Ten days to save Kade's life.

But…no. Ten days is when Kade hangs. Marguerite Broderick gets murdered a few days before that. But when?

I wracked my brain, trying to remember.

Ughh. Nothing.

Church! The thought hit me. The article said she had gone to church that morning. Church was held only on Sundays. I did some quick math. There was only one Sunday left before Kade's hanging.

Marguerite was to die on January 17. Six days.

I tried to calm my racing pulse. Six days was more than enough time to stop Kade from getting framed.

I can do this.

And then I wondered, why did the rift bring me back to January? Shouldn't the rift have delivered me to March 31st as it did the letter?

Maybe it couldn't. Maybe Time knew Kade was dead by then, and it simply brought me to a point where he was still alive and well.

Or…my brain whirled…maybe it was more about the talisman-nature of the letter. It seemed logical for the letter to draw me to the point in time where Kade had just sealed its counterpart inside of Maui. Imagine the sheer power there, I mused. Two talismans—one that had already traveled through time clutched in my hand, the other sealed inside the rift. The two might have been drawn together like magnets.

Kade was talking and I snapped back to attention. "Sorry, what?"

"How do I die?"

Oh. Feeling tongue tied, I twisted my hands together.

"Aviva. Tell me."

My voice was hoarse. "You're hung."

"Hung for what crime?" Again, his voice carried a forced-calm.

I stalled, my voice coming out in a half-whisper. "For the murder of Marguerite Broderick."

His face paled. "No." The short syllable came out in a choke. He lurched out of the chair and stood over the bed, towering over me. "No! That is impossible! You are lying! Treacherous girl!"

I clutched the blanket to my chest, surprised at the sudden change in his demeanor.

"You are leaving," he ordered.

"What? Kade, I—"

He grabbed my wrists and hauled me out of the bed. "There is an inn at the southwestern corner of town. I am sure they will be glad to let you stay the night. In the morning I suggest you leave this town. You have overstayed your welcome."

With that he released me and walked to the side table. Before I could protest, he picked up our miracle-letter that had traversed back and forth between two centuries, and tore it to pieces.

Tears sprang to my eyes as he stormed out the door.

Seventeen

*The people you love
become ghosts inside of you,
and like this you keep them alive.*
Rob Montgomery

Sunday, March 31
Present Day

"WHAT'S TAKING Aviva so long?" Phee complained.

Krystal tapped her empty cup against the table, feeling the same impatience. Where was her sister? Copper's Kettle would be closing in twenty minutes. She understood that Aviva was upset, but it was unlike her to take off like this.

"Do you think she's still upset by what you guys said?"

Phee huffed. "If she is, she's being way too touchy about it."

"Well, you did kind of imply that a guy she cares about is possibly a murderer."

"Don't act all innocent Krys," Phee said. "Just because you didn't say it out loud doesn't mean you don't agree with us."

An abrupt laugh sounded nearby. Krystal peered over to

see the sound came from some guy, probably twenty or twenty-one, sitting about three feet away at a small round table, reading what looked like a journal or field log.

Had he been there the whole time? How much had he heard?

Phee crossed her arms. "Um, excuse me. Do you have a problem?"

Heat fanned Krystal's face. Phee's tendency to be confrontational with people—especially strangers—always unnerved her.

He tore his eyes from his book and lowered his thick reading glasses, revealing intense hazel eyes. "No, no problem. By all means, continue to rehearse your play."

"Play?" Krystal kept her voice polite.

"Is there any other reason teenage girls would be sitting here at a coffee shop on a Sunday night talking about time-travel and murderers?"

So he *did* hear everything.

Phee narrowed her eyes. "And who might you be?"

"I'm Owen." He didn't bother to reach out and shake hands, instead, choosing to return his attention to his journal.

"I've seen you somewhere before," Taz pointed out.

Owen didn't bother looking up from his book. "I was a student of your dad's. He helped me with a research project after graduation. I actually had dinner at your house. Twice. But that was a few years ago...I don't expect you to remember." He laid the book down and glanced over at Phee. "Especially you, Sunshine."

Phee cocked her head. "Why, 'especially' *me*?"

"If I recall, you were too wrapped up with your nails and hair to be bothered by a guest in your home."

Phee bristled. "Well, *Owen*, how about you get back to your coffee and mind your own damn business?"

Owen shrugged and continued reading.

Phee leaned in, her voice soft and seething. "Can you believe that guy?"

She would never say it out loud, but Krystal wondered if Phee was more mad over Owen's words, or the fact that he wasn't falling at her feet like most guys.

"Yeah, he's a jerk," Taz agreed, "but…it's getting late."

They all knew Taz's implication. Where the heck was Aviva?

A vague feeling of unease settled over Krystal. "I think we're gonna have to hunt her down."

Taz and Phee nodded their agreement and stood to put on their jackets. Krystal zipped up her sweater and dumped their empty cups into the trash. Phee shot one more dirty look at Owen before walking to the door. He never looked up from his book, but Krystal did see his lips quirk into a small smile. The door chimed behind them as they slipped outside into the bright night.

"Where should we look?" Krystal asked.

"Let's try there," Taz pointed to Patty's Critters. "When I'm upset, animal memes always cheer me up. And this is the real thing."

"What are you, three years old?" Phee quipped.

"You have a better idea?"

"Uh, no."

Krystal doubted that Aviva was drowning her sorrows in rabbits, but she didn't have a better suggestion either, so she followed her sisters inside the store. Once inside, they decided to split up to look.

Krystal walked the back of the store and was just stepping

into the aquarium section when she heard Taz holler, "Hey, check this out!"

Curious over the excitement in Taz's voice, Krystal hurried through the shop. She found Taz in aisle six, pointing at a multi-tiered rat cage, complete with large tubes, ramps, and a hammock on top.

"It's on sale," Taz grinned.

Krystal refrained from smacking Taz in the head. "What the heck does this have to do with our missing sister?"

"Well, nothing...but wouldn't this be an awesome birthday gift for Stryder? Poor Miss B is still in that fish tank."

"Stryder's birthday was over a month ago."

"Fine. It can be a gift for our quarter-anniversary."

"Because that's a thing," Krystal mumbled.

"Huh?"

She sighed. "You're never going to save up money for a car if you keep buying Stryder stuff. And you do know that he's rich, right? He can buy a hundred of these cages himself."

"Yeah, but it'll be more thoughtful coming from me. Here, help me grab this box."

Krystal sighed again--a nice hotty puff of air to make sure Taz knew she was only doing this under duress--and squatted down to help her with the box on the bottom shelf.

A few minutes later, Krystal and Taz left the pet shop, holding the rat cage between them in a large bag. Phee sauntered in front of them.

"Let's drop this off in your car," Taz suggested to Phee, "then get back to looking for Viv. We can cover more ground if we're not lugging this thing around."

"You don't say," Phee noted. Like Krystal, she didn't

appear entirely enthused by Taz's purchase.

"We're parked over on Greenwich, right?" Krystal asked between breaths. She wasn't really as winded as she was letting on. She just wanted to make Taz feel guilty for making her haul her boyfriend's ridiculous unbirthday gift. "If we sneak behind Copper's Kettle, we can get there faster."

"Too dark and creepy," Phee said. "Let's cut across the courtyard."

Most of the time, her sisters never questioned or doubted Krystal when it came to directions, having learned a long time ago that their little sister was a mad genius when it came to geography. Unlike Phee and Aviva, who couldn't decipher east from west. But in this case, Krystal agreed. Creeping through dark alleys near the abandoned railroad tracks probably wasn't worth saving a few minutes.

Maui began her musical caterwauling as they stepped into the square, reminding Krystal how late this evening was stretching. Her arms starting to throb, she quickened her pace, but then stopped. A sharp tang tickled her nose. She sniffed the air, trying to find the source of the thick, cloying smell. She set down her half of the gerbil cage (ignoring Taz's protest of "Hey!") and followed the scent to a brick planter in front of the square's enormous fountain. The planter was stuffed with vibrant orange and yellow snapdragons, buried in a bed of white lilies, much like a sunrise peeking through puffy clouds.

Weird. Aviva had always been able to smell the snapdragons, but Krystal never could. Krystal just assumed it was a spring-thing, since Taz and Phee weren't very attuned to nature's aromas either. Yet tonight, somehow, she could smell the snapdragons. Maybe it was that one phenomenon she learned about in her biology class. They watched some documentary about these "insomniac" flowers that release strong odors at night time, or if they are in distress...whatever "distress" means for a flower. Now she understood why Aviva wrinkled her nose every time she walked past the fountain. The scent was thick and sickly-sweet.

"What are you doing?" Phee demanded. Krystal turned around, startled.

Taz popped up behind Phee, dragging the giant bag. "Thanks a lot Krys," she grunted.

"Sorry, I was smelling the flowers," Krystal said.

"So you literally stopped to smell the roses," Phee snorted.

"What roses?" Taz set her load down.

"Not roses. Snapdragons," Krystal corrected, turning to point to them. Then she gasped. She crouched down, trying to make sense of what she was seeing.

Save for one little clump on the edge, the vibrant orange and yellow snapdragons that she had just been gazing at were...well, they were gone. In their place, laying in a bed of white lilies, were shriveled gray twigs covered with miniature skulls. Tiny, screaming skulls.

Fascinating. She fought the urge to scoop up a bouquet of them to display in her room.

Taz and Phee dove down next to her, trying to figure out what had captured her attention.

"Look," Krystal pointed.

"Those are just dead snapdragons," Taz said.

"No way." Each skull, with its empty eye sockets and gaping mouth, looked like it was in agony.

"That's normal," Taz said. "I know they're creepy as all

get-out, but I swear that's just what snapdragons look like when they die. Here, watch." She narrowed her eyes at the last cluster of snapdragons on the edge of the planter.

Krystal watched as the vibrant orange of the snapdragon slowly bled from the flower, the ashen-gray petals shrinking and tightening into the shape of a skull. "Wow," she breathed. "What a beautiful and morbid flower."

Phee was swiping images on her phone. "Ew, I just googled it, and it's true. They all look like tiny skulls when they die. How'd you know snapdragons do that, Taz?"

Taz gave her a withering look. "Come on, you know I'm like the Queen of Death. And do you really have to google something you just saw with your own two eyes?"

"Sometimes I trust Google more than my eyes. Anyway, let's go find Aviva and have her revive these things."

And then Krystal remembered, and her pulse quickened. She grabbed Taz's arm. "You guys, these flowers were alive like, three minutes ago."

"What? You mean the ones I just drained?"

"No. All of them. They were all colorful and healthy right before you walked up. They even smelled...flowery. I turned around to talk to you, and when I looked back, they were dead."

Taz's brows shot up as she considered what Krystal told her. "It is kind of weird that these snapdragons are dead when all these lilies are still alive. I don't get it. What would make healthy flowers suddenly die? I mean, besides me using my powers on them, which I didn't. Even frost doesn't work that fast. Plus, it's been so warm this month."

Phee yawned behind them. "I don't really care what killed the flowers. Let's get on with this. I need my beauty sleep."

Taz gazed down at the flowers, looking lost in thought. A small roach crept from the shadows of the planter.

"Nope," Taz told the roach. It immediately rolled over, legs sticking up in the air.

"You're scary," Phee said.

Krystal grabbed a small twig from the planter and used it to nudge the roach. "It's dead."

Taz paled. "I didn't mean to kill it." She put her palm against her forehead, and her body swayed. Though it was a mere roach, absorbing its life essence had taken a toll on her.

A veil of quiet dropped on them. Neither she, nor her sisters, cared much about one less roach roaming Pendulum Square, but Krystal knew it was the implication of what had just happened that rendered the three of them wordless. Within two seconds Taz had killed a living thing without so much as touching it. Her power was…creepy.

For the umpteenth time, Krystal felt a pull of jealousy over Taz's gift. Not that she wanted to kill things…she loved animals and nature almost as much as her sisters did. But she found Taz's life-draining ability disturbing and darkly fascinating.

Krystal finally broke the silence. "We need to find Aviva." She reached down to grab her half of the rat cage when a spark of light winked at her from the clocktower.

"What's that?" she pointed.

Before her sisters could answer, she walked over to investigate. Two small objects were lying neatly next to each other on the ground, as if placed there on purpose, right next to a dirty wooden box. One of the objects glinted lewdly in the dim bath of nearby twinkle lights. "It's…." She plucked it from the ground. "It's a knife." She turned it around in her hand. "American Centennial," she read from the handle.

Taz hurried over. "Can I see?"

Krystal passed it to her.

Taz rubbed the dull handle with the pad of her finger. "What on Earth is this doing out here? It looks like an antique."

"Hey, check this out," Phee set her purse down and reached for the other object. She held it out between her glossy pink fingernails; a tiny pewter soldier.

"What the...?" Taz's voice trailed off.

"Um, guys?" Krystal said. She ran to the base of Maui and plucked a third object from the ground.

Purple prescription glasses. The left lens was cracked.

Krystal's stomach heaved. There was only one person she knew who wore purple glasses.

"Oh no," Phee stuffed the soldier in her pocket and swiped the glasses from Krystal's hand. She examined them closer, her face turning pale. "They're Aviva's. Which means...which means she's been kidnapped! Some creepy bastard has our sister!" Her body trembled in anger.

"Phee, calm down. Let's think this through—"

Before Taz could finish her thought, Phee pounded her fist on the tower. She had barely hit the bricks when her body shimmered, then disappeared right before their eyes.

"What the hell?" Taz exclaimed, her voice high-pitched. "Where'd she go?"

Confusion and fear paralyzed Krystal for five seconds. But in the sixth second, she understood. "Oh. Oh no."

"What?" Taz asked, her voice still a shaky squeal.

Krystal lunged toward the clock tower and pounded the bricks with her hands in wild movements. "This is the rift.

It's right here. Maui is the rift!"

She continued to scratch and dig at the bricks, her short fingernails growing ragged with the effort.

"Remember why we drove to Poplar Glen today?" Taz's voice was now eerily quiet, causing Krystal to stop her assault on Maui. "To look for an object of Kade's. You need an object belonging to someone in the past to get through."

She was right, Krystal thought. When Phee touched the rift, the little soldier she was holding pulled her into the past. She wondered what object Aviva had used. There must have been another trinket besides the knife and the soldier.

Krystal glanced up at Taz to share her thoughts, but then took in a sharp breath. She was massaging the knife's script with her fingers, a thoughtful expression on her face.

"Taz, I know what you're thinking. Don't you dare."

"I have to save them."

"Taz, no. NO. Please--don't leave me here alone."

Taz ran up and gave Krystal a quick, tight hug. "I'm sorry. Find Dad. Go get help. I love you Krys." She paused, then breathed, "Tell Stryder I love him."

Before Krystal could reply, Taz jumped toward Maui and slammed her hand against the brick.

With a heavy vibration, she disappeared.

"Taz! No!" Krystal wailed, lunging for the clock. "Let me in! Damn you Maui! Let. Me. *In.*" She banged the clock with each word. It was fruitless. She needed an object to get through, but the trinkets were swept into the past with Taz and Phee.

She eyed the dirty wooden box lying nearby and grabbed it, took a deep breath, and placed her hand on the clock.

Nothing. The box must not belong to anyone, only the items within.

What about Phee's purse? Would it take her to Phee?

She whisked it from the ground and slammed her palm on Maui.

Again, nothing.

Of course. Aviva had mentioned earlier that the object must belong to that time period. The purse was Phee's, but it belonged in this century, not in the past.

A cold chill washed over her body. Never in her life had she been separated from her sisters.

Never in her life had she felt so alone.

Find Dad. Go get help.

Krystal, feeling frozen, looped Phee's purse over her shoulder, then forced her numb legs to move, dragging Taz's enormous Patty's Critters' bag behind her. A crow cawed from a nearby tree, a ghostly sound that echoed through the square. The bird's beady eyes followed her as she trudged past the fountain. She turned to glance at the flowerbed one more time. Somehow she wasn't surprised to see that, like the snapdragons, the lilies were now dead too. No more sun rising through puffy white clouds.

All that remained were skulls resting in a grave of black lilies.

Eighteen

You are the piece of me
I wish I didn't need.
Zedd

January 11, 1886

THE WALK BACK into town was cold and made longer by the fact that the world was fuzzier and scarier without my glasses, though at least my anger toward Kade was proving to be a nice distraction.

How could he? I fumed. After everything I had done to get to his time period; the risks I had taken. The risks I was still taking. Well, to hell with him. If he didn't want my help, there was nothing I could do. No way was I staying in this time period just to watch him be hanged. I was marching straight to Maui and going back to my own time where I belonged. My dad was right. Trying to intervene with history was a bad idea.

I clung onto my anger like a life preserver, knowing the second I let it go I would be drowning in the pieces of my broken heart. Pieces as shredded as our precious letter, I thought through tear-streaked vision.

The blurry silhouette of Maui loomed in the distance. Thank goodness I knew the landscape well enough to navigate myself to this point. Everything in this century was so different and weird—the charming victorian and colonial structures, the outhouses and pump stations dotting the landscape, the open spaces where businesses should be, the unpaved roads with the occasional horse-drawn wagon clopping by—yet it felt surprisingly normal at the same time. I half-expected for the world to be shaded with rustic ivories and browns like those old-time photos you see in novelty shops, or for classical music to serenade me everywhere I go. Shouldn't I *feel* like I was in the late 1800s? But the pine trees were as green as they were in my time period, the late afternoon sun just as bright, making it easy to forget.

Approaching the clock, I pulled Phee's lip gloss from my apron. Or, rather, from the apron of the dress Kade had given me. At least he had the decency to loan me some period clothing so I wouldn't stick out like a sore thumb. After storming out, he had come back briefly to push a bundle of clothes into my arms, his lips set in a straight line. I asked him where they had come from. Without looking at me, he said, "From our former housemaid. She was petite like you." Then he left me to change in a washroom of sorts that was so tiny it must have once been a closet. I had planned to keep my own clothes, but deciding at the last minute that I didn't want to carry them around, I ended up leaving them behind, being sure to pull my cellphone from the pocket of my jeans. When I stumbled upon Phee's lip gloss, I grabbed that too, and stuffed both into my apron.

The lip gloss was important. Uncle Kiel did a good job explaining to me how to sneak into this century, but he failed to tell me how to get back home. I thought it was a little odd that he neglected such an important detail.

Probably because he never expected me to actually make it this far. No matter, I was sure the process of getting home was the same as getting here. I simply needed an object from a person of my own time period to pull me back into the present. My cellphone wouldn't work, since I was here in the past. But Phee's lip gloss…it was perfect. I vaguely remembered stuffing it into my pocket in frustration back at Copper's Kettle. Thank goodness for happy accidents.

What time of the day would it be once the rift spit me back out into my own time period? I wondered if for every minute that passed here, a minute passed in my own time. I hoped too much time wouldn't pass or else my family would be crazy with worry. I remembered Uncle Kiel's warning that talismans aren't always reliable. Unreliable didn't mean overshooting my own time period by like, fifty years or something, right?

People milled about Pendulum Square, strolling in and out of various shops. Most of the shops were small and quaint with hand-painted signs in careful handwriting. A woman with two kids stepped out of a rustic store called "Switzer Brothers Quality Merchandise." The girl, about six years old and dressed like a porcelain doll, gave me a curious glance as she passed by. This was the closest I had been to any person from this century in broad daylight, and I tried not to stare at the little girl's fancy costume.

They're not costumes, I chided myself. I'm pretty sure in this time period they call them "clothes."

Too many people were out and about for me to go jumping into a time rift, so I decided to explore a bit. I had come all this way; might as well take in some of the sights from this century before heading back home.

Stuffing the lip gloss back into my apron, I set off. The

streets here in Pendulum Square weren't dirt like the outlying roads leading into town, rather, they were paved with what looked like newly-laid bricks. I was too intimidated to walk into any stores, but I felt my spirits lifting just from looking at the signs. This was more of the 1880s-vibe I was hoping to experience. Right past the Quality Merchandise store was *The Letter Depot: Saddle & Harness Maker*, followed by a little store called *E.L. Smith's Daily Papers, Stationery, Laundry Agency, Candy, Cigars, & Ice Cold Drinks*. Catchy. I guess the nineteenth century had yet to embrace the acronym fad like KFC and IHOP.

Passing a *Guns, Pistols, & Ammunition* store and *J.C. Cunningham's Merchant Taylor*, I rounded the corner and stopped short at the quaint little business across the road. A wooden sign proudly displayed the name "Oaks & Son Studio" in large, bold font, with the words "Portrait & Event Photography" painted right beneath in a slanted orange script. Oaks & Son…. Kade Oaks….

This shop belongs to Kade's family! I remembered him spewing out all sorts of facts about developing film and stuff when he was a ghost, right after he saw the camera app on my cellphone. His instinct was right; he really was a photographer. Based on the addition of the word "Son" on the sign, it was definitely Kade's profession too, not simply his father's. I was surprised photographers even existed in this century. I sort of imagined family portraits being captured by oil painters or something. I wondered how complicated it was to be a photographer in this time period, without cellphones or digital cameras. Did they use film? Or was there something before film? Hadn't Kade said something about glass plates?

Curious, I was struck with an urge to go into the store.

Kade couldn't possibly be in there, right? He had just evacuated me from his house, and since none of his family was home while I was recovering from the rift, they wouldn't recognize me. I'd be nothing more than some random girl browsing through their store.

Unable to talk myself out of it, I darted across the brick-paved street and, taking a deep breath, stepped inside.

The store was much lighter than I expected, with several small windows letting in natural light. Black and white photos lined the walls, and an array of gadgets and parts cluttered a dark wooden counter to the left. At the edge of the counter was a camera—a monstrosity of wood and metal—resting on a tripod. I walked over to it and grazed the copper scope with my fingertips. It looked like something you'd see in a museum.

"Can I help you, miss?"

I yanked my hand away and looked up to see Kade's older doppelgänger. The man had Kade's light blue eyes and ash blond hair, though his was shot with streaks of silver. Lines creased his forehead and tiny wrinkles gathered in the corners of his eyes.

I opened my mouth to say I was just looking around, but then a thought occurred to me. This wasn't some mall in the twenty-first century. I was dressed like a housemaid, and I doubted servants wandered into these kinds of stores in the nineteenth century to check out expensive cameras.

Maybe coming here wasn't the best idea.

Think fast. "My, um—" what was the 1880's word for boss? Was it supervisor? Head honcho? Big cheese?—"My employer wants me to price cameras for him. He is unwell and not fit to go outside."

"Ah, very well. Selling cameras is not our specialty—as a

studio our specialty is to provide photographic services—but I do have a few options."

"Great. What is this one?" I pointed to the giant one on the tripod, trying to get into the role I had unfortunately cast myself into.

"Surely you have seen a Maddox camera before?" he noted, walking over to the counter to stand across from me.

"I'm not from around here," I stammered. "The cameras where I come from are… different."

"How so?"

"They're, um, smaller."

"Perhaps, but only when compared to the Maddox, which is our studio camera and not actually for sale. Unless your employer is a professional photographer, he would never be able to use this camera. This, on the other hand…" He pulled out a black box from a low shelf and placed it on the counter. It was about the size of a small shoe box, though the material and handle looked like something you'd see on a briefcase. "This is my latest model, and I guarantee none from your region are more compact. I'm calling this the Oak Box camera," he smiled proudly.

I leaned in, noticing a hole in the front of the box where I assumed the lens must be. "It looks kind of…plain."

"It is indeed basic in appearance, but it is quite remarkable." His voice took on a salesman quality, and I could tell he had given this pitch before. "Unlike other cameras, this one uses a special flexible film for capturing photos. No glass plates required." He picked up the box and pointed it my direction to demonstrate. "Not only can photographs be captured with a click of a button, but this is the lightest and most portable camera in existence."

"Wow, that's amazing," I gushed, not sure if it really was amazing or not. "How much is it? I will pass the information on to my employer."

"Oh, this is a mere prototype, miss. One of several. It is not quite ready for the market."

I tried to look disappointed.

"But it will be available soon," he assured, "so be sure to tell your master to check back regularly. My business is currently under negotiations for a merger that will allow the Oak Box to be available across the country. And have no doubt, this camera will revolutionize photography, allowing the most inept layperson to capture photos."

Mr. Oaks' speech reminded me of what Kade had told me in my room…something about inventing a camera that anyone could use.

"Didn't your son invent that camera?" I blurted out.

His face darkened.

Oops.

"Sorry. I mean, that's just what I heard," I tried to cover.

"Blasted babble merchants," Mr. Oaks scowled. "My son may have invented this contraption, but it'd go nowhere without me. That bleeding-heart louse has no business sense."

I inwardly flinched. What a loving father this man was.

He cocked his head and looked me over, curious. "Where are you from? I can't place your accent."

Shoot. When Kade ordered me to leave, I hadn't considered creating a backstory. I thought I was marching straight to Maui and going home. My brain raced to think of details from my history class that might help me. I remembered that a lot of immigrants migrated from northern and western Europe during the nineteenth century, because I just crammed for that test last month.

"My family's from Sweden," I finally replied.

"Ahhh, that explains your appearance."

"Yes. I'm very…Swedish-looking." I wanted to smack myself. Good job with the eloquent speech, Aviva. I needed to get out of here before he pushed for more information. "Well, I had better get back to my, uh, master. Thanks for showing me your new camera!" I pushed out the door before he could ask any followup questions.

"Good-day, miss," his voice followed me out.

I walked the same way I had come, garnering a few stares as I passed shops that were closing their doors for the day. I may have lied when I told Mr. Oaks I was from Sweden, but I was definitely feeling like a foreigner in this town. I quickened my pace and didn't slow down until I reached the town square. Maui towered ahead with her warm, knowing face.

I thought about Mr. Oaks. He had seemed like a decent person, until his disdain for his son crept into our conversation. That probably explains why Ghost-Kade didn't seem to like his dad too much. Either way, talking to people in this century was…tricky. I felt like a bumbling idiot.

I passed an evergreen shrub, some of its needles brown beneath small heaps of snow. I gently touched the branch and focused my energy into healing the plant.

The branch twitched a bit. Then…nothing.

I concentrated and concentrated until the dizziness became too much to bear, yet the needles remained brown.

What?

Confused, I tried my powers on a few other plants and shrubs in the square. Each time the result was the same.

Nothing. My powers didn't work here. The knowledge settled uncomfortably in my gut.

Luckily I was leaving now anyway. I could put all of this behind me. I'd go back home, my powers would work again, and all would be right with the world.

Looking back and forth to be sure there were no witnesses, I sauntered up to Maui. I gazed up at her solemn face. It was remarkable, how in a century where everything was so different, Maui was the same. Sure, there were no benches or fountains around her, no shrubs with twinkle lights, no structures crowding in on her tower, no electric wires running to and fro from her face…but the clock herself was unchanged. Still stoic. Still golden. Still strong.

I turned around, nice and slow, one last time, engraving into my memory as much of my surroundings as possible. I reached into my apron and touched my cellphone, wishing it wasn't dead so I could at least snap a few quick pics. Seeing the large clumsy cameras in Oaks Studio—even the supposedly cutting edge "box camera" that Mr. Oaks spoke so proudly of—gave me a newfound appreciation for the miracle of my cellphone camera app. I would never be back here again, and a part of me wasn't ready to say goodbye to this century. The other part of me felt like a fish out of water and couldn't wait to be reunited with my sisters in a land where I wasn't Swedish.

I was also eager to apologize to my sisters for leaving Copper's Kettle in such a huff. They had done nothing but help and support me, and I had acted like a spoiled brat. An ache uncurled in my stomach. I was already missing them.

I released my cellphone and leaned forward, my left hand clutching Phee's lip gloss, my right hand hovering over the clock's brick surface.

Do it. I took in a deep breath. Do it now.

What was wrong? Why couldn't I move?

Tears pricked my eyes, and just like that, Kade flooded into my brain. No matter what he did or how mad I was at him, I wanted him to live.

He tossed you out onto the streets, I reminded myself.

I replayed our conversation earlier. Could I really blame him? I crashed into his quaint little life, telling him that he was going to die in ten days. If that wasn't enough to rattle a person, I also told him he was going to kill his own fiancé. How would I feel if the tables were reversed? If Kade had come to my school that first day and told me I was going to be executed for whacking my step-mom, how would I have reacted?

I would have been furious, I admitted to myself. I would have demanded that he leave. Shoot, I had demanded that his ghost-self leave several times, simply because he was annoying me.

My hand dropped away from the clock tower. I shoved the lip gloss back into my apron.

I might be furious with Kade, but it didn't matter. Because he mattered. I had come here to save his life, and that's what I was going to do.

Caring about someone really sucks.

I heaved a heavy sigh, realizing that since I was no longer going home, life had become a lot more complicated. Where would I go? I couldn't go back to Kade's house. Even if Kade was cooled off by now, his dad would recognize the weird little blonde from Sweden who pretended to be interested in his cameras. Kade had mentioned an inn southwest of town. If only I had

Krystal's sense of direction! I turned around and scanned Pendulum Square, half-hoping to find one of those giant theme park maps with a "You are Here" arrow.

"Do you need help, miss?" a man approached. He was wearing pinstripe pants, a long slim coat, and a tall hat that reminded me of Abe Lincoln. His face was gentle, his brown eyes warm.

"Yes, thank you!" I exclaimed. "I've just arrived to town. Can you point me to the inn?"

"Sure thing. It's just two whoops and a holler that way."

As he gave me the directions, I realized he was describing where the De' Chancor Hotel was located in my time period.

"Would you like me to escort you?" The man offered.

"Oh, no, no need," I told him. "Thank you sir for your help!"

"My pleasure. Safe travels, miss," he tipped his hat.

I walked for what must have been nearly an hour. Once I left the main town square—what would be known as Clockworks Village in my time—the crowds of people walking about thinned dramatically. Houses were spread amongst snow-covered pastures, and candlelight began to spark through the windows of small, quaint houses dotting the open landscape. I was starting to feel nervous over the darkening sky, when the inn loomed ahead. It looked more like a tavern than a hotel, with its rustic reclaimed wood structure and large wagon wheels hanging as decoration. I quickened my pace. The dark in the nineteenth century was much darker than the dark in the twenty-first century, I decided, and the golden glow coming from the curtained second-story windows looked terribly inviting.

A small bell tinkled as I entered. Two oil lamps cast

muted light across the front counter, and several candles were set in copper fixtures along the paisley walls.

An elderly woman in a large bustle dress with frizzy pinned-up hair hurried down the stairs. "What canna do fer you, lass?" She spoke with a thick Irish brogue and, though her words were polite, her sharp eyes seemed to shrewdly assess me.

"I'd like a room for the night."

"Of course." She opened a leather bound book and lifted a steel pen. I was a little disappointed it wasn't one of those giant feather quill pens. Man, I was hopeless when it came to historical trivia.

"Board and lodgin' fer one night is fifty cents," she said. "That's includin' supper an' breakfast."

"Fifty cents? That's all? Wow."

She tilted her head curiously at my words. Oops. When was I going to learn that the less I opened my mouth in this century, the better?

The bell chimed behind me, which thankfully distracted the innkeeper long enough for me to slide a dollar bill from the small billfold of my cellphone case without her seeing. A quick glance informed me that two women had entered behind me.

"I'll help you lassies in a moment," the innkeeper said before returning her attention to me.

"Here," I handed her the bill. "Put me down for two nights." *Hopefully after that I will have convinced Kade I'm not a crazy person.*

The innkeeper's eyes narrowed as she examined my crisp dollar bill. She passed it back to me. "You tryin' to pull the wool over my eyes, lassie?"

"Huh?"

"I ain't no dolt. This ain't acceptable currency."

My pulse skittered. I was such an idiot! Of course a dollar bill from the twenty-first century would look totally different from its nineteenth century counterpart. *Cover story, quick.*

"I'm so sorry ma'am, I swear I'm not trying to trick you," I sputtered. "I'm newly immigrated from Sweden and this was the money my aunt gave me before I left. It must be from a different state?"

Her face softened. My story was a lie, but my panic was genuine, so maybe in that sense she could hear sincerity in my voice. "No harm, lassie. But I still canna take yer payment. Do you have any coins, perhaps?"

"No. Just bills." I started sweating at the thought of having nowhere to sleep tonight.

Sympathy laced her voice. "My apologies, but my rooms are reserved fer payin' customers only. I gotta make a livin' ya know."

"I understand," I said, trying to stay calm. "Do you know of anywhere else I can go?"

"Mother," a voice behind me said, "are we not looking for a new housemaid?"

I swung around, then stopped cold, feeling the air knocked out of me. The young woman standing behind me was quite pretty, even more so than she was in her grainy, black and white photo.

It was Marguerite Broderick.

Marguerite Broderick, in the flesh, who would be murdered in cold blood in less than a week.

Somewhere in my muddled shock, the realization crept up on me that if I could get close to Marguerite, maybe I could save her…thus saving Kade too. If Marguerite never gets murdered, Kade can never be wrongfully accused of her death.

But then Kade would marry her.

That didn't matter, I decided. I had to save Kade. If that meant losing him to Marguerite, well…he was lost to me either way. At least with this plan, he and Marguerite would both get to live. Have a life together.

Images of a happy Kade with his beautiful wife and adorable kids pranced around in my head. I ignored the pang in my stomach.

I couldn't let this opportunity slip by.

Swallowing hard, I mentally shook off my daze and forced myself to speak, keeping my voice composed. "I'll be your maid person! I can do all sorts of stuff. Cook. Clean. You name it."

"My," the woman who must be Marguerite's mother observed, "your manner of speech is quite peculiar. Does everyone from Sweden speak like you?"

She obviously overheard me telling the innkeeper I was Swedish. Might as well stick with the same story. "It depends what part of Sweden they're from," I faltered. "I'm from the…um, Voonderschnine region." My cheeks grew hot. Voonderschnine?

"Let us employ her, Mother," Marguerite said. "How I would love to have a servant from Sweden. Imagine all of the stories she can tell us!"

I kept a straight face, already wondering how I was going to manufacture a bunch of Swedish stories. Oh well. I'd cross that bridge later.

"Very well, Molly, but let me first speak with Mrs. Cudahy to be sure she hasn't seen our Clair."

A shadow flickered across Marguerite's—or Molly's— eyes, but disappeared a second later. I must have imagined it.

I stepped aside as Mrs. Broderick spent the next five minutes talking with the innkeeper. She told Mrs. Cudahy that her servant girl had disappeared a few days ago, and asked the Irish woman if she had seen the girl at all. "Since you come across so many travelers," Mrs. Broderick explained, "I was hoping you might have heard some news regarding her whereabouts."

Molly wrung her hands next to her mother.

"Sorry ma'am, I ain't heard a thing 'bout yer servant's whereabouts. But now that I know yer lookin' fer her, I'll be sure to let you know if I hear any news."

"I appreciate that, thank you." Mrs. Broderick turned toward me. "The job pays four dollars and fifty cents a week, room and board, with Sundays off. Do you accept these terms?"

I wouldn't be buying a car with that kind of salary, but still, my chest swelled with pride at having nailed my first job interview. I nodded eagerly. "Yes, I accept those terms."

Molly beamed.

"Well, then, come along, girl."

Nineteen

*What looked like morning
was the beginning of endless night.*
William Peter Blatty

Sunday, March 31
Present Day

"WE NEED TO call the police and report them missing!" Krystal finished her story hysterically.

She could barely recall the events of the past hour. She had fuzzy memories of navigating her way to Phee's car, where she had briefly considered driving it home before realizing that her first time behind the wheel probably shouldn't be when she was an emotional basket case. She decided to follow Phee's advice and call her dad. He and Daphne raced over to Clockworks Village to pick her up, with Daphne driving Phee's car home.

On the ride home, she told her dad everything that happened in a speech so fast and unorganized it might as well have been verbal vomit. She repeated the whole story again, for Daphne's sake, once home. Now, she didn't understand why they were both sitting at the table, doing nothing.

Daphne and her dad looked at each other, faces grim. "And say what, exactly?" Dad asked slowly, in response to her plea to call the police.

Krystal's panicked brain scrambled to come up with a response before she was hit with the bleak realization that her dad was right. Even if the police believed that her sisters had disappeared into a time rift—which they wouldn't—what could they possibly do about it?

"Dad, you're Father Time," she argued. "Let's go back in time and get them!"

"I can't," he said, his voice strained. "I can't physically transport myself anymore. I used to be more powerful, and could travel to any time period on a whim, but ever since you and your sisters were born…." he trailed off, his troubled eyes shifting to Daphne's. "Never mind, that's not important. All you need to know is that it takes a special ingredient for me to physically travel back into time. One that I don't presently have. Otherwise I'm subject to the same rules as you. I need an object from a person from the past to use as a talisman."

"Then let's go to Uncle Kiel's antique store and find something from that century," Krystal said.

"Sure," her dad said, "But we'd end up God-knows-where and God-knows-when. We could undercut your sisters by twenty years and end up smack in the middle of the Battle of Gettysburg. Unless we know the exact person an item belongs to, it makes for a dangerous and unreliable talisman." He creased his forehead. "Though if I can't come up with another plan, we might have to take our chances and use a talisman, despite the risks."

Daphne had been listening intently, anxiety lining her forehead. "We don't even know for sure if Taz and Phee ended up in the same time-period as Aviva," she said, her words hesitant and pained, "or if the three of them are spread all over the place in different times."

"Can't you at least use your crystal ball type skills to look for them? I remember you said you looked into Taz's and Stryder's loops."

"I already am," her dad replied. "I've been concentrating on finding all three of your sisters ever since we got home. Every human being has a unique energy that supernatural beings such as myself can sense and identify. It's like a metaphysical fingerprint of sorts. When Taz was trapped in the curse with Stryder, I used Taz's 'fingerprint' several times to peek into her loops. She was easy to find. But when I search for Aviva's fingerprint now, it's…." he stopped. Stress lines pulled at the corner of his eyes.

Krystal felt her fists clench. "It's what, Dad?"

"Gone. Her fingerprint is gone. It's like she doesn't exist."

Krystal's heart sank in her chest like a heavy stone. "Does that mean she's…."

"Oh no, honey," Daphne comforted in a gush. "It just means that she lost her powers when she stepped into the past."

Her dad nodded. "Without her powers, her identifying energy is completely changed. There's no way for me to find her. Or your sisters."

"Why would they lose their powers?" Krystal asked.

"Well, if the daughter of Gaia is still alive in the past—" Daphne broke off when Dad shook his head at her in warning.

"Daughter of Gaia?"

Dad peered at Krystal over his coffee mug. "We don't speak of Themis." An almost unnoticeable shudder rolled through his shoulders. "Daphne's simply trying to say that because your sisters aren't supposed to exist in the nineteenth century, neither do their powers."

Krystal didn't bother hiding her skeptical expression as she stared at her dad. Who is this Themis-person? Why don't they speak of her? And why is her name so bothersome to Daphne that she had refused to even say it, instead referring to her as the daughter of Gaia?

If her sisters weren't missing, she might have pressed the issue, but there were more important things to worry about at the moment.

All Krystal cared about was getting her sisters back.

"What about the special ingredient you mentioned Dad? The one that allows you to travel to the past? Can we get some?"

Daphne's face darkened. "Your dad used to have unlimited access to it, but it's locked away now."

Something occurred to Krystal. "Is this 'special ingredient' the stuff that was in Taz's necklace?"

Daphne's face lit in surprise. "How do you know about that?"

"Taz overheard you and Dad talking about it during one of her loops and told me and Aviva about it. You guys said something about 'the Sands'."

Daphne looked over at Krystal's dad, her eyebrow arched in question.

"Yes, the Sands is the magical ingredient," her dad admitted. "And we believe that Taz's necklace might have contained some. We think that's why Taz was pulled into Stryder's curse."

"The necklace was a gift from Uncle Kiel," Krystal mused, remembering when Taz had opened it. It was New

Year's Day, the morning after Stryder had played the horrible rat-prank on her. Strange how all of that felt like events from a different lifetime. "If this sand is locked away, how'd Uncle Kiel manage to get some? And if it's magic, why did he want Taz to have it?"

Daphne's shoulders dropped. "We don't know."

"We've been inviting your uncle to things, trying to get some kind of hint as to what he's up to," her dad added.

"Wait—are you guys saying Uncle Kiel is *bad*?"

"Not bad," her dad said. "It's more like, he has such a different view of the world. He sees so many things that we hide from ourselves and there is part of him that simply cannot abide by that. Sometimes he has to jump up on the table and scream truth to a world that doesn't want to hear it. Except, instead of screaming, he plays pranks. He reminds us that things are not what they appear."

"And perhaps during one of his pranks, he did something careless," Daphne added. "Maybe he didn't know what was in that necklace. Or maybe he thought it was funny."

Dad nodded. "Either way, the necklace is lost. As well as the magic that might have been within."

"So what do we do?" Krystal asked.

"Daphne and I need to talk about it for awhile," her dad said. "This is complicated. Try to get some sleep tonight. We'll reconvene in the morning."

In bed, Krystal overheard the hushed and anxious tones of her parents. Eventually pink and lavender streaks seeped through Aviva's half of the window, spilling dull light across her ceiling. Dawn was normally a cheery affair full of hope and new beginnings. Today's dawn was dreary.

She finally drifted into a gloomy, restless sleep and dreamed about flowers withering in the frost.

Twenty

*High dive into frozen waves
where the past comes back to life…*
Zedd

January 14, 1886

"I'M EXHAUSTED." I collapsed with a basket of bulky dresses on an armless chair in the laundering quarters, eager to rest my throbbing legs. "How do you guys keep up with all this work?"

I had been up since dawn hauling and boiling water, stoking fires in various woodburning stoves, and getting the house in shape before the "gentry" arose. My back hurt, my knees hurt…pretty much my everything hurt. Somehow I had pictured life in this century a little more glamorous. Like, frilly dresses, fans, and those fancy lacy umbrellas you see on TV. Not back-breaking labor.

"Up with you, lazy girl," Maude swatted me with a rag. "You may have lived a cushy life in Sweden, but here in America yer expected to work."

I tried not to huff. I had already heard this speech several times. Maude was Molly's lady servant, but she took on other household roles when she wasn't tending to Molly, including that of a supervisor. Though her station was considered equal to the other servants, her years spent with the family gave her status and authority that she was more than happy to wield.

"And why, child, do you say 'guys' when we clearly ain't?"

"Aw, Maude, I've told you already. Where I'm from we all speak different, okay? Guys can mean girls, wicked means cool, sweet means cool, tight means cool...actually," I scratched my head, "we have way too many words that mean cool."

"Voonderschnine must be colder than a witch's brazier on a shady side of an iceberg to require so many words fer it."

I couldn't hold in my laugh at her creative metaphor, not to mention her careful pronunciation of my make-believe hometown. "No, the word 'cool' isn't actually a temperature." I clarified. "Well it is, but in this case it means...oh geez, never mind."

I could see a smile flitting beneath the surface of her foul expression. Maybe the nonsense I spewed all day amused her.

"Up, child," she swatted me with the rag again, this time square in my face. Luckily I blinked or she might have impaled my eyeball. "This laundry ain't gonna wash itself."

I groaned and hauled myself up from the chair, resisting the impulse to tell her that where I'm from the laundry actually does wash itself. I grabbed the basket from the top of the old block table.

A few minutes later, washboard in tow, I lugged my cumbersome load across the yard toward the laundering buckets. I was concentrating so hard on my balance that I failed to notice the young man in my path until I nearly pummeled into him.

"Whoa." He grasped my arms to steady me.

"I'm sorry," I said, regaining my footing. "My mind was a million miles…" I trailed off when I saw the gorgeous face that was smiling down upon me. Gold-streaked chestnut hair, soft hazel eyes, killer dimples…*wow*. He looked about Kade's age, maybe a year or two older.

He cocked his head at me. I realized that I had never finished my sentence.

"Um, a million miles away," I stammered.

"That is a curious expression." He gently released my arms. "You must be our new housemaid from Sweden. I've heard about you."

"Yeah, um, yes. I'm Aviva." Smooth. "Nice to meet you." I reached forward to shake his hand.

"The pleasure is mine, Miss Aviva." He took my hand and brushed it against his lips, planting a feather-light kiss on my knuckles.

Again, *wow*. Why couldn't the boys at school greet me like that?

"I am William Broderick." He did a gallant bow that I knew was overly-dramatic even for this century. I couldn't resist smiling at his performance, and he grinned in response. "I believe you have met my mother and sister."

"Yes, I have. Hi, William." I politely retracted my hand, the thin skin across my knuckles tingling at the contact of his lips.

William Broderick…this must be Kade's friend William, the one who had helped to plant the time capsule. Which meant…whoa. Kade's best friend was also Molly's brother. The world here in Sezona Hills—Valley—kept getting smaller.

"Well, Miss Aviva. What brings you across the ocean?" William's voice was light and conversational, and his eyes shone with humor.

"Oh, you know…." my mind clambered for a decent response. "The usual. In my hometown of, um, Voonderschnine, America is considered the land of opportunity."

"And has it been fortuitous thus far?"

"Oh yes!" I bluffed. "I feel very grateful to be here."

His cocked his head, seeming to study me with interest. "Interesting. You remind me of someone."

"Oh?" I kept my voice casual. "You remind me of someone, too. You're a lot like my friend Brett, back in my time per—er—my time in Voonderschnine." I realized as I stumbled over my words that they were mostly true. William, with his easy manner and bright smile, really did remind me of Brett…though a much more formal version of him. And a more charming version, too.

A heaviness swathed my heart at the thought of Brett. I missed him. But more than that, I missed my sisters, and Dad, and Daphne. We had only been apart for mere days, but days stretch for an eternity when you're a millennium away.

What if the rift was already closing? A sliver of fear spiked through me at the thought of never seeing my family and friends again.

"Well, this Brett-fellow sounds like a jolly good man," William winked, distracting me from my thoughts. "Likewise, you and my lady acquaintance have similar accents and mannerisms."

"Who is she?" I asked, wanting to keep our conversation going.

He seemed to assess me for a few seconds. "Her name is Aurora."

"Pretty name. That's my sister Taz's middle name. Maybe your friend is a long-lost relative of mine," I joked.

"Likely not. Aurora is a recent transplant from Ireland, not Sweden, so it is unlikely that you and she are even acquainted, let alone related. She arrived a short time ago as well, but alas has come down ill from her travels, and is presently recovering." An odd note crept into his voice that made me wonder if he had some kind of crush on his lady friend. "Count your blessings that you arrived in good health," he added.

"I will for sure count my blessings," I said, immediately feeling like an idiot. Literal much, Aviva? "So…you said you heard about me?"

"Ah, yes, indeed." His eyes sparkled with mischief. "A little bird told me that you are entertaining and unorthodox, and somewhat uncouth."

I leveled him with a wry look. "Does that little bird go by the name Maude?"

"Do I look like I walk about introducing myself to birds?" he ribbed.

Laughter pealed from my lips before I could stop it.

"You have a pleasant laugh." His comment was straightforward and rang with sincerity.

Blushing, I changed the subject. "Do you always talk with the help? Aren't there rules against that?"

"Perhaps unspoken ones. But I have always found it refreshing to escape the confines of stuffy conversations with the gentry to interact with more down-to-earth folks with interesting pasts. Plus I can tell by your articulate speech that your education exceeds that of a common servant." He stared at me again, with more intensity than before. "There's something fascinating about you, angel."

My stomach did a little flip at his compliment and his term of endearment. I guess all of my 'ums' and 'ers' didn't make me sound like a total idiot, after all.

"Sadly duty calls and I must be off now." He tipped his hat at me. "It was a pleasure conversing with you, Miss Aviva. Perhaps I will see you at supper this evening, once I have concluded my business."

"If I'm not buried in laundry," I smiled.

Chuckling, he headed off to the carriages. Once a few yards away, he turned around. "You seem like a nice girl, so I'll offer you some quick advice. Stay away from my father." Before I could ask him what he meant, he strode away. I felt a twinge of disappointment at his departure. Although I was surrounded by people, keeping up with this fake life had lent itself to a strange sort of loneliness these past two days, and it was refreshing to talk to someone pleasant like William whose sole purpose in life wasn't to crack a whip at me.

Then the thought occurred to me: William's sister was going to die in three days. William was such a happy, lovable guy—he didn't deserve to have that kind of tragedy thrust upon him. Really no one deserved it, but meeting some of the loved ones who would be impacted by Molly's death made my mission here feel that much more important. It was no longer Kade alone I was saving, it was the happiness and well-being of William now too, along with the rest of the Brodericks.

Two days wasted now. Over forty-eight hours, and I still couldn't figure out a way to get close to Molly. Things were different here; I couldn't just walk up to her and start a conversation. Servants didn't chat with their employers. If only I could swap jobs with Maude for a few days. I'm sure Molly disclosed things to Maude all the time, considering Maude waited on the girl twenty-four-seven. But there's no way Maude would be giving up her comfy gig as Molly's personal servant anytime soon.

Hours later, I draped wet clothes on racks to dry, then snuck back into the tiny servants' bedroom I shared with Ruby, the household cook, hoping I could sneak in a nap. My legs and back were aching from being crouched over a tub for so long, and my upper-arms were on fire from scrubbing all those clothes against a washboard. I definitely was not cut out for manual labor.

Our sleeping quarters were tiny and could barely be called a "room." It was more of a hovel. With the two small beds and dresser in the middle, it had less floor space than Daphne's walk-in closet. Maude got her own room—tiny like ours, but hers alone. Sharing with Ruby wasn't too bad though. Ruby looked to be close to the same age as me—maybe a year or two older—but we'd had little time to get to know each other since she spent most of her time in the kitchen prepping meals. Once she and I were back in our servants' quarters for the night, we were both so exhausted that we exchanged only small pleasantries before collapsing in bed.

I poured tepid water from a blue and white pitcher into a basin sitting on the dresser and splashed it on my grubby face. Feeling somewhat refreshed, I collapsed on the bed that had been dubbed mine and closed my eyes. For the dozenth time I wished my cellphone was still working so I could set an alarm. If I napped any longer than twenty or thirty minutes, I'd likely get busted by Maude. Before I could ponder the matter any further, warm tendrils of sleep drifted over me and I slipped into a cozy blackness.

A knocking startled me awake sometime later. I jolted up in bed, my migraine-excuse on the tip of my tongue for Maude.

But it wasn't Maude. The door swung open and the large figure of a man stood in my doorway. I hastily rubbed the sleepiness from my eyes, trying to clear my blurred vision. The man stepped into the room further. With Molly's nearly black hair and sharp nose, and William's hazel eyes, it was easy to recognize Mr. Broderick.

Stay away from my father.

I tried not to let William's warning freak me out. After all, I had already run into Mr. Broderick while serving the family during mealtimes, though we had never been formally introduced. He wasn't bad looking for a man that had to be in his forties, his age apparent around his eyes but having not yet crowded in on the rest of his face. Of course my lack of decent vision made everyone look more attractive. Nothing like experiencing life through a soft filter.

Before I could say anything, he crossed the room and glowered down at me. "Is there a reason we're paying you good wages to sleep?"

I scurried out of bed into a standing position, my heart in my throat. "I'm sorry, sir. I came down with a migraine and decided to lie down for a few minutes. Can I help you with something?"

His scowl softened, though he still wore a vague expression of disapproval. "Unfortunately it is too late now. I needed my suit readied for supper this evening and Maude was forced to delay her responsibilities with Molly in order to take care of it on your behalf."

Based on his softening expression I could tell he responded well to meekness, so I tried to sound as contrite as possible. "My apologies again, sir. I had no idea you were expecting guests. It won't happen again. Is there anything else I can help you with?"

His eyes ran across my face and slipped down the bodice of my dress, eventually making their way back up to my face again. "Perhaps there is."

Oh crap. The innuendo beneath his words seemed pretty clear. I crossed my arms in front of me, trying to hide myself.

Hunger darkened his face. "Beneath these layers of fabric and filth, I wager you are quite lovely, my dear."

My chest clenched as he leaned in to touch a loose lock of my hair. I cringed away, but that didn't seem to deter him. He stepped forward, forcing me to step back until my legs hit the bed. He traced my jawline with his finger and I held my breath, trying to decide whether to knee him in the balls now or wait until he tried to do something worse. He leaned in and whispered, "I can make life here very pleasant for you, my dear, if you will allow me." Before I could react, he stepped back. "We have guests coming for supper tonight. Be sure to clean yourself. I anticipate seeing you out there assisting Ruby with the service. You are more pleasing to the eye than Maude." He strode out the door.

Okay, this century officially *sucked*. My brain reeled. I tried to catch my breath while simultaneously containing the revulsion rolling through my body. What was my recourse here? It's not like I could file sexual harassment charges on the bastard. How did women deal with living in such a suffocating time period? I had to leave *now*. As convenient as this arrangement was, it wasn't worth walking around on pins and needles.

I stuffed my hand beneath my mattress to retrieve my cellphone. Instead, my fingers touched something soft, and I pulled it out. It was a tiny knitted sock. More like a baby's bootie, white with blue trim. I reached under the bed and found a second one. The second one was only half-finished with two knitting needles impaling the delicate yarn. I sat on the bed, pondering the two delicate booties resting in my hand. Who did they belong to? Why were they left under my mattress?

A strange feeling of melancholy settled over me. I knew I was overthinking it, but there didn't seem to be a scenario in the world that would make never-used, forgotten baby booties anything other than sad.

I dropped the first little sock into my apron and stuffed the half-knitted one back beneath my mattress, then fumbled around for my cellphone. I needed to get out of here.

But where would I go? Other than Kade, I knew no one in this time period, and what little money I had was no good. Despite what had just happened with Mr. Broderick, the thought of stepping through the rift without saving Kade tore at me.

I can make life here very pleasant for you, my dear, if you will allow me…. Mr. Broderick had said "if you will allow me." He wouldn't have used that wording if he intended to force himself on me, right? Even though he was a creep, it sounded like he would only proceed with my permission.

I stuffed my cellphone back under my bed and formulated a plan. Tomorrow I would befriend Molly no matter what. I had already wasted two days here waiting for a convenient time to approach her. It was time to take action. I would learn as much as I could about her life, and hopefully get some kind of clue as to who wanted her dead. I might call attention to myself, but it was a risk I needed to take. Meanwhile, I would avoid being caught alone with Mr. Broderick. It shouldn't be too hard. Not only was today the first time I had run into him alone, but this century was very social…it seemed like there were always people around. As long as I stopped slipping into this little room during the day where he might catch me, I should be fine.

Feeling more calm, I headed to the kitchen to grab a hunk of bread to relax my nervous stomach. Ruby, her shiny black curls held back by a blue tied scarf, was plucking feathers from a dead chicken when I entered, while Maude prepared Molly's afternoon tea.

"Where did you disappear to?" Accusation laced Maude's words.

"I'm sorry Maude. I got a migraine and just needed to lay down for a sec." I pulled out the baby bootie, hoping to distract her from her irritation at me. "Hey, do you know who this belongs to?"

She eyed the sock. "I've never seen it before. Where did you find it?"

"Underneath my mattress."

Ruby let out a "Hmmm" as she turned the chicken over.

"Do you know anything about it, Ruby?" I held the bootie out for her.

"I ain't seen it before, but I suspect it may've belonged to Miss Clair."

"Who's Clair?"

"She was the last housemaid. You're sleepin' in her old bed."

"Oh," I replied, looking down at the bootie. "Where'd she go?"

Ruby paused in her plucking to glance around, as if to make sure no one was listening. Her amber eyes shone brightly against her bronze skin. "She left. Don't know beans about it. She never said nothin' 'bout why she was leavin' or bothered with goodbyes. But I did notice one night when we were donnin' our sleepin' gowns—before she disappeared--that her stomach looked awfully round. Quite a scandal for an unwed girl."

"Wow, I guess that explains why she left in a hurry," I said. "Who do you think the father was?"

Maude gasped, the tea splattering from the pot as she dropped Molly's tray on the counter. "We do not speak of such things!"

"Oh. Sorry."

Maude clucked her disapproval before sweeping out the door with her tray.

Ruby continued to nonchalantly pluck feathers until Maude was well out the door. Then she dropped the bird and said in a low conspiratorial voice, "There've been whisperings about Clair's child. Some think Charlie, the stablehand, was the babe's father. He ain't even a man yet —only fifteen—which might be why Miss Clair fled."

"You don't seem convinced," I pointed out, noticing the skeptical look on her face.

Her shoulders tensed and she continued to pull feathers.

"You know something, don't you Ruby?" The confrontation with Mr. Broderick suddenly turned in my head. "Does this have something to do with Mr. Broderick?"

Ruby turned to me with her mouth agape, her face

unable to hide the truth.

I nearly dropped the sock in my hand. "Does he, um, try to…you know…with all the servants?"

A blush crept up her cheeks.

"Oh my gosh Ruby, have you and he…?"

She picked up the bird and continued to pluck, ignoring my question.

"I'm so sorry."

She looked at me, her shoulders stiff. "I don't need your pity, missy. I ain't no dolt. I know what I'm doin'. Mr. Broderick gives favors to the servants he beds. It's my choice." She grabbed a paring knife and began to meticulously skin the creature. "Things are different in these parts than where you're from."

"Well, um…okay." I was so out of familiar territory here, I didn't know what to say. "But what if you end up pregnant too?"

She leaned in close to me and whispered, "I use *Madame Dresler's Preventative Powder*. It don't make a lick of sense to me that Clair weren't more careful. Sometimes I think that girl was as blind as a post hole. Here," she said, handing me some potatoes. "Chop these."

I piled the potatoes onto a cutting board and grabbed a knife. "What about William?" I asked. "He seems so nice, but he kind of hinted to me about his father. Does he know this is happening?"

"He knows, but he's far too worried 'bout his inheritance to get involved. Pretty sure Clair was smitten with William at one time too…but aren't they all? He's a looker for sure, and he's nice to the help…" she shrugs and adds some seasoning to the now-naked chicken as I started slicing the first potato. "You know, it won't take long for Mr.

227

Broderick to notice that you're comely, too."

"Comely?"

"Ya know, handsome. Fetching."

"Oh, like pretty."

She nodded. "Do you want me to get you some of Madame Dresler's powder?"

I jolted and nearly cut my thumb off. What was this, a freaking harem? I'm not sure what I expected from this time period when I was swept into the rift, but being offered nineteenth century birth control (made with God-knows-what kind of mystery-voodoo ingredients cooked up by 'Madame Dresler') was not on my list.

"No, I think I'm good."

As I slipped into the mindless task of slicing potatoes, my mind drifted to the knitted bootie in my apron. Was Clair pregnant with Mr. Broderick's child? Did she find a place to raise her baby?

In this century, was there any possibility for an unwed mother to find a happily ever after?

Twenty-One

If I found a way to stay with you tonight
It would only make me late,
for a date I can't escape.
Lord Huron

January 14, 1886

KADE STEPPED INTO the Brodericks' foyer, allowing Molly's lady servant, Maude, to take his coat and hat. Molly and her parents stepped into the room to greet him. Mr. Broderick grinned broadly, slapping Kade on the back. "Come now, let's not dally," he said after greetings were exchanged. "The Hendersons and your folks are already here." He turned toward Molly. "Would you care to escort Kade to the dining room, sweetheart?"

Molly clasped Kade's hand, her eyes smiling into his. "Of course." She was beautiful, her dark curls gleaming against the pale lilac satin of her evening gown. Kade wanted to feel his heart thump at her loveliness, but instead, an image of the mysterious girl with platinum hair flashed through his mind, her small helpless form sprawled on the ground in front of Maui in that unseemly and disheveled manner. His chest dropped for the hundredth time. Irritated with himself, he sighed.

The girl appearing from nowhere with a letter he had just sealed within the clock, not to mention her knowledge of trivial details about his life…even he had to admit that it gave some legitimacy to her fantastical claim that she was from the future. He wasn't a fan of science fiction, but he didn't know how else to explain everything that had happened. Talking to the strange girl, he could feel himself being pulled closer to her by some unexplainable magnetism.

But when she told him he would murder his own fiancé, he felt so angry.

Why did he get so angry? Was it because he was offended that someone would suggest he was capable of murder? Or was it guilt? Because on some level he knew Molly's death would free him—and just the mere thought was like committing murder with his heart. In that moment, it felt like this Aviva-girl was playing some kind of insidious game, trying to expose his weaknesses, and he felt like sending her away was the only way to avoid her wicked little trap.

Yet thoughts of her had twisted like a knife in his brain from the moment she left. He couldn't stop thinking about her. The shock that sparked her soft sage eyes when he ordered her to leave, the betrayal that had flitted across her face. It left a dull ache in his chest. Wicked or not, he had a feeling that the girl did not know the ways of life around here and could very well be eaten alive if left alone.

Whatever her intentions, he should have shown more gallantry. Instead, he abandoned her. There was no nobility in that. So a few hours after forcing Aviva to leave, he searched the town for her. Turning up empty-handed, he remembered telling her about the inn. Perhaps she had found shelter there? If so, he would take her back home with him, talk more gently with her…try to figure out exactly what was happening.

But no, she wasn't at the inn. According to the innkeeper, she had gone home with the Brodericks. Kade had promptly made arrangements with Molly's mother for supper with the two families. Mrs. Broderick was delighted by the idea, and decided to invite the Hendersons to join them in the festivities.

But Kade's true motives had nothing to do with enjoying an evening of fine dining. It was the rumors. There was talk around town about how Mr. Broderick treated his servants. Kade had to convince Aviva to leave with him, somehow. He would never forgive himself if something happened to her here. Whoever—or whatever—she was, she didn't deserve to be mistreated.

Molly guided Kade through the parlor, where Kade spotted his Oak Box camera prototype displayed on the Broderick's dark, gleaming mantle. He fought the urge to take it back. It was the first successful model he had created, and half of the film had already been used on snapshots that Kade himself had taken. Photos he did not want to give up. But Kade's father had insisted that Kade, in a gesture of good faith, give the camera to Mr. Broderick, back when they were trying to close the business merger between the two families. "Let him play around with your invention, son," Father had commanded him. "He needs to see for himself how incredible it is." So Kade had relented.

They passed the study and entered the dining room where Kade's friends, William and George, along with their parents, stood up to greet him. Once everyone was seated, polite conversation commenced about the spring-like

weather the town was experiencing—surprising for January
—followed by talk about the Hendersons' latest champion
horse. Kade tried to concentrate on what was being said.

"Dawn's Run, they call him," George was saying. "He
was bred at Oxton Hall near Tadcaster in North Yorkshire,
and is the second of three Derby winners sired by his
champion father. You can imagine the effort and cost my
father and I underwent to bring him here to the States."

"Certainly sounds like he was worth it," William said. Mr.
Broderick nodded his agreement.

Mrs. Broderick harrumphed.

"Why the derision, Mother?" William peered over at her.

"You and your father, collecting prized horses like they're
coins."

Mrs. Henderson chuckled. "I believe that is all men,
Sally. My husband is known to say "Like firearms and fine
cigars, a gentleman can never have too many horses." She
paused. "If he was still a bachelor I am certain he would
add 'women' to that list."

The party laughed.

"Well, I must respectfully disagree," Mrs. Broderick said.
"When you have so many horses they no longer fit into
your stable, I say enough is enough."

"Ahhh, you are now boarding your horses?" George
asked.

"Indeed," Mrs. Broderick replied. "Over at the McCleran
Stables."

"We have a few of our stock there, as well," George said,
taking a sip from his wine glass. "Wise choice."

William agreed. "They have the largest and best
maintained facility in the county, as far as I've seen."

"Yes, though we do hope it is a temporary arrangement,"

Mr. Broderick said. "William and I have plans to build a new barn in the spring."

The servant Maude came in at that moment to make sure everyone's drinks were full, and let them know that their supper was still being prepared but would arrive shortly.

"Tell me gentlemen," Mr. Broderick said once Maude departed to help in the kitchen, "What is the latest developments on our camera? No pun intended, of course," he laughed at his own joke.

Kade sipped from his wine glass while his father regaled Mr. Broderick with the latest, inserting an affirmative head nod or "Yes, indeed" here and there to keep his portion of the conversation alive. In reality his mind was nowhere in that room. His thoughts were stretching outward, searching the house for Aviva. Why hadn't he seen her yet? Was she still employed here? Or had the innkeeper been mistaken?

"...eh, Kade?" Mr. Broderick's speech cut into his thoughts. "At this point I believe the only thing that could improve upon your camera design is if it captured photographs in color."

Molly giggled. "Oh my, colored photographs? Can you imagine such a thing?" The table hummed with laughter.

"My son claims it will happen some day," Kade's father stated.

"I believe him," Mr. Broderick said. "Unlike William here who has no ambition, Kade knows how to make things happen." He elbowed his son playfully, but William just rolled his eyes.

Kade, realizing he wasn't contributing to the conversation, lifted up his glass. "Mark my words, a day will come when photographs will be as imbued with color as the world we live in."

William lifted his glass. "Let us toast, then. To health, love, and…a future rich with color."

Molly's eyes glowed with merriment as she raised her glass.

"Cheers!" everyone sang, clinking glasses.

The door swung open as two servants backed into the room with a serving cart. Kade, eyeing them unceremoniously, pulled in a long drink of the heady wine when one of the servants turned around to serve Mr. Broderick at the head of the table. The wine, instead of sliding down Kade's throat, sprayed out of his mouth in a glorious garnet-colored geyser. His glass toppled down onto the table.

It was her! Aviva. Even knowing she might be here hadn't lessened the shock of seeing her in the flesh again.

She raised her head at his wine accident, then jerked when she saw him. Her eyes mirrored his own surprise.

The occupants at the table gasped at Kade, who was now sitting erect in his chair with Pinot Noir dribbling down his face.

"Darling, are you well?" Molly exclaimed.

Wiping his face and neck down with the linen napkin from his lap, he took a deep, calming breath, attempting to slow down his beating heart, then pretended to cough a few times. "Yes. My apologies. I appear to have had something stuck in my throat."

"Well, don't just stand there, girl," Mr. Broderick turned toward Aviva. "Go fetch our guest a hot towel before that wine sets into his suit."

Aviva, her face stone-cold pale, snapped to attention and nodded to Mr. Broderick. "Yes, sir," she replied before hastily leaving the room.

A coldness seeped into Kade's chest. He had to get Aviva out of here.

He coughed roughly into his hand a couple more times, then pushed back his chair. "Please excuse me while I go to the washroom and attempt to hack out this frog." He chuckled and shook his head, then coughed a few more times for good measure.

"Heavens, me, I hope he isn't coming down with an illness...." He heard Molly's voice trail behind him as he hurried from the dining room. Once out of sight, he veered toward the direction of the kitchen. He had never been in the Broderick's kitchen before, but it was easy to follow the sound of voices and clattering dishes.

He walked through the kitchen door. Maude was helping the cook with supper preparations at a butcher block counter, while Aviva was setting a pan of water on a burner.

Maude gasped when she saw him. "Mr. Oaks, sir, there is no need for you to come into the kitchen. Miss Aviva is boiling water now and will bring warm linens to the table." Her pudgy cheeks were rosy pink, with beads of sweat dotting her forehead. It was highly unorthodox for a guest to enter the kitchen—especially with supper being staged—and her anxiousness at his presence was written all over her face.

Aviva glanced up from her pot, confusion marbling her features.

"I simply need to speak to your new housemaid for a moment," Kade said. Maude's mouth dropped open, a question on the tip of her tongue but wisely not spoken. "Privately, please," he added.

Maude, with no other recourse, nodded her permission to

Aviva. Aviva, shaking her head, followed Kade out of the kitchen into the study.

Checking to be sure they were completely alone, Kade turned toward Aviva. Before she could utter a word he said "You can not stay here."

She gaped at him. "Excuse me?"

"There are rumors about Mr. Broderick."

Her eyes narrowed. "I've heard the same rumors," she said cooly, "but I don't really have a choice, do I?" It was more of a statement than a question. "You kicked me out and I'm not exactly rolling in cash right now."

He ignored her awkward phrasing. "Forgive me, Aviva. My behavior was dastardly. Will you let me remedy that now?"

Hurt and resentment gleamed in her eyes. "You tore up our letter."

"I know." He couldn't keep the regret from seeping into his words. "I wish I hadn't."

"You threw me out into the cold with no food or...or anything!" Angry tears pricked her eyes. He had hoped apologizing would soften her, but instead it was digging into a wound that she had probably spent days trying to ignore. And now her tears were like daggers in his chest.

"Bloody hell. I'm sorry, little one. I never meant to hurt you like this. I was a fool." He took her arms and implored her with a stare. "But do not punish yourself because you are angry with me, or because you are too proud to accept my help. I beg you. Do not stay in this household with that...predator stalking about."

She glared at him, saying nothing.

"Come to my home," he persisted. "Sneak out tonight. I will bring a carriage."

She shook him off and crossed her arms. "What will you tell the Brodericks when I suddenly disappear from their house and show up in yours?"

Kade stepped back and raked his hands through his hair. Damn. His family and the Brodericks were closely knit. She had identified a real problem.

"I do not know. We may have to keep you hidden in the servants' quarters." His voice was firm. "All I know is you can't stay here."

Aviva bit her lower lip, seeming to consider all that he said. Then her face dropped with disappointment. "I can't."

"You must."

"No. You don't understand. I can't save your life if I'm stuck cowering in some servants' closet all day."

He felt his eyes widen. She wanted to save his life? Even though he had thrown her out?

"I know you don't believe me," she said, "but your fiancé is going to die in three days unless I do something about it. Here at the Broderick's, I'm close to Molly. I can talk to her, feel things out. Try to figure out who wants her dead. That is, if I can somehow get near her. But the point is, by staying here I'm in the best position to solve the mystery of who frames you for her murder."

"Wait." Kade stepped in closer to her. "The other day, when you told me I would be hung for the murder of Molly, you thought I was framed?"

"Yes. I mean, I don't know if you were purposely framed, or if someone just conveniently let you take the blame for their crime. But I know you didn't do it."

"How do you know?"

"I just know. Okay?"

Kade's stomach dropped. Quiet stretched between them. She had assumed his innocence this whole time. If he hadn't been so busy behaving like a cad with his brains in his bollocks, perhaps he might have noticed that.

And then he realized he believed her. The truth scared the devil out of him, but he could no longer deny the truth of her words. Perhaps he had believed her all along, and that was why he behaved like such a coward.

He knew he shouldn't touch her again, but the impulse to do so was too strong for him to squelch. He reached his hand out. She drew back, but then relaxed as his fingers grazed her cheek. His voice came out hoarse. "I am sorry, clever girl. I am sorry for not believing you. I am sorry for tearing apart our letter."

She opened her mouth as if to argue, but then sighed instead. "Okay."

"Is there anyway I can convince you to leave with me tonight?"

"No." Her features hardened. "I'll be fine. I'll stay away from Mr. Broderick."

Kade could see her mind was made up. He contemplated sneaking back in the middle of the night to abduct her— it'd be easy as pie given that she likely weighed less than a bag of flour—before realizing the absurdity of that thought.

"Very well." He dropped his hand from her cheek. "I will talk to various people in town to try to deduce who might want to harm my betrothed. Meanwhile I must visit here frequently to be sure you are safe. The Brodericks will likely tire of my presence."

"Ahhh, just like when you were a ghost," she ribbed. "It'll be nice to have my annoying stalker back."

Twenty-Two

Encourage me, and I will not forget you.
Love me and I may be forced to love you.
William Arthur Ward

January 14, 1886

I COULD SEE Kade's lips quirking into a smile, in spite of himself. "My ghost sounds quite persistent," he commented.

"Oh, he is," I grinned. "That is, *you* are. Now if we're all finished here, I have to get back to serving dinner—er, *supper*—before Maude and Mr. Broderick have my head."

"Of course," he said. "But one more thing before we part. I didn't want to offend you by giving this to you right away, but I…" he paused. "I've brought you a gift."

"A gift?"

"Of sorts. Nothing fancy. Just something I made." He pulled an object from his pocket and pressed it into my hand.

I looked down at the trinket, and my heart skipped a beat. "Glasses?" I examined them, bewildered. The design was rudimentary, with thin silver frames looping two round lenses, a curved bridge, and small scoops at the temple ends. A silver chain dangled from the right lens, with a tiny hook on the other end of the chain. "But how…?"

"I noticed when you first awakened that you were squinting a lot. It was easy to deduce that you have trouble seeing."

I stared at the delicate spectacles, incredulous. "How do you know how to make something like this?"

"I melted down some old cutlery to forge the frames. And the lenses…well, I'm no optician, but as a photographer I know how lenses and magnification work. Unfortunately, even if these help, they will not be a match for your vision. But I'm hoping the magnification I applied is enough to help you see items far away, even if only a little."

I slipped the glasses on and, surprisingly, they worked, though it was kind of like looking through a pair of binoculars rather than my normal glasses. Still, I could see the titles of books on the shelf across the room, and I no longer felt like I was underwater. I peered up at Kade, startled by the brightness of his eyes.

He leaned forward, his warm fingers grazing the soft skin of my ears as he adjusted my glasses. He pulled back and stared into my eyes. "That's better." His voice was gruff.

"They're perfect."

Tension hummed between us. "Hey," I finally cut the thick, lingering current. "I've been dying to know, how did this happen?" I stepped back and pointed to the rugged scar tracking its way from his coat cuff to the bone of his right thumb. "All your ghost could tell me was that it had something to do with pumpkins."

He tilted back his head and laughed. "When I was about ten years of age, Will dared George and I to steal a pumpkin from Mr. McGregor's farm."

"Will…? As in, William Broderick?"

"One and the same. He seems a gentleman now, but do not be fooled, he was quite the scoundrel as a boy." Kade's eyes shined with humor. "Neither George nor I felt particularly inclined to steal a pumpkin, but it was All Hallows' Eve and neither one of us wanted to come across as yellow-livered. We waited for nightfall, and the three of us crept onto Mr. McGregor's property. McGregor's Farm is surrounded by osage orange trees, so we had to be careful."

"What's wrong with osage orange trees?"

"They're covered with vicious thorns. Farmers use them to create a protective border around their property."

I nodded, and Kade continued. "Will, George, and I each swiped the largest pumpkin we could carry. We reached the edge of the pumpkin patch, thinking we'd gotten away scot-free, when suddenly Mr. McGregor comes tearing across his farm with his shotgun—"

"No way!"

"Indeed. He was waving that shotgun, his face beet red, bellowing out enough swear words to make his grannie turn in her grave. At this point George and I dropped our pumpkins and went running as if our lives depended on it, because truly, they did. I heard the shotgun blast behind me, and I scrambled my way through those osage trees faster than green grass through a goose. Thankfully it was dark, lest Mr. McGregor's aim be spot-on. I escaped Mr. McGregor's wrath, but not before a nasty thorn wreaked its vengeance on me." He pointed to the scar. "Sliced my hand clean to the bone."

"Wow." I shook my head, marveling at how different nineteenth century childhoods were from my own.

"I got off easy. Poor George," he grinned. "One of the pellets from McGregor's shot gun wedged itself into his…," he coughed, "derrière."

"Derry-what?"

"His buttocks."

I pressed my hand against my mouth to avoid howling with laughter.

"The best part is he knew if he told his folks about it, his father would beat him well-into-Sunday."

"So what'd he do?"

"Nothing."

"But how did he get the bullet out of his butt?"

Kade chuckled. "He didn't. He tried, but it was too deep. And he saw no way of seeking help from Dr. Harris without his folks finding out."

"Wait, you're telling me that the sophisticated man sitting in the dining room right now, eating and drinking with the Brodericks and talking about racehorses, has a shotgun pellet buried in his ass?" I blanched when the unapproved curse word popped out of my mouth, but I was too caught up in the moment to correct myself.

"Yes."

Now I really did howl with laughter.

"Your mannerisms are most unladylike," he pointed out.

"Yeah, you keep saying that. But I don't think you mind. I think you just think you're supposed to mind."

Humor still shone in his eyes, but something else was there, too. Some kind of raw intensity. He looked away and cleared his throat. "If you insist on staying here, little one, tell me what I can do to help you. It makes no sense for me to be uninvolved in saving my own fiancé." His face darkened. "And evidently my own life, as well."

I thought about it for a few seconds, but drew a blank. Given how little I knew about Molly's murder, it was nearly impossible to come up with any kind of strategies to prevent it. Well, other than tying her to a chair in three days to keep her from going to the stables.

We'll call that Plan B, I thought.

As simple—though inelegant—as it sounded, forcing Molly to stay away from the stables might simply postpone her murder rather than prevent it. If someone wanted her dead, who's to say that person wouldn't simply try again… and again?

No, the best strategy was to figure out who wanted Molly dead. Which meant I needed to talk to Molly.

"If you can figure out a way for me to get close to Molly, that would be a huge help," I finally told him.

Kade contemplated my words. "That is a difficult request given your status as a servant, but I will think of something."

I nodded.

"We should talk very soon, Aviva, about all of this."

Footsteps sounded nearby. Both of us straightened. He leaned over, the stubble on his chin grazing my cheek. "Stay safe," he whispered, his breath tickling my ear.

I took a long detour back to the kitchen, my heart skittering over my confrontation with Kade and my brain a confused muddle. Finally reaching the kitchen door, I pressed my hand against my still-tingling cheek and took a long cleansing breath before stepping inside.

Ruby looked like she was preparing dessert, while Maude filled a pitcher with water.

"There you are," Maude looked up at me, her expression livid. "I can't believe how cocky that chuff is, stormin' in here and whiskin' you right away as we're servin' the main course!" She harrumphed. "Supper's nearly over now. Here," she shoved the pitcher in my hands. "Make yerself useful. Clear plates while yer out there too. I'm s'posed to be a lady's maid. I ain't no common house servant." She snorted and stormed out.

I looked over at Ruby, who started chuckling as she added bits of dried fruit to the custard she was preparing. "Maude's madder than a March hare, ain't she?"

"What's her problem anyway?"

Ruby considered my question. "Jealous, mayhap? You're all young and fetchin', and now you have the attention of that handsome fella." She looked at me, giving me a once-over. "When did you start wearin' spectacles?"

I ignored her question. Kade's gift felt personal, somehow, and I didn't want to cheapen it by sharing.

Undeterred, Ruby continued pressing me for gossip. "Ain't cha gonna tell me why Mr. Oaks pulled you away? Your face looks all dreamy, so don't go tellin' me it was nothin'."

Crap. I scrambled to think of a response.

"I just reminded him of someone," I said slowly.

"And he felt it necessary to pull you aside during supper preparations to tell you?"

"I guess so."

Her eyes narrowed skeptically. "He said so?"

"Um, yes?"

She shook her head. "He's plainly smitten with you and was lookin' for a reason to talk to you."

She huffed, "And to do so with his betrothed sittin' right in the next room! What a heel."

"Wow, do you really think that's what he was doing?" I

asked, feeling a pang of guilt for throwing Kade under the bus, but not knowing what else to do. "Ughh."

Ruby's face softened. "It ain't yer fault, what with you all dainty and easy-on-the eyes. You just gotta be more aloof if you want to keep all those randy men at bay."

"You know Ruby, you're pretty too," I pointed out. "I bet men are falling at your feet all the time. Am I right? And I mean hot, young guys, not just old perverts like Mr. Broderick."

The words were out of my mouth before I could take them back, and for a second I was worried I had offended her. But after a brief shock, her face split into a grin. "Miss, yer not supposed to talk in such a forward manner! 'Tis quite unladylike." She shook her head. "Do they not teach you to mind your manners in Sweden?"

"Not in Voondershnine," I elbowed her playfully.

She laughed, the sound peeling from her lips like music. "I should like to visit Voondershnine." She stepped back to her dessert station and started placing the little bowls of custard onto a serving tray. "Now skedaddle, before Maude makes a die of it."

When I entered the dining room, William, not to be outdone by George, was regaling everyone with stories of their prized thoroughbred, Northern Dancer. His hazel eyes shone when he saw me.

Unlike Mr. Broderick, who leveled me with a glare, one I could see clear as day now that I was wearing my new glasses. "I expect prompter service in the future, Miss Aviva." Then, as if trying to avoid embarrassment over my deplorable performance, he chuckled at the rest of the group. "Our new housemaid seems to be struggling to deduce her place."

William opened his mouth as if to defend me, but Kade beat him to the punch, keeping his voice light. "Ah, I respectfully disagree. Your new servant is quite efficient. She caught me on the way to the wash room with some fresh warm linens, and fetched me some lozenges for my scratchy throat."

Mr. Broderick's eyes lit with surprise. "Very well, then. I was wondering where she disappeared off to. I am glad she was able to be of service." The man gave me a subtle nod of approval, and I knew Kade had just saved me.

"I didn't realize you wore spectacles, my dear," Mrs. Broderick's voice rang out.

My hands darted up to touch my frames. "Oh, these?" *Think quick.* I was pretty sure no one in this room would be thrilled to hear Kade had made them for me. "I've always worn them. They've been lost, but I finally found them, thank Go—er—Heaven." I continued to casually clear dinner dishes and refill water, not trusting myself to make eye contact with anyone. Especially Kade.

Kade's mother, Mrs. Oaks, swallowed a delicate bite of food, then spoke. "Sally, were you able to find out what happened to your previous servant?"

Mrs. Broderick looked at her husband and shook her head. "No. Such a strange thing too, the way our Clair took off in the middle of the night." She frowned.

I paused at her words and stuffed my hand into the pocket of my apron, gently massaging the baby's sock between my fingers. I glanced up to see Kade eyeing me. He shook his head slightly and nodded toward Mr. Broderick. I released the sock and snapped back to clearing dishes.

"At least you found a swift replacement," George spoke

up. Earlier in the meal, I had recognized George as the young Abe Lincoln look-alike who had kindly given me directions to the inn. Now I knew he was Kade's childhood friend, too—one of the three that had buried the time capsule.

The one with a bullet buried in his butt. I tried not to grin.

"A coincidence, too, I'd say, as we acquired a new servant this week as well." George shook his head and laughed. "Though ours is quite the disgruntled worker. I have never seen a migrant lacking so greatly in useful skills."

George's parents, Mr. and Mrs. Henderson, nodded their heads in agreement.

William dabbed at the corner of his mouth with his linen napkin. "Shame your latest acquisition is so unskilled. But you ought to have no problem replacing her, should it come to that, as it seems that foreigners are dropping from the sky."

William's eyes met mine. What did he mean by that? Did he somehow know about me?

Kade's jaw tensed, his face expressionless.

"Indeed," George agreed. "There does seem to be an influx of immigrants as of late."

I let out the breath I didn't realize I was holding. Based on George's reply, 'dropping from the sky' sounded like nothing more than a metaphor. William was simply saying that a lot of foreigners had come into the town recently.

George turned to face me as I reached for Mrs. Henderson's empty plate. "Where are you from, Miss? You have similar features to our new servant."

My eyes widened, and I tried to contain my surprise at being directly spoken to by a guest. I was getting used to living life in the background, and had been adamantly practicing the skill of keeping my mouth shut. Mrs. Broderick had addressed me earlier, but she was the 'missus' of the house. Was it taboo for a guest to address a servant? Would it be inappropriate for me to reply? Would it be rude to *not* reply? I was struck with that feeling you get when the teacher yanks you from a daydream to ask you a question in front of the class, and you have no idea what the answer is.

I looked for help from Mr. Broderick, who intimidated me but would certainly have an opinion on how I should respond to his guest. His chin tipped down in a slight nod. I took that as his permission to speak.

"I'm from Sweden," I offered. "The Voondershnine region." I had mentioned Voondershnine so many times now that I was starting to convince myself that it was a real place. Maybe I could talk Dad and Daphne into taking us there over summer break.

Kade recognized the lie, but of course said nothing.

George cocked his head. "Hmmm. I have never heard of it before."

"It is very small," I explained.

"Plus you have no sense for geography," William poked at his friend.

"Are you claiming you have heard of Voondershnine, Mr. Knows-Everything?" George poked back.

"Indeed, upon my honor I swear I have heard of Voondershnine before," William said solemnly, sipping his wine. After a pause, he added, "Of course that is because Miss Aviva mentioned her hometown to me earlier today."

He grinned as the table burst into laughter. I shook my head and smiled, stacking William's plate on top of Mrs. Henderson's, allowing myself to feel more relaxed. Maybe servants in this era feel nervous around the elite, but in my world, these were just "people."

"Does your new servant hail from Sweden as well?" Mrs. Broderick asked George.

"No, she is an expat from Ireland," George replied.

My gaze shot up to William, waiting for him to say something about his friend Aurora, who was also from Ireland. Instead, William leaned back and took a long sip from his wine. There was something curious in his demeanor. I briefly wondered if there was any connection between Aurora and George's new servant. Maybe they both 'dropped from the sky.' Or maybe they were the same person. William did say that he enjoyed talking to people who weren't all uppity and rich, didn't he?

"Interesting that I, too, have never heard of the Voondershnine region," Kade's father spoke, interrupting my thoughts. His voice carried an edge and was lacking William's good humor.

Realizing his implication, I almost gasped but managed to squelch it. I had been so overwhelmed meeting all these new people and trying not to do anything clumsy, I had nearly forgotten my encounter with Kade's dad. My mind raced, replaying the conversation between Mr. Oaks and myself in his studio. I had lied to him! And he knew it. I had told him that my employer was ill and had sent me out to browse for cameras. At that time I didn't care, because I was planning to jump into the rift and go back home. Never had I imagined that I would be confronted by him later, with said-employer in the room.

I dared to peek at Mr. Oaks. I wasn't feeling very comforted to see him eyeing me suspiciously.

Mr. Oaks turned to Mr. Broderick. "Did your new servant tell you that she and I met previously?" His voice was still laced with an edge sharp enough to cut Ruby's chicken from earlier.

The plates rattled in my hands. Now would be a great time to disappear back into the kitchen, I thought. Or better yet, disappear into Maui.

Before I could move, Mr. Broderick's eyes narrowed on me. "What is he referring to?"

My body froze. I looked over at Kade. His fists were clenched, muscles taut, as if he were going to spring out of the chair at any second.

Well, the jig was up, I decided. Might as well go out with a bang. "He's referring to the day you sent me into town because you were not feeling well. I went into the studio as you requested, where I met Mr. Oaks for the first time."

My stomach clenched. Even I could hear how ludicrous it sounded—trying to convince Mr. Broderick that he sent his servant to scope out cameras when he clearly never did. If a genie popped up right in this moment to grant me three wishes, my first one would be for a nice fat hole to crawl into.

Mr. Broderick stared at me, his hazel eyes darkening. A hush trickled through the dining room. Then, to my utter shock, he laughed. "Ah, yes. In actuality I had but a mild headache, but I thought it would be a good opportunity for our new servant to explore our town."

Icy relief rushed through my body. I glanced over at Mr. Oaks in time to see his skeptical expression turn to one of resignation. Who knows whether he believed Mr. Broderick or not—either way, there was nothing he could do about it.

But why would Mr. Broderick lie for me? It didn't make sense.

As I turned toward the door with my load of plates, I

peeked over at Mr. Broderick. His dark gaze held mine. It might have been my imagination, but his stare seemed to say "You owe me for this one, sweetheart." Kade was staring at Mr. Broderick with his lips in a firm line, his jaw tightening. Did he interpret the man's expression the same way I did? A shudder rolled through my body as I hurried from the room.

Ruby had all of the bowls of custard ready for delivery, but something about my face stopped her short.

"What's ailin' you?" her voice rang with alarm as she set down her tray.

"I, um…" I sighed, dropping my stack of dishes onto the narrow butcher block table. "Ruby, do you think *Madame Dresler* wards off men too, or just babies?"

She laughed, a sad sort of sound, and stepped forward. Then, much to my surprise, she wrapped me in a hug.

Don't cry, I told myself, trying to control the trembling of my chin. *You've got this. Don't cry.*

But then I thought about my sisters, and my parents, and Brett's adorable haiku, and the comfort of my new attic room, and the refreshing release of reviving flowers, and ghost-Kade lighting up over mint n' chip ice-cream, and flesh-and-blood-Kade with his somber expressions and beautiful gift and upcoming hanging….

I collapsed into my new friend's embrace and let the tears take over.

Twenty-Three

*Watch with glittering eyes
the whole world around you
because the greatest secrets are always
hidden in the most unlikely places.*
Roald Dahl

Monday, April 1
Present Day

KRYSTAL WOKE TO the sound of her cellphone chirping low battery. In all of last night's chaos, she had forgotten to charge it. She plugged it into the charger, then sat on her bed, staring at the screen.

We don't speak of Themis, she remembered her dad's warning from the night before. She pushed her phone's center button. "Who is Themis?" she spoke clearly.

"Here is some information about Themis," her phone told her in its clear British accent.

Themis is an ancient Greek Titaness, the words on the screen said. She is described as "of good counsel" and is the personification of divine order, fairness, natural law, and custom....

Krystal rubbed her sleepy eyes, feeling impatient already. She refocused on the screen, trying to find something that would make sense to her. Scanning the text, she paused

252

when she got to the list of Themis's family members. The name of Themis's mother jumped off the screen: Gaia.

Gaia. Krystal remembered that Daphne had called Themis "the daughter of Gaia."

Krystal clicked on the small arrow next to Gaia's name. She was awarded with pages of information. Scanning through the text, she learned that in Greek mythology, Gaia was the Mother Earth goddess. In the same way Krystal was the person of winter, Gaia was the person of nature.

Interesting.

She returned her search back to Themis, Gaia's daughter. She scrolled through the list of Themis's family.

Parents: Uranus and Gaia.

Children: Horae, Epimetheus, Prometheus, Hesperides, and Menoetius.

Krystal stopped at the list of siblings to click the arrow next to the first child listed: *Horae*. Scanning the text, she was surprised to discover that *Horae* was not actually one child, but four separate children whose identities were so obscure they did not even have their own names. Intrigued, she went back to the beginning of the text to read it more carefully.

In Greek mythology the *Horae, or* Horai, *or* Hours, *were the four goddesses of the seasons and the natural portions of time…*

Her heart stopped. The hair on her arms stood on end.

The Internet may not know the names of the *Horae*, but she did. The *Horae* was her. She and her sisters were the *Horae*. The names of the four obscure entities were Phoenix, Topaz, Aviva, and Krystal.

And Themis was their mother.

That would make Gaia, Mother Nature, their

grandmother.

Why hadn't her dad ever told her?

Krystal sat staring at her phone, unable to move, unable to think a coherent thought. She barely noticed the frost crawling across her phone's screen, spreading and crackling over the keypad.

Her sisters were trapped in the past. Her parents were keeping secrets. And to top everything off, she was a goddess.

Twenty-Four

January 15, 1886

RUBY SHOOK ME awake at first light. "Up and at 'em!"

I sat up in my bed and rubbed the sleepiness from my eyes. I've always been a morning person, but three days straight of rising at the crack of dawn to work my butt off without so much as a drop of caffeine was pushing it.

I reached for my new glasses on the nightstand, feeling relieved for the umpteenth time that Kade had made them for me. My new job as a servant was grueling enough without adding handicaps into the mix. Being half-blind in a foreign century sucks.

Ruby was standing at the dresser between our beds, cleaning her face in the wash basin.

I tossed my blanket aside and stepped onto the cold floor. "Brrrr, it's freezing!"

She looked up at me through a small vanity mirror, her eyebrows quirked in amusement. "Sweden has been too soft on you, Vivvy girl. Oh, you don't mind if I call you Viv, right? Your full name is too fancy on the tongue."

"Viv is fine. My sisters call me that. And sometimes my friend Brett."

"Is he a looker?"

"Oh, yes. He's sweet too. But I'm not into him like that."

"Like what?"

"Well, you know…romantically. He's a good friend."

She looked at me curiously.

"What?"

She tied her scarf around her head with impressive efficiency. "Interesting that men and women in your hometown can be casual friends and all."

Another period difference that I take for granted, I thought.

I dressed quickly, shivering the whole time. I'd give up my entire life savings right now for a hot shower. My thirty-two dollars and twelve cents probably wouldn't amount to much, but still. It was a moot point anyway because though the Broderick's home featured one shower—a garish thing of exposed pipes—servants weren't allowed to use it. We had a portable tub and a privy out back.

"So what's on the agenda today?" I asked, twisting my hair into a messy bun. "Wait, let me guess. Washing rich people's clothes. Followed by…more washing of rich people's clothes."

Somewhere in all that, I was going to find a way to talk to Molly today. Doing laundry wasn't bringing me any closer to finding her killer.

"Rightly so," Ruby replied with a grin. "Or fer me, it's makin' rich people food. Followed by making rich people more food."

I finished fixing my hair as Ruby hurried out the door.

She had to get moving faster than the other maids every morning to get breakfast underway and start planning for dinner (as they called 'lunch' in this century) and supper. As crummy as my lot was, at least I wasn't hired to be the household cook. I'm sure if there was a way to screw up plucking a dead quail, I'd figure it out.

I threw on a shawl and followed Ruby to the cold, rank privy to relieve myself, then hurried back to our room. Leaning over the now vacated basin, I scooped some toothpaste out of a jar and used my finger to scrub it along my teeth, cringing at the goop's soapy flavor. I gargled and spit into the basin right as the door swung open. My heart jumped in my throat. Wiping my mouth with a hand towel, I steeled myself for another encounter with Mr. Broderick.

Relief poured through me when Maude entered instead. I let out a heavy breath. "Don't people in this century knock?"

Maude put her hands on her hips. "Now doncha be gettin' cross with me, missy. I'm in a hurry."

"Sorry. What's up?"

Maude glanced up at the ceiling, then looked back at me with a peculiar face.

I rolled my eyes. "It's an expression in my hometown. I mean, what's the big hurry?"

"The Oaks have requested my services. The youngest, Bess, is comin' out and will now be goin' to social events with the missus, so she needs my help this morn' to help 'er prepare."

"What does 'coming out' mean?" I knew what it meant in my time, but I doubted it had the same meaning here.

"It's when a girl has come of age and is acceptin' suitors for courtship."

"Oh. Like she's old enough to date?"

"Date?"

"Never mind," I said. "So the Oaks are borrowing you for the day then? Is that normal for servants to be sent to other families?"

Maude frowned. "You ask a lot of questions, girl, and I ain't got the time nor the patience. I need you to fill in fer me as Molly's lady servant. I already finished yer mornin' chores."

"Really?" My face broke into a grin. It took every ounce of willpower to not jump up and down with excitement. I'd be able to talk to Molly without having to get sneaky about it! Plus I would get to escape the evil throes of laundry.

Maude clucked disapprovingly. "You ought to be more quiet and genteel with yer feelin's."

"How come?"

She cuffed me in the ear. "You also ought not question yer elders."

"Sorry," I said through my ear-splitting smile.

Her lips quirked in the way they did when she was trying not to come over to the dark side with me by smiling back.

Maude spent the next ten minutes giving me the lowdown on how to care for Molly (you'd think I was watching over a newborn baby rather than a young woman) before she finally departed the house to meet her carriage. I wished I was her, getting into that carriage to spend the day with the Oaks. The warmth that spread inside of me at the thought of seeing Kade last night thawed some of the morning chill. But I knew I had been handed this opportunity on a bright, shining platter and it would be foolish to not jump at it.

I wondered if Kade had anything to do with

orchestrating this whole Maude-leaving-for-the-day thing. He had assured me, after all, that he would try to get me close to his fiancé.

I tied on my apron and headed over to Molly's bedroom. I tapped lightly on her door and entered, but her curtains were drawn and the room was dark. Molly mumbled something into her pillow about leaving her alone, so I slipped back out. Maude had warned me that Molly tends to sleep in due to all of her late-night social engagements, so I wasn't surprised to find her still asleep. Softly closing Molly's door, I contemplated what I should do next. If I saw one more basket of laundry I might have to stab myself in the eye. Maybe I could help Ruby prepare breakfast. Decision made, I swung around to head toward the kitchen, when I hit a brick wall.

Except for the brick wall was Mr. Broderick.

"Good morning, my dear."

I swallowed. "Uh, good morning, sir. If you'll excuse me, I have to help Ruby in the kitchen." I tried to step around him, but he side-stepped to block me.

"You used my name to deceive Mr. Oaks."

My chest clenched at his accurate accusation. I knew he was going to try to cash in his favor of not blowing me in. I was just hoping I could avoid running into him alone before he had the chance.

And then I made a decision. If he tried anything, I'd let out a blood curdling scream. We were, after all, standing right in front of his sleeping daughter's room. I didn't know much about Mr. Broderick, but I knew enough to suspect that he wouldn't want his little servant fetish paraded in front of his family.

Having a back-up plan filled me with confidence. "Well,

technically I never used your name," I hedged. "I hadn't met you yet. I simply told Mr. Oaks that my *employer* had sent me into his store."

He grabbed my elbow and leaned in. "Are you arguing with me, girl?"

"Oh, no, not arguing," I back-pedaled. "I'm actually really grateful for what you did. Thank you for covering for me in front of Mr. Oaks. Anyone else would have sold me out right then and there, and man that would have been embarrassing. But you spared me for whatever reason. That was really cool."

His expression hovered somewhere between a glower and confusion, and I realized I had slipped back into modern-speak again.

His hand slipped from my elbow. "I don't know what to make of you."

"You could just make nothing of me and allow me to pass?" I suggested.

Mr. Broderick shook his head, as if trying to clear it. "We're not finished with this, young lady," he finally said. Then he stepped to the side. "Hurry along, then."

I scurried down the hall, not pausing until I reached the kitchen. Bursting through the door, I sagged against the counter.

"Viv! Are you not feeling well?" Ruby asked. She was turning flapjacks on a grill, and had a smudge of flour smudging her left cheek.

I grinned triumphantly. "I figured out what preventive powder works on Mr. Broderick."

It took her a second, but then understanding dawned on her features. "What?"

"Confusing words. He doesn't know what to do with a girl

who talks too much."

Ruby burst out laughing. "Of all things. Why in tarnation would talkin' do anything?"

"I don't know. But seriously. Just talk in circles until he tires of you."

"Well, I'll have to give that a try sometime."

"I thought you liked his attention?"

"I do. But not every gosh-darned minute." She stuck her ample hip to the side and gave it a smack with her spatula. "A girl this saucy needs a break once in awhile."

I laughed.

"Now are you here to help or not? Start crackin' those eggs into a bowl."

I got to work on the eggs. Ruby and I spent the next half hour making breakfast, a comfortable air of companionship stretching between us as we worked side-by-side.

Once the food was ready, we both crammed down a quick plate, then I helped her load up the serving cart. "Do you mind if I leave now?" I asked. "I want to go check in on Molly." As much as I enjoyed Ruby's company, I needed to get on with the more important task of digging for information.

She waved me away. "I got this. Thanks for helpin'."

I loaded some food on a tray for Molly and headed to her chambers. I knocked, and a soft voice said "Enter."

The room was still dark, but Molly was sitting up in bed now, her face traced with faint wisps of sleep.

"Good morning!" I set the tray next to her on the nightstand. "Mind if I open these curtains? It's kind of depressing in here."

She quirked a brow. "By all means."

I pulled open the drapes, feeling instantly cheered by the

light pouring in the room.

Molly yawned and stretched her arms up over her head. "Where's Maude?"

"She's at the Oaks' home for the day," I said. "Bess is coming out and needs help getting ready for some fancy party."

She frowned.

"What's wrong?" I asked.

"I'm merely surprised that I was never told about Bess's coming out." She paused. "You are quite bold for a servant. Did they not teach you etiquette in Sweden?"

I cringed. This seemed to be the theme of my life here. I had overstepped my bounds again, though I wasn't sure how. "We have a different way of doing things where I come from."

"I suppose," she looked thoughtful. "But you are new to this household, yet you marched into my chambers like you own the place. Are you not intimidated by me?"

I cocked my head. I probably should be, but I wasn't. Maybe it's because I knew I wasn't staying here in this time period, so even if I made a fool of myself, no one would be around to remember it once I was back home.

What happens in 1886 stays in 1886.

Or maybe it was because I couldn't get myself to put importance on the thick, bold lines that seemed to divide the classes here. Molly may be rich, but she was still a person like me, trying to figure out her place in the world. I bet Stryder was just as rich as the Brodericks, but that didn't stop him from dating Taz or being a friend to me and my sisters.

Or maybe my lack of intimidation was because Molly was destined to be murdered in a matter of days. How do

262

you fear someone whose expiration date was right around the corner? Sympathy was the most I could muster.

Whatever the reason, I needed to convince Molly to open up to me. I remembered how excited she was at the inn, when she was begging her mom to hire me as a servant. The fact that I was (supposedly) from Sweden had made me appeal to her like an exotic pet. I wondered how sheltered her life must be, living as a young woman within the constraints of nineteenth century high society.

A memory flashed in my mind. My sisters and I broke out into a fight once, over the last maple donut in the fridge, which escalated to all of us dragging each other to the kitchen floor. I was toward the bottom of the dog pile, and when I tried to scream and dislodge myself, Phee shoved my hair in my mouth and lunged for the donut. Taz had armed herself with the sink's spray hose, which she shot at full impact directly into Phee's face, then swiped the donut. Phee screamed, yanked the hose from Taz, and sprayed all of us. By the time Daphne stepped into the room, the donut was nothing but soggy mangled pieces all over the kitchen. My sisters and I were panting, bruised, and drenched; laughing and crying at the same time.

Daphne grounded us for a week and refused to buy us donuts for the rest of the year.

My heart lurched, and I ignored the pricks of moisture in my eyes. People like Molly never get to wrestle with their siblings, or laugh over a slice of pizza, or cower within the warmth of a cozy blanket during a scary movie.

And the worst was people like Molly never knew what they were missing.

"I'm not afraid of you," I finally said hoarsely, trying to keep my voice light as I blinked back the homesick tears that threatened to invade. Was the rift still open? Would I ever see my sisters again?

Stop. Of course you will.

I swallowed, realizing Molly was staring at me. "I mean, you and I are nearly the same age," I explained, blinking my emotions away. "Where I come from, we'd be friends. So if you want to talk, I'm here. You seemed upset by the fact you didn't know about Bess's coming out. Why does that bother you?"

A ball of awkwardness tightened in my stomach. I knew I sounded like a freakin' psychiatrist, but I was getting desperate for some information and was at a loss as to how to get it.

She stared at me for a moment more, then to my surprise, admitted, "I've never had a sister before. Or any other girl I could talk to."

Relief swelled inside me and I plopped down on a chair near her bed. "See? Here's your chance! Let's start over. Hi Molly, I'm Aviva. Your temporary lady servant— and friend…maybe?"

She smiled reluctantly. "I suppose I can talk while eating breakfast. I've nothing else to do."

I ignored the guilt I felt over my ulterior motives as I passed her the breakfast tray. She started chatting between delicate bites.

"I was upset because I do not understand why Kade failed to tell me about something so important as his sister coming out."

"Maybe he only just found out himself?" I suggested. "Or maybe it didn't interest him enough to share it with you."

"Perhaps," she mused, picking at her plate. "But this has been his way. He is distant with me. We are to be married in two weeks time, yet he regards me more like a polite cousin than his fiancé." She looked over at me, sadness flickering across her toasted almond eyes.

Weird twinges of emotion tangled inside me. Molly's words made me feel sad, yet relieved at the same time. The sadness was easy to define. Molly's fiancé didn't love her back, or at least Molly was convinced he didn't. The fact that Molly believed she was about to spend the rest of her life in a loveless marriage was clearly heartbreaking.

But the relief bothered me, because in its happy wake I was left swimming in guilt. I shouldn't feel grateful that out of all the different personalities Kade had presented to me, 'polite cousin' was never one of them. What kind of monster was I, that Molly's suffering was bringing me any kind of relief?

I felt a tug in my stomach. My next question, I was ashamed to admit, had nothing to do with her murder investigation. "Do you love him?"

She nearly choked on her bite.

"Sorry," I said, "It's hard for me to get used to your customs here. Where I come from we talk about every thing with our girlfriends."

"Surely you jest. There is no way you share everything."

"Okay, maybe not everything, but a lot."

She took a gulp of tea. "Well…since you asked, I think I do love him. In a way."

"In a way?"

"I love the man he presents to others." She paused, thinking. "He is of strong character, and witty, and kindhearted in unexpected ways. He contains all of the ingredients to be a wonderful husband. But his disinterest in me has me forever questioning how I feel about him. It can be difficult to love a man who has no love for you."

I considered her words. This was all very telling as far as understanding her troubled relationship with Kade, but unfortunately none of this was helping me solve her murder. All I was accomplishing was feeling more relief, followed by more guilt. And I couldn't outright ask "So hey, know anyone who wants you dead?"

Then a thought occurred to me. A jilted lover might want Molly dead. She was a catch and probably had several men disappointed that she was about to be married. What better motive for murder than jealousy and resentment over not having been chosen? And framing Kade for the murder would be the perfect icing on a revenge-flavored cake.

"Is there a man out there who you do love?" I asked. "And who loves you back?"

She blinked and pushed away her tray. "It is time for me to dress for the day."

Damn. I had pushed too far. "Sorry. I ask too many questions. Let's talk about something less personal."

Molly hesitated. "Very well. What would you like to know?"

"Oh, I don't know. How about your family? What are they like?"

She chuckled. "Ah…you're smitten with my brother too."

My mouth dropped open. "Of course not!" Then her words replayed back to me. "And what do you mean, 'too'?"

She shook her head and swiped a piece of cornbread from her plate. "Oh, all the servants are head-over-heels for Will. He's handsome and relates well with the lower class."

I vaguely remembered Ruby saying something about Clair having a crush on William, which apparently was nothing out of the ordinary in the Broderick household.

"Have you met his friend Aurora?" I asked.

She scrunched her nose questioningly. "Aurora? No, I've never heard of anyone by that name. Is she someone Will mentioned?"

"Yeah," I affirmed, "but I'm starting to think she doesn't really exist." Between William not mentioning Aurora during supper and Molly never hearing about her, I wondered if William manufactured a fake girlfriend just to break the ice with me.

"What about your father?" I hedged. "What's he like?"

Her face darkened as she swallowed her bite of cornbread. "I'm sure you know. Everyone knows."

"Yeah, I've kind of noticed." I really wanted to hear more about Mr. Broderick, but I didn't want to spook Molly away from the conversation.

"My father tries to keep his indiscretions a secret," Molly bit out, "but it is so obvious. I am sure the whole town knows. It is rather embarrassing." She shook her head.

I remembered the blue booties, and my conversation with Ruby about Mr. Broderick's relations with the servants. Not to mention *Madame Dresler's Preventative Powder*.

"Do you think your dad might have had something to do with Clair leaving?"

Her face grew pale. "I am done talking for the day." She forced a tight smile. "But thank you for the lively conversation. I assume you will keep the confidence of everything I have shared with you." It was a statement, not a question.

This time I knew beyond a shadow of a doubt that I had pushed too far, but at least I now had a lead. Was Clair carrying Mr. Broderick's child? Did Mr. Broderick force

Clair to leave—or do something worse—to protect his secret? And what, if anything, did this information have to do with Molly's impending death?

"Of course I will," I assured Molly. "Your secrets die with me."

No need to say that those secrets would die with her in two days.

Twenty-Five

The ghosts
of things that never happened
are worse than the ghosts
of things that did.
L.M. Montgomery

January 17, 1886

MOLLY'S DEATH DAY. The words taunted me as I crunched through last night's snowfall toward the stables. The fact that I still hadn't figured out who was going to kill Molly pressed sickly against my chest. Solving crimes on TV always looked so easy. The hero questioned a few people, followed a few clues, and bam, mystery solved. I, on the other hand, was sitting here the day of the murder, trying to navigate my way through my own murky confusion. At this point my biggest suspect was Mr. Broderick, but I still couldn't fathom why an affair with the house servant would lead to Molly's murder.

I needed to know more. There was one person on the property I still hadn't talked to: Charlie, the stablehand. Though Ruby hadn't sounded convinced, she did mention the possibility that he might have been the father of Clair's unborn baby.

The day, bright and cloudless, was cloying in light of the

violent crime that was supposed to take place today, with the sun's rays blinding against the white snow. At least it was Sunday, my one and only day off. It felt liberating to not have Maude breathing down my back.

Trying to keep my skirt from dragging in the snow, I was so deep inside my head that I didn't notice the solid body striding toward me until I nearly smacked into it.

"Whoa," William said, his hands gripping my elbows right before I stumbled into him. "I'm beginning to think you are purposely trying to mow me over, Miss Aviva."

Wow, was he a sight for sore eyes, with his golden hair and easy smile. "Shoot. Sorry. I was deep in thought." I laughed. "And how do I know *you're* not the one arranging these chance meetings?"

His eyes sparkled. "You are a charming thing, aren't you? No wonder Kade is smitten by you."

My heart stopped. "What?"

"Come now, angel. You can not be so daft to not have noticed the way he looks at you."

My face suddenly felt tingly and numb, and I knew it wasn't from the cold. "But he's engaged," I stammered.

"Kade is a noble man and will do what is right for his betrothed, but being under obligation does not stop the heart from wanting what it can not have." He stared at me, his bold eyes appraising. His next words came out soft. "Your face gives you away. I can see your heart belongs to him, as well."

I slid my arms away from his gentle grip and stepped back. "Why are you saying these things when there is nothing to be done about it?"

William looked contrite. "Apologies, angel. I mean you no distress. I was under the assumption you knew."

"I didn't know." The words came out choked.

Was William telling the truth? Did Kade have feelings for me?

I stiffened. Really, did it even matter? Kade was getting married.

Molly.

The thought of her hit me like a ton of bricks. I didn't have time to be distracted by my so-called feelings for Kade; I needed to save his life—by saving hers.

"Do you know where Charlie is?" I asked, realizing a second later that my question was totally out of the blue.

William tilted his head, looking perplexed at my sudden change of subject. "He is in the stables, readying the mares."

"Oh, where are you off to this morning?" I asked, curious.

"Church." He paused. "You ought to come along."

"No thanks." Church was personal, and the idea of encroaching upon his family's outing made me feel all squirmy. "But I hope you and your family enjoy the service," I added, hoping I hadn't offended him by turning down his invitation.

I turned toward the stable when details from the newspaper article I had read in Copper's Kettle bombarded my brain.

Marguerite Broderick goes to church today.

That's right. If I was remembering the article correctly, Molly attends church with her family, then later proceeds to some stables to meet Kade for a horseback ride. If I tagged along with the family to church, maybe I could talk Molly out of going to the stables. Or at least I could follow her and try to stop the killer.

I swung around. William was still standing there, watching me with a contemplative look on his face. "Actually, I'd really like to go." I searched my head for a quick explanation. "I just don't have anything nice to wear."

William grinned. "I'm sure we can find something suitable for you from my sister's wardrobe."

"Great! I'm just going to talk to Charlie for a minute, then go get ready."

If William was curious about why I wanted to talk to the stablehand, he did a good job of hiding it.

The stable was cool and smelled dank and musty when I stepped in. The horses nickered softly in a cozy, welcoming chorus. Two stalls to the left, a tall, lanky kid was sitting on a wooden milking stool, using a metal tool to dig into the hoof of a gray speckled mare. With his tousled brown hair and ruddy, dimpled cheeks, he looked like any somewhat-cute-but-awkward teenager you'd see in my century. My gaze roved over the light scattering of pimples on his chin and cheeks, visible even in the shadows. Acne in this century struck me as funny, somehow. I always assumed my breakouts were due to french fries and chocolate shakes, but I guess not.

I took a deep breath and sauntered toward him. He was so deeply engrossed in the task in front of him that I doubted he even knew I was there.

"Charlie?"

He jerked and glanced up, pausing in his hoof-cleaning. "Yea, I'm Charlie. What's it to you?" His voice, deep at first, ended on a high note in the manner that characterizes boys in the throes of puberty.

"Hi, I'm Aviva," I said, leaning against the stall door.

"Yea, so?" He stood up, stretching to his full height as if he were trying to make himself as tall as possible.

Okay, awkward. Charlie obviously wasn't much of a talker. I cleared my throat. "Um, what's his name?" I asked, gesturing to the horse, trying to break the ice.

"*Her* name is Clementine," he informed me with a look of disdain. "Cant'cha tell a stallion from a mare?"

I looked over at Clementine. Her eyes were deep brown and oh-so-gentle. "Well, I wasn't exactly looking for a pair of balls or anything," I said defensively.

"A pair of…what?"

"Nothing." I could feel my face reddening. This wasn't going well. Time to get to the point. "Uh, Charlie, I was wondering if I could ask you something?"

He sighed and set his hoof-cleaning tool on the stool. "Carry on, then."

"Well…" I trailed off, trying to decide how much I should tell him. I really should have rehearsed this conversation first before approaching him. "Did you know the last house maid, Clair?"

He wiped a small piece of straw from his forehead. "'Course I do. I know all the staff here." Impatience edged his voice.

I decided not to point out the fact that I had been here for five days and yet he didn't know me. "Do you know why she went away?"

His even stare turned into a glare. "She was carrying a bastard child."

I cringed. Wow, people in this century were savage when it came to kids growing in a single mom's uterus. "Do you know whose child?"

His already ruddy cheeks flushed with red. "That's all we

need around here, another clatterfart." He grabbed a brush hanging from a nearby nail. "I have work to do."

"Wait, Charlie, I'm sorry," my words came out in a rush. Anything with the word 'fart' in it couldn't be good. "I swear I'm not trying to say you're the father. I honestly don't know who is."

He turned back toward me. "What's it to you then?"

"Because…" I realized there was no way I was getting any information from him unless I inserted a little honesty into my next words. "I know it sounds crazy, but I…well… I sort of know things. Things about the future."

His eyes lit up. "You're a diviner?"

Sure, why not? "Yes, I guess you could call me that."

"My mother used a diviner to predict the genders of all my brothers and sisters. That woman was correct on four out of five of them! And really, she was only wrong about Mabel because Mabel ended up being such a tomboy."

"Wow, that's interesting." I needed to get him back on track. "But, the reason I came to talk to you is because my…divining…has told me that Miss Marguerite is in big trouble if I don't figure out a way to help her."

His whole body stiffened. "Molly?" he whispered.

I cocked my head at him, my brain instantly alert. Something about his tone and body language piqued my senses. I hadn't been in this century very long, but I knew enough at this point to understand that members of the household staff were not on a first name basis with their employers. Yet he had referred to Marguerite as "Molly." Not just her first name, but her very familiar nickname. And the way his body stiffened….

"You're in love with her."

Charlie's face paled. He clutched the stall door. "S'pose

there's no point in denyin' it, since you're a diviner and all."

"How long have you felt this way?"

"Since the first time I laid eyes on her." His voice took on a shrill note. "But it ain't only me! She loves me too!"

"Has she told you that?"

"Not in words. But I know it. She's always so kind to me."

I ignored the impulse to roll my eyes. Charlie was only—what had Ruby said?—fifteen years old? Yet he had his eyes set on a woman who was way out of his league.

"So you never had a relationship with the former housemaid, Clair?"

His face scrunched up, as if tasting something bad. "Clair was nothin' but a gowpenful-o'-anything, always proddin' into things that weren't none of 'er business."

"That doesn't really answer my question…."

"Will this help keep Molly out of whatever danger you're divinin'?"

"Yes, it will," I affirmed. Who knows, I could be telling the truth.

He let out a puff of air and shifted from one foot to the other. "I may've kissed Clair, but only once. It was when I found out Molly was goin' through with her marriage to that fool who don't even love 'er. I was tryin' to make 'er jealous."

I ignored the defensive feeling in my gut over the reference to Kade as 'that fool'. "A kiss, then, that was all?" I said my next words as a statement. "So there's no chance her baby might have been yours."

He frowned. "You think I'm some kind of dalcop? I ain't in no position to raise no bastard child."

I flinched. I never knew Clair, but I couldn't help but feel bad for her. Even if she was a gowpenful-o'-whatever.

"Is Molly gonna be okay?" Charlie's question intruded my thoughts.

"I hope so."

I said goodbye, then left the stables, feeling guilty for the state I was leaving him in. I hurried across the yard toward the Brodericks' house, hoping I wasn't too late for church. My conversation with Charlie had delayed him getting the horses ready, so that might buy me more time.

As I crossed the yard, I thought about everything the troubled stablehand had shared with me. Charlie was in love with Molly. That meant he was innocent of her impending murder, right? He wouldn't kill someone he loves.

Something was bothering me. I tried to pinpoint it, but it kept fleeing every time I got too close.

It didn't hit me until I reached the servants' quarters.

Charlie has motive for murder.

I almost fell back from the dresser's vanity where I was attempting to pull a rough hairbrush through my tangles.

Yes, Charlie loved Molly. But how quickly does love turn into jealousy, and jealousy into hate? He admitted to being angry when he found out Molly was still going through with her marriage to Kade. Molly's kindness toward him had convinced him that his love for her was reciprocated.

Would his jealousy and anger toward Molly's looming marriage provoke him to kill her in a crime of passion, and frame Kade for the murder?

My blood felt chilled as another thought occurred to me. What if my conversation with Charlie prompts Molly's murder? Charlie was going about his business this morning without a care in the world (though he did seem grumpy), but then I walked into his life and put all these ideas in his head. I brought all of his raw feelings for Molly to the surface.

No, I argued internally. Charlie seemed deathly afraid of anything happening to Molly. There's no way he will set out today to hurt her.

But...*he might*, the thought whispered with a hint of malice. Maybe he doesn't set out today to hurt her, but after our conversation, he might seek her out to talk to her, to make sure she's okay. Then when he sees her happily preparing for a horseback ride with her fiancé, he might lose his temper, go into a fit of rage and kill her...

Whoa, I reeled back.

Get a grip. The murder was published in newspapers that I had found in my time, and in *my* time, I hadn't gone back into the past to interfere. So there's no way my conversation with Charlie changed the course of history and caused Molly's murder. According to Brett, that kind of timey-wimey stuff happened in Dr. Who, but this was real life.

So that left Mr. Broderick as my prime suspect.

I finagled my hair into something between a braid and a french twist and headed towards Molly's quarters to ask about a church dress. Shoving all of my dark thoughts aside, I allowed myself to feel excited for the tranquil normalcy of going to church. I was desperate for something familiar to remind me of home. The somber reading of scripture might not hit the spot the same way a Quarter Pounder with Cheese would, but it was still its own kind of comfort food.

He was silent as a lamb being led to the butcher.... The verse came to me from nowhere. Was that from Isaiah? Great comfort food, I thought. I wondered who my sub-conscience considered the lamb here. Molly? Kade?

Either way, after the service ended, it was do or die time.

I ignored the persistent thought that maybe the one being led to butcher was me.

Twenty-Six

Nothing burns like the cold.
George R.R. Martin

Monday, April 1
Present Day

HOW MUCH TIME had past. Minutes? Hours? Glancing down at the giant ice-blob where her cellphone used to be, Krystal knew it was time to move. But she wasn't quite ready to talk to Dad and Daphne about her *Horae* discovery. She threw on jeans and a hoodie and, remembering the dead blossoms from last night, walked outside to check the flowers in Daphne's garden.

Huddled in her hoodie, she felt the biting air but didn't mind it, other than the fact that it was out of place. Their springlike weather had taken a turn overnight, with April bringing a spatter of dreary gray clouds and temperatures that felt more like winter.

It was like even the weather could sense something was deeply wrong.

Likewise, Daphne's flowers, freshly planted last week, were shriveling and turning black, just like the snap dragons and lilies in Pendulum Square. Only the roses stubbornly clung to life.

She gazed at the brown and withered tulips and gladioli. Was it the sudden backslide into cold weather that was causing them to die? Admittedly Daphne had planted them too early. The general rule of thumb in Sezona Hills was to wait until Mother's Day to plant flowers, to be sure the last of the frost had past. But Daphne, with a thumb almost as green as Aviva's, had cheated this rule for years without any issues. Sometimes Krystal wondered if Daphne was more than she seemed, too.

It seemed fitting that today was April Fool's Day. As if nature itself was playing some kind of mean joke. "Haha, y'all thought it was spring. Gotcha!"

April Fool's Day was Krystal's least favorite day of the year. She had never been a fan of pranks, even before Stryder played his horrible joke on her. Pranks did nothing but trick and deceive people. Why would anyone find that fun?

Coincidentally it was also April Fool's Day—or night—that Joe was the victim of a hit-and-run accident, an event that left his foot permanently deformed. He told her he didn't feel sorry for himself, so neither should she. But she still couldn't help think about how that night had stolen everything from him.

At least authorities were able to arrest the true driver. That awful girl Shana was arrested and charged with a felony hit-and-run. Her rich dad was able to get her out of juvenile hall on bond until her trial, but with barely a leg to stand on, Shana was likely going to be spending several years behind bars. Stryder was considered to be an accessory to the crime since he withheld information about the hit-and-run, but Stryder's attorney was able to work out a plea deal, and now Stryder was serving community service. The other guy involved, Lance, claimed ignorance to the entire incident. Since he technically wasn't in the truck when the accident happened, he got away with it.

Despite Lance being let off the hook, Stryder never acted bitter about it. In fact, Krystal suspected Stryder actually *wanted* to serve community service, *wanted* to have a black mark on his record for the rest of his life. It was like his weird way of coming to terms with what he did...for atoning for his sins or something.

Krystal got it. She was similar to Stryder in that way. She liked to beat herself up over things, too. Well, maybe 'like' was the wrong word. It was more that she had a habit of beating herself up over things.

Krystal wasn't like her sisters. Her heart tugged as she thought about them now...the daydreamy and optimistic Aviva, always seeing the silver lining and working under the assumption that everything would work out for the best. Or Taz, the pragmatist, who was guided more by logic than by fantasies. She was the levelheaded one—the mediator of the family—trying to resolve problems from a rational place.

Then you had Phee, who was above it all...too grounded in her self-confidence to care one way or another. When Phee was confronted by problems, she usually shrugged them off.

But not Krystal. Krystal was a pessimist. Maybe fear was a touch colder in Krystal's mind, just like her power, which made it hard in the past to share a room with a bubbling, happy Aviva.

Krystal didn't *want* to be gloomy; she'd love to be more like her sisters and adopt any one of their attitudes. But against her will, her brain gravitated into dark corners, picking at the one thing that could go wrong and anxiously kneading it between the heavy fingers of her thoughts like a rough stone pressed ruthlessly by the wild river until it's ground smooth.

And that's what she did now. Except for instead of one rough stone, it was dozens of them.

No, she had never liked April Fool's Day, but now that it had played the biggest trick of all time by stealing away her sisters, she could safely say that she hated the holiday. She'd take Aviva's moth invasions and Phee's self-centeredness all day long if she could just have her sisters back.

Krystal bent down to examine the flowers closer, rubbing a cluster of crispy brown petals between her fingertips. Without meaning to, she froze the petals. She dropped the icy clump and pulled away, realizing she needed to be more careful. First her cellphone, now the petals. Why was it so hard to control herself? Was it because she was upset? Dad said that being the youngest of her sisters gave her the least mastery over her abilities, and this was especially true when she was feeling emotional (which was, like, ninety percent of the time).

Could she be causing this weather?

She was an *Horae*, after all.

A crow cawed, and she straightened to a stand. The crow watched her from its low perch on a nearby mulberry tree. She stared at it. It seemed unperturbed, assessing her with eyes that were both piercing and intelligent. She could swear that it was the same crow who had cawed at her last night in Pendulum Square. She shivered, then realized the ridiculousness of the thought. It's not like one crow looked any different than another. She stared at the crow for another few seconds. It cocked its head at her. Uncomfortable, she looked away.

She returned to her task of examining flowers, the chilly air bleeding through the thin fabric of her hoodie. If she were a normal person, she'd be shivering by now. Luckily being the human embodiment of winter gave her an amazing cold tolerance. She could feel the cold, but never felt bothered by it. Even holding ice for long periods of time never phased her.

She was about to go inside when her ears tuned into a muffled, high-pitched cheeping. When she stood again, the unmoving crow was still watching her. She ignored the crow and followed the noise to the back patio. The cheeping was louder here, and coming from above. She looked up toward the underside of the roof, where she saw the dove Aviva had revived last week. The bird was up in the rafters, hovering on top of her nest.

Of course. Her babies must have finally hatched.

Turning to go inside the house, Krystal stopped when the cheeping turned into a faint but unnerving squeal. It sounded like one of the baby birds was in distress. Krystal glanced up again, where she could see the mama dove pecking with a fervor that seemed almost violent.

Krystal drug Daphne's wooden step ladder over and climbed to the top, trying to get a better view of the nest. What she saw made her gasp.

The mama bird was pecking madly at the head of her baby. And based on the blood spreading along the baby bird's head, she intended to kill it.

Without thinking, Krystal reached inside the nest, sending the mother into a panicked flurry of flapping, and grabbed the squealing baby bird. One more glance inside the nest revealed to Krystal that the dove's only other baby was already dead.

With the baby bird clenched in her hand, Krystal jumped off the ladder and ran into the house. Dad and Daphne were finally awake, though barely, staring at each other with blank expressions over mugs of black coffee.

"Morning Krys," Dad muttered.

"Morning, " she said, moving to rush past.

Daphne was a little more observant than her dad. "What have you got there?"

Krystal halted briefly. "A baby bird. I'll explain later though because I think it's in trouble." Before they could ask any more questions, she hurried upstairs to her room and pulled a shoebox from her closet. With the bird in one hand and the box in the other, she walked to the bathroom. She set the shoebox down on the counter, swiped a hand towel from the rack on the wall, and stuffed it inside the box.

"There, you have a nest," she told the bird, placing it gently inside. "Now let's patch you up."

She moistened a wad of toilet paper and used it to gently wipe the blood from the bird's head. Once she patted it dry, she pulled a small tube of Neosporin from the medicine cabinet and smeared a generous amount on the open wound. The bird cheeped the entire time, but the sound no longer had the panicked quality from earlier. She wondered if the little guy—or girl—knew she was trying to help.

The final step was bandaging the bird's head. Krystal didn't have healing powers like Aviva, but she had watched Daphne treat scrapes and cuts so many times as a kid that she knew a gaping wound could get infected if it wasn't protected from dirt and grime. She scanned the bathroom, trying to find something that could be used as a bandage. She nearly shouted in victory when she found little round spot Band-Aids, the kind you use to cover a blister or a shaving nick. Peeling off the wax backing, she gently pressed the tiny circle onto the bird's head. It looked comically big, but it would do the job.

Krystal swaddled the baby bird loosely in the hand towel and took a step back to look over her work. "Well, your Band-Aid looks more like a helmet, but I think you might live."

The bird squeaked its response.

Krystal walked the baby bird back to her room and got it settled on her nightstand. She wondered how she would feed it, and if she would need a heat lamp to keep it warm. Stryder might have one she could borrow, since he kept Miss. B in some kind of reptile tank. But the feeding thing…she'd have to ask Daphne for help.

She exhaled a heavy puff of air. Now that the immediate task of saving the bird's life had passed, the weight of her missing sisters pressed upon her chest again, not to mention the revelation that she was an *Horae*.

She trudged down the stairs. It was time to confront Dad and Daphne about all of this. But more than that, it was time to figure out how to save her sisters.

Twenty-Seven

*Do not fall in love with people like me.
I will destroy you in the most
beautiful way possible.*
Caitlyn Siehl

January 17, 1886

CHURCH WASN'T WHAT I expected. I naively
thought I'd be sitting with the Brodericks, but servants had
their own section in the back. The Civil War may have
ended, but segregation was still very much alive in the
privileged town of Sezona Valley.

As nice it was to blend into the background without
having to make small talk with the Brodericks, this wasn't
boding well for me following Molly after the service. I
couldn't even see her in the congregation. The whole town
must be piled into this little building.

Singing Creek Episcopal Church was somewhat like
church from my time, but so …unlike it, too. The sermon
was solemn and formal. I fought to stay awake during the
reverend's detached tirade, in which the most exciting thing
that happened was when he thumped a prayer book to
drive his point home. Did that man ever crack a smile?

The clothes were more formal, too. The men wore straight, trim suits, their jackets hemmed around the thigh, some featuring short rounded tails curving around the back. The women's Sunday finery included the usual gorgeous dresses, but with bustles under their skirts to make their rear ends stick out at such a drastic angle that from the back they looked like walking sofas. Apparently people in 1886 liked big butts. *When a girl walks in with an itty bitty waist and a round thing in your face you get sprung…*

I coughed and cleared my head. But seriously, I couldn't fathom how women in this time period sat down in those monstrous things. It looked like it involved a lot of patting, smoothing, and fussing. Some carried small prayer books with their thin, collapsed parasols, and all of them wore hats adorned with feathers, flowers, and lace.

Much like my church, there was worship music…sort of. I was used to standing and clapping along—sometimes even dancing a little— to more upbeat songs. But here, between the heavy notes chiming from a pipe organ and a choir that sounded like they were auditioning to be in an opera, the songs were somber and grave. I tried to imagine what would happen if I spontaneously broke out into cheery clapping.

It probably wouldn't go over well.

Whatever happened to "Make a joyful noise unto the Lord…"? These people sounded like they were lamenting at a funeral.

It wasn't until *Amazing Grace* that I finally perked up. The last time I heard this song was in my own church, with Kade's ghost sitting next to me, his voice a beautiful bass as he sang the lyrics that traversed time. That was a mere week ago—or had yet to happen, depending on how you looked at it. I wondered if Kade had struggled to sing along with the more modern version that my church's worship team had performed. It sure hadn't sounded like it.

Humming along to this slower, more melancholy version, I became lost in the melody. The voices of the congregation lifted and mingled together, and the result was something so poignant and emotional, it gave me chills.

Maybe this serious, formal church wasn't the worst thing in the world.

In the midst of this thought, something made my back stiffen.

A voice, I realized. A male voice, rich and deep, trying to blend with the rest of the congregation's, but too distinct to not rise above them.

Kade.

I shifted myself into a taller seated position, peering over the dozens of frilly hats trying to block my view. Following the sound of his voice, I turned my head and scanned the far side of the chapel until I finally spotted him. He was on the left side of the church, sitting next to his family, impossible to notice if one didn't have motive to crane her neck.

He was true to his word that he would make himself a nuisance, as I had seen him several times these past few days. But unfortunately it was nearly impossible for Kade and I to talk alone. Servants didn't go meandering off with the gentry.

The service ended a few minutes later and, still unable to find Molly, I hurried outside, eager to catch Kade before he left with his family. Hopefully he had learned something about who might want to murder his fiancé.

The morning was brisk and bright blue when I exited the

church, with the snow tamping softly beneath my feet. My breath came out in white puffs. It was one of those days that infect a person with joy, though it did not have that effect on me now.

"Hello, clever girl."

My body jolted at his familiar ghost-greeting. He was leaning on the wood-sided wall near the doorway, arms crossed in front of him, looking as if he had been waiting for me. He wore his usual self-assured expression, but I sensed something uneasy flickering beneath his calm facade.

I was uneasy, too. Molly's Death Day wasn't exactly a day at the park.

"You knew I was here?"

"You're hard to miss."

I blushed and glanced down, feeling a little ridiculous in the sage green dress Molly had loaned me. With its high lace collar and soft, ruffled fabric that gathered at my hips before dropping to the ground, I felt like I was attending a costume party. She had chosen it because she said the color of the dress set off my eyes. Luckily she hadn't tried to loan me the Butt Plumper 2000 to go along with the dress. Apparently servants' booties are fine the way they are.

"You're lovely, Aviva." The words came out so softly I wondered for a brief second if I had heard him correctly. Startled, I returned my eyes back to his. It was like he read my mind about how silly I felt in this stupid dress.

I cleared my throat. "You never thought that when you were a ghost," I ribbed him, trying to cut the tension that threatened to suffocate us. "I guess my jeans and t-shirts don't have the same effect."

"I am relatively certain that the spirit version of myself

thought you were rather fetching too, but did not feel it pertinent to tell you so."

"And it's 'pertinent' now?" I asked.

"Somehow, yes. It is."

I swallowed hard. Was Kade getting out his last words, like a man being escorted down death row?

The air grew thicker between us. I wondered if Kade could feel it too.

"Did you learn anything about Molly's killer?" I asked, keeping my voice low. I looked around, hoping the Broderick's were distracted elsewhere, and dropped my voice down to a near-whisper, "I have two possible suspects, but I just don't know."

"I've met with the same luck," Kade said. "My questioning these past few days has accomplished nothing more than casting suspicion on myself. Who are your suspects?"

"Charlie, the stablehand, and Mr. Broderick."

"I had considered Mr. Broderick myself, but I do not see how he benefits from murdering his own daughter. Charlie, on the other hand…." He considered it. "No, I do not believe he is capable of such a thing. Charlie does not have the gumption to kill a person. He is somewhat of a cringeling."

"I agree, but don't you think people will do crazy things when they're in love?"

"In love?"

My stomach tightened. I was beginning to feel like the Archangel of Bad News. "Charlie's in love with Molly."

Kade pondered that information quietly for a moment. "I suppose that makes sense. Much like her brother, Molly has always been kind to the servants. Between her comeliness and good nature, it'd be difficult for a lad such as Charlie to not be taken by her."

Okay. He took that better than I thought.

He glanced around, then gestured for me to follow him. I trailed after him until we were behind the chapel. Thick vegetation grew in wild abandon back here. Kade took my hand and pulled me into a thicket of tall brush, brown and dry for winter. Molly was going to kill me when she saw all of the twigs and thorns caked on the hem of her dress.

If she was alive to kill me.

"Now we are no longer in view of prying eyes," he explained at my questioning look.

"Won't the Brodericks wonder where I have disappeared to?"

"Servants live their own lives on their days of rest. They will assume you are enjoying dinner with an acquaintance, or have decided to walk home on this lovely day."

I started to ask him why I would be eating dinner so early in the day, when I remembered that in this century, dinner meant lunch.

"What about your family?" I asked.

"When I saw you in the chapel earlier, I told them I had an errand to attend to after the service and I would see myself home."

"Oh. Okay."

A tree rustled above us, and I whipped around to see a small brown squirrel alight on one of the branches. Poor fellow was probably desperate to find one measly acorn on these barren trees. When I turned back around, Kade's eyes were fixed on my own. My heart thudded with more intensity than the reverend pounding his prayer book earlier. "Will you stop doing that?"

"Stop doing what?"

"Staring at me."

"Presently you are the only person in my company. At whom would you have me stare?"

"I don't know. How about that squirrel?" I pointed toward the tree.

He laughed. "Are you always so amusing?"

"Occupational hazard," I muttered.

"Come again?"

"Nothing," I said. "Let's figure out how to save your fiancé."

"Yes." He coughed uncomfortably. "I think knowing the details of her death is of the utmost importance, so let us begin with you telling me everything you know."

"Well, I remember the newspaper article I read on my cellphone said—."

"What's a 'cellphone'?" Kade interrupted.

I leveled him with a stare. I had told ghost-Kade what a cellphone was, but never living-Kade. "If I'm going to get through this, you can't interrupt me every time I talk about something from my time period that you don't understand."

"Or, you can narrate your story in a way that a man from 1886 can understand." A smile played on his lips.

"Fine," I sighed. "The article I read on my tiny handheld rectangular-shaped communication device—."

He rolled his eyes at me.

"—said that Molly was killed at the Mc-something stables. She was meeting her fiancé—that would be you—for a horseback ride."

Kade's face went pale.

"What's wrong?" I asked, alarmed.

"Oh. It is nothing."

"Kade. Come on, just tell me."

"It is only that…although I believed you about all of this, it feels strikingly real when you recall details that have yet to transpire."

"Like what?"

"Molly and I are indeed scheduled to go on a horseback ride today. We are meeting at the McCleran stables. How would you know that? It's like listening to a diviner. It *is* possible you spoke to Molly about all this, but…."

My heart dropped. "I thought you said you believed me."

His blue eyes dimmed as he gazed at me. He leaned over and pulled a small twig from my hair, his cold fingers grazing my cheek as he did so. "It's not that, little one," he said, his voice low. "I do believe you, but at the same time my rational mind is trying to find a reason not to believe you. Because the things that you say will happen…I'm afraid they will break me if they come to pass. And that's assuming I don't hang from a noose first."

His words were a painful beating on my chest. How could I be mad at him for doubting my words, when believing them caused him so much pain?

The answer was, I couldn't.

But we still had a job to do.

"Kade," I said in the same pleading voice Taz always used when she's mediating arguments between me and my sisters. "I *am* from the future. You know in your gut I'm telling you the truth, and I don't have time to convince you anymore. This is happening today, whether you believe it or not."

He opened his mouth as if to argue, then clamped it shut. His eyes hardened with resolve. "Very well. Tell me more about the article."

"Okay. Like I said, you meet Molly for a horseback ride. Someone reports hearing a scream from the stables, and the sheriff arrives. He finds you standing over Molly's dead body."

"It sounds like I'm guilty."

I glared at him. "You're not."

He stared at me, wordless.

I tried to remember anything else that would help us, but the effort was starting to hurt my brain. What I would pay to have that newspaper article in front of me right now!

"What time does all this happen?" Kade asked quietly.

"Oh, I know this one! 3:20. I only remember that because my birthday is March twentieth. Anyway, I think that's when someone reports a scream to the sheriff."

"3:20. Molly and I agreed to meet at 3:30." Kade pondered aloud. "Why was she alone? She always has an escort with her. Something about this feels...peculiar."

"Honestly, I barely remember the article and I'm probably messing up the details."

He frowned. "Even so, something's not adding up."

I silently agreed, but I didn't know how to make the equation make sense when we were missing so many pieces. I tried to tamp down the annoyance I was feeling at myself. If Krystal had been the one to read the article, she would remember every detail.

Kade pulled out his pocket watch and gave it a glance. His face grew taut. "We still have a few hours. Enough time to change into more suitable clothing and head over to the stables."

"Or you can just not go?" I suggested, regretting the words the second they slipped out.

"Aviva. I can not allow my betrothed to die. Especially in the hands of a cold-blooded killer."

"I'm sorry," I said. "I didn't mean that. I'm overwhelmed and trying to think of every option. There's no way I'll let her die either, Kade."

"I know." He stared at me, his eyes a midnight storm as they traveled across my face. "Though I do not understand why you would dedicate yourself to such a risky venture." His voice was husky. He stepped in, closing the space between us. "What is your motive, Aviva? Why are you risking so much to help me?"

I froze as his hand reached out to touch my cheek. It was the gentlest of caresses, barely discernible, his fingers the kindling that set my nerve-endings on fire.

"I only wish…" he whispered, a look of tortured pining flickering across his features as he let the thought trail off.

My pulse skittered. "You wish what?" I breathed.

I gasped as he wrapped one arm around my waist and pulled me against his body, while his other hand wound its way up my neck through my hair, pinning me in place. Angling his head over me, his lips crashed down upon mine, hungry and hard. Unable to rationalize what was happening, I parted my lips, welcoming him in. The kiss, desperate and aggressive, slowly dissolved into something warm and sensual, and every muscle in me weakened as I melted into his arms.

He tore away from me with a groan and stumbled back a few steps.

"Blasted hell." He stormed to the edge of our thicket, shaking his head. Turning back around, he took a deep breath. "I don't know what has come over me. My actions are deplorable. Aviva, please forgive me."

I staggered, trying to regain my senses. Breathless, my brain fuzzy, I already missed the warmth of his hard body pressed against mine. I didn't want to forgive him. I wanted him to do it again and never stop.

"I forgive you," I managed to croak.

He stared at me, looking aghast. "You should not be so quick to allay my shame, sweet girl. What I did was dishonorable. I am betrothed! I took advantage of your youth and naivety to steal a moment that I wanted."

His words sobered me. My cheeks flushed with aggravation as I put my hands on my hips. "You're nineteen," I bit out. "I'm sixteen. We're practically the same age. Quit acting all high and mighty and treating me like some stupid kid who doesn't know what she's doing."

"Apologies for offending you, little one," Kade said, "but I get the distinct impression from your mannerisms that sixteen years of age in your era is much younger than sixteen in mine."

I opened my mouth to protest, but then closed it when I realized his point was true. Sixteen-year-old girls in Kade's time period were 'coming out' to suitors, preparing for marriage and getting ready to start their own families. Well, the rich ones were. The poor ones were buried in the throes of farm life and daily chores, or servitude to other families. Likewise, sixteen-year-old boys were slaving away in some kind of laborious job, farming, or, if they were from a wealthy family such as the Broderick's, attending universities and starting apprenticeships, or going into business with their fathers.

Unlike the teenagers in my time period, who were all playing video games and swiping at their cellphones. So yeah, there was a wee bit of difference in maturity between the two eras.

Not to mention that in my century, it wasn't even legal for Kade to be intimate with me. He was an adult in the strictest sense of the word, while I was still a child.

But I didn't care. I wanted Kade to love kissing me. Because those twenty seconds in his arms made me feel like, no matter what happened today, it was worth taking that leap of faith into Maui.

Kade was engaged. Logical-me—the one whose knees weren't full of jelly, and whose toes weren't still tingling with sensation—knew it. Kade kissed me, knowing he was marrying another woman. I forced my thoughts to narrow in on this fact, basking in the surge of anger it brought.

"You're right," I finally said, my face smooth and my tone firm. "That was a douche move of yours, Kade. I forgive you, but do not ever kiss me again."

If my words confused him, he didn't show it. "I promise you, I will not."

I ignored the sinking feeling triggered by his promise.

Something inside of me wept as Kade and I stepped out of the thicket. For a short time this place, though wild with brambles and thorns, was our pocket universe. Time, space, impending death…none of it mattered here. There was just us. And now we were leaving it behind, and I knew we would never be back.

That thought was cut short as I rounded the corner toward the front of the church to find Mr. Broderick a few yards away, leaning on the building close to where Kade had been waiting for me earlier. His expression was dark, his eyes narrowed. Crap. How much did he see?

Kade might be in trouble. And so was I.

Twenty-Eight

True love is like ghosts,
which everyone talks about
and few have seen.
Francois de La Rochefoucauld

January 17, 1886

KADE'S HOUSE WAS only fifteen minutes on foot from the church, so we decided to walk.

I could have rode home with the Brodericks, but seeing the murderous look on Mr. Broderick's face, I opted for a more classy approach. That is—I bent my head down and covered the side of my face, pretending not to see him as I scurried past. I'm sure that made him even more mad, but I didn't have time to ponder the consequences. And, much to my relief, he obviously had no intention of creating a scene with so many churchgoers still mingling about.

If things went according to plan, I'd be jumping into Maui tonight anyway and returning to my own time period.

I let that thought sink in. By this time tomorrow, I'd be back in my own room, in a world with microwaves and wifi and hot showers, where the only back-breaking labor I had to suffer through was writing haikus for Ms. Frost's class. It sounded like heaven.

I only hoped it was a world in which a murder obituary for Marguerite Broderick didn't exist. A world where a man named Thurston Kade Oaks had once lived a long, happy life.

A life without me.

An unpleasant ball of…meh…curdled in my stomach. I ignored it.

We arrived to Kade's house. I waited outside while he changed from his Sunday suit into more casual clothing and readied our horse. Once finished, he helped me into a small, horse-drawn buggy, tucking a blanket around my legs as he apologized for the fact that his parents had taken the more spacious family carriage.

The space was tight. Once Kade took his seat, I was hyper aware of his right arm and leg pressed against me, his body heat managing to seep through all of my layers.

The ride was quiet for the first few minutes, each of us deep in our own thoughts.

Kade was the first to speak. "What was I like as a ghost?"

I glanced over at him, surprised. I had assumed conversations about ghost-him were off limits, given they were coming dangerously close to talking about a topic no one wanted to think about: his death.

"You were…" I searched for words, "confused, but still confident. Cocky, even. Like, you didn't really know what was going on, but somehow you seemed okay with that."

He tilted his head. "Being a ghost sounds very unsettling. I'm surprised I was comfortable with it."

"Well, you didn't really know you were a ghost. Most of the time you thought you were dreaming. It was weird.

Like you had some kind of filter preventing you from seeing the whole picture of what was actually happening to you."

"Was my personality the same?"

I considered that. "Yes and no. As a ghost, you were more obnoxious, and playful. Again, I think that filter-thing kept you from taking things too seriously. But…" I trailed off, my heart feeling a small pang. "I got used to having you around. It felt…empty…when you were no longer there, pestering me."

"Did you…" he gave me a sidelong look and trailed off.

"Did I what?"

"Did you have feelings for me when I was a ghost?"

My heart fluttered. "Um…" I stammered. "Shouldn't we talk about our plan for saving Molly?"

He stared at me for a moment, then nodded. "Yes, we should."

Whew, dodged that bullet.

He flicked the reins, his mind already switching gears. "I think the best course of action is to arrive to the stables early, well before Molly is supposed to show up. I am hoping we catch the killer there before she is in any kind of danger."

I considered his idea. "But what do we do with him once we catch him?"

"What do you mean?"

"Do we tie him up? Torture him until he confesses his evil plan?"

Kade frowned.

"You see what I'm saying Kade. It's not like we can have him arrested when he has yet to commit a crime. And we're obviously not the torturing type."

He pursed his lips. "Hmmm."

300

"Instead of showing up at the stables," I said, "what if we simply stop Molly from going there in the first place? I'm sure as her fiancé you can cancel your date today. Fake a migraine or something. I would have suggested this idea before, but I was worried it would only postpone Molly's death. Like, if she doesn't show up to the stables today, the killer will still be running around loose and might murder her on a different day." I took a deep breath. "But at this point in time, we're running out of options, and this seems like the safest one."

Staring ahead at the road, Kade's knuckles tightened around the reins. "It's a legitimate plan, except for the fact I've no idea where Molly is."

"What? Isn't she home from church by now?" I thought about Taz and Stryder. Even when apart, they were constantly texting each other a play-by-play of their day. But I guess here, in 1886, you wouldn't have that dynamic.

"Molly was attending a luncheon and tea at an acquaintance's house after church today," Kade explained, "but she never told me which acquaintance."

"Can't you make an educated guess?" I asked. "How many friends can she possibly have?"

Kade pulled the left rein to gently guide our buggy before leveling me with a bemused stare. "She's a socialite, sweet girl. She has dozens and dozens of friends." He checked his pocket watch. "And unfortunately there is no way we have time to seek out each one."

"Ugh," I muttered. My back-up plan had always been to simply prevent Molly from going to the stables. I had even entertained the notion of tying her up, if it came to that. The fact that my reliable Plan B was now as useless as Madame Dresler's Preventative Powder left me feeling uneasy. "That means we have to do it your way and go to the stables."

His eyes darted over to me before returning back to the road. "Worry not, little one. The element of surprise gives me a big advantage. And if I do not confront Molly's killer tonight, it will be as you say; a murderer will remain on the loose. I need to resolve this now." He paused and leveled me with a gaze. "I will make sure no harm comes to you. I give you my word."

I tried to let his promise comfort me, but instead a heavy pit took residency in my stomach. I wasn't worried about being hurt. It was *his* fate I was worried about. And why did he keep saying *I* and *me*, instead of *we* and *us*?

Twenty minutes later, Kade steered our buggy around the backside of the Brodericks' property to avoid a possible confrontation with Mr. Broderick. It occurred to me that if Kade survived this week without getting hung—*which he will*, I insisted inwardly—he'll have to explain to Mr. Broderick why he was sneaking around with me in the thicket behind the church. *Not fun.*

My toes tingled at the thought of our kiss. *Let it go*, I told myself.

We rolled up near the stables.

"I'll be right back." I shimmied from the cramped space and dropped clumsily to the ground. "I'm going to sneak into the servants' quarters and change out of this horrible dress."

"Wait." Kade jumped from the buggy. I tried not to feel impatient as he walked over to my side. "Come with me to the stables where it is warmer, so we can talk a little more. I also want to look for something I can use as a weapon."

"A weapon?" I stared at him.

"Yes. It would be foolish to arrive to this situation unarmed. I need a tool to use against the killer in case things go awry."

He was right. And there were probably all sorts of sharp, pointy objects in the stables. I nodded my agreement, and Kade took my arm and guided me into the building.

Other than the peaceful nickering of the horses, the stable was quiet. Clementine's stall was empty, I noted, so the pretty gray-speckled mare must be out for a ride.

Kade gazed at me, his expression troubled. "I must tell you something I previously had no intention of disclosing. But I have decided I can not betray you the way I had planned."

"Betray me?" I asked, unable to hide my unease. "What's wrong?"

He removed a bunch of leather cords from a nearby hook, wringing them absently within his hands. "I am proceeding to the McCleran Stables without you."

"What? No you're not."

"You are staying here. Molly is already in danger, and there is nothing I can do about that other than try my damndest to catch her killer before he fulfills his intentions. But I refuse to put you in harm's way. I previously intended to drive off in the buggy while you were inside the Brodericks' home changing your dress, but it feels too cruel. After everything you have done for me, I can not leave you without telling you goodb—"

"You're not going without me," I interrupted icily.

"Aviva, please, listen carefully. Once I leave, I need you to stay away from Mr. Broderick. Do not trust him. Especially with these latest developments. If you must go near him, be sure that Mrs. Broderick or one of the other servants is nearby. Do not put yourself into a situation where you can be caught alone—"

"You're not going without me!" I repeated, louder this time.

"Yes, I am."

"The hell you are," I bit out. "I followed you to this century for this reason. To save Molly. And to save you. If you leave without me, I'll figure out a way to follow you. I'll saddle up one of these damn horses myself if I have to."

Kade sighed. "I feared you might say that." His face hardened. Before I could comprehend what he was doing, he lunged forward and grabbed my wrists, yanking me against his body. I shrieked and struggled in his arms, but he easily overpowered me with his vice-like hold, forcing me down onto the wooden stool.

"Quiet, Aviva," he ordered, pressing his hand against my mouth, his other arm securing my body against his own. My spine ground painfully against the small wooden back of the chair. "You must know I intend you no harm."

I shook my head back and forth, ignoring his command as I shrieked and bit into the flesh of his palm. Sighing, he pulled his hand away and, using the leather cords he had been playing with earlier, pulled my arms behind me and strapped my wrists to the back of the chair with smooth efficiency. I continued to scream my head off and kick at him.

Without saying a word, he yanked a rag from a nearby shelf and tied it around my mouth. It tasted grimy, like ash and grease. I tried to spit it out, but it was too tight.

With silent precision, he caught my flailing feet beneath my skirts and bound my ankles together with the straps and tied them, also, to the stool.

"Forgive me," he stood, towering over me, not sounding sorry at all. "I do not care for handling you in such a brusque manner, sweet girl, but you have given me little choice. You may have come here from another century, but this was never your fight. I only want to protect you, but you are too stubborn to stay out of this."

I glared at him with as much hatred as I could muster and lashed against the leather straps, my screams now muffled and pointless beneath the filthy rag.

"Before I leave, I need to tell you…." His eyes, as deep as the ocean, penetrated mine. "Aviva, regardless of what happens tonight, I have decided to break off my engagement with Molly. It is not fair to either one of us to go through this sham of a marriage when we clearly do not love each other."

Curious, I stopped struggling against the leather straps to listen to his words.

"And it is even more dishonorable to make a vow to love, honor, and cherish her when, in fact, I love, honor, and cherish…" he stopped and looked away. "…someone else."

Despite the cords digging into my wrists and the oily rag in my mouth, I felt my knees turn to water at his words.

Was that someone else me?

His eyes returned to mine, assessing. "It matters not that this someone else and I are star-crossed. That we can never be. The fact that I feel what I feel about her means I would enter into a marriage contract having already betrayed my new bride. Unfaithfulness with your heart is still unfaithfulness."

I stared at him soundlessly, my body trembling, knowing any words I tried to say would be muffled and indecipherable against the rag.

"I am telling you this, my sweet, clever girl, so you will leave this place knowing that I tried to be an honorable man. I will do everything in my power to save Molly—not because I love her, but because I care about her, and because if something happens to her I will never be able to live with myself knowing that I could have prevented her from harm. I know you loathe me right now, but I also know you are intelligent enough to understand I am doing this for the right reasons. I want you to go back into your clocktower with the knowledge that, not only did I do what is right for the women with whom I do not love, but I also did what is right for the one I do."

Did he just confess that he loves me? My mind frantically replayed his words, but it was hard to focus with my pulse racing.

He stepped out of my line of vision, then came back a minute later with a heavy woven blanket that I could only assume was used to keep saddles from chaffing the horses. He crouched down before me and wrapped the blanket around my shivering body, his face mere inches from mine. My body froze as his eyes pinned me with his dark gaze. He reached forward and grazed my cheek, his fingers caressing me softly until they worked their way up into my tangled hair. Fire raced across my skin. He leaned in and whispered, "I should love to rip this gag from your mouth, little one, and kiss you like there is no tomorrow." His hot breath grazed the sensitive flesh of my ear, sending goosebumps racing up the nape of my neck. "It is good," he continued, his voice low and husky, "that you made me vow to refrain." He pulled back, his deep gaze roving across my face, then back to my eyes. He let out a tortured groan and, without another word, turned around and left.

My heart was drumming a frantic beat, and blood roared in my ears.

He loves me. The words pounded over and over again in my brain, reaching a lunatic's pitch.

He never saw the tear trickle down my cheek.

And because of that damn nasty rag pressed into my mouth, he never heard me say the words, Kade. *I love you, too.*

Twenty-Nine

January 17, 1886

TEN MINUTES WHEN you're tied to a chair feels like hours. I stopped fighting against the leather cords after the first three or four minutes, realizing the effort was doing nothing but rubbing off precious skin cells and leaving my wrists chaffed and burning. Instead, I focused my attention on listening to the soft sounds outside of the barn, straining to hear the tell-tell crunching of footsteps. My plan was, upon hearing footsteps, I would rock on the stool until I fell against the wall. I was hoping the big *thump* would cause someone to come investigate…without knocking me out.

That's your big plan? Fall against a wall and hope you don't knock yourself out?

Okay, maybe it wasn't the best idea, but it was all I had.

What if no one ever came by? My mind railed. What if I was stuck here all night and Molly was murdered and Kade was arrested for the crime? Everything I had gone through would have been for nothing, and I would have to live forever with the knowledge that Kade is hung for a crime he didn't commit.

Or, what if Kade confronts the killer and gets murdered himself? I never saw him grab a weapon. I knew now that the whole weapon-thing was a ruse to get me into the barn. But did he still find something to defend himself with before he walked out?

Despite the blanket Kade had wrapped around me, a shudder ran through my body, causing my stool to wiggle. Operation Fall Against Wall might happen too early if I didn't calm myself down.

I need to get out of here. It was almost like I could hear Maui ticking all the way from town square. Each second brought me closer to Molly's murder. Each second brought me closer to Kade's death. Each second brought me closer to being trapped forever in this century. Was the rift even still open? If so, how much longer did I have before it sealed itself shut?

Don't panic.

I thought about my powers, before remembering they were useless here. And how would I use them anyway? Revive that half-dead moth over there and ask him to untie me? Even if Mr. Moth could help, I could only revive things by touching them, and my wrists were otherwise occupied right now.

Kade I love you but how I hate you I hate you I hate you…

A rhythmic clopping of hooves sounded near the barn. Hooves! It's go time!

Using the weight of my body to rock the stool, I inched myself closer to the wall.

The clattering hooves sounded louder, and were now paired with the soft thump of footsteps. I stopped. If

someone was actually coming into the stable, maybe I
didn't have to bang my head after all—

"Miss?"

I jolted in the chair, my eyes darting to the speaker.
Charlie! It was Charlie, escorting Clementine into the
stables. I felt a spike of fear. I still hadn't ruled Charlie out
as Molly's murderer.

But then it occurred to me that if Charlie was the killer,
he would be at the McCleran Stables—or at least on the
way—not here.

"Help!" I shouted. It came out as a muffled
"Hmmphhh!"

He dropped Clementine's reins and ran forward, yanking
the blanket from my body and the rag from my face. "Sakes
alive! What in tarnations are you doin'?"

I inhaled a deep breath and shot him a venomous look.
"You think I tied *myself* up?"

He looked at me in bewilderment. Shaking his head, he
scurried behind me to unbind my wrists. "Blazes, these are
too tight." He fumbled around behind me, and then I felt
the pressure of the cords being sawed through with a knife.
I held my breath, hoping he wouldn't slip and cut *me*, but
still wanting him to hurry. Once my wrists were free,
Charlie untied my ankles. I jumped from the stool, pausing
for a moment to rub my chaffed wrist.

"Who in Sam Hill done this to you?" Charlie demanded.
"You need to tell Mr. Broderick."

"It was Kade," I said, feeling out of breath, my words
coming out in a panic. "Please Charlie, saddle up a horse. I
don't have time to explain. Molly's in trouble. I'm going to
sneak into the house to grab…something."

His face clouded with red, but the desperate tone in my

voice must have set him in motion. "Take Clementine," he said. "She just came back from a ride, so she's saddled and ready to go." His paused. "Mr. Kade Oaks done this to you?"

I heard the judgement creep into his voice. "It's not like that. Kade's a good guy. Where's the McCleran Stables?"

Charlie gave me the quickest route. With a little luck I could actually beat Kade there, since he was stuck traveling at a slower pace in the wagon. I ran toward the gray-speckled mare waiting at the entrance of the stable. Thank God for those horseback riding lessons Dad and Daphne had surprised me with for my eleventh birthday.

"Any special instructions for riding her?" I asked Charlie in a rush.

"Nope, just the usual," he said. "Tap 'er with your heels to start movin'. Flick both reins to go faster; pull back to heel. To turn left, pull back all gentle-like on the rein in yer left hand. Same fer right."

I stepped onto the stirrup and clumsily swung my leg over Clementine's back, bunching the skirts of my dress into my crotch. No way I was riding side-saddle the way Molly did. "Do you want to come with me?" I asked. "I could probably use the help."

Fear flickered in his eyes. "Mr. Broderick will tan my hide if I don't start cleanin' these stables."

I didn't bother telling him that Mr. Broderick might be too busy burying his daughter's body to worry about the stables. What a coward, I thought. Charlie proclaims to love Molly, gets angry when he hears Kade is involved, but when push comes to shove, he refuses to risk his life for the woman he loves.

"Er, Miss Aviva?" he said as I turned the horse around.

"What? I'm in a hurry."

"Did you ever think that Mr. Kade Oaks might be the one to hurt Molly?"

I leveled him with a stare. "I have to go." I kicked my heels into Clementine's massive sides, steering her toward the house. We stopped behind the servants' outhouse.

"I'll be right back, Clementine," I told her, patting her large neck. The horse nickered her response as I dismounted.

I wished I had time to change out of my church clothes, but there was no way I could take the chance. Not only might I run into someone on my way to the servants' quarters, but the time it would take me to get out of this ridiculous dress might get Molly killed.

No, I was going inside the house to find a weapon. Kade might have the strength to use a horseshoe or some other tool to bludgeon a bad guy, but I needed something a little more reliable.

Once inside the house, I crept through the back corridors toward the kitchen. I found Ruby there, turning over a quail on a large tray. She looked up and grinned as I stepped inside. "How do ye, Vivvy-girl?"

"Hi Ruby!" I said brightly. I flung open drawers until I found what I was looking for. A large knife.

A mystified look crossed over Ruby's face. "What in tar —?"

"Bye Ruby!" I waved the knife at her and shot out the door before she could ask any questions.

I stuck to the servants' corridors again as I edged toward the back of the house, hoping to avoid any of the Brodericks. An idea struck me. Something I had spotted a few days ago in the Brodericks' parlor. I retraced my steps, passing the kitchen, dining room, and study. I took a deep breath, knowing I'd be fully exposed once I entered the parlor. Before I lost my nerve, I stepped into the space. I saw what I was looking for sitting on a dark, mahogany mantle.

The Oak Box Camera. Kade's prototype. It looked like the one Mr. Oaks had shown me in his studio, but slightly larger, and not as clean.

So easy to use that "anyone can be a photographer."

Man, I hoped that slogan was true, because this beast was a lot more to handle than my cellphone camera app.

I grabbed the camera and pulled the long strap over my head and shoulder, securing it to my body. A voice sounded from nearby, followed by another. Then the thump of footsteps. Oh no! Feeling like I might explode with nerves, I ran from the parlor, the knife clutched in my sweaty fist, blowing past the study, dining room, and kitchen, through the servants' corridors, and out into the backyard. I didn't stop running until I reached Clementine, who was still waiting for me behind the outhouse. I mounted her in a chaotic flurry of sage green ruffles.

"Let's go, Clementine!" She twitched her ear at me. I dug my heels into her flanks and flicked the reins, and Clementine lurched forward into a gallop. My stomach was in my throat as she and I flew like the wind across the valley.

The air, already cold before I had mounted Clementine, was positively frigid now, whipping against my arms and face, chapping my lips and stinging my eyes. The scenery passed by me in a blur. I was unsure of how much time I spent tied to a chair, but based on the position of the sun, it was getting late.

Too late? With the shorter winter days and gloomy clouds gathering in the distance, it was hard to tell if it was late afternoon, or early evening. "Come on Clementine," I urged, though I knew I couldn't make the poor horse run any faster.

A dark blur in the distance captured my attention. From this distance it looked to be a carriage or wagon blocking the road. Trotting closer, I realized it looked like the same horse-drawn buggy I had ridden with Kade. My ears tuned to the sound of voices. Not wanting to be spotted, I yanked Clementine's reins to the right and we detoured into the trees.

I inched Clementine forward through the wild roughage parallel to the road, until we were lined up with the buggy. The voices sounded louder now. I peered through the scraggly tree branches and saw two men arguing.

It was Kade and his father. An untethered tawny mare stood next his dad; he must have been riding that horse when he came across Kade on the road. Ignoring my hammering pulse, I strained my ears to hear what they were discussing.

"….the disgrace you have brought upon our family! Do not try to deny that you were cavorting with that blowsabella, given that Mr. Broderick saw it with his own two eyes."

"I am not denying anything, Father. I simply do not have time to discuss this right now. I must attend to Molly—"

"Liar. You are hurrying off to be with that hedge whore."

I clasped my hand over my mouth.

Kade's next words came out in a low growl. "Call Aviva that again, Father, and I will not be responsible for my actions. Now step aside so I can save my intended."

The two stared each other down, both of them with clenched fists. Finally, Mr. Oaks broke the contact and unhitched the horse holding Kade's buggy.

"What are you doing?" Kade said quietly.

"Go," Mr. Oaks said. "Go be with your servant girl. But you are no longer welcome in my house. And you are no longer entitled to the use of my horses."

"Bloody hell." Kade stepped toward Mr. Oaks. "Do not make me take that horse by force, Father."

Mr. Oaks flipped his suit jacket open, then quickly closed it. I couldn't see what he had flashed at Kade, but Kade took a step back.

"Very well," Kade's deep voice barely controlled his anger. "Take the blasted horse. You will not stop me."

With that, Kade turned away from Mr. Oaks and stalked down the road.

My head spun dizzily. I fought the urge to trot after Kade and rescue him. Now we could save Molly together!

But…no, I thought. He had tied me up in the barn to prevent me from being involved. If I went over there to help him, he'd steal my horse and leave me behind. I already learned the hard way that Kade had no problem manhandling a girl if he thought it would keep her safe.

On the other hand, with him horseless, stuck sprinting alongside the road (and no hope of Uber giving him a ride), he wouldn't make it to the stables in time to be framed for Molly's murder. It was perfect. Without even trying, I had affected the future. In the original timeline, Mr. Oaks never stopped Kade on the road to argue about me, because I didn't exist in that world. But in this version of history, Mr. Oaks had probably saved his son's life.

My gut lurched with longing as I forced myself to steer

Clementine back through the woods to bypass Kade. If I didn't move now, I knew that I'd forget everything, and I'd be a weepy thing running into his arms.

Sorry Kade, my thoughts whispered. *You left me for my own protection, and now I'm doing the same.*

"Yah!" I commanded Clementine, bringing her to the fastest trot I could manage to navigate through these brambly backwoods.

I tried to ignore the sinking feeling that followed me through the austere trees. *You did the right thing*, my head reasoned. You saved Kade. Now you're going to save Molly. It's what you came here to do.

If only I could convince my heart.

Thirty

*A chill swept through the air,
the sort of graveyard kiss promising
bad news to follow.*
Katherine McIntyre

Monday, April 1
Present Day

DAD AND DAPHNE were still sipping coffee when Krystal came downstairs. They stared up at her vacantly as she approached the kitchen table.

Krystal plopped down in one of the chairs. "What would cause a mother bird to kill her own babies?"

Daphne's eyes widened at the question. "Is that why you brought in that baby bird?"

"Yeah," Krystal said. "The mom was pecking it to death. Her other baby was already dead. Aren't mama birds supposed to protect their babies? Why did this one go all psycho on hers?"

Dad looked thoughtful. "During one of my lifetimes, we raised carrier pigeons when I was a kid. I remember one year we had a false spring. The weather was unseasonably warm for a few weeks, despite it technically still being winter. One of our pigeons, fooled by the warm spring-like weather, laid eggs and hatched babies."

Krystal pulled at a thread on her sleeve. "What does that have to do with anything?"

"Because when winter finally came back to reclaim its throne, the new mother bird pecked her babies to death. I don't think she was being 'psycho.' It's just something that happens in nature. She instinctively knew that she could never provide enough food and warmth for her babies in winter, so she took care of the problem."

"That's horrible," Krystal said.

"A lot of horrible things happen nature," her dad said. "And though each one is a crude, ugly thread, together they weave the beautiful fabric of life."

Krystal blinked. "Dad, what the heck are you talking about?"

Her dad sighed. "I'm simply saying your dove laid her eggs while it was still warm, but this sudden cold spell probably has her thinking that she made a mistake—that winter's back—so she decided to kill her babies to prevent them from dying later of starvation."

"Oh. Okay, I guess. But it's still seems wrong. Can you imagine if my mother Themis had decided to slaughter me simply because I was born in the wrong season?"

Daphne and Dad gasped, mouths dropped open.

"Sorry," Krystal said. "That was my way of letting you know I know the truth."

Dad squirmed. He always got squirmy whenever she mentioned her biological mother, which happened more often than it should because, unlike her sisters, Krystal had no memories of her mother and was darkly obsessed with the topic. But this last comment from Krystal had taken the cake.

"What exactly do you know?" Dad hedged.

"I know Themis is my real mother." She glanced at Daphne, realizing how thoughtless her words were. "Sorry. My biological mother," she clarified. "I know that Gaia is my grandmother. She's Mother Nature. I know that me and my sisters make up the *Horae*. What I don't know is, why'd you keep all this a secret Dad?"

His eyes were dim and rimmed with red. "To protect you."

"From what?"

"From everything that the Internet can't tell you. I never wanted you to know how your mother…died."

"You've always said she died in a boating accident."

"Yes, I did. But that's not the truth. Your Uncle Kiel invented that story on the spur of the moment many years ago when we were staying at his beach house. Little Phee was asking questions, and the lie just rolled right off his tongue. I think being a manipulator of outcomes makes it easier for him to lie."

Krystal was stunned. Her entire childhood felt like it was unraveling before her. Was there anything real about her life?

"So how did my mother die?"

He ran his hands down his weary face. "I can't talk about that right now. It's…complicated. We need to focus on saving your sisters. We're running out of time."

"Is the rift closing?"

"The rift seems to be holding. For now."

"So why are we running out of time?"

He gazed at her with watery eyes, his cheekbones looking hallowed.

She thought about the bizarre chill this morning. "Is it

something to do with the weather?"

Dad coughed, took a long sip of his coffee, then set his mug down.

"Oh my God, I'm causing this, aren't I?"

"Yes," he said hoarsely.

Her stomach dropped. "How do I stop it?"

"You can't," Daphne said. "Your sisters powers are neutralized in the past, leaving only yours in the present."

"I don't understand. I'm not using my powers right now." Krystal knew this for sure, because she always felt fuzzy or tired after freezing things.

"The *Horae* have both active and passive powers," her dad explained. "Your active powers are the ones you consciously use, like when Aviva revived that dove, or when you froze my goldfish. Your passive powers, on the other hand, require no deliberate choice on your part to activate. Much like a heart beats without any conscious effort, your passive powers work like an involuntary muscle, doing the same. As long as you are alive, they are always 'running' in the background. You can't turn them off."

Krystal was beyond feeling surprised. Every time she thought she finally knew everything about herself, another revelation was dropped. She adjusted quickly to this new development. "So what exactly is my passive power?"

He looked at her as if she were dense. "You're winter."

"I already know that," Krystal grumbled.

Daphne offered a better explanation. "You and your sisters are each the embodiment of a season, so your passive powers work together to maintain the seasons in our world: summer, winter, spring and fall. Phee's powers bring warmth, while yours bring cold. Sixteen is generally the age of full-power acquisition and mastery. Right now it's

Spring's season, and Aviva, finally of age, was doing a fine job compelling leaves to bud and flowers to bloom, without even realizing she was doing it. But now, with your sisters' powers neutralized in the past, all we're left with is winter."

"Not just winter," her dad's voice was full of gravel. "Winter when it's not Winter's turn. Winter unchecked by any other seasons. Winter that is still young, unstable, unactualized…."

"A winter the likes we've never seen before in this lifetime," Daphne summed up.

"An ice age," Krystal whispered.

Her dad, his stare frozen onto some distant thing only he could see, nodded. "The ice is coming."

Thirty-One

I'll be the blood
if you'll be the bones
I'm giving you all
Of Monsters and Men

January 17, 1886

THE STABLES WERE not what I expected. I had
imagined an old, dilapidated building, like a haunted
house...with horses. This was, after all, supposed to be the
setting for a murder. Instead I was greeted by a large,
cheery structure, freshly-painted red with gleaming white
trim. A large hand-painted sign on the front of the building
pronounced "McCleran Stables" in bold, black letters. A
few small outhouses—equally as charming—were scattered
across the property, but otherwise there were no homes as
far as my eyes could see. I pulled my homespun glasses off
my face—they were covered with dust and film due to my
crazy horseback ride—and wiped them off the best I could
with my skirts.

"Okay, this isn't so bad," I told Clementine, cramming
the glasses back onto my face. Swallowing hard, I guided
her through the large double doors in the front of the

stables. After her long ride, I'm sure she was ready for some water and rest.

The inside of the building was the complete opposite of the outside, gloomy and damp, with dirty sunlight slanting in through gaps in the wood. Much more befitting for a murder. Stepping deeper into the building, I spotted an opening two stalls down. I led Clementine into the stall and guided her to a trough half-full of water, then tried to decide where to go next. I wanted to hide somewhere and wait for Molly's killer, but I had no idea which direction he would come from. Would he enter through the front of the barn? How long would I have to wait? I wished I had a way to tell the time. A watch. A sundial. Anything.

If it was Mr. Broderick, maybe I could talk some sense into him. I had, after all, convinced him to calm down once before, that one time in front of Molly's bedroom. Something about my speech seemed to get him to pause. Maybe I could use that to my advantage.

What sounded like voices niggled at my ears, and I caught my breath. I strained to listen.

Nothing. Was I just hearing things? Or maybe a stable hand was making his rounds?

I squeezed the kitchen knife, reassuring myself it was still there.

I padded past a few stalls. Something rustled to my left. I yelped and jumped back. Two chestnut mares nickered softly, looking at me with soft brown eyes as if they were amused by my reaction.

Get it together, Aviva. I chided myself. I fought to grip my knife, which was now slippery in my sweaty palms, and turned down the right corridor. The Oak Box camera—the strap designed for a much taller person—was sliding and banging heavily against my groin. Annoyed, I yanked the strap off and hung it on my shoulder like a purse.

Someone screamed.

The sound was so muffled at first that I barely comprehended it. Was it the whinny of a horse? But then a shred of it escaped from whatever had it smothered, and for a split second it was piercing. My blood turned to ice.

Move, I inwardly screamed. *Move now*!

I leapt forward, running toward the direction of the bloodcurdling sound. The building was one giant U-shape, and my stomach sank with dismay when I realized I was on the wrong side of the stables.

It's too late, the thought pressed into me, squeezing my chest, immobilizing me. I got here too late. Molly's going to die.

By sheer will, I forced myself to round the corner. Molly was crouched against a wood-planked wall in front of an empty horse stall, her red-splattered arms held above her head. A man—his broad back facing me—lifted a knife and plunged it into her chest. One final, gurgled scream escaped her lips as a stream of blood poured from her ruby mouth. She collapsed to the ground, her head hitting the dirt with a thud. A frozen gaze migrated across her eyes.

The shock of my failure hit me in violent waves. This couldn't be happening. I was supposed to save Molly. I couldn't be watching her die. Bile forced its way up my throat. I heaved, nearly dropping the camera. Realizing my mistake almost instantly, I scrambled to regain my grip on the sweat-slicked box as I swallowed down my vomit.

Mr. Broderick, his back still facing me, kneeled down in front of Molly and used his finger to trace something in the dirt, directly over her head.

My temples pounded. Snap a picture. Then *run!*

Terror clawed over me as I aimed the viewfinder on the grisly scene in front of me, positioning my finger over the button.

He turned around, the bloody knife still in his hand. "Hello, Miss Aviva." His smile was warm, his tone friendly, as if we were merely bumping into each other at church.

It was Mr. Broderick, alright. But not the Mr. Broderick I was expecting.

The camera slipped from my hands. I watched, mesmerized, as it hit the floor, the shutter clicking right before it smashed into pieces.

"William," I croaked. I took an involuntary step back. I clutched the knife inside the folds of my dress. "It can't be you."

He stepped forward, his smile still warm, but his hazel eyes strange and cold. "Are you not happy to see me? I assumed you were smitten with me like the other servants."

I took another step backwards, my senses searching for the empty space behind me where I might swing around and escape.

"You will not outrun me, angel," he said, seeming to read my thoughts. "My legs are much longer than yours."

Ice burrowed sickly into my stomach. My muscles tensed to spring away from him, but sensing my intentions, he lunged for me. I yelped and spun away. He barreled into me before I could get three steps away, body-slamming me. My glasses were knocked from my face, and the knife slipped from my hands, clinking to the ground before being pinned underneath my body. Had he heard it?

I screamed as he rolled me onto my back. He grabbed a fistful of my hair, yanked my head up, and brutally ground his other hand into my mouth to silence me. The damned dress tangled around me, its heavy fabric trapping my legs.

I wondered for a split second why he hadn't killed me yet.

His knife. He had dropped it when he lunged for me. He would either have to let me go to grab it, or drag me over to where it lay. Either option might give me enough time to grab my knife, if I could only reach it.

"If you're thinking about escaping, love," he whispered, as if reading my mind again, "I can kill you quite easily with my bare hands." To demonstrate, he released my mouth and wrapped his large hand around my throat. Then he started squeezing.

Feeling my air supply cut off sent me into a panic. Every cell within me screamed bloody murder as I pushed and flailed with the frenzy of a wild animal caught in a trap.

My mind flashed to a memory. I was six years old, vacationing with my family at the beach. Phee badgered me into going further into the frothy blue waters than I had ever gone before. I was about chest-deep when a powerful wave crashed over me. When it receded, I could no longer reach the ground with my toes. Angry water rushed over my head, and I tried kicking to the surface, but I was stuck in some kind of riptide, and I couldn't tell up from down.

I was reliving that terror now—desperately searching to break through an unseen barrier, dark salty waters swirling around me, confusing my senses, my lungs building with explosive pressure as I tried to pull in air…

Gray spots crept into my vision.

Oh my God. I'm going to die. I looked over to my left, where I could see Molly's vacant, frozen expression. Soon I would join her.

Phee had been the one to pull me from the riptide. She

was pissed, and had yelled at me as I sat sputtering and coughing up water on the warm sand, telling me I was a "big baby" and ordering me to "Learn to swim, already!" But as she turned to storm away, I saw something else in her eyes. Fear. And shame. I knew in that moment that Phee had been scared for my life, and felt guilty for convincing me to go that far into the water. Lashing out at me was her defense mechanism. She wasn't mad at me; she was mad at herself. We never spoke about the incident after that.

And now I would never see her again. Or sweet, moody Krystal. Or smart, level-headed Taz.

I'm going to die. And I couldn't even tell my family goodbye. My sisters were probably crazy with worry, and I had no way of telling them how much I loved them. Tears stormed my eyes as I grew lightheaded.

"Shhh. It's okay, angel." William released my throat and shifted his weight so he was straddling me. He pinned my wrists painfully over my head in a vice-like grip. "I'm not ready to kill you. I should love to talk to you, actually. Does that sound agreeable? If you so much as whimper, however, I will of course have to strangle you. Understand?"

I could feel the tears streaming as I nodded, gasping for air.

"Good." His eyes roved over my face. "You are a curious little thing. Why did you come here this evening?"

I stared at him, my vocal cords paralyzed with fear.

His eyes darkened. "My time is limited here, angel. Either answer me or my business with you is concluded."

I swallowed the thick glue-like saliva that had wedged itself in my throat. "I knew someone was going to try to kill Molly," my voice came out in a whispered croak, my vocal

327

cords still recovering from being squeezed. "I wanted to stop them."

William narrowed his eyes. "And how could you possibly know that? I never shared my intentions with anyone."

"How can it be you, William?" I whispered, changing the subject, knowing there was no way he'd believe I was from the future. He might kill me on the spot if I brought it up, thinking I was messing with him. "Why did you kill her? Molly's your sister! I don't understand. You can't be a murderer. You just can't. You've been so kind to me. I really liked you."

"Flattery will not save you, love." He paused. "But I suppose I may as well tell you, since my secret will die with you soon. I do enjoy conversing with someone of your divinity."

A shiver wracked through my body. My *divinity*? Is this because, like Charlie, he thought I was a diviner?

"It is quite simple," he stated. "I escorted Molly here to the stables before she was scheduled to meet Kade so I could attempt one more time to talk some sense into her."

I squirmed under him, trying to find a position that would make it easier for me to breathe. Feeling my struggle, he pushed harder against me. I flinched as the knife wedged beneath my body dug further into my back. Thank God for the thick fabric of the dress, which I had been cursing earlier.

"Talk some sense into her…about what?" I managed to say.

He sighed. "About what she witnessed. Sadly my efforts did not work. She said she was going to tell our father, and I could not allow that. I would lose my entire inheritance. And do you know who would be awarded my share?" A bitter note edged his next words. "She and Kade."

"But Kade is your best friend, isn't he?"

"Yes, angel, he has been a dear friend in the strictest sense of the word. But it has become such a nuisance in my life, the way my father fawns over him. 'Why are you not talented like Thurston's son?' Father says. Or, 'Why do you not have Kade's business prowess?' It matters not to me. I am an aristocrat. I come from money; I do not need to work. But Father has never understood this. And if my dear sister decided to tell our father what she witnessed, I would be written out of his will. As if it was not enough that the lowlife Oaks family was getting half of my father's business. Now they would get his entire fortune."

My heart was in my throat. "What did Molly witness?"

"Ahhh, yes. I had relations with our housemaid." He gazed at me darkly. "Now, now, do not look so judgmental, love. I cared about Clair." His eyes softened for a moment before returning to their strange vacantness. "But then she went and got herself with child. I told her I would pay to take care of the problem. I know a specialist in Chicago. She refused. Sweet Clair was always a romantic. Obviously I could not allow her to give birth to our bastard child. It would ruin me. So I corrected the situation."

"By corrected it, you mean…?"

He tilted his head, his expression deceptively kind. "What do you think I mean, angel?"

Nausea coursed through my body in torrents.

"Shame, too, because Clair had a heart of gold. Though I can not lie, love. A euphoria came over me as I squeezed her slender throat. It was an ecstasy of the likes of which I have never experienced before. I felt like my body was rising to the stars. I did not understand it at the time, but I realized it later; it is because Clair was an angel. And I was the savior destined to send her delicate soul back to Heaven where she belonged."

I heaved beneath him, feeling sick. He was insane. Killing Clair had...what...*turned him on*? Fulfilled some kind of perceived divine purpose?

A frenzied excitement glittered across his dilated pupils. "The best part, love, is I soon realized there are more angels walking amongst men, each one waiting for me to send her back to Heaven. It is only through the pain I inflict upon their earthly bodies that their souls rise to glory in their ethereal form."

What? I vibrated with fear. William had started off sounding so rational, even for a murdering lunatic. But he had officially stepped onto the crazy-train and was dragging me along for the ride.

"Is Molly an angel?" I breathed.

"Sadly, no, though I have marked her as such, simply to honor the life of my dear sister. Angels have a soft aura around them, nearly impossible to see, but I have been blessed with the Sight."

I looked over again at Molly's lifeless body. That's when I noticed it. The circle he had traced over her head in the dirt.

A halo.

A cold awareness spread through me. "You're the Angel Killer."

He looked at me questioningly, and I realized that at this point in history, he had not yet been given that title. "Not a killer, love. If you must give me a name, Angel Deliverer is more accurate."

Fear squeezed me like a vice. William was the Angel

Killer. Authorities in this time period had never connected Molly's death to the Angel serial case, probably because Molly's halo was barely noticeable, scratched into the ground the way it was. It would be easy to miss it if you weren't looking for it. But as history would show, William would switch over to drawing his victim's halos with charcoal, and eventually, with their own blood.

And Molly wasn't even the first! The first true victim of the Angel Killer's murdering spree was a poor unknown housemaid named Clair. Killed not because she had some kind of 'aura', but because she was pregnant with the Angel Killer's lovechild.

The worst part was history would never know. Because the one person who could enlighten them was about to be victim number three.

Keep him talking. Buy yourself more time. "Molly saw you kill Clair," I said. "And she was going to tell your father."

"More accurately, Molly 'heard' me bring Clair to absolution. She confronted me a few days after it happened. She became hysterical and threatened to divulge my secret." He shook his head. "Women."

I tried not to choke on my next words. "Don't you miss Clair?"

He laughed. "Oh precious angel, I was indeed fond of Clair. But I am over her now. I am presently quite smitten with another woman. Aurora."

"The one from Ireland? The one who was sick from her travels?" I asked.

"Yes. Presently she does not share my affection. But I believe that will change in time."

I would have feared for the life of this Aurora-person if I wasn't so scared for my own life at the moment.

Keep him talking. Just keep him talking long enough for Kade to get here….

I vehemently wished I hadn't left Kade behind on the road.

It was probably going to be the last thing I ever wished.

"By the time Kade arrives, I will be long gone," William continued, reading my mind again. "The sheriff will find Kade alone with Molly's dead body, and now, yours. Given the fact that the whole town is aware that Kade does not want to marry his betrothed, there will be enough evidence to damn the man."

I gaped at him, the depth of his premeditation shocking me. He wasn't just crazy. He was diabolical. "And you will have killed two birds with one stone," I finished for him. "Molly can no longer spill the truth about Clair, and Kade will be out of the picture, ensuring your inheritance is safe."

"I knew you would understand, angel." He brought his fingers close to my face, and I flinched, but he simply lifted a lock of my hair and rubbed it between his fingertips. "Now I need to bring you to absolution."

Horror clawed at my insides.

"Your aura was evident the moment I saw you, and even more pronounced with your unusual features. Your flaxen hair…" he trailed off, still massaging the lock between his fingers. "And your eyes. But it is your spirit that truly gives you away. It does not mingle with this world."

My temples pounded, and blood roared in my ears. If my heart wasn't banging in my chest in terror, I might have felt impressed that William was so damned perceptive. His rationale might be insane, but he *had* accurately picked up on the fact that I didn't belong in this century.

Maybe this same intuition would allow him to believe the

truth. The real truth.

"I'm not an angel," the words gushed from my lips in a panicked torrent. "Please, believe me. I'm from the twenty-first century, and I am far from an angel. I lie, I cuss, I wear clothes you'd consider scandalous, I think unholy things about cute boys…please William! That's why you sense a spirit in me that doesn't mesh with this world. I don't belong here."

He gazed down at me, his expression heated as his eyes roamed my body. "I should like to relieve you of that dress, love, and take my time with you. The more pain I inflict upon you, the higher your soul will elevate. Imagine how beautiful your naked flesh would look carved with my blade."

Cold, sick dread twisted through me.

"But sadly we do not have as much time as I would like. Kade is scheduled to arrive for a romantic horseback ride soon. I must guide you to actualization quickly."

"I'm not an angel! I'm just a girl in the wrong place at the wrong time!"

"The interesting thing about angels is they do not know they are angels." He yanked me up and pinned me against his body, twisting my arm behind my back. "Let us get on with it now, love."

My knife no longer trapped, I grazed it with the fingertips of my free hand and slid it into my palm. He drug me across the dirt toward an empty stall. Spotting his knife, he released my arm for a split second to grab it. I saw my opportunity. Tensing my muscles, I swung my arm forward, aiming my blade straight toward William's chest. Sensing my movement, he turned at the last second and twisted away. Instead of stabbing him in the chest, my blade glanced off his arm. Without a word he yanked the blade from me and threw it to the ground. He grabbed my neck, shaking me. Then he raised his knife.

"Get off her!" a deep voice roared.

William whipped around. I took advantage of his distraction by tearing the knife from his hand, slicing my own hand in the process. Before I could second-guess myself, I flipped the blade around and plunged it into William's shoulder blade. I knew it wasn't fatal and honestly I wanted to kill the bastard dead, but it was the only thing I could reach.

William howled in pain. Kade ran forward, his face contorted in rage, and ripped the madman off of me, punching him in the face with fists of steel and kicking him in the chest until he lay unmoving on the ground.

I crawled to my glasses a few yards away and plucked them from the dirt. I jammed them on my face, not even bothering to wipe them off. Then I struggled to stand. My dress was torn, my body was bruised, and my head felt like it had been battered by a baseball bat.

"Aviva! Oh Holy God." Kade's face looked drained of blood as he rushed over to me, grabbing my elbows and helping me stand. He pulled my quaking body into his arms and pressed my face against his chest.

My body sagged into his arms like a rag doll, and I let myself sob into his chest. I was out of 'tough' and I didn't care.

Thirty-Two

I wanted his words to make
my heart sing, but instead,
like the cold breath of a grave,
they cut into my very soul.
Aviva Aevos

January 17, 1886

I COULD HAVE stood there for hours letting Kade soothe me with his gentle touch and calming words, had the pounding of hooves not intruded. A gun blast ricocheted from the stable roof, the sound sending me jumping about a mile into the air.

"Back away from her!" a male voice ordered. I looked over to see a Texas Ranger charging into the space, pointing a pistol. Except for we weren't in Texas, so I guessed he must be the town sheriff. The dim light filtering through the wood slats highlighted the creases on his time worn face. His posse entered behind him, mounted on horses.

As if it caused him pain, Kade slid his hands from me and stepped back. He raised his arms. His eyes darted toward Molly. In all of the chaos, this must have been the first time he truly noticed her, as I saw the shock of her death roll through his body. He leaned over and heaved onto the ground. Wiping his mouth, he stood upright again, moisture fogging his eyes.

Keeping his gun trained on Kade, the sheriff stepped forward, grabbed my elbow and pulled me away.

"What are you doing?" I demanded, shaking my arm free.

"Miss, I need you to keep back," the sheriff warned. His posse surrounded Kade and drew down on him with rifles.

"No!" I yelled. "You have it wrong! He's innocent!" I lunged toward Kade, but the sheriff gripped me by the shoulders and yanked me against his chest, wrapping me in a reverse bear hug.

"Don't be gettin' hysterical, miss."

"I am NOT hysterical!" I stomped his foot as hard as I could with my boot.

He grunted, but did not loosen his hold. "Jim, Harry, restrain the girl."

I flailed and squirmed as two of the sheriff's cronies bound my wrists together. Once finished, the one called Harry lowered me to a seated position on the floor, next to the broken pieces of the Oak Box camera. "No more trouble from you now, Miss," he ordered, though his voice was kind. He pointed toward my sliced hand. "We'll get the doc to look at that."

I barely noticed my throbbing hand. My eyes wandered toward William, bruised and battered on the ground. I gasped when his finger twitched. Then his left foot jerked.

He was waking up. Even surrounded by lawmen, a chill seeped into my bones.

Kade, his own wrists now bound in front of him with

rope, leveled the sheriff with a murderous glare. "Sheriff Barlow, what the hell is the meaning of this?"

"I ain't gonna lie, this ain't easy for me. I've known you since you were ye' high," he held his hand level with his knee. "Hell, I know yer whole family. But I've gotta job to do. A witness heard a woman scream, and I come a'runnin' to see one girl dead and another man stabbed and beaten within an inch of his life. Yer the only one who's still standin', and by the looks of it you were about to drag yer next victim away—"

"I stabbed William," I interjected. "William tried to kill me, and I stabbed him. Kade came running in and defended me."

William was now hauling himself up into a seated position. He groaned and clutched his bleeding shoulder. His eyes darted around the room, seeming to assess the situation, until they landed on me. He held my gaze, his lips quirking into a faint smile.

A shiver rolled through me.

He glanced at the sheriff. "Sheriff Barlow, what's happening?" His voice was raw with emotion. Fake emotion. "Tell me it was all a dream." He trembled, making a show of standing on wobbly legs. "My sister. She isn't…she can't be—" His voice broke off, choked.

Damn, he was convincing.

"I'm sorry for yer loss, Will," the sheriff said gently. "I'm afraid there ain't nothin' we can do for your poor sis now. Can you tell me what happened?"

"He killed her." William shot a murderous glare at Kade and advanced forward a step, as if he was going to attack him in righteous rage. One of the sheriff's lawmen stepped near William and placed a warning hand on his arm.

"From the beginning," Sheriff Barlow prompted.

William glanced over at Molly's body, and a cry escaped his lips.

"This whole thing is an act!" I yelled from my corner on the ground. "He's the Angel Killer! Look at the halo drawn over his sister's head. If you don't arrest him, he'll keep killing! He'll kill fourteen more girls!" I knew I sounded like a maniac, but I didn't know what else to do. Other than Kade, who looked over at me with deep concern, everyone ignored me.

William pulled in some air, as if trying to compose himself. "My sister asked me to escort her to the McCleran Stables. She told me that she and Kade were having some troubles. They decided to go on a horseback ride together to work things out before their wedding."

Kade's eyes darkened, his muscles tense. "That's a lie. Molly and I were simply planning to enjoy each other's company. We never had any plans to discuss issues."

William pressed on, ignoring Kade. "When Molly and I arrived to the stables, Kade was already here. She asked me to leave so that she and Kade could talk privately. Under normal circumstances I would never leave my sister unchaperoned, but with their wedding right around the corner and the poor girl trying to make things right, I didn't see the harm." He sobbed and allowed his head to collapse into his hands. "I should have never left her alone."

The lawman standing next to William patted his shoulder, careful to avoid his injury.

Kade gaped at William. I felt sick.

"So I left. As I walked away, I overheard my sister and Kade break out into an argument. Molly accused Kade of cavorting with a servant girl, though I never heard the girl's name." His implication was clear as his eyes pinned me in my corner. "It was all very personal. Not wanting to intrude, I hurried out of the stables. The last thing I heard was Molly telling Kade that if he broke off their engagement, she would make sure he never saw one shilling from our father. Kade seemed angry. Once I was a short distance away, I heard screaming. I turned around and ran back into the stables. When I rounded the corner, Kade was plunging a knife into my sister's chest." He broke into sobs again.

"When did the girl enter the scene?" Sheriff Barlow asked, gesturing to me.

"I--" William's face contorted, his voice raspy. "I can't."

"I know this is rough on ya Will," the sheriff said, "but the more you tell us, the better we're able to bring justice to your sister."

William looked up into the room, tears streaming his cheeks.

I was stunned by his amazing performance, almost convinced that he believed his own story. Almost. That faint smile he had tossed my way as he had awakened told me he knew exactly what he was doing.

William lifted his head, looking around the room, as if trying to recall the information the sheriff had requested through his gut wrenching grief. "When I ran to save Molly, Kade turned the knife on me and stabbed me in the shoulder. I knocked it out of his hand, and he quite vigorously punched me in the face and kicked me to the ground." He paused. "I am ashamed to confess I was catawamptiously chewed up by him. I have failed my sister and my family."

The sheriff's patted William's shoulder again.

"The girl--she is our housemaid, Miss Aviva." His hazel gaze raked over me. "She ran into the stables—I have no clue why she was here—and saw Kade beating me. As I collapsed to the ground, I saw Kade run to her and throw his arms around her. He soothed her, telling her that he had attacked me because he had come upon me murdering my sister. Of course this was a lie. That is all I remember before everything went black."

"He's lying!" I was livid, my whole body shaking. "Everything he's telling you is a lie! He killed Molly, and he tried to kill me. I stabbed him in the shoulder, not Kade." I held up my bleeding hand. "Look, here is where his knife cut me when I tried to escape."

The sheriff shook his head, his lips pursed in concentration. "If you stabbed a man, miss, we're gonna have to take you in."

"I stabbed him," Kade said, his lips pressed together in determination.

"No you didn't Kade!" I cried. "Don't try to protect me!"

"I believe Miss Aviva is in love with Kade," William said in a steady voice. "It is the only thing that explains why she is covering for him." He scratched his head, and then his eyes widened as if a thought had just occurred to him. "Sheriff, I'd bet money that she's the servant Molly was talking about! The one Kade was cavorting with."

My mouth fell open. I pulled against my restraints, the bloodied slice on my hand burning at the motion.

It didn't matter—what did I think I would do if my hands were free?

"Are you sayin' she's an accessory to murder?" the sheriff asked.

340

"Not at all. I believe the girl is innocent. But I do believe she was under the impression that Kade was going to break off his engagement with my sister. Perhaps that is why she showed up to the stables this evening."

"It's not true," I said meekly, my heart dropping lower and lower. What else could I say? That I showed up to the stables because I was a time traveler who knew Molly was going to get murdered?

"I'll be honest with ya Will," the sheriff said. "There's a lot of sense in the story yer tellin'. But without more evidence, it's yer word against your servant girl and Mister Kade Oaks. I have to bring all of you in."

William nodded. "I understand, sir. I only want justice for my sister. You and I are on the same side."

"I'm glad you feel so. I take this to mean you will come with us willingly?"

"Of course." He walked over to the deputy, holding out his wrists to be tied.

The sheriff waved away the man. "I don't think the rope will be necessary."

Yet they thought rope was necessary for Kade, I mused. This wasn't looking good.

"Take 'em in, boys," the sheriff gestured toward Kade. "Harry, get the girl, and have Dr. Harrison dress her wounds, but don't let her out of your sight. Jim, grab that broken contraption," he nodded toward the camera pieces. The posse hauled Kade up onto one of the horses.

Harry took my wrists and pulled me to a stand. "No!" I cried. This couldn't be happening. I had come to 1886 to save Kade. But Molly was dead, and now Kade was being arrested for her murder. How could things have gone so wrong? "Kade is innocent! Please!"

Kade's eyes, burning with fury and dread, softened when they peered down at me. "All is well, sweet girl." His voice was quiet. "Everything will turn out for the best. The truth is on my side."

Lovely words, but I knew from past—or future— experience that the truth would not save him from hanging at the end of a rope. "I'm sorry, Kade," I said, my voice hoarse with emotion.

I failed him, but I couldn't tell him that. I also couldn't tell him that I would never stop trying; that before the sun even finished setting tonight, I would be working on a new plan to vindicate him.

But worst of all, I couldn't tell Kade that I loved him. Because that would cement his fate.

As if reading my mind, Kade uttered the words I would not say.

"I love you, Aviva."

I gasped. Harry and the sheriff whipped their heads around, wide-eyed, and stared at Kade. William's lips curved into a soft, satisfied smile.

"Kade, no…" I whispered. My head fell into my tied hands. I wanted his words to make my heart sing, but instead, like the cold breath of a grave, they cut into my very soul.

Because by admitting he loved me in front of all these people, he had just hammered that final nail into his own coffin.

"Thank you, Mr. Oaks," the sheriff said. "You've given us a motive for murdering your fiancé."

Thirty-Three

*A true friend is one who walks in
when the rest of the world walks out.*
Walter Winchell

January 21, 1886

KADE WOULD HANG today. The thought struck me like a semi truck and dragged me through the gutters of my own personal hell.

I sat on the small hard mattress in the Oaks' servants' quarters, hunched over the blue baby bootie knitted by Clair. Staring into some vacant space while kneading and grinding that bootie in my hand had taken up the better part of my day. I should be grateful for the small things. Like the fact that after hearing Kade's and William's testimonies, the sheriff released me, deciding I wasn't an accomplice to Molly's murder. Or the fact that Mrs. Oaks had hidden me in their tiny servant's quarters so I'd have a warm place to sleep, and was sneaking me food.

But it was getting harder and harder to appreciate the small things.

The court proceedings were a joke. What would have lasted for weeks in my time period was accomplished in a single day. The Brodericks hired an expensive lawyer—the best of the best--and the man ate Kade alive. Charlie, under oath, was forced to confess his illicit kiss with Molly, which gave the jury yet another motive for Kade murdering his fiancé.

But even more damaging was Mr. Broderick's testimony. After placing his hand on the Bible, William's father claimed to have seen me and Kade kissing behind the church. He looked straight at me while giving his account, his eyes shining with what I swear was glee.

I always knew that man had it in for me.

Afterwards, the prosecution called up a second witness, a gray-haired widow with shrewd eyes and a sharp tongue. She corroborated Mr. Broderick's testimony, saying that she, too, witnessed Kade and I being intimate behind the church. At this moment of the trial I wanted to jump up and scream "'Liars!" But I couldn't. Because everything they said was true.

The most damning evidence, of course, was submitted by Sheriff Barlow, who testified that Kade was heard professing his love to me in front of several witnesses.

By this time the jury knew two important things: One, Kade didn't want to marry Molly. Two, Kade claimed to love me. In my time period, all of this evidence would have been considered circumstantial. Fingerprints would be required, or DNA samples, or something more concrete. But modern forensics didn't exist in 1886. So for the jury, this was an open-and-shut case. Kade's family was forcing him to marry a woman who he didn't love, so he took matters into his own hands and killed her.

The jury deliberated for less than an hour before coming back with their guilty verdict. It took the judge less than two minutes to sentence Kade to the death penalty.

That was another big difference between Kade's time period and mine. In the twenty-first century, a prisoner can sit on death row for over ten years. But not here. Justice was swift in the 1800s. Kade was handed his sentence a mere two days ago, and his hanging was tonight.

"Miss Aviva, you have a visitor." Mrs. Oaks, her eyes rimmed with red, had a kind, but crestfallen, look on her face as she popped her head in the door. Kade's mother had been so compassionate and wonderful these past few days, but I knew she was going through her own personal hell right now with her son about to be hung tonight. Dealing with the stress of keeping me hidden from her husband couldn't be helping much, either. I couldn't fathom why she was being so kind to me when her husband couldn't stand me, but there was no way I could ever go back to the Brodericks, so I was grateful for her help. Maybe she sensed my feelings for her son, and that mattered to her.

I stuffed the bootie into my apron and stood. "Thanks, Mrs. Oaks."

Mrs. Oaks led me to the parlor where I assumed yet another one of the sheriff's cronies was waiting to ask me more questions. Though with the hanging scheduled tonight, shouldn't the interrogations be over?

Maybe it was the Sezona Valley Herald, wanting to do an interview for their newspaper. Wouldn't that be something. Returning back to present-day to find my own name in a newspaper from the 1800s.

But it was neither an investigator or a reporter waiting for me in the parlor. The girl's face broke out into a grin when she saw me, and she rushed forward to give me a hug.

"Ruby! What are you doing here?" I exclaimed, hugging her back.

She slapped me in the arm. "That's the greetin' I get?"

"Sorry. But you know what I mean."

"I talked Maude into doin' the cookin' today so I could see you. I stayed up late doin' all the prep work last night." She pulled back and examined me, her warm eyes shaded with concern. "Are you feelin' alright, Viv?"

"I—" my traitorous eyes formed tears, "I don't know."

"Oh no…don't start cryin' girl. You're tougher than that. If you start cryin', I'll cry too." She took my hand and pulled me to the lounge, where we both sat down. "You gotta tell me what happened. Everyone in the Brodericks' house has gone plumb crazy."

"Do you want the real version, or the version that makes me seem less insane?"

"What do you think?" She leveled me with a stare.

I stared back at her. Did my big secret really matter at this point? What else did I have to lose?

I took a deep breath. "I'm from the twenty-first century. I came to this time period to keep Marguerite Broderick from being murdered. I failed."

Her mouth gaped open.

For the next twenty minutes I regaled her with my crazy story. I told her about Kade visiting me in my time period as a ghost, the rift, my confrontation with William in the stables…I told her how William had killed Clair, then his own sister. I told her how he tried to kill me, and how he was now on a vendetta to kill "angels" and send them back to Heaven. I even told her about my powers.

She paled. "Sakes alive."

"Do you believe me?" I asked.

"I ain't sure." Her voice was shaky, and it occurred to me that for her to believe me, she'd be forced to acknowledge that she was living under the same roof as a psychopath. "Can you prove it?"

"How?"

"You said you had powers. Show me."

I sighed. "That's the thing. They don't work here in the past."

"That seems awfully convenient."

"Tell me about it," I huffed. "How about...you ask me anything you want to know about the future? I can tell you everything I know."

Ruby scrunched her dark brows together. "I ain't gotta clue what to ask."

Arghhh. I could see her point. How would people from this time period have even a small inkling of what they're missing? They can't wonder about things like flying cars or teleporters or machines that magically materialize food when they don't have even the basic versions of these ideas, like Jeeps or elevators or microwaves. Not to mention there's no sci-fi shows feeding them these fantasies.

I felt a small, heavy weight in the pocket of my apron. I reached in and pulled it out. "Here."

She took it and cradled it in her hand. "What's this?"

"It's a cellphone. I wish I could turn it on to show you how it works, but the battery's dead."

Ruby's eyes were lit with wonder. She gingerly touched the smudgy, black screen. "What's it do?"

"It lets me talk to anyone in the world. I can also take pictures with it, listen to music, play games...."

"You gotta be yankin' my chain. What yer describin' is magic."

"Not in my time period. We call it 'technology'. But yeah, for you guys, it really would seem like magic." I paused. "We also have cars in my time period—they're like carriages, but they move themselves forward with engines instead of horses. We have TVs that play movies--which are like moving pictures," I clarified when I saw her look of confusion. "It would be like watching your favorite play in the theater, but on a screen instead. And we have fast-food, and the Internet…." I trailed off, realizing I had no idea how to explain the future to someone who didn't even have a modern-day light switch. "Segregation is gone in my time period," I finally said.

"What does that mean?"

"It means, the color of your skin doesn't matter. You can sit anywhere you want in church. You can even run for president, if you want."

"A colored servant can run for president?" Disbelief was written all over her face.

"You wouldn't be a servant. You'd go to the same school as me, and with as smart as you are, you'd continue on to college to do whatever you wanted to do."

Ruby's eyes grew wide. "It sounds amazing."

"So you believe me, then?"

"Mayhap. Though I can't tell if it's only 'cause I want to believe you. Though…anyone can tell there's something peculiar 'bout you. You don't even talk right."

"Gee, thanks."

A grin spread across her face. "Didn't say I hate it. Though you'd be rather off-puttin' to some folks. Probably best for you to return to your own time, if your story is actually true and you ain't mad as hops. You'll be eaten alive here."

"Thanks again."

Her face smoothed over in thought. "Really, your story is too detailed for you to be pokin' bogey. And, now that I'm thinkin' it over…" she paused, her face darkening, "everything you said about Will Broderick rings true."

"Oh my God, Ruby," I grabbed her hand and clenched it. "You can't go back there! He's a serial killer!"

She raised her brows in question. "'Cereal' killer?"

"Yes, serial killer."

"Since you ain't from this time, you should know that 'cereal' is a grain that folks eat."

I rolled my eyes. "Not 'cereal' with a 'c'; I mean 'serial' with an 's'. And you guys seriously have cereal in this century? Like Cap'n Crunch and all that?"

She stared at me blankly. "Who's Captain Crunch?"

"Never mind. All I'm saying is that William will kill over and over again. It's an obsession, and he's not going to stop. What if he sees an aura around *you*? You'll be next on his hit list."

Ruby laughed. "I ain't no angel, Viv."

"Ruby. It doesn't matter. None of his victims are actually angels. He's a psychopath, looking for a reason to justify a sick addiction. The way he talked…I swear he gets off on causing pain."

She shivered, but covered it quickly. "I *have* to go back to the Brodericks. Don't matter if the whole family has lost its marbles. I'll starve if I don't."

At that moment I wished with a vengeance that I had the Internet so I could look up other victims of the Angel Killer. Was Ruby one of them? If she continues working for the Brodericks, will her life be in danger? I clenched her hands in my lap, staring at her, worry seeping through my pores. She was the one real friend I had in this century. The one person who liked me despite my twenty-first century weirdness. The one person who knew who I truly was and had accepted me.

I already failed Molly; I couldn't fail Ruby, too.

"Then we need to put an end to this. Today."

"How do we do that?"

"Are you off all day?"

She nodded. "I said to Maude if she did all my cookin', I would do all the launderin' for her on the morrow."

"Okay." I scrunched my nose, thinking. "What does this time period consider 'solid' evidence that someone is guilty?"

Ruby considered this. "Someone who saw the crime."

I frowned. "They already have a witness. Me. But no one believes me."

"'Course they don't believe you. Them Brodericks are big bugs 'round here, lining the sheriff's pockets. You ain't nothin' but a servant, and a foreigner at that."

I let that sink in. I never considered the fact that the town had nothing to lose by believing William, but a lot to lose by believing me. Whatever evidence I dragged up would have to be unarguable.

If only I hadn't dropped the Oak Box camera in the stables. There was a reason for the expression "A picture is worth a thousand words." A snapshot of William hovering over Molly, brandishing that knife, would be all the evidence I'd need. My heart sank all over again, remembering the way I had fumbled it in my hands, trying to snap a picture, and then watched, as if in slow motion, the box smash into pieces. All my hopes had smashed with it.

Out of nowhere, something clicked in my memory. Literally, *clicked*. Fresh hope zipped through me.

The camera. Right before it broke into pieces, it clicked. It had *clicked*!

Ruby was staring at me, seeming to notice the change in my mood.

"I'm going to break into the sheriff's department and steal a camera," I said.

She cocked her head at me, as if wondering for a few seconds if I was joking. "Alright. I'm comin' too."

I could hardly believe my ears. "Yeah?"

"Well someone's gotta keep you out of trouble."

In that moment I realized I had a truer friend in Ruby than I had ever had in any person from my own century. Though to be fair, Brett had never been given an opportunity to dive headfirst into a crime spree with me.

"But…" she said, interrupting my thoughts. "If we're gonna go breakin' into places, we need help."

"Who?" I asked.

Ruby's eyes drifted toward the ceiling, thinking. "We need someone who has ties with the sheriff. Someone who believes Kade is innocent."

I considered this. I thought about my conversations with Kade back when he was a ghost.

The time capsule.

His two closest friends had contributed to the time capsule with him. One turned out to be a killer. The other was…George. The Abe Lincoln look-alike with the kind eyes who had given me directions to the inn. The man who had boasted about his new prized horse during dinner at the Brodericks'. The man with a bullet in his butt.

Was it possible that George believed in Kade? Was it

possible that he was devastated that one of his best friends was getting hung tonight, and was searching for a way to vindicate him?

"Does George Henderson have any ties with the sheriff?" I asked.

Ruby's eyes lit up. "Pretty sure George's pa and the sheriff fought in the Civil War together."

My heart thumped with hope. "Let's go talk to him."

A LITTLE OVER an hour later, Ruby and I disembarked from our wagon and stood on the front porch of the stately colonial. My hand hovered over the door.

Peering over at Ruby, I could tell from the look on her face that she was nervous, too.

I swallowed and lifted the knocker, rapping it three times against the door. I took a breath, waiting for a servant—or maybe George himself—to greet us.

The door swung open. A servant's smock hung loosely on the thin frame of the figure on the other side of the door. My eyes traveled from her clothes, to her pale, ashen face. I gasped.

Ruby, alarmed, asked "What in tarnations, Viv?"

I rubbed my eyes, took a step back, and gasped again. Then I'm pretty sure I had a minor stroke.

The dim blue eyes staring back at me across the doorway mirrored my own shock and awe.

Breathing hard, I lunged through the doorway, tears storming my eyes. "Phee!"

Thirty-Four

*Sweet is the voice of a sister
in the season of sorrow.*
Benjamin Disraeli

January 21, 1886

PHEE AND I JUMPED in crazy circles, hugging each other. I knew I was missing my sisters, but I didn't realize how deeply the emotion cut until Phee was standing in front of me, in the flesh.

Phee's dark blonde hair was twisted into a greasy braid, with strands poking out in every direction. Her face was paler than usual, and her eyes, normally sharp, were duller —closer to slate than blue. She had also lost weight, her collar bone and elbows more pronounced on her thinner frame.

Didn't matter, she still looked beautiful. Clinging onto her, nothing could go wrong. Like the time she pulled me from the riptide, I was overwhelmed with the feeling that everything was going to be okay.

We finally calmed down and Phee, after being introduced to Ruby, guided us into the parlor. Ruby and I sat down on a stiff, formal sofa the color of Pepto-Bismol. Phee perched across from us in a wooden chair boasting a burgundy velvet cushion.

"What are you doing here?" I asked at the same time Phee blurted out "Where the hell have you been?"

We both laughed.

She smoothed her hands across her apron. "After you ran out of Copper's Kettle, me and Krystal and Taz went searching for you. Krystal found your glasses by the Face of Maui. I grabbed them from her and...well, I blacked out and woke up here."

Ruby looked back and forth between me and Phee, her eyes wide, as if realizing for the first time that the crazy story she had chosen to believe might actually be true.

"Did you touch the clocktower?" I asked.

Phee scrunched her nose, thinking. "Yeah, I think I punched it or something."

Ruby leaned in, curious. "When you say you woke up *here*, are you talkin' right in this-here house?"

"Yes. In the study, to be exact. I woke up right when George—he lives here with his parents—stepped into the room, though I didn't know who he was or what was happening at the time. You can imagine how well that went."

I frowned. "Why would my glasses take you here?" Uncle Kiel had mentioned that the talismans could be unreliable, but still...shouldn't my glasses have brought Phee closer to me?

"I don't know, but I'm guessing it has something to do with this." Phee pulled a small object from her apron and held it out. It was the tiny pewter soldier I had found in the time capsule. "Oh, and here are your glasses." She passed them to me. One of the arms was bent, and both lenses were cracked. I sighed and stuffed them into my apron. I'd stick with Kade's for now.

Ruby studied the soldier. "I never saw that figurine 'afore, but I'd venture to guess that it belongs to the Hendersons, since Mr. Henderson senior fought in the Civil War an' all."

"So George was the one who put the tiny soldier into the time capsule," I mused out-loud. "And it took you here."

"I think that's right," Phee said. "While dusting the house I've come across all sorts of war memorabilia."

"You *dusted*?" I couldn't hide the incredulity in my voice.

"Sure. I can dust."

Ruby ran the pad of her finger across the side table's surface, then flashed her grime-covered finger tip at me and Phee.

Phee rolled her eyes. "I didn't say I dusted *well*."

I asked the question I was afraid to ask. "Are they not treating you well here? You look…different."

"Oh no, they've been great!" She ran her fingers through the roots of her messy braid. "I've been sick, though I'm feeling better today. This place is the pits. Not George's home—" she corrected, "—just this century. How do people survive here? I feel like if I go one more minute without a running toilet I might drown myself in a horse trough."

I wanted to roll my eyes, but honestly I could totally relate. "So what happened when you got here?"

"Well, like I said before, I woke up with George walking into the study. He totally flipped out, wondering how I had gotten into the house. But he calmed down pretty quick. I think it was because I was super dizzy and drowsy and, okay, I'm hot, too, and he realized I wasn't any kind of threat. He thought I was 'unwell'—as he put it—and went into gentleman mode, treating me like a damsel in distress —"

"That must've driven you nuts," I interrupted.

"You'd think so, right?" Phee fiddled with a lock of hair that had slipped from her braid. I noticed several of her nails were broken, with the normally immaculate polish chipped away. "Usually I hate it when guys treat me like I might break any second. But…I don't know. In this century, it feels different. Chivalry is kinda hot."

"If I didn't know any better miss," Ruby said, "I'd say you were smitten with Mr. George Henderson."

If someone had blurted out my crush, I would have had the decency to blush or…something. But not Phee. Instead, she grinned.

"Um, yeah. He's all dark and cute in that computer-geek sort of way, with gorgeous eyes…a little too skinny for my taste, but once he starts in with all those 'Can I get that door for you, my dear' and stuff like that…" she fanned herself off with her hand to illustrate her point.

I couldn't stop the smile from teasing my lips. Even under-the-weather nineteenth century Phee was still very much Phee.

"You know he's spoken for, don'cha?" Ruby said.

Phee sighed. "Yeah, I know. And man is she boring. She's this little goody two shoes who's all 'How are you today, my darling?' and giggles at everything he says. He needs someone with a backbone. Someone who can keep him on his toes."

"Phee," I leveled her with a stare.

"I'm kidding." Her voice was totally unconvincing. "I'm not into chasing men who are already taken. I just like fantasizing, okay? Anyway, George was worried if he threw me out in the street I'd be eaten by wolves or something, so he gave me some clothes to change into and told his family he had hired me on as a house servant."

"You don't clean."

"Will you stop with that? Geez. I can clean." She paused. "Okay, maybe George had to cover for me a few times."

"You sayin' that man picked up a dust rag?" Doubt crept into Ruby's voice.

"No, nothing like that. He just defended me to his family, saying that I was feeling unwell since my travels and to give me time to adjust. He told them I came highly recommended from my last employer and I'd be well worth keeping on as a servant once I recovered from my traveling-fatigue."

Wow. George Henderson sounded like a decent person. A feeling of hope swelled inside me.

Maybe he would help us.

"Once I recovered from the time travel sickness—" Phee was saying, "that's what I've been calling it in my head—I told George I wanted to get to know the town. He already thinks I'm a little crazy, so no way I could tell him that I was hunting for my sister from the future. Anyway, I went out looking for you. I wasn't even sure if you had made it to this time period, but I knew if you had, the first thing you would do is find Kade. Since this is one of those creepy little towns where everyone knows everyone, it only took me a few hours to hunt down his family. When I came to the door, an older guy answered. I'm assuming he was Kade's dad. I didn't tell him who I really was. I've been keeping my identity here a total secret. Don't want to get burned at the stake or whatever."

"They haven't burned a witch at the stake for like two hundred years," I pointed out.

"Yeah, and I don't want to be the reason they pick that hobby back up again."

Ruby arched her brow. "We do like our hobbies 'round here."

We all laughed.

Phee continued. "So I told the guy I was an out-of-towner looking for a childhood friend who might be here. He said he had run into a girl with 'similar mannerisms' as me in his photography shop, but he hadn't seen her since."

I thought about this. Kade's dad *had* seen me since then, so Phee must have questioned him before he and the Hendersons came over for dinner.

And then I remembered—during that dinner, George Henderson was joking around about a new servant they had hired that week, saying something about her being a crummy worker. The whole time he had been talking about Phee!

I leaned back into the hard velvet of the lounge, feeling awed.

"After that dead-end, I got sick," Phee continued. "Like, sick for real. Not time traveling sickness. I've been puking for days. Today is my first day out of bed. Do you think the water in this century is full of parasites or something?"

No wonder she looked so pale and thin when she opened the door. This century had already put us on the world's worst crash diet, but Phee not being able to keep any of it down was adding salt to the wound.

"I've been drinking the water," I pointed out, "and I'm not sick." I thought about it. "Although I stayed at the Broderick's most of the time, and they have running water.

Sort of. You have to pump it, but maybe it's got some kind of filtration."

"Yeah, we have none of those fancy luxuries here. The Henderson's water is scooped straight from the well."

Phee considering pumped water a luxury and me agreeing with her signified a huge change in both of us that I didn't have time to contemplate.

"So you haven't left the house since you got sick?"

"No," Phee replied. "I tried stumbling out of here once, but George stopped me. He's been waiting on me hand and foot, even cleaning out my gross bedpan. He's really the nicest man I've ever met." Her eyes got all distant and dreamy, but then she snapped back to the present. "I've been stuck in a dark, smelly room the size of a closet for days, and I never heard anything about you, so I was starting to wonder if I was in this time period alone. I thought maybe the girl that Kade's dad saw was someone else."

"But didn't you hear about the murder?"

"What murder?"

Ruby and I looked at each other.

Phee's eyes traveled back and forth between us. "Did the murder already happen? The one Kade gets hung for?"

I nodded, swallowing hard.

"Oh crap. No wonder George has been acting so weird. He's normally all happy and upbeat, but the last couple of days he's been super serious and looked like something was bothering him. Did you know that George and Kade are, like, best friends? Well, there's three of them actually. He told me all sorts of stories about the antics they used to get into when they were kids."

I tried not to let the numbness take over again.

Phee eyed me. "Are you okay?"

"I…" my shoulders started to shake. "I don't know."

Ruby, sensing my struggle, spoke up. "Our Viv saw the murder happen. The bastard tried killin' her, too."

"Oh my God," Phee's face paled. "Who's the killer?"

"William Broderick," I whispered.

"What? No! That's George's and Kade's other best friend."

I could do nothing but nod.

"Wow." Phee looked a little shell-shocked. She reached across the small coffee table and squeezed my hand. "You don't have to talk about it." She looked over at Ruby. "So Kade still got arrested? Even though Aviva witnessed it?"

Ruby nodded. "His hanging is tonight."

Phee processed this for about three seconds, then jumped from her chair. "Well, let's go!"

"Go where?" I asked.

"Save him. We'll…break him out of jail, or…something."

My mouth curved into a faint smile. I wished I had the faith to run head first into danger with no real plan. "How exactly will we do that?"

She paused. "I'll create a distraction. I'll use my powers to blow something up near the jail, and while everyone is running over to deal with that, we can break him out."

"Have you tried using your powers lately?"

"No." Phee said. "Like I told you, I'm trying to avoid getting burnt at the stake, plus I've been sick."

"Try them." Who knows, maybe it was just me who was powerless here.

Phee fixed her gaze on a matched set of silver candlesticks on a nearby mantle. She squinted at the pillars, and I could feel the intensity of her concentration. My skin crawled as the air around us vibrated. Ruby gasped, and I realized she, too, could feel the energy Phee was emanating. I returned my gaze to the candlesticks. The tiniest ember sparked on one of them before almost immediately being snuffed out, leaving a tiny wisp of curly smoke.

"Whoa," Ruby muttered under her breath. "People in these parts really just *might* burn y'all at the stake."

"Told you we had powers," I couldn't resist pointing out to Ruby.

"What the hell?" Phee swung over to me and Ruby. "Why aren't mine working?"

"I don't know. Mine aren't working either," I said.

"Maybe since y'all ain't supposed to be born yet, yer powers don't work in this century," Ruby suggested.

"That's as good a theory as any," I said.

"Hmmm." A thoughtful look crossed over Phee's face.

"What?"

"When you disappeared, the flowers started dying."

I stiffened. "What? What do you mean?"

"When we were in Pendulum Square looking for you, the snap dragons went from bright orange to black-as-death within minutes."

"What does that mean?" I asked.

Phee cocked her head, thinking. "Your birthday fell on the first day of spring this year. Flowers had started blooming. Then you left, and it's like…I don't know. Do you think when you went through the rift, spring disappeared with you? And that's why the flowers started dying?"

"So I have…what? The power to keep spring going?"

"Something like that."

"But ain't you a season too?" Ruby said.

Phee looked at Ruby, her eyes growing wide.

"What's wrong?" I stood. This conversation had gotten too crazy for me to be able to sit still.

"Ruby's right. If you're controlling spring, I'm controlling summer."

"It's not summer in Sezona Hills right now," I said. "It's springtime."

"Yeah, but with you stuck in the past, once the flowers started dying and the weather started getting colder, wouldn't the next season in line try to take over? Stabilize things a little? That would be me. Summer. But with you and I both here, we just knocked out the two warmest seasons."

Understanding dawned on me. "It's just Taz and Krystal holding down the fort. Fall and winter."

Phee nodded.

"Okay, that's not great. Things might get a little cooler in Sezona Hills. But Taz is older and more powerful than Krystal, so I think her power will take over, and fall isn't too different from spring, right? I mean, it sucks that the flowers are dying and stuff, but at least the temperature should be close to the same."

Phee looked unsure. "I guess. I just wish there was a way to know what's happening back at home."

"We'll find out as soon as we save Kade and go back through the rift," I inserted optimism in my voice.

She crossed her arms. "Well, duh. But since our powers aren't working, what do you propose?"

I glanced over at Ruby. "We were thinking that we should ask George Henderson for help."

I heard a shuffling of feet near the doorway. "Ask my help for what?"

The masculine voice rang across the room. Standing at the entrance to the parlor was the trim, dark-haired man, his Abe Lincoln hat clutched in his hands, his expression stern. "And what in heaven's name are you young ladies doing gabbing away in my parlor?" His eyes visibly softened as they lingered on Phee. "Are you feeling well now, Miss Phoenix?"

My pulse raced a mile a minute. I didn't know George the way Phee did, so I had no idea how to approach this. With no time to formulate a better plan, I blurted out the truth. "We're going to save Kade."

He narrowed his eyes.

"Wanna join us?" I added, my voice croaking at the end.

A thick silence descended the room as George's eyes roamed each of our faces, as if trying to decide whether this was some kind of joke. I held my breath.

He placed his hat back on his head and stepped into the room, then said two words that were pure fuel.

"Very well."

Thirty-Five

We hold the history of blood and promises.
We are speaking. Are you listening?
Will you hear?
Libba Bray

January 21, 1886

THE FOUR OF US, a most unlikely party of criminals, hid behind the thick foliage near the sheriff's department.

Even with my heart racing, I couldn't help but acknowledge the fact that there was something special about our group. Phee and I, two teens from the twenty-first century, were working together with some random guy and an underprivileged servant in 1886 to save an innocent man from being hung. When exactly did life get this weird?

"How long do we have to wait?" I whispered to George, who was crouched over to my right, peering over the bush.

"It shouldn't be too long," he said, keeping his voice low.

"This place ain't like the ones in the city," Ruby chimed in from my left. "It ain't got no modern plumbin'. The sheriff's usually got a brick in his hat by high noon, so he'll be shinning around that outhouse in no time."

I glanced at her questioningly. "He's that predictable,

364

huh?"

"He likes to tip that ole' whiskey bottle," Ruby explained.

I sighed, trying to control the impatience thrumming through my nerves. Kade was going to hang in a matter of hours, and we were hiding out in the bushes waiting for the town sheriff to pee. Couldn't we come up with a better plan?

But when I was honest with myself, I knew listening to George was probably a better gamble than trying to wing it on our own. Phee had suggested that we simply ask the sheriff to hand over the camera. Since George's dad and Sheriff Barlow had fought side-by-side in the Civil War—as Ruby had told us—there should be a trust between George's family and the sheriff, right? But George informed us it wouldn't work. He told us that though his family was close to the sheriff, Sheriff Barlow was a law-abiding, upright man, and in his eyes the letter of the law comes before all else.

So, building from my idea to break into the sheriff's office, George suggested that we simply wait outside for the man to relieve himself. When Phee arched a critical eyebrow at this, George had calmly told her, "I know you ladies want to storm in there like batty-fangers, but sometimes the simplest plan is the best plan."

So here we were.

I shivered in the late afternoon chill, pressing my cloak closer to my body. "Why are you helping us, George?" I asked, trying to distract myself from the cold.

He peered over at me. "I know Kade is innocent."

"How do you know?"

He thought for a few seconds. "I've known him my whole life. Kade is far from perfect, but he is incapable of killing someone in cold blood."

"You've known William your whole life, too. You don't think the same about him?"

George shuffled his body to face me. "When I was a lad, I walked over to the Brodericks' house one morning to see if Will wanted to play a game of jacks. He was breaking in a young mare when I showed up."

"What's wrong with that?"

"Normally, nothing. But it was the way he was doing it. Instead of using a standard crop, he was using a heavily knotted whip, with nettles fashioned onto the last knot. He struck the poor creature mercilessly, over and over. And I swear I saw the oddest smile creep across his face. It doesn't seem like much, but even at the age of twelve, the sight unnerved me."

Goosebumps unrelated to the cold crept up the nape of my neck, and my stomach felt sick for that poor horse.

"I am not suggesting that I ever imagined Will could kill another human being, much less his own sister," George said. "If I had guessed his true nature, I would never have maintained a friendship with him all these years. But that memory has stuck with me…a small, easily ignored cloud. Thus, when you invaded my home declaring Kade's innocence, something inside me told me to believe you." He pulled a twig from his coat, fiddling with it. "Honestly, dear girl, I am heartbroken. I have lost my two closest friends. One to insanity and the other to the gallows. If I have a chance to save one of them, I will do it." He glanced down at the ground and swiped moisture from his eyes, quickly, as if hoping I wouldn't see. His next words came out like gravel. "Kade would do the same for me."

"Oh…." I blinked, at a loss for words. "You're a good

friend, George."

He nodded, his smile strained. We slipped into a comfortable, cold silence and continued to wait.

I counted seven hundred and forty Mississippis by the time Sheriff Barlow finally swaggered out of the building.

"Now," George prompted as the sheriff slipped into the outhouse. He and I surged forward, with Ruby and Phee a step behind. George and I ran into the small sheriff's building, while Phee and Ruby crept around the corner to play lookout and create a distraction—if it came to that.

My heart leaped when I saw the small jail cell inside the building. I found my body gravitating toward it against my will. A hand pulled me back.

"He's not here," George said, his tone gentle. "They've already taken him to the courthouse to ready him for the hanging."

I blinked back the moisture in my eyes and nodded, remembering our mission. "Let's look in those." I pointed at two heavy oak desks sitting in the center of the room.

"That'd be a good place to start."

Voices sounded from somewhere outside. Distant, but not distant enough.

George's eyes widened. "We best hurry." He dashed over to the furthest desk and started flinging drawers open. I darted to the closest one. The first two drawers yielded nothing but papers, a box of long matches, and a clear glass flask that was about a quarter-full of amber liquid. The third and largest drawer on the bottom was locked.

"Damn," I muttered.

"It's a trick desk," George told me from across the room. "Close the top center drawer as tight as it will go, and it will release the bottom one."

I followed his directions, and to my surprise, the bottom drawer glided open. Nestled inside, bundled in thin, plain cloth, were the pieces of the broken Oak Box camera.

"Yes!" I yelped, holding the bundle in the air like a trophy.

The voices outside grew louder. George and I eyed each other. He held a finger in front of his mouth in a "shhh" gesture. I froze, straining my ears to hear what was happening outside.

"Young lady," I could hear a male voice say. "I appreciate yer kind words, but I gotta get back to work."

Oh crap! The plan was for Phee to use her "feminine wiles" (as George put it) to flatter the sheriff if he stepped out of the outhouse too early, but it obviously wasn't working.

"Oh, Sheriff Barlow..." Phee's sultry voice slipped through the gap of the slightly ajar door. "You poor, overworked man. How about you take a much-needed break from all this law-enforcement stuff? You and I can go for a little walk..."

I cringed and waited, hoping her shameless flirting would work.

"Now there, Miss, this is startin' to feel rather inappropriate...."

My panicked gaze darted to George. I mouthed the words "What do we do?"

He pointed at the front door. "Run," he whispered. "I'll distract him. On the count of three."

I quickly wrapped the towel as tight as possible around the camera bits and tied the ends.

"One..." George whispered. "Two...three!"

I bolted out the front door, clinging onto my bundle for

dear life, and tore for the woods.

"You there! Stop!" Footsteps pounded after me.

"Sheriff Barlow, I have a dire situation happening over here—" I heard George say.

"Not now, Henderson!" the sheriff yelled. "I have to catch that girl! She was pokin' 'round my station—"

Crap crap *crap*! George's distraction wasn't working, either. I quickened my sprint. A painful cramp sprouted above my groin. Why couldn't I have put more effort into the monster mile during PE? My panting took on a frantic pitch, and the frigid air around me whooshed inside my stinging ears as if it was being blasted through a stereo. I knew I couldn't last much longer. I rounded a bare tree to see a giant bush beckoning me. Without giving it a second thought, I tucked the camera pieces close to my chest, closed my eyes, and dove headfirst into the twiggy mass, my hair getting torn by its dry, sharp edges.

Ouch.

Trying to calm my breathing, I reoriented my body until I was in a more reasonable crouched position, then peeked through a thin spot in the bush, my lashes brushing against its snagging fingers. I could see the large figure of the sheriff bumbling his way through the brush. Every few seconds he would pause to examine a broken twig, or bend down to gaze at the ground.

Dang it, the man was some kind of professional tracker.

"Sheriff," George and Phee were following right behind him. George's voice was pitched with desperation. "If you follow me back to your desk, I think I have more information about your intruder."

"Or you and I can go for that walk…?" Phee suggested lamely.

The sheriff, struck with tunnel vision, ignored them both.

The distance between him and my bush was shrinking rapidly. At about eight feet away, he stopped and stared in my direction. Did he see me? I jerked my head back behind a thicker branch and held my breath.

"Sheriff Barlow," George tried one more time, "I really think you ought to—"

"What on Earth is that?" I heard Phee's voice say. She sounded genuine.

Unable to resist, I lifted my head back up to the thin spot of the bush and peered out. Luckily I was greeted with three backsides. George, Phee, and the sheriff were turned around now, all three staring at something in the distance. I craned my neck until I finally saw it.

Smoke. Thick, black smoke uncurling a short distance away, from the direction of the sheriff's station.

"Blasted hell," Sheriff Barlow said. He glanced again toward my hiding spot, and, with a dejected sigh, turned away and jogged back toward the smoke.

A quiet minute passed.

"Aviva?" George finally said, creeping forward.

I waited a few seconds more, wanting to be sure the sheriff was totally gone, then popped my head out.

"Hi guys!"

Phee jumped about a mile into the air, then glared at me. "Do you have to be a freakin' Jack in the Box? Geez Viv. You gave me a heart attack."

George stepped forward, took my hand, and helped me crawl clumsily out of the sticky mass. My other hand gripped tightly onto the bulging towel, refusing to yield it to the sharp sticks trying to snag it away. Back on my feet again, I looked over at Phee and George. "Where's Ruby?"

"I don't know," Phee said, "but for the record, I would've totally had that sheriff eating out of my hand if this flu didn't have me looking like a hot mess."

George and I eyed each other knowingly, both of us understanding that Phee's pride was wounded. Poor girl wasn't used to looking one micro-grain less than gorgeous.

George reached out and squeezed Phee's hand. "Any man who's not instantly wooed by you, my dear, ill or not, has something wrong in his head."

Phee broke out into a grin. "Thanks, George."

"But seriously guys. Where's Ruby?" Worry over her was gnawing at me. "And why is there smoke?"

"Cus' of me," a familiar voice said from our right. All three of us whipped around to see the dark, slender figure sashaying from the trees.

"Ruby!" I shouted, running forward to give her a hug. "You started that fire?"

She squeezed me, then stepped back and waggled her brows. "I could see things were goin' south. None of your distractions were workin'. I got the fire idea from Phee."

Phee's mouth fell open. "But how? You don't have any powers."

Ruby grinned and pulled a tiny object from the pocket of her apron. She held it up. It was a matchstick. "You know, girls, you ain't gotta have powers to be powerful."

I looked over at Phee. Phee looked over at me. Then we both lunged for Ruby and attacked her with a ferocious embrace. The three of us fell to the ground in a fit of giggles. George shook his head at the spectacle we were creating. He leaned over and snatched the camera bundle from my hands, a trickle of a smile on his face.

Kade was getting executed. Molly was dead. A serial

killer was loose. I could be trapped in this time period forever. These thoughts bombarded me one after the other, trying to bruise me into numbness. But in this moment in time, rolling around in laughter with these two girls I loved, our small beacon of hope nestled in George's hands, I felt… happy. It was a maniacal sort of happiness. Maybe I was suffering from some sort of PTSD, and I was actually going crazy. Either way, I closed my eyes and tried to cling on to the feeling.

This might be the last time I ever feel this way, I thought. Maniacal or not, I needed to soak it in for a minute. Just… treasure it. Because if Kade died tonight, I knew I would never feel happy again.

ABOUT THIRTY MINUTES later, George steered our carriage into Kade's yard.

"You're sure about this?" George pulled the reins back, bringing us to a stop.

"Yes," I said. "He'll help. Won't he?"

George shook his head. "I think you and I have seen two different versions of this man."

"Okay, he's a jerk," I conceded. "But he's Kade's dad. There's no way he wants to see his own son hang."

George nodded, his lips setting into a straight line.

I paused at the front door.

"Something wrong?" George asked.

"Well, I don't think anyone in this house knows I've been staying here, except for Mrs. Oaks. I haven't seen Kade's dad at all. So I feel weird just walking in. Like I'm an intruder or something."

"Shall we knock, then?"

"I think so."

We knocked on the front door and waited. I gripped the camera bundle. Thirty seconds or so later, a servant swung open the door.

George tipped his hat. "Good afternoon, Ms. Griselda. Might we request the company of Mr. Oaks for a few minutes?"

"Come to pay your condolences?" She sniffled, and I noticed her eyes were rimmed with red like Mrs. Oak's had been earlier. "Sure thing, Mr. Henderson. 'Tis a horrible thing, it is. How my heart hurts for Mrs. Oaks! To lose her only son…." A silent sob wracked her body as she guided us into the sitting room. Phee looked over at me apologetically.

A few minutes later, Mr. Oaks entered the room. He stood stiffly by the door, his eyes narrowing when they crossed mine.

So he was home.

I jumped up before anyone could speak. "Hi, Mr. Oaks. Do you remember me? I met you at your camera store last week, and then I waited on you at the Brodericks."

"I remember you." His voice was sharp. "One does not easily forget a…*young lady*…like you."

I cringed at his scathing tone. I knew this wasn't going to be easy. The man hated me. I remembered him calling me a whore or a hedgehog or something, when I had overheard his conversation with Kade on the road. Still, I was counting on his love for his son being bigger than his hatred toward me.

I brushed off my nervousness and walked over to him, opening the towel to reveal the broken camera pieces. "I know this is a difficult time for you right now, but I have reason to believe that this camera could prove your son is innocent of the crimes he's accused of."

Mr. Oaks glared at me for a moment, then pulled a pair of spectacles from his pocket and slid them over his nose. He gazed at the broken contraption. "This is one of our prototypes."

"Yes, it is," I confirmed. "That's why I came to you. I'm hoping you can fix it?"

He peered down again, examining the pieces. "This camera is beyond repair."

My heart dropped. "Are you sure?"

"Yes."

I looked over at George, Ruby, and Phee, their faces instantly blurring as tears pooled inside my lids. Ruby had her hand over her mouth, as if trying to squelch a gasp of horror. Or sympathy, maybe.

Blood roared in my ears, keeping me from hearing what Mr. Oaks said next.

Something-something-blah-blah-blah-photographs.

Photographs?

"What?" I asked, trying to calm the pounding in my head.

"I said, you do not, however, need to repair this camera in order to view the photographs."

My heart leapt. "I don't?"

"No. The Oak Box camera captures images by exposing photographic film to light."

I stared at him blankly.

He blinked at me. "No glass plates reside in this camera. Rather, it uses film. Film flexes, it does not break. And this piece—" he pointed to a brown cardboard canister—"is still intact. Which means the film has not been compromised by light exposure."

I tilted my head at him. "So the film is still good? Even though the camera is a mess?"

He sighed his exasperation at my stupidity and handed me the canister. "Your film is safe. You simply need to develop it."

I almost yelped my joy.

George stepped forward. "Will you help us develop it, Mr. Oaks?" He pulled out a pocket watch and glanced down. "Our time is waning."

Mr. Oaks shook his head. "I'm afraid not."

I felt my mouth drop open. "What? Why?"

Mr. Oaks moved toward the door. "It is a worthless endeavor. Kade's own dearest friend, William Broderick, caught him red handed. We all know how Kade felt about Molly. He was marrying her to ensure the merger of our two businesses. And despite all of the arguments my son and I have had over the matter, at least he was willing to do the honorable thing for his family. That is—" he paused, his eyes shooting black darts my direction, "until he met *you*."

My eyes widened.

"He was to wed in nine days. In nine mere days, we would have had the Brodericks' entire empire funding my son's invention. We were to be rich! But instead, he fell for you. A penniless driggle-draggle."

I thought driggle-draggle sounded kind of cute, but Phee clenched her fists.

Mr. Oaks continued. "I now have no way of paying off the debt I have accrued. My family will fall into ruins. We will lose everything. Thus, as far as I am concerned, you, young lady, can hang in the gallows right along with my son."

"You asshole!" Phee shouted, lunging toward Mr. Oaks.

George leapt forward and pulled Phee back, pinning her to his chest. "Phoenix, let us go."

"You're lucky I can't fry your ass right now," Phee spat as George maneuvered her toward the front door.

My mind spun. *He's not going to help us.* Kade was going to die at sundown, and his own dad was going to let it happen.

Numb, I allowed Ruby to guide me out the door.

Thirty-Six

*I don't believe in ghosts
but they blindly believe in me.*
Amit Abraham

January 21, 1886

QUIET SHROUDED our carriage. The horse's gloomy clop clop clopping echoed my current mood.

"I can't believe that asshat won't help his own son," Phee broke the thick silence.

I nodded mutely, clutching the worthless film can in my hands as if I could squeeze it into being the magic potion it had promised.

"I can't believe how much filth comes out of women's mouths in your era," Ruby said.

"Not all mouths," I said in a flat tone. "Just Phee's. And sometimes mine. And sailors. Not that sailors is some big profession in our time…." My voice wavered, and my eyes misted. I stuffed the canister into my apron. The lump it made on my lap was about as big as the lump in my throat.

Ruby squeezed my hand. "Don'cha go losin' faith now, Vivvy girl. We still have the film."

"But what difference does it make?" my voice squeaked.

"None of us know how to develop it."

"And it's not like YouTube can help," Phee chimed in. Ruby stared at her. "Sorry. Not helping."

"Let's not give up the ghost yet," George said. I almost smiled at the duel-interpretation of his words. "Perhaps once we arrive to the studio, we will be able to deduce how to develop the film. Kade and his father likely have a book laying around, describing the process."

"Yeah?" Phee said hopefully.

George sighed. "Lord, I hope."

The streets were a scurry of activity as our carriage rolled through the small town of Sezona Valley. Shop owners were turning their 'CLOSED' signs early in order to get good standing space at tonight's festivities. Tonight's festivities being Kade's hanging, scheduled for sundown.

A rock settled in my gut.

We passed the *Guns, Pistols, & Ammunition store* and *J.C. Cunningham's Merchant Taylor,* rounded the corner, and slowed to a stop in front of *Oaks & Son Studio.*

Departing the carriage, George, Phee, Ruby and I scurried to the front of the shop. George pushed through the front door.

A woman sat at the side-counter, crying over a framed photo.

I gasped. "Mrs. Oaks, what are you doing here?"

She looked up, tears streaming down her face. "He loves it here. Photography is his passion. I…." She set the frame down, pulled out a hankie and blew her nose. "They won't let me near him. I came here to…to…feel close to him."

George stepped around the counter and took the crumpled woman into his arms, where she sobbed on his shoulder for several minutes. My own eyes were burning from crying so much today, yet I still felt the tell-tell signs of more tears.

Mrs. Oaks finally pulled away, her body trembling. "I suppose I ought to get on over to the courthouse now. I'm not going to let my son die without his mother."

I was too choked to reply, but Phee, thank goodness, spoke up. "Mrs. Oaks, we have film from a camera that was on the crime scene when Kade's fiancé was murdered."

I pulled the canister from my apron, and Phee took it gently from my clenched hands. "I don't want to give you false hope, but Aviva says she heard the camera click right before it broke. We were hoping we could try to develop the film?" She swallowed, then said, "It might be for nothing. But we might as well give it a shot, right?" She held the canister out, as if it was some kind of peace offering.

Mrs. Oaks swiped her eyes, smearing dirty tears across her face. She took the can from Phee. "Do you know how to develop film? It is a sensitive process."

I froze, feeling a small seed of hope sprout in my stomach. "Wait—do you know how?"

Mrs. Oaks looked at me with a strained smile. "Who do you think taught Kade about photography, dear child? Certainly not his father; that self-absorbed oaf. The man has only ever cared about money. Kade and I, on the other hand, we love the art of it." Her forced smile dissolved to something more real. "Photography began as Kade's passion. But because his father refused to teach him, I was forced to learn. Eventually it became my passion, too."

I stared at her, daring to hope. "Will you—will you help us?"

"I'm not as good at it as Kade." She gazed down at the canister and tilted her head, then met my eyes, her own shimmering with fresh tears. "But yes, it would be my honor to try."

DESPITE THE STRONG bitter odors wafting the room, I was surprised to discover that I loved the Oaks' photo lab— or whatever you'd call it in the late nineteenth century. It was dark and peaceful. A perfect atmosphere when the man you love is going to die soon and you're tired of bright lights and noises mocking your pain.

Upon entering the small space, Mrs. Oaks moved quickly to light a row of oil lamps lined against the wall behind a set of sheer, red drapes hanging from a clothesline. The effect was spooky, with the candlelight filtering through the drapes, tinging the entire room in deep crimson.

"Why the red curtains?" Phee asked. "Aren't you worried about them catching fire?"

"The lamps have glass shades and are a safe distance from the drapes," Mrs. Oaks explained as she poured a bottle labeled *Distilled White Vinegar*, along with some other chemicals, into several different trays. "We call this 'the dark room.' If the film is exposed to light, it will ruin it. Thankfully black and white paper has a difficult time seeing the color red. Thus we use red light to see what we're doing."

In my time if we needed red light, we would have used a red lightbulb, like the kind you see on a strand of Christmas lights. The fact that the Oaks had thought to use oil lamps and red drapes to create the same effect awed me. Somehow this pre-technology process impressed me more than anything I had ever seen in my more advanced world.

We got to work, helping Mrs. Oaks cut the film into strips

and dipping each segment into the various trays. With no clue what I was doing, I went into autopilot mode, simply following her orders.

Once finished, we used clothes pins to hang the wet, developing photos on thin ropes strung across the room. My eyes watered in the cloud of chemicals as we waited for them to dry.

Finally, the photos were ready.

We gathered at a worktable in the center of the room, piling the photos into one messy stack. Mrs. Oaks yanked open the red sheers and lit a few more lamps so we could see better. I tried to keep calm as I reached for the stack, planning to look at each photo carefully. But, unable to control my frenzy, I found myself tearing through them.

A picture of a willow tree. A wren. The sun setting behind Singing Creek Episcopal Church…or was it rising? Molly standing in front of The Face of Maui, shadows playing across her beautiful, solemn face (did no one smile in this century?). George and William, standing in front of a carriage with stoic expressions. I shivered when I saw William and tossed that photo on the floor.

A few pictures of random household objects; a milk jug, a marble, a chair. It looked like someone was playing around with shadows and light. I wondered who took all these photos. I couldn't imagine Mr. Broderick being all that into photography.

It had to be Kade, I decided. This was, after all, his prototype. He probably played around with it quite a bit before handing the camera over to Mr. Broderick.

The next picture confirmed my suspicions, and my heart just about stopped. It was the letter I had written to Kade. The camera wasn't zoomed in close enough to read the words, but I recognized the modern paper with the fringed edges, along with my loopy handwriting. The letter was perfectly positioned on a nightstand beside a pillar candle, the flame casting what would probably be golden shadows across the creased paper if the photo wasn't in black and white.

He must have clicked this photo before he buried the letter in the time capsule. I shook my head, trying not to smile. He had been so determined to bury all vestiges of me to do what was right for his fiancé, yet he still cheated a tiny bit, in his own little way.

An ache pulled at me from deep inside.

I continued to flip through the photos until I reached the one I was looking for.

Nausea punched me. I must have heaved or something, because Phee and Ruby appeared at my side, with George and Mrs. Oaks peering over my shoulder to see what I had found. I gripped the photo with both of my trembling hands. Despite the awkward angle of the shot, I recognized the slats of rustic wood in the background; the way the dirty sunlight filtered gloomily through the cracks.

This was it. This was the one and only picture captured by the Oak Box camera in the stables. This was the one accidental image, frozen in time, depicting Molly's murder.

My saliva was thick like glue in my throat. In the forefront of the photo was a large hand, clear as day, holding a knife stained in black. Molly's blurry, broken body was visible beyond the knife, slouched against the slatted wall.

Phee and Ruby gasped beside me.

I swallowed down my bile, concentrating on the image. "It's…" I whispered, tilting the photo. "The angle's wrong.

It's just his hand. I need his face."

I held it up to the light, desperate for William's face to materialize next to that knife. I stared, adjusted the glasses Kade had made for me, and stared some more. That was *William's* hand. The camera had done its job. Though black and white, it had captured the murder weapon in the killer's hand in perfect clarity. Yet…it was worthless. This picture was supposed to vindicate Kade; instead, the stupid thing had done nothing more than capture Molly's grisly last moments and force me to relive my worst nightmare.

George sighed heavily behind me, putting his hand on my shoulder. "I am sorry, Aviva."

Tears stung my eyes. "It can't be," I croaked, the photo vibrating in the air as my hands shook. "It just can't."

I pulled my glasses off to wipe my burning eyes. Memories of Kade flashed through my mind. The first time I saw him, sitting in Mr. English's class. The first time he called me "sweet girl." The first time he touched me, his hands reaching for my face, his fingertips grazing my cheek with such shock and tenderness….

My muscles froze. I jammed my glasses back on my face and returned my gaze to the picture. "George, is this the left hand or right?"

"What difference does it make?" Phee asked.

I ignored Phee. "Left. Or. Right."

George leaned over for a closer look. "The right."

"You're sure?"

"Yes, I am certain. See the angle of the elbow? And the thumb? But—my dear—both William and Kade are right-handed. This does not help anything."

I swung around. "How much time 'til the hanging?"

George pulled out his pocket watch. "Sundown is in

about ten minutes. Perhaps less."

Ruby spun on me. "What do you see in the photo?"

"It's what I don't see. George, unhitch me one of the horses."

"Where are you going?" Phee demanded.

I snatched the photo from the table. "I'm going to prove Kade is innocent."

Thirty-Seven

Ghosts aren't white and bright.
Ghosts are shadows of someone
or something gone wrong.
Paul Tremblay

January 21, 1886

DARKNESS COULDN'T HIDE the throngs of jeering
faces crowding the gallows. Candlelight danced about,
casting amber shadows through the spectators.

Kade, guided by Sheriff Barlow, stepped out into the
courtyard, taken back by the throng who had shown up to
his hanging. It felt like there were more bodies here than
the population of his entire town. A sound erupted as he
moved across the space, something between applauding
and heckling. Excitement pulsed and writhed through the
mob like a hungry snake.

Kade ignored the crowd and fixed his gaze straight ahead
to the freshly-built gallows at the edge of the courtyard.
The structure was a stark silhouette against the crimson
puddles bloodying the dark horizon as the sun dipped to its
final resting place. Hangings were rare in Sezona Valley,
the last one having been in 1852 for a man who killed an
acquaintance during a gambling dispute, so the sheriff was

forced to commission local carpenters to erect a structure specifically for Kade.

He wondered if he should feel flattered.

Wrists bound loosely in front of him (as his good behavior had rendered him a low escape risk), Kade reached the narrow steps leading to the platform. His heart hammered as the sheriff prompted him up the steps. Glancing up, Kade could see the shadows of several men waiting at the top. He wasn't sure what their roles were or why so many were needed, but the lanterns flickering above revealed that one of the men was wearing a robe and holding a book.

Reverend Sunderland, he grimaced. The man had christened him as a babe, baptized him in his youth, and was supposed to preside over his and Molly's nuptials one week hence. Instead the reverend had lowered the young bride into her eternal earth bath, and was now seeing the groom hanged for her murder.

If only he had ignored his father when he came upon him on the road, he might have made it to the stables in time to stop the murder before it happened. Or if he had believed Aviva from the very beginning. If he had acted sooner.

He had lost everything. His mother. His sister. His betrothed. Granted he never loved Molly in the ways that mattered, he did care about her, and now she was dead.

His eyes burned with tears that he could no longer shed. He had dried out days ago.

Molly didn't deserve to die.

Everything, lost. His future. His life.

His...Aviva.

Surely she is safe and sound in her own time period by now, he told himself, trying to find solace in the knowledge that she would live on.

Indeed, he knew she was safe, because she had sought to comfort him in this exact moment through her letter.

Her letter. The words came to him now in a torrent. He had read that letter every day, sometimes several times a day, since he was nine years old. He had every word of it memorized, a fact that he never shared with Aviva. Tearing it to pieces had been symbolic at the time; he did not need the letter to remember all it held.

Dear Kade, the words echoed softly in his mind. *I know this letter will never reach you, but as I stare at the Face of Maui, this amazing thing that you named, I feel like you are here with me, somehow…*

He wished he could feel her presence, but instead he felt nothing but the chill of fear.

He threw his shoulders back as he stepped onto the platform. Fear would not change anything. If he was going to die in dishonor, he would do so honorably, without any groveling or bitterness.

Or he'd do a damned fine job pretending.

The men, under the direction of the sheriff, fussed with various pulleys and ropes while the reverend began reading passages from his Bible.

"The Lord is my shepherd; I shall not want. He maketh me to lie down in green pastures: he leadeth me beside the still waters…."

His last rites, Kade realized, ice clutching his chest. The din of the crowd grew, nearly drowning out the reverend's intonations. Kade finally dared to peer into the throng. Staring back at him were familiar faces, such as the Barnard family and the widower Mrs. Thornber, along with unfamiliar ones—people who had traveled from the next county over for an evening of unbridled entertainment. An array of emotions shone from the crowd. A few faces seemed drawn with sympathy, but most glowed with glee. Molly had been loved by all, so it was natural for the townsfolk to feel grateful that justice was being served. But he still couldn't control the swift blow of anger and burning pain that punched him in the gut. Yes, the evidence stacked against him was damning, but many of these people had known him since he was a babe in his mother's arms. It was he who had repaired Mrs. Knowles' roof when she was recently widowed, and he who had helped Farmer McMullen rebuild his stables after a lightning strike burnt the structure to the ground. Shouldn't the character by which he had lived his life speak louder than all else?

But perhaps it was meant to be this way. Perhaps this was his penance for not loving Molly the way he should have; for not keeping her safe.

No, his mind whispered in stifled disagreement. *Hanging you means the true killer goes free.*

William goes free. He lives on, able to hurt others.

The scene in the stables flashed through his mind. Kade convulsed, a scythe of hatred burrowing into his chest.

"Yea, though I walk through the valley of the shadow of death, I will fear no evil...." Reverend Sunderland monotoned as Kade spotted his sister, Bess, a few rows back, bawling into a handkerchief.

She was only just entering womanhood; she should not have to bear the crux of her brother's death.

He tore his eyes from her and continued to survey the crowd, searching for his mother. She should have been standing next to Bess, yet she was not. Perhaps she was in the rear of the mass somewhere, and he simply could not see her, though it would be difficult for anyone to hide from him from this height.

When he was sincere with himself, he hoped his mother was not here. He had grown up wanting nothing less than to lasso the sun for her, just as Chief Maui had done. His mother should not be forced to watch her only son die in shame, and her enduring such a heartache was enough to break Kade's resolve to die an honorable death.

His father was nowhere to be found, either. This observation prompted no emotion within him.

But where was George? No man wants to see his close friend hanged, but Kade felt certain George would subject himself to this torment to be here for him.

Would he not? Or did George, too, believe he was guilty?

What would Kade believe if the situation was reversed?

I would know George was innocent, Kade decided.

"Surely goodness and mercy shall follow me all the days of my life: and I will dwell in the house of the Lord for ever."

Kade recognized that the reverend was nearing the end of his recitations. He was reading one of Kade's favorite passages, but it was doing little to comfort him.

Was there anything that could bring him comfort?

His eyes darted through the crowd again, frantically this time, as he realized the answer to his unspoken question.

Aviva. How he longed to see her, but simultaneously did not.

Instead, he found William. Their gazes locked. Will's expression remained stoic, with the slightest quirk turning up the corners of his lips.

Kade leveled him with a dark stare that surely spoke hatred, but a chill pierced his heart at the thought that

William might still hurt Aviva.

Fear not, he reminded himself. She is safe within her own century.

Kade broke his gaze from William—refusing to sacrifice precious few seconds on the evil, vile traitor—and let himself sink into the words of Aviva's letters as he faced his final moments of life.

I probably shouldn't like you.

But I do, Kade...I more than like you. I feel...something stronger than 'like'. My uncle calls it love. Is it possible to feel love for someone I barely know? For someone who I've never met in the flesh?

I don't know. But I do know that your disappearance is a stabbing ache.

Kade felt himself stabbed mercilessly by this same ache now. The pain twisting through him was more than he thought he could bear.

"Amen," the reverend said, and Sheriff Barlow reached toward Kade with a dark hood.

"No," Kade jerked back. "I do not want it."

The sheriff cocked his head. "If you refuse to don the hood, Kade, yer death will be that much more ghastly for the spectators. Consider yer loved ones, son." He paused. "Think about Bess."

Kade flinched, but then met the sheriff's anxious gaze. "I understand. It is, however, my wish to face my accusers as I die." The sheriff looked uncertain. "Please, Sheriff Barlow, you have known me my whole life. Grant me this one request."

The sheriff glanced at the reverend, who shrugged apathetically, then looked back at Kade. He stared for a moment too long, and Kade noticed the moisture clinging into the corner of the tired man's deep eyes.

Sheriff Barlow doesn't want to hang me, Kade realized. Maybe he didn't believe in my guilt, after all. Or perhaps it was simply because hanging any person is an ugly matter. Either way, this ordeal looked like it had aged the man by years.

"Alright then, Kade."

Kade sighed his relief. Little did the sheriff know the true reason he refused the hood. In her letter, Aviva had commanded him to look for her. How could he do so if he was blinded by a hood?

I'll be an angel watching over you. Her soft voice whispered the words to him now. He knew it was impossible, but was it more impossible than anything else that had happened? Aviva's very existence in his life was an impossibility, yet somehow, she had touched him in a way no person ever had. Perhaps it was foolish, grasping onto the one small hope that Aviva would appear to him as an angel when she had yet to be born. But it was a tiny spark of hope that gave him strength. Thus he would cling onto it until his last dying breath.

Sheriff Barlow prodded him to the center of the platform, moving Kade on top of the trapdoor. He then strapped Kade's legs together at the ankles and above the knees—to prevent him from bridging the trap with his legs, Kade supposed.

A time might come when you will be forced to pay a price you don't deserve. If that happens, I'm begging you, please let these words wrap around you, and protect you from pain.

He forced himself to relax his muscles, imagining cool soothing water running through his hot veins. *Let these words wrap around you....*

The sheriff lowered the noose over Kade's head. Kade's

heart thrummed sickly in his chest. A light breeze stirred, chilling the slick of sweat that coated Kade's neck.

And remember as you look across a sea of mocking, accusing faces, that I'll be with you.

Kade tuned out the shouting and jeering. He visualized Aviva amongst the horde, reading the words of her letter, soothing him, telling him it was going to be okay.

The sheriff nodded to a man Kade couldn't see. He swallowed the paste-like saliva coating his mouth, but it wedged itself in his throat, gathering at the noose. A sound cracked Kade's ears—something that sounded like sandpaper running across wood. The floor beneath Kade's feet disappeared. Then, he was falling. He nearly howled out loud when he hit the end of the rope and it snapped painfully against his neck.

Something was wrong. Sheriff Barlow had assured him that he would die instantly. The rope was supposed to snap his neck. Yet he was alive, dangling in the frigid air, feeling everything. The terror. The pain.

He tried to pull in air, but could not. The coarse rope twisted painfully into his neck, strangling him. His brain screamed its want for oxygen. Desperate, he thrashed in his binds with a nearly inhuman strength until he twisted one of his hands free. The spectators gasped, but he barely noticed as he pulled at the rope that was squeezing his neck.

It was useless. Even with his hand wedged between the rope and his neck, he was merely prolonging a painful death.

I'll be an angel watching over you.

He searched for her. Spots formed in the corners of his vision. He couldn't breathe.

How long did it take to die this way?

Air. Air. *Air.*

And then…he saw her. Far away at first, then closer, and closer. Candlelight danced around her, reflecting from her bright wild locks like a halo. She was an angel with alabaster hair, glowing with light.

Was she real? Did it matter? If she was a hallucination, he heartily thanked his dying brain for it.

His angel. She had come, just as she promised.

Find me, and take my hand Kade.

She was closer now, shouting up toward the podium, waving something furiously in her hand. Convulsions were taking over his body. He wanted to touch her. One last time. She was so vivid. So real. He yearned for her to be real.

…take my hand Kade. We'll get through this together.

He twisted on the rope and reached for her.

So close. So close…

The words "Stop the hanging!" rattled dimly through his fading mind. Then everything happened in flashes.

A gunshot rang through the cold, dark night.

A yelp surged through the crowds.

The noose slackened around his neck.

Air. Space. Falling.

Aviva's beautiful flushed face filling his vision.

Those around you might betray you. But I'm here. And I believe in you.

Falling…falling….

Thirty-Eight

If I lose myself tonight,
it'll be by your side.
OneRepublic

January 21, 1886

"KADE, WAKE UP." I tried to control the panic building in my chest as I smacked his pale cheeks. Mrs. Oaks squeezed my arm. She and Ruby had shown up out of nowhere, and I was grateful for their presence.

"You are certain he will live?" Mrs. Oaks turned toward Dr. Harris, her body shaking beneath her shawl. The four of us were kneeled over Kade beneath the gallows where he had fallen. Ruby was almost finished untying Kade's legs. George and Phee were standing off to the side, talking to Sheriff Barlow and gesturing to the creased and battered photograph. The sheriff's men—the same ones who had conducted Kade's hanging—were now shooing away the remaining bystanders, with the exception of one stocky man, who, per the sheriff's orders, was guarding us with a shotgun. The reverend lingered nearby, praying.

"Your son will have a blazin' headache when he comes to, Mrs. Oaks, and his neck might be scarred for life. Other than that, he ought to pull through. His heart is beatin' good an' strong."

She exhaled a happy puff of air. I smiled at the doctor's words, but held my joy on standby. It all felt too good to be true, and every time I caught a glimpse of the red and purple gouges burned into the flesh of Kade's neck, I could feel the panic rise again.

Don't be all dark and pessimistic like Krystal, I chided myself. Since when was I so dramatic?

Since you witnessed a young woman brutally murdered, my brain answered for me. Since you yourself were almost killed. Since you witnessed the man you love hanging by a noose.

I shivered, wondering if it was from the frigid air, or from the image of Kade dangling from that rope, slowly twisting around, reaching for me…

Just like the shadow had done at Mel's Diner.

Whoa. The dejavu was dizzying.

A low groan interrupted my thoughts. Kade's lashes brushed against his cheeks. His eyes fluttered opened, a deep cyan blue beneath the glow of Dr. Harris's lantern.

My heart skipped a beat. I wanted to throw myself at him but I knew he was probably confused and hurting all over, so I forced myself to simply take his hand and squeeze it in my own.

His eyes found my face, then widened. "Aviva." He wheezed out in broken syllables.

"Kade," I whispered.

He reached up and touched my cheek. "You're here."

"Yes. I'm here."

Tears pricked his eyes. Or maybe they were mine.

"Your letter. All these years, you said you would be

here…." Kade shook his head, bewilderment lighting his face. "And you're here."

I laughed. "Yes. I'm here."

Kade's curious gaze traveled across the others leaning over him. "Mother?"

She wept over him. "I can't tell you how happy I am that you're safe."

He squeezed her hand with his free one. "Where is Bess?"

"Mr. Barnard escorted her home. She was struck with hysteria, not knowing if you were alive."

He started to sit up, then moaned. He let go of Mrs. Oaks' hand and grabbed his head.

"Easy, now," Dr. Harris encouraged. "You suffered a bit of a fall from the gallows. I'd be surprised if it didn't rattle your brain. You may be concussed."

Ruby set aside the ropes that had been wound around Kade's legs, and she and the doctor guided Kade into a sitting position. I sat in front of him, unable to let go of his hand, unable to peel my eyes away from his living and breathing face.

"I don't understand," Kade said through breathless gasps. "Why am I alive?"

Mrs. Oaks eyes glowed with merriment. "Aviva saved you."

"We *all* saved you," I corrected.

"How?" Kade rasped. "And what in blazes is wrong with my voice?"

Dr. Harris chuckled. "You were strangled by a noose. A rope squeezed your vocal cords. You expect to sound normal?"

"Is it permanent?"

"Mayhap."

"It's okay, Kade," I comforted. "You sound sexy like that. All gruff and throaty."

Doctor Harris gaped at me.

"Viv! You ain't s'posed to say untoward things like that, 'specially in front of gentry." Ruby glanced sideways at Mrs. Oaks.

I peered up at Kade's mother, expecting to be reprimanded, but instead she smiled. "Kade is going to have his hands full with this one, isn't he."

A tingle rushed through me. It was subtle but…did Mrs. Oaks give me her blessing to be with her son? Even though as far as she could tell, I was nothing more than a poor servant?

Kade laced his fingers through mine. "Is someone going to explain how this little wisp saved me?"

Sheriff Barlow chose that moment to approach our group, with George and Phee right behind him. He held the photo.

"We explained everything to the sheriff," Phee assured me. I nodded.

"I know you're in a state right now, son," the sheriff leaned over Kade, "but I need to take a gander at yer right hand."

Tilting his head, Kade offered the sheriff his hand. Even in the dim lighting, the pearly lavender of Kade's thick, puckered scar shone brightly against his skin.

The sheriff nodded. "It's more of a formality. I've seen this scar since you were a young'n. Lucky for Henderson here that I have seen it, or I would've had him arrested on the spot for the stunt he pulled." He chuckled. "Who'd've thunk that one measly scar would someday save your life?"

Kade looked at George, then back at the sheriff. "Am I

missing something? What stunt did George pull?"

Sheriff Barlow glanced down at the photo again. "Yer innocent of all charges, son. That ain't yer hand holdin' the murder weapon."

Kade frowned.

George tried to explain. "When Aviva confronted our friend William in the stables, she had your Oak Box prototype."

"You don't say?" Kade asked.

I nodded. "When I realized it was too late to save Molly, I tried to take a picture. I dropped the camera. It broke into pieces. But right before it hit the ground, the shutter clicked."

Phee, not wanting to be left out of the reveal, leaned in. "So we all decided to break into the sheriff's office and steal the camera. Sorry, Sheriff Barlow," she grinned in his direction.

"I should throw the whole lot of you in the barracks," he replied, his strained smile betraying he had no intention of doing so.

"We were almost caught," Phee told Kade. "But Ruby created a..." she coughed, "diversion."

"*You* were the ones who started that fire?" the sheriff exclaimed. "You might've burned the whole town down!"

"Now keep in mind Sheriff," Mrs. Oaks said in a calming voice, "the actions of these young people prevented the death of an innocent man from being on your shoulders. Can you imagine carrying that burden for the rest of your life?"

Sheriff Barlow nodded toward Mrs. Oaks. "You ain't wrong 'bout that, ma'am."

"The camera was broken, but the film canister was

intact," Phee continued, still talking directly to Kade. "So we took it to your studio, and your awesome mom helped us develop it. Then Aviva found a picture of…." Phee trailed off, the story no longer fun now that she was broaching the topic of Molly's death.

"She found a picture revealing Miss Marguerite's final moments." George finished for her, his voice solemn. "I'm sorry, my friend."

"The problem was the photograph didn't show the killer," Mrs. Oaks said. "Only a hand, holding the murder weapon."

Kade nodded in understanding.

"Miss Aviva was the one who figured it out," Ruby chimed in. "The hand in that photo is as smooth as a baby's bottom. If you were truly the killer, the hand in the photo would bear that nasty scar."

"I'm glad you told me that story, Kade," I said. "Even though I had seen your scar a couple times, I don't think I would have given it a second thought if it hadn't been for the hilarious story behind it."

"Wait, does this mean she knows about the shotgun pellet…?" George trailed off.

"Lodged forever in your ass?" I finished for him. "Why yes, yes she does."

"Damn you to hell, Kade."

We laughed.

"Y'all are getting off topic," Ruby complained.

"Apologies, Miss Ruby," Kade said. "Continue, please. I am truly chomping at the bit to learn what happened next."

Ruby looked pleased as she took over the story. "Once Viv saw the photograph, she jumped on Mr. Henderson's horse and went tearin' off to show the sheriff. But that's as far as I can tell since we parted ways after that. Mr. Henderson and Miss Phee unhitched Mr. Henderson's other mare and followed after Viv. Me and Mrs. Oaks took the family's wagon, but it was slower going, and we only just arrived. We heard a gunshot when we were approaching the square."

"George and I were racing only a few minutes behind you, Viv," Phee supplied.

"You were?" I asked, surprised. I realized then that I had no idea what had happened to all of them when I went flying off to the courtyard. All I remembered was seeing Kade dangling from a rope as I waved the photo around and screamed Kade's innocence into the night air. Then I heard a gun shot, and Kade fell from the gallows. Phee found me in the chaos, and I shoved the photo in her hand, telling her, "Give this to the sheriff. Tell him to look at the hand holding the weapon." Then I ran to be with Kade.

"Of course," Phee said, answering my question. "How else do you think we got here? You took only one of the horses, so George unhitched the other one and we came after you. I thought about taking George's horse alone— you know, flying off into the night all heroic like you did— but no way was I riding by myself. Not all of us were lucky enough to get horseback riding lessons as a kid."

"You hated horses when we were little," I told her. "You said they were big, horsy, and smelled like horse."

She waved my words away. "George wasn't going to let me go by myself anyway. You know how the men are here. Annoyingly gentleman-ish."

George cocked his head, his eyes lit with amusement.

"When they're not trying to kill you," I muttered, thinking of William, who was a master of chivalry.

400

She ignored that. "When we arrived to town square, we saw you waving the photo at Sheriff Barlow and shouting at him to stop the hanging, but he was all the way at the top of the gallows. We knew he couldn't hear you. Especially with the crowds going nuts. They released the trap, and Kade dropped down. We thought he was a goner."

Ruby, listening in awe, shivered. She and Mrs. Oaks had missed this part.

"But then we saw that Kade was still moving, and his hand had escaped his ties." Phee leaned forward. "And then...you're gonna love this. Without saying a word, George whips out an antique rifle and shoots the rope holding Kade with one shot."

"Once again, Miss Phoenix, it is not an antique rifle," George said. "My 1885 High Wall is brand new."

"It's totally antique," Phee assured me.

"Wait a sec," I turned toward George. "You *shot* Kade down?"

"Yes."

Kade shook his head. His hoarse voice carried a note of astonishment. "You are a good friend, George."

"You would have done nothing less for me."

Kade nodded. I felt something pass between them. A brotherly love of some kind; that kind of bond that happens on battlefields.

"We were inordinately lucky," George broke the silence. "This county hasn't seen a hanging in decades. It's not surprising that the hangmen miscalculated the length of the rope. Had they done their job correctly, Kade's neck would have snapped instantly, and he'd be dead." I shuddered, but George smiled. "Thank God for incompetence."

"Should I take offense to that?" Sheriff Barlow asked, and

we all laughed. But then the sheriff froze. "If Kade ain't Marguerite Broderick's killer, that means…"

"*William* is the murderer," I finished for him. "Like I told you all along."

"Bloody hell. Where is he?"

"He was at the hanging," Kade said lowly.

"That means he'd've seen Mr. Henderson shoot you down, and seen you vindicated." The sheriff paused. "He knows he's been had."

All of us looked around. The air seemed to grow colder.

"Where do you think he's gone?" Ruby finally broke the silence.

The sheriff glanced around again. "A part of me hopes he's still nearby. But another part of me hopes he's long gone."

Tension rolled through our group in heavy waves. In my world, the Angel Killer had killed fourteen women in Sezona Valley and the surrounding counties. But that was in a timeline in which no one knew his identity. Because I had interfered, the people in 1886 now knew the killer was William Broderick. His identity had been revealed before he had the chance to become a serial killer. Would that help? Would William's reign of terror end here, with Molly?

Optimistic-Me wanted to believe so. But I felt uneasy.

"He's probably long gone by now," I said, hoping saying it out-loud would make it true.

Phee nodded her agreement. "Once he saw the jig was up, he probably bolted. I bet he's halfway to Chicago by now, where he can blend in. He has money, right?"

"Yes, he does," Sheriff Barlow confirmed. "If he plays his cards right, he could very well start a new life. Which is what we do *not* want. I'm gonna round up the posse and do a man-hunt for him." He gazed over at Mrs. Oaks. "Ma'am, I don't know why Mr. Oaks ain't here, but I'll be happy to help you and yer family get back on yer feet again, if need be. Don't hesitate to holler a whoop my way." With that he jogged away toward the courthouse, leaving us beneath the gallows.

"Is the sheriff married?" I mused aloud.

"Widowed," Mrs. Oaks replied, her eyes following him into the dark.

With the courtyard vacated, the darkness deepened.

"Now what?" Ruby asked.

"We have to get to Maui before the rift closes," Phee answered.

I shook my head. "No. No way. I'm not leaving Kade."

Kade squeezed my hand tighter. "I'm not leaving Aviva, either."

Both Mrs. Oaks and George looked utterly confused, so Ruby told them the short version of all they had missed.

"Well *great*," Phee huffed, once Ruby had finished. "What are we supposed to do?"

"Leave me here?" I suggested, but I immediately knew I couldn't do that. I couldn't bear the idea of never seeing my family again.

"Aviva," Kade intervened. "You will not sacrifice your whole world to be with me."

"Not to mention I'm not leaving without *you*," Phee put her hands on her hips. "Krys and Taz would kill me. Plus I'm pretty sure life would literally suck with Taz absorbing the essence of everything and no Spring to put it back."

"I have a suggestion," Kade said, his voice husky.

Our group turned to give him our attention.

"I was supposed to die tonight."

"Yes," I said, wondering where he was going with this. "But you didn't."

"Precisely. This could be a sizable problem."

"What do you mean?" Mrs. Oaks asked.

"I'm not supposed to exist past tonight. That means every action I make can put the universe in peril."

Mrs. Oaks tilted her head, confused.

"Let me illustrate," Kade put his elbows on his knees, drawing in a deep breath. I couldn't imagine how battered he must feel right now. "Suppose Aviva returns back to her own time period, and someday down the road I marry a woman named Anna, though I can never imagine such a thing. But, for the sake of making my point, let's imagine I do. Let us assume now that Anna was fated to marry Charles. Anna was never meant to meet me. I should not exist. But now she and I have married, and the offspring she was intended to have with Charles cease to exist. Consequently her children's children no longer exist, and her grandchildren's grandchildren…. In Aviva's and Phee's world, this could lead to folks inexplicably ceasing to exist. I do not know what this would look like—perhaps they would vanish into thin air?—but I know it can't be natural. Aviva and her sisters may be rendered nonexistent themselves because of a decision I make here in my own time."

I reeled back, shocked by the truth in Kade's words, and even more shocked that I had never considered these ramifications myself.

"One may argue, 'Simply avoid marriage, you simpleton,' and I would gladly agree. There is only one woman I can envision myself being happy with." He reached over and squeezed my hand. I felt my cheeks warm. "But any action I take from this point forward will, at the best, tamper with the future world, and at the worst, wreak havoc on it. I may save a man from a runaway horse who was never fated to live. Later he beds a woman intended for another…leading to more folks existing that were never meant to be, and others disappearing. Imagine what these changes will look like after a hundred years."

"So…what do we do?"

"I see only two options," Kade replied. "Option one, I die tonight."

I gasped.

He squeezed my hand again. "I said two options, little one."

I nodded, trying to calm down and listen.

"Option two…I go to your time period with you."

"Kade, no!" Mrs. Oaks cried.

"Mother, consider this from my point of view. Is it worth living a life where I must be invisible? Where one tiny ripple from me may have disastrous consequences? Simply steering our wagon left when it should have gone right could tear the world apart. Whereas if I live in Aviva's time period, decisions I make there should have no consequences on the future, as it has yet to be written."

"Kade…." Her eyes flooded with tears. "Your future here hasn't been written yet, either."

"But it has. Aviva's very presence here proves that we are living out a story that has already passed. Now that I have subverted my own death, I am forever off-script. "

"Would you not be causing the same ripple effect by going with Aviva and Phoenix into the future?" George asked. "After all, you are not supposed to exist there, either."

"No," I answered quietly. Everyone turned to look at me. "Maui allowed me and Phee to come into the past," I explained, "but my dad and uncle never said anything about it allowing us to travel into the future. I think the timeline stops at my present day. I know it sounds egocentric, or time-centric, or whatever, but I don't think anything beyond my and Phee's time has been written yet." I couldn't be sure of this, but it felt right as I was saying it. Maybe the timeline stopped at us because that's where my dad—Father Time—existed in his current human form. No way was I going to say that aloud, though.

"There you have it," Kade said. "Authors may make as many changes as they desire to a story that is still being molded."

He gripped my hand tightly, scooted forward, and stood, wobbling at first before gaining surer footing. He stepped toward Mrs. Oaks and wrapped his arms around her.

"I don't want to leave you." His voice was soft. "But the life I have here…it is gone now. And…" he paused, looking uncomfortable. "Folks whom I have known and trusted my whole life; they were mocking me, Mother. Their eyes shone with glee while I was hanging. They had no faith in me, in my character. Even my own father has disavowed me." He took a breath and squared his shoulders, resolute. "I no longer have a home here."

She nodded, sobbing into his shoulder. I knew in that moment that she was going to let him go. Tears burned my eyes.

We all made a silent, mutual decision to give Kade and his mother space, our group meandering toward the courthouse while they said their goodbyes. Phee was in the middle of complaining about yet another sister being involved in a supernatural relationship and "Can't any of you date like normal people?" when we passed the reverend, who nodded our direction before lifting his robes and departing the square.

I felt too many emotions to process at once. But one thought stood out above the others. *I'm going home.*

And the ghost I loved was coming with me.

After several minutes had passed, Kade waved us over. His eyes were rimmed with red. "George and Ruby, will you escort my mother to the wagon and see her home?"

"Certainly," George said.

"Wait, why are you sending them off without us?" I asked. "There's no way we're going to the rift tonight. You're in no shape for time travel, Kade."

He turned toward me and took my hand, imploring me with his eyes. "If I am to do this, I must do so now before I lose my courage. I have said my goodbyes to my mother, and she is going to pass my well-wishes to my sister. If I attempt to tell Bess goodbye in person, she is likely to go hysterical again. Bess is not hearty like you and Miss Phoenix. She is fragile."

I stared at him. "What about your father?"

"The man is dead to me. Sheriff Barlow will help my mother and Bess get through this difficult transition. The sheriff has wanted a family to look after for a long time." His shoulders stiffened. "It must be now, Aviva. You heard your sister. We need to go before the rift closes."

Reluctantly, I nodded.

Ruby stepped toward me, and I couldn't stop the tears from burning my eyes.

"Now, now, none of that Vivvy-girl," she said, pulling me

into a tight hug.

I swallowed. Pulling back, I looked deep into her warm, intelligent eyes. "For what it's worth Ruby, you're the bestest friend I've ever had."

She squeezed my hands and swung away from me before I could see the tears prick her eyes, not realizing it was too late—I saw them.

Phee flung herself at George and, with reluctance (as I'm sure this was considered 'untoward' behavior), he wrapped his arms around her.

"You're going to make some unlucky bastard quite lucky someday," he joked, a trace of fondness creeping into his voice.

"You know you'll miss me." She smacked a kiss square on his lips before pulling away. George's cheeks flushed, his lips twitching into a smile as he grazed the freshly-kissed spot with his fingertips.

Finally, George and Kade stepped toward each other. They shook hands, then quickly embraced, patting each other on the shoulders.

"Thank you for all you have done for me," Kade said to George. "And thank you for having better aim than I with a rifle."

The two chuckled.

"You will not be forgotten," Kade said, his smile turning sad.

George nodded. "I will send a letter to you to let you know how life is faring for all of us here. Check the loose brick where our time cache is buried."

Kade grinned. "Wish I could send one back. Perhaps I will find a way."

They patted each other's backs one last time, then

George and Ruby departed with Mrs. Oaks toward the family's wagon.

"Are we ready?" Phee asked. "Honestly, I won't miss this place one bit. This century is one big armpit. First thing I'm doing when I get home is taking a nice, hot shower." Despite the words coming out of her mouth, I noticed her eyes were rimmed with red, too. It occurred to me at that moment that all three of us had been irrevocably changed by the events that had happened these past ten days. None of us would ever be the same.

"Yes." I looked from Phee to Kade. "Let's go home."

Thirty-Nine

*There's no road that will lead us back
When you follow the strange trails
…who knows where.*
Lord Huron

Monday, April 1
Present Day

KRYSTAL PUSHED the dropper into Bobo's beak, trying to hear the evening news over his eager chirping and the loud hum of the space heater keeping his nest warm. Even though it had only been a few hours since she had rescued the baby dove, she had already given him a name, and he seemed to already consider Krystal his new mama. He stretched his neck and body out as far as he could, standing on the tips of his clawed feet and nearly toppling out of his box with excitement over his dinner. Daphne, who was used to working with wildlife through her job, had created a temporary formula for Bobo from lay mash, kitten chow, and warm water. She said they would all go to the feed bin tomorrow to get better food and supplies for him, but Krystal had a hard time imagining doing anything normal with her sisters missing.

At least taking care of Bobo was giving her a distraction from the anxiety flooding her mind every minute of this long, cold night. Dad and Daphne were gone now, having driven to Uncle Kiel's antique shop in search of items that might bring them to 1886. When she had pointed out to her dad earlier "I thought you said using a talisman was too dangerous," her dad had replied in a weary voice, "We've been brainstorming for hours and have officially reached a point where inaction is more dangerous."

Krystal opted out of going with her parents tonight, still hoping that her sisters would find their way back through the rift. She wanted to be home if they showed up. They'd have a good laugh over this; drink some hot tea at Copper's Kettle while admiring the newly perked-up flowers and basking in the fresh springy weather.

"…in an unprecedented cold snap that appears to be centered here in Sezona Hills," a reporter was saying, as if trying to be ironic. Krystal pushed another bite of mush down the bird's throat. Daphne told her she couldn't be gentle about it, because in nature mama birds weren't gentle. They just got the job done. As if to prove her point, Bobo squalled almost angrily as he was force-fed his bite, but then stretched his neck and wiggled his body in anticipation for more.

"Sandra," a male anchorman interjected, "can you explain why this particular weather system is causing alarm for some of the locals?"

Krystal glanced up from feeding her bird to see the screen switch to the on-location reporter who was standing in Whisper Park, wearing a fuzzy cream-colored beanie with matching scarf and gloves. Behind her, the camera's light illuminated the ice woven through the young springtime grass like spider webs, thinning to mere threads as they reached toward the pond. Fog rose like steam from the silver, gently rippling water, disappearing into the night sky. Soft waves lapped against the muddy shore.

"Off-season cold fronts aren't uncommon, Tony. But this particular anomaly concerns meteorologists due to the lack of a storm system associated with it, and the fact that the frigid temperatures are so localized."

They wouldn't be localized for long, Krystal thought. She had overheard her dad telling Daphne earlier during their brainstorming session that Sezona Hills was only the beginning. "If we don't get the other seasons back, there's no stopping it," he had stressed.

She wondered if any meteorologists had figured out yet that the ice could be followed from Whisper Park to her front door.

"Flash freezes of this nature are rare," the reporter, Sandra, continued, "and the ice you see here in the park appears to be spreading at an alarming rate."

The camera zoomed in toward the ground to give viewers a close-up of the icy lace that had crept like bacteria through the grass. Sandra gasped suddenly, and the camera returned to the reporter's profile.

"Folks," she glanced back at the camera, "take a look at this." She pointed toward the pond.

Krystal's stomach clenched as the camera zoomed in.

What was delicate waves lapping against the shore only minutes before was now frosty and solid. The center of the pond continued to ripple beneath a layer of fine mist, but the water closest to the shoreline was frozen.

Her eyes burned. Ice was spreading like a virus in her own neighborhood, and without her sisters here to balance nature, there was nothing she could do to stop it.

Her dad mentioned that her emotions were aggravating the problem. But how does a person force herself to stop feeling?

Hopelessness seeped into her very pores. She should run away to a desolate place before the ice hurt anyone. Like the Sahara Desert, or Death Valley. Funny, she had always hated the Disney movie *Frozen*, but now she found herself relating with the ice queen, Elsa, and her urge to take her freezing problem away from civilization.

Krystal jolted at a tap near the window. She swung toward the sound and gawked.

A large crow with gleaming feathers, precariously perched on the window ledge, peered in.

Krystal slowly put the plunger down and stared at the crow, an ominous feeling creeping over her as its glimmering beady eyes tracked her movements. Was this the same crow she had seen in Daphne's garden earlier? And the same one from Pendulum Square?

Was this crow following her?

She shook her head, realizing the stupidity of the thought. Crows don't follow people. She stood up and forced herself to move across the living room. Avoiding eye contact with the crow, she jammed the two curtain panels together, covering the window.

There. No more crow.

A knock on the door startled Krystal. Was it the crow…? She chuckled darkly, then moved to the door and opened it about an inch.

"Stryder?"

He was wearing a heavy jacket and bouncing restlessly on the porch with his hands stuffed in his pockets. His breath came out in icy puffs. "Where's your sister, Krystal? I'm going nuts."

She must have blanched a bit, because Stryder immediately looked contrite. He took a deep breath. "I'm sorry. I'm losing my mind. Taz hasn't responded to any of my texts since last night, and she wasn't at school today. I finally got ahold of your dad and he said she's sick, but something in his voice tells me he's lying. And I know your sister. Even if her thumbs fell off she'd still text me."

Krystal stepped aside and opened the door the rest of the way. "Come in and I'll explain. Hurry before that stupid crow follows you."

He arched an eyebrow at her but stepped quickly in. Just as she was closing the door, headlights flooded the drive way. Once parked, Dad and Daphne stepped out of Dad's truck, arms loaded with various objects and trinkets. Stryder and Krystal ran out to help them. The crow watched from a nearby fence post. Krystal ignored it.

"There's more in the back," Dad said.

After bringing in an armful each of various antiques and dumping them carefully onto the dining room table, Stryder finally said, "I don't get it. Why'd you guys bring home all this junk? Why would anyone want to go antique shopping during this freaky weather? And where's Taz?"

Dad and Daphne looked at each other.

"She isn't sick, is she."

"No, she's not," Dad said. "I told you that because I didn't want you to do anything crazy. Not until we formed a plan, at least."

"Where is she?" Stryder looked around wildly, as if he might storm the house looking for her.

"Somewhere in the past with Aviva and Phee," Krystal

said quietly.

Stryder's mouth dropped open. "All three of them are missing?" His voice came out in a growl.

Krystal nodded. "They found the rift."

Dad gestured toward the table. "We're hoping something in this pile of junk will help us find them."

Stryder straightened his shoulders. "Okay, let's get started. We can cross-reference all of these objects with their time periods online, narrow them down to the most viable options, and try each one at the rift."

Determination burned in Stryder's eyes, and Krystal could feel the energy emanating from him. It was contagious. For the first time today, she felt hope wiggle inside her. It felt good to have a plan, even if it was only mere seeds of a plan.

"We can go through the rift together," she suggested. "That way if we accidentally travel to a dangerous time period, we'll have strength in numbers."

"Really, we only need to stay in each time period for as long as it takes to find one person who can tell us the date," Daphne added. "Then we'll just race back to the clock if it's the wrong time period. Though…" she paused and rubbed the back of her neck in worry. "These trinkets could take us anywhere in the country."

"That's why we need to do our research," Stryder said, nodding toward the table of antiques.

Dad rubbed his forehead with the back of his hand. "Okay, if we're going to do this, not only do we need a talisman to get us through the rift, we'll also need one to bring us home."

"What do you mean?" Krystal asked.

"We need to bring an item that distinctly belongs to

someone who is physically in this time period. It's the only way to get home. It can't belong to any of us, because we'll be in the past."

Stryder's eyes darted toward Krystal. "Did your sisters have an object to get them back home?"

Krystal's shoulders dropped. "I don't know. They didn't exactly wake up Sunday morning planning to fall into a rift." She paused. "If they *did* have a talisman to come back home, wouldn't they be back by now?"

Stryder swore under his breath.

"Let's not panic," Dad said. "We'll figure this out. We'll find them."

The group stared at each other.

"So what should we use as our talisman to get back home?" Dad broke the silence.

Stryder sighed. "I've got nothing. Everything in my truck is mine."

"We don't have anything either, Horace," Daphne said. "Almost everything in this house is either ours, or the girls. Since the girls will be in the past with us, their belongings won't work as talismans." She paused. "We have keepsakes belonging to old relatives, but those won't take us back to the right time period."

"I can swing by my house real quick," Stryder said. "Grab something that belongs to my mom."

"I'll go with you," Krystal said. "I need to borrow your reptile heater for Bobo, anyway. I can't keep this space heater running all night. You have one, right?"

Stryder nodded. "Yeah, it's on the top shelf of my closet. Miss B. doesn't use it. Who's Bobo?"

Krystal pointed toward the shoe box sitting on the side table where the space heater was still running. Stryder peeked in. "Of course you'd have some random baby bird. Why do you have it in a box? It needs to be in a glass tank so the warmth from the heat lamp can create a greenhouse effect."

"I know, Daphne told me the same thing. But all of our glass tanks have lady bugs and moths in them right now. I have Aviva to thank for that." Her heart gave a tug at the mention of her sister.

"Unfortunately my only tank is occupied by Miss B. right now…" Stryder mused aloud.

"Wait a sec," Krystal remembered. She spotted the large bag sitting near the front door where she had dropped it the day her sisters disappeared. She walked to the bag, grabbed the top of it, and dragged it over.

"This is your quarter-anniversary present from Taz."

Stryder slid the bag down to reveal the large rodent paradise within. He shook his head, then gazed up toward Krystal. "Want to help me set this up for Miss B. while we're at my house?" The question was simple, but his voice was hoarse with emotion. "Then we can transfer your bird to the tank. I'll let Hilda know to take care of both Miss B and your baby bird while we're gone."

Krystal nodded.

"Great, it's settled then," Dad said. "While you two are gone, Daphne and I will start researching these items." He turned toward Stryder and spoke in a slow, serious tone, "Be sure the item you choose has never belonged to anyone else other than your mother. If it's something that, say, used to belong to a deceased relative, the object can very well take us back to that person in the past rather than returning us safe and sound to our current time period."

"Her bra is always a safe bet," Daphne offered.

Stryder cringed. "I'll come up with something."

The four of them looked at each other, wordless for a moment. Each saw reflected in the eyes of the other a fiery conviction. And hope. And fear.

"Let's do this."

Outside in the dark night, the temperature dropped by another three degrees.

Forty

Hold still right before we crash
'Cause we both know how this ends
Our clock ticks till it breaks your glass
And I drown in you again
Zedd

January 21, 1886

AS WE SCURRIED through the dark night toward Maui, I wondered vaguely how Dad was going to feel about all this. He was very much against changing anything from the past. How would he feel when I showed up with a man from 1886? One who was supposed to die in his own time period?

I cringed. He might actually kill me dead.

And how would Kade feel when he found out that my sisters and I had powers? Ghost-Kade took it pretty well, but he also thought I was a figment of his imagination. Would living-Kade be so understanding? I mentioned my powers to him when I had first awakened in this century, but it was jumbled in with so much other information. Then we had been so occupied in saving his life…the fact I commune with flowers never came up again.

Another worry crawled over me. What was Kade going to do in modern day Sezona Hills? He had no identity in my time period. No driver's license, no social security number. No way to enroll in school, or work a job….

I probably should talk to Kade about these things before we stepped into the rift, but he seemed so determined. I didn't want to shake his confidence.

Or maybe I was being selfish.

I shook these thoughts away as we approached the clock tower. Maui loomed tall and formidable, the moonlight glinting from her face, the rest of her body shrouded in thick dark. Kade reached over and squeezed my hand, then the three of us stood in a sort of quiet homage in front of her.

"Tell me you have a plan for getting back home," Phee finally broke the silence.

"I do," I said, reaching into my apron and pulling out Phee's lipgloss. "Uncle Kiel said that any object belonging to a person in the time period you're traveling to can be used as a talisman, so I figure it'll work for going back home, too." I showed her the half-empty tube. Then I felt the blood drain from my face. "Oh no."

"What's wrong?" Phee asked, alarmed. "Do *not* tell me we're stuck here."

"This is your lipgloss. This whole time I was planning on using it to get me home, but you're here with me in the past. It only works if you're in your own time period where you—and it—belongs. It won't work!"

Phee took the lipgloss, examined it, and laughed.

"Why are you laughing?" I asked, dismayed.

"This isn't my lipgloss," Phee said. "I borrowed it from Taz. Well, stole it from her purse might be more accurate."

The relief was so intense I thought I might cry.

"We are able to travel through the rift, then?" Kade clarified.

"Assuming Aviva's correct about how talismans work, then yeah, we're good to go. See Aviva, aren't you glad now that I'm a brat who borrows your guys' stuff?"

"I've never been gladder."

Kade looked at me, excitement and nervousness warring across his face. I squeezed his hand. "Kade, are you sure you want to do this?" I swallowed, the fear of losing him suddenly a living, breathing thing crushing my chest. But I knew I had to be honest with him or I'd never be able to live with myself. "If you go through this rift, life's not going to be easy for you. You'll have no identity in my time period. Not until we can figure out how to get you one. Maybe my uncle can help with that. But until then, you'll have no schooling, no job…and life in my world is more… complex. It's going to be like another planet for you."

Kade tugged me forward, his eyes burning with blue fire. "Life will be hard whether I stay here or go with you. But at least the latter allows me to be with the person I love."

I hesitated. "What if the person you love is…a little more than you signed up for?"

He cocked his head.

"What if she has the ability to, um, heal things? And her sisters all have weird powers, too?"

He stared at me. "I would tell her that I already knew she was more than meets the eye. And I would say she and her family sound fascinating, and I'm eager to learn more about them, and about her."

Relief poured through me like cold lemonade on a hot summer day. I did my due diligence. He knew, and that was that. Now we could cross each complicated bridge once we got there, one step at a time.

Together.

A look of awareness crossed Kade's features, and he pulled something from his pocket and leaned over to place it on the ground. A small pile of shredded paper.

"What is that?" I asked.

"Our torn apart letter." He glanced over at me. "I wanted it with me while I was hanging."

Warmth seeped into the uncertain spaces of my heart. "Why are you leaving it here?"

"Now that it has served its purpose, I want it returned to the breeze in this time period. It belongs here."

I elbowed him playfully. "You are so dramatic."

He smiled and took me into his arms. "I do not need a letter anymore, little one, when I have the real Aviva right here in my arms."

It occurred to me that a perfectly whole version of our letter existed a mere few steps from us, since Kade had sealed it inside of Maui the morning of my arrival. It would be over a hundred years before present-Me found his letter in the time capsule. Kade had ripped up the future letter—the one I was carrying—but not his own. A part of me wanted to tear into the clock right now to retrieve it. Take it with me to the future. Hold it forever close to my heart.

But if I pulled the letter out of the time capsule, future Me would never receive it, and would never be able to use it to get through the rift. That would create a paradox, right?

I decided that the letter would remain in the clock, forever caught in some strange time loop. The thought made me smile.

"By the way," I said, searching Kade's eyes. "I never had

the chance to tell you this since you stuffed that disgusting gag into my mouth, but…" I paused, my cheeks warming. "I love you too, Kade."

His eyes lit up like a clear summer morning.

"You shoved a gag in her mouth?" Phee questioned next to us, unruffled by our personal moment. "Kinky."

Ignoring her, I wrapped my arms around Kade's neck. His eyes darkened with hunger as his arms circled tightly around my waist and our mouths melded into a slow, warm kiss. My body turned to liquid as Kade worked his magic, tracing lines of heat across my lips with his own. Goosebumps unrelated to the night's chill traced my neck as his fingers left my waist and tangled their way through my hair.

"Bloody hell," he uttered huskily. "I broke my promise."

I knew he was referring to his promise to never kiss me again. I also knew he'd happily break that promise over and over again if given the chance.

"Why does this always happen to me?" Phee sighed impatiently.

Kade and I sighed and broke apart.

"My apologies, Miss Phoenix," he said.

"Sorry," I said, not really sorry.

"Whatever." She waved the lipgloss. "Can we go home now?"

My heart skittered. Home! My heart hungered for it. I ached for the familiarity of the twenty-first century. I ached to see the rest of my family again.

"Shall we all hold the talisman, to ensure it works?" Kade suggested.

"Couldn't hurt," Phee nodded. We three lined up directly in front of Maui. Staring up at the clock, Phee passed the lipgloss to me since I was in the center. Phee and Kade both placed two fingers on the talisman.

My heart drummed against my chest. Tears misted my vision. This was it. We were going home.

"On the count of three?" I asked.

Kade and Phee nodded.

"One," Phee said.

"Two," Kade said.

"Three." We all placed our free hand against the brickwork of the clock while clinging to the lipgloss. I closed my eyes.

Maui released a dull *bong*. The world around me vibrated, and then an invisible wall slammed into me. I toppled backwards.

Something was wrong. I knew it before I hit the ground. The rift should have taken me home, wherever Taz was. But it didn't feel right. I felt like I had been…rejected, somehow.

Landing hard on my tailbone, my eyes popped open. Phee and Kade were on the ground next to me.

"Ouch," Phee said, rubbing her lower back.

Maui towered in front of us. I stood up and turned around, searching for the Pendulum Square I knew and loved, full of benches, flowers, shrubs, and fairy lights, with a giant fountain as the cherry on top.

But none of that was here. Pendulum Square looked the same as the one we had just left. Plain. Empty. Dark.

"I—I don't understand." I stammered.

"Where are we?" Phee asked as she and Kade stood.

Kade turned around, squinting as he examined the world around him. "We're in the same place."

"What?" Phee demanded. "What do you mean, we're in

the same place?"

"Look," Kade said, stepping toward a small pile of shredded paper lying on the ground. "I left this torn letter in this spot a mere few minutes ago. If we were in any other time period—even if only a day into the future—these fragments would have scattered with the breeze."

"I don't get it," Phee said, her face visibly pale beneath the moonlight. "Why didn't we leave?"

"You suggested earlier that the rift may be closing." Kade told Phee, putting voice to all of our fears.

A knot of dread uncurled sickly in my stomach. But then a thought nibbled in the corners of my head. "No, I don't think it's closed. Not that I'm all knowledgeable about this stuff, but I felt my skin vibrate when we touched the clock. And then I felt a wall push me out. It's like...the rift was open, but then it kicked us out."

Phee pursed her lips. "I felt some kind of force pushing me out, too. If it were closed, nothing would happen at all, right? It would be just a normal clock tower, wouldn't it?"

Kade nodded his agreement. "Despite the fact that we are still here in this time period, the clock certainly did *something*. I don't know what time travel is supposed to feel like, but I experienced the sensation you ladies are describing. The sensation of being...physically rejected."

"Then...what? Maui might have rejected us if our talisman is no good," I waved the small tube of lipgloss at Kade and Phee, "but this is a perfectly good talisman! It belongs in the twenty-first century with Taz. And we all felt ourselves entering the rift right before it kicked us out. Why would it do that? It's like the talisman thinks Taz...." I stopped as a disturbing thought sent goosebumps racing up my neck.

"Is here," Phee finished for me.

"Oh my God." A hush descended upon our group.

"Is it possible?" I asked Phee after a few chilled seconds of silence.

Phee's eyes shifted sideways, as if searching her memory. "I went through the rift first. I wasn't around to see what happened with Krystal and Taz once I disappeared." She gulped. "So yes. It's possible."

Kade's brows furrowed in concentration. "Aviva, you were holding my letter, and it brought you to me. Phee was holding the pewter soldier, and it brought her to George. There was only one item left in that cache." His face paled.

"The knife," Phee supplied.

"The Schrade pocket knife," Kade said softly. "Inscribed to mark our first centennial."

My brain scrambled through the clues. The reference to a mysterious friend "Aurora." The one from Ireland, who was ill from her travels.

Taz's middle name is Aurora. The red highlights in her hair would make her look Irish. She would have blacked out after going through the rift. *Ill from her travels.*

Maui refused our entrance fee into the rift because the owner of the talisman was here, in 1886.

Phee gaped at me, her eyes mirroring the shock I felt ricocheting through my body. "We're trapped here."

I nodded numbly. "And the Angel Killer has Taz."

TO BE CONTINUED
in the final installment of the
Chasing Echoes Series
Spring of Crows

Visit Jodi online for updates!
https://twitter.com/perkjo
facebook.com/AuthorJodiPerkins
www.jodiperkins.com

Reviews are Hugs for Authors

Enjoy Black Lilies?
How about leaving a quick review?
It doesn't have to be fancy;
one or two sentences is awesome!
Simply go to amazon.com/books
and type in 'Black Lilies Jodi Perkins'.

Review or not, thank you
from the bottom of my heart
to all my readers.

♥

Acknowledgements

THANK YOU to the following wonderful peeps who have done nothing but enrich my writing and my life:

To my editor Dylan Devine who is seriously underpaid. You're not only an editor, you're a stand-up comedian.

To Naj Qamber for yet another slam-dunk cover.

To Simon Graeme, for serving as my research consultant for life in the nineteenth century, and for being the most supportive friend a girl could ask for.

To my forever-writerly-buddy Krystal Jane Ruin for all of her valuable writing tips, her sharp insight on how to smooth out my prose, and for always making me smile.

To Thomas Mattheos, for being the voice of Uncle Kiel. Thanks for taking my hand and guiding me into those dark crevices that I'm too scared to travel alone.

To Richard Moore. 'Cause…everything.

To my amazing dad in-law Carey, who put in weeks of back-breaking labor to build me the most amazing writer's lair. Springfluff Manor is my happy place and this book would not exist without it!

To Trinity and Elijah, for putting up with your mother's insanity yet again. Trin, thanks for letting me run so many ideas past you and reading my first draft with such enthusiasm! Elijah, thanks for trekking through rain, sleet and snow to replenish my wine. ;)

To my parents (Penny, Michael, Teri and Carey) and my Shosho, for always rooting me on and making me feel like I can accomplish anything.

To Roger Williams for always 'talking shop' with me, and for that great pellet-in-the-arse story…that was pure gold.

To Gus, who cuddled at my feet during the entire drafting process and let me bounce ideas off his furry head. (Yes, I'm including my dog in my acknowledgements).

Beans, you did nothing. You were a blob of fur.

To all of my beta readers: The valuable feedback you provided helped transform Black Lilies from a sloppy chorus to a finely tuned melody. Love you all!

And of course, a huge shout-out to my hubby for being a book-formatting ninja, a "What if…" master, a she-shed extraordinaire, not to mention the sweetest, most thoughtful and supportive spouse EVER.

And lastly, to God. It all belongs to You.

Made in the
USA
Lexington, KY

55434158R00265